NIGHTMARE ABBEY

Thomas Love Peacock

edited by Lisa Vargo

broadview editions

Library and Archives Canada Cataloguing in Publication

Peacock, Thomas Love, 1785-1866.
  Nightmare Abbey / Thomas Love Peacock ; edited by Lisa Vargo.

(Broadview editions)
Includes bibliographical references.
ISBN-13: 978-1-55111-416-3
ISBN-10: 1-55111-416-X

  1. Peacock, Thomas Love, 1785-1866. Nightmare Abbey.
I. Vargo, Lisa, date II. Title. III. Series.

PR5162.N5 2007   823'.7   C2006-906590-X

Broadview Editions

The Broadview Editions series represents the ever-changing canon of literature in English by bringing together texts long regarded as classics with valuable lesser-known works.

Advisory editor for this volume: Jennie Rubio

Broadview Press is an independent, international publishing house, incorporated in 1985. Broadview believes in shared ownership, both with its employees and with the general public; since the year 2000 Broadview shares have traded publicly on the Toronto Venture Exchange under the symbol BDP.

We welcome comments and suggestions regarding any aspect of our publications—please feel free to contact us at the addresses below or at broadview@broadviewpress.com.

North America
Post Office Box 1243, Peterborough, Ontario, Canada K9J 7H5
3576 California Road, Post Office Box 1015, Orchard Park, NY, USA 14127
Tel: (705) 743-8990; Fax: (705) 743-8353
email: customerservice@broadviewpress.com

UK, Ireland, and continental Europe
NBN International, Estover Road, Plymouth, UK PL6 7PY
Tel: 44 (0) 1752 202300; Fax: 44 (0) 1752 202330
email: enquiries@nbninternational.com

Australia and New Zealand
UNIREPS, University of New South Wales
Sydney, NSW, 2052 Australia
Tel: 61 2 9664 0999; Fax: 61 2 9664 5420
email: info.press@unsw.edu.au

www.broadviewpress.com

Broadview Press acknowledges the financial support of the Government of Canada through the Book Publishing Industry Development Program (BPIDP) for our publishing activities.

PRINTED IN CANADA

NIGHTMARE ABBEY

broadview editions
series editor: L.W. Conolly

Thomas Love Peacock, by Roger Jean (1805).
Courtesy National Portrait Gallery, London.

Contents

Acknowledgements

This edition owes its existence to the generosity of Mical Moser and Don Le Pan and to the patience of Julia Gaunce. It was completed under the most pleasant circumstances I can imagine, as the Leonard Slater Fellow, University College, Durham University during Epiphany Term 2005. Living and working near Durham Castle was the ideal location in which to edit a novel set in a castellated abbey. I wish to thank the Master Maurice Tucker, Acting Master Paula Stirling, and especially the Fellows of the Senior Common Room, who were so kind and welcoming. During my fellowship I delivered presentations about my edition to the Department of English Studies, Durham University, to the Fellows of the Senior Common Room, University College, Durham University, and to the Northeast Graduate Forum on the Long Eighteenth Century. The questions and suggestions I received from my audiences were immensely useful. Particular thanks to Corinne Saunders, George Boys-Stones, and Michael Rossington for organizing these occasions.

In carrying out the work for this edition, I am happy to have the opportunity to thank a number of individuals and organizations for their assistance. My debt to Thomas Love Peacock scholars, especially Marilyn Butler, Nicholas A. Joukovsky, James Mulvihill, and the previous editors of *Nightmare Abbey*, David Garnett and Raymond Wright, is noted with respect. The Interlibrary Loan Department of the University of Saskatchewan provided their usual efficient assistance. The Carl H. Pforzheimer Collection, New York Public Library and the Cambridge University Library Rare Books Department provided copies of the first edition and other research materials. A grant from the University of Saskatchewan Publications Fund contributed financial support. I wish to thank Pamela Clemit, Keith Crook, Nora Crook, Doucet Devin Fischer, Helen Griffiths, John Lumsden, Carrie Ann Runstedler, Thomas Steele, and Stephen Wagner for their assistance. Leonard Conolly and Jennie Rubio from Broadview Press deserve special thanks.

Perhaps the best thing I can say about editing *Nightmare Abbey* is that the text continues to provide me with great pleasure and amusement as well as to serve as a source of thought and inspiration. With this in mind, I wish to dedicate this edition to my nephew Daniel Sidney Vargo.

Introduction

1. The Spirit of the Age and "Lived Romanticism"

Critical opinion about *Nightmare Abbey*, Thomas Love Peacock's third novel, has taken the perspective that the novel is more concerned with ideas than people, and with matters that are narrowly literary rather than encompassing a wider political interest. Peacock himself seems to confirm this in his account of the inception of the novel: "At present I am writing a comic romance with a title of Nightmare Abbey and amusing myself with the darkness and misanthropy of modern literature, from the lantern jaws of which I shall endeavour to elicit a laugh."[1] Once he had worked on the novel, he was more specific about the particular source of the irritation and its effects: "I have almost finished Nightmare Abbey. I think it necessary to 'to make a stand' against the 'encroachments' of black bile. The fourth canto of Childe Harold is really too bad. I cannot consent to be *auditor tantum* of this systematical 'poisoning' of the 'mind' of the 'Reading Public.'"[2]

Peacock alludes to topical matters relevant to the year of the novel's composition and publication, 1818. In fact Humphry House calls Peacock "a man whose true value cannot be seen apart from this context in history. His books are unintelligible without it. For he was not primarily an artist or a novelist, but a critic, a critic abnormally sensitive to the important movements of the mind and spirit in his age."[3] House looks to one of the most accomplished critical essayists of the day, William Hazlitt, by way of explaining Peacock's writings as achieving

> the same sort of thing that Hazlitt was doing in the essays that were published as *The Spirit of the Age*; and Hazlitt is the best introduction to Peacock. What neither of them could do was done by John Stuart Mill's two essays on Bentham and Coleridge. Between the three of

---

1   Joukovsky, Nicholas A. *The Letters of Thomas Love Peacock* 2 vols. (Oxford: Clarendon P, 2001), 1.121–22.
2   Joukovsky, *Letters of Thomas Love Peacock* 1.123.
3   Humphry House, "The Novels of Thomas Love Peacock" (*The Listener* 42 [1949]: 997).

them there was the material for a great analytical satire that none of them ever wrote; yet in a way Peacock was nibbling at it all his life.[1]

Peacock's particular sense of the times is central to the writing of the novel and represents the approach taken in preparing this particular edition (Excerpts from Hazlitt's *The Spirit of the Age* can be found in Appendix C [202–09].)

House's view of Peacock as a sensitive critic examining movements of mind while working in the medium of a particularly gentle and comic form of satire captures some of the value of *Nightmare Abbey*. And yet in the novel Peacock may be said to be doing rather more than "nibbling." Peacock claims that the goal of his novel is "to bring to a sort of philosophical focus a few of the morbidities of modern literature;"[2] we need to understand what is meant by these alleged "morbidities." Links can be forged with a similarly titled novel that also appeared in 1818 and which also satirizes literary excesses of the age—Jane Austen's posthumously published *Northanger Abbey*. Ian Jack suggests that "unlike Jane Austen, Peacock is more interested in ideas than in people."[3] In Jack's view, Austen is able to transcend literary and cultural contexts in a manner that Peacock's writing cannot.

But there are other ways to view the matter. Howard Mills contends that Austen keeps romanticism within books and distant from "real life," while Peacock "diagnoses inside Scythrop romanticism as it fuses with individual character and directs one's life" to what he terms a "lived romanticism."[4] "Scythrop romanticism" refers to the fact that, as with two of his previous novels (*Headlong Hall* [1816], and *Melincourt* [1817]), Peacock gently ridicules the idealism of his friend Percy Bysshe Shelley. In *Melincourt* the character of Mr. Forester embodies a more mature and serious version of the poet, who movingly argues that "the history of the world abounds with sudden and

---

1   House 998.
2   Joukovsky, *Letters of Thomas Love Peacock* 1.152.
3   Ian Jack, "Peacock." *English Literature 1815–1832.* Vol. 10 of *The Oxford History of English Literature.* (Oxford: Oxford UP, 1965), 213. See also Nancy S. Struever, "The Conversable World: Eighteenth-Century Transformations of the Relation of Rhetoric and Truth." *Rhetorical Traditions and British Romantic Literature.* Ed. Don H. Bialostosky and Lawrence D. Needham (Bloomington: Indiana UP, 1995), 233–49.
4   Howard Mills, *Peacock: His Circle and His Age* (Cambridge: Cambridge UP, 1969), 164.

extraordinary revolutions in the opinions of mankind, which have been effected by single enthusiasts." By contrast, in *Nightmare Abbey*, Scythrop, with his interests in secret societies and gothic literature, is largely a target for comedy.

Such comparisons suggest that *Nightmare Abbey* is a lighter and less significant work than its predecessor *Melincourt*, not to mention less politically engaged. But this is not the case. I wish to differ somewhat with received critical opinion and view the novel as the work of a writer who remains steadfast in his interest in people and his commitment to politics. Marilyn Butler suggests that the portrait of Shelleyan idealism in *Melincourt* presents an ideal of the "radical intellectual," and explores the kinds of roles that society's intellectuals should play.[1] *Nightmare Abbey* develops this theme. As such the concept of "Scythrop romanticism" is not incorrect. However, Peacock presents a young intellectual who is tempted by the dilettantes around him to engage in fashionable perspectives that advocate solipsism and withdrawal. Peacock's point is that Scythrop's elders should represent better models of the committed intellectual than they do. The novel's "lived romanticism" is made evident by Peacock's particular concerns: that which is "too bad" about *Childe Harold*; comic romance; an objection to the darkness, or "black bile" of modern literature; the evolving notion of the reading public; and a desire to evoke laughter. And for all their topicality, these matters suggest that *Nightmare Abbey* is not merely the work of a "critic abnormally sensitive to the important movements of the mind and spirit in his age." It contains much that is relevant beyond Peacock's times by way of a statement of the importance of writing and conversation in determining the quality of our lives.

2. Making a Stand against *Childe Harold*: A Summary of Peacock's Life

Peacock's mention of the fourth canto of Byron's *Childe Harold's Pilgrimage*, a quasi-autobiographical poem about the poet's own wanderings in continental Europe between 1809 and 1817, is revealing. The reference suggests that he is taking issue with excessive

---

1 Marilyn Butler, *Peacock Displayed: A Satirist in His Context* (London: Routledge, 1979), 98.

introspection and the belief that an artist's life is inextricably bound up in his works. The first cantos of *Childe Harold*, published in 1812, inspired Byron to comment, "I awoke one morning and found myself famous," and marked the beginning of his astonishing celebrity as much as for the man he was as for his poetry, which promotes a melancholic world weariness and a disillusioned perspective. Peacock's dismay at what is to us a very familiar form of celebrity is matched by his desire for reserve. He is also clearly concerned with the increasingly close connection between authorship and fame in the minds of a reading public that formed the market for literature.

The "morbidities" described by Peacock refer to the melancholy subjects and perspective of contemporary literature (such as Byron's account of Italy as a place of decline and decay [see Appendix C, 193–98]). But Peacock also sees a connection here to notions of literary authority that exploit the renown of the author. As the creator of a series of novels that foreground dialogue and multiple perspectives, Peacock eschews the belief that individual celebrities should set the fashion for ideas or attitudes. He prefers a more collective and multivocal world; and his vision bears some consideration as an alternative to our own celebrity-obsessed world—which is after all a legacy of the fame of Byron.

Peacock presents a model of intellectual community that involves collective discussion of ideas; here, individual points of view are shown to have potential for corrective, through consideration by others. At the same time, Peacock was publicly reticent. As Nicholas Joukovsky suggests, he "despised, on principle, the increasing violation of privacy in the new literary journalism that emerged in the 1820s."[1] It was only late in life that he reluctantly wrote about his friendship with Percy Shelley. But there are other reasons beyond a desire to keep his life and that of his friends private. Unhappy family circumstances (poverty, his wife's mental illness, and the scandal of his daughter's adultery) might also have led to his reticence. Another factor may have been that, like Charles Lamb, Peacock was employed by the East India Company: he might have wished to escape association by critics with the "Cockney School of Poetry" of Keats and Leigh Hunt.[2] In fact it was only with the publication of

---

1 Joukovsky, *Letters of Thomas Love Peacock* 1.xxxvii.
2 Joukovsky, *Letters of Thomas Love Peacock* 1.xxxix.

Peacock's surviving letters in an edition by Nicholas A. Joukovsky, which appeared in 2001, that some information about the life of this very private man has come to be known. More details about Peacock's life can be found in the introduction and chronology to the Letters.[1]

It is important to recognize that in an age where writing was a profession, Peacock did not earn his livelihood as an author. Peacock was born in 1785. He falls between his contemporaries, being closest in age to Byron (born in 1788). Wordsworth was fifteen years older, and Coleridge thirteen years older, while his friend Shelley was seven years younger. His father, Samuel Peacock, was a London glass merchant, who died in 1793 or 1794.[2] Peacock's mother, Sarah Love, was an admirer of the historian Edward Gibbon and herself wrote verse. In 1791, she moved with her son to Chertesy, twenty-two miles from London, and kept house with her father, a retired naval officer who had lost a leg while fighting in the West Indies. Peacock attended a school until he was thirteen; here he learned some Latin and Greek. Thereafter he educated himself, writing poems and essays while he worked as a clerk in the City of London. He became engaged at twenty-two, but the woman's family prevented the marriage; she married another man, and died within a year. Peacock followed his grandfather's footsteps and joined a ship as clerk to Admiral Sir Home Riggs Popham on the H.M.S. *Venerable*, but the venture did not last long. An important connection began in 1807 when he met Edward and Thomas Hookham, the sons of bookseller Thomas Hookham; Nicholas Joukovsky notes that the Hookham library and reading rooms at 15 Old Bond Street were recognized as "the habitual resort of the litterateurs of the day."[3] The Hookhams were known for their republican views, and it was Thomas who introduced Peacock to Percy Shelley in 1812 (Thomas would later be the one to inform Shelley

---

1 Information about Peacock's life can be found in the "Biographical Introduction" to the *Halliford Edition*. There are two biographies, Carl Van Doren, *The Life of Thomas Love Peacock* (London: J.M. Dent; New York: E. P. Dutton, 1911) and Felix Felton, *Thomas Love Peacock* (London: Allen and Unwin, 1973). James Mulvihill's *Thomas Love Peacock* (Boston: G.K. Hall, 1987) is also helpful. The introduction and lengthy chronology that preface Nicholas Joukovsky's edition of the letters are invaluable.

2 Joukovsky, *Letters of Thomas Love Peacock* 1.cxvii.

3 Joukovsky, *Letters of Thomas Love Peacock* 1.l–li.

that his first wife, Harriet Westbrook Shelley, had committed suicide in 1816). The brothers helped Mary Shelley with uncovering some forged letters in 1845–46 and Thomas later assisted her son and daughter-in-law, Sir Percy Shelley and Lady Shelley, with acquiring letters by Shelley.[1] The Hookhams gave Peacock access to the lending library, assisted him in receiving grants from the Literary Fund, and published *The Genius of the Thames* (1810, rev. 1812), *The Philosophy of Melancholy* (1812), *Sir Proteus* (1814), *Headlong Hall* (1816), *Melincourt* (1817), *Rhododaphne* (1818), *Maid Marian* (1822), *The Misfortunes of Elphin* (1829), and *Crochet Castle* (1831).

His acquaintance with Percy Shelley was, as Joukovsky terms it, "in many ways the most momentous event of his life."[2] After the introduction by Thomas Hookham their friendship developed over the next year; they remained in regular contact until Shelley left for Italy in 1818. Throughout he served as an agent and advisor for Shelley, who in return helped him financially. When Shelley died in 1822, Peacock was literary executor along with Byron (who died in 1824). He was also given the delicate task of arranging for support for Shelley's widow and son from Sir Timothy Shelley, Shelley's father, who neither approved of Mary nor of Shelley's career as a poet. Peacock remained a friend of many of the Shelley circle, including Mary's stepsister, Claire Clairmont, and Shelley's Oxford friend, Thomas Jefferson Hogg. It is commonly accepted that *Nightmare Abbey* touches upon events in 1814 when Shelley left Harriet and eloped with Mary Godwin. Peacock liked Shelley's first wife, but understood that Mary, the daughter of intellectuals Mary Wollstonecraft and William Godwin, was more suited to Percy's intellectual interests. Peacock's lack of a stand on the issue of Harriet's abandonment, which was followed by her suicide in 1816, is considered a curiosity and sometimes seen as evidence of his coldness or opportunism. It is probable that like many people who are faced with the foibles of a friend, Peacock was willing to overlook

---

1 George Byron (1810-82), who claimed to be the son of the poet Lord Byron, came into the possession of a number of letters by Byron and Shelley via a bookseller. He made copies of the letters, along with others that had been published and sold these forged versions to Mary Shelley and her son. See Joukovsky, *Letters of Thomas Love Peacock* 1.liii and Betty T. Bennett, *Letters of Mary Wollstonecraft Shelley* 3 vols. (Baltimore: Johns Hopkins UP, 1988), 3. 245n, 248, 250-1, 252n, 278, 279, 279n, 280, 282, 297, 297n, 298, 298n.

2 Joukovsky, *Letters of Thomas Love Peacock* 1.lv.

what might seem like serious failings for the affections of friendship. Yet Scythrop's entanglements with Marionetta and Celinda offer a kind of quiet statement—Scythrop gets neither woman, and perhaps this is Peacock's comment on what might have made for a happier outcome. During this period of close friendship he published his first two novels, *Headlong Hall* (1815) and *Melincourt* (1817), both of which contain Shelleyan figures. Peacock published a long, ambitious classical poem, *Rhododaphne*, in 1818; and in October of the same year, after the Shelleys left for Italy, *Nightmare Abbey* made its appearance. None of these works attracted any remarkable critical attention.

In 1819, at the age of 33, Peacock was appointed to the East India Company as Assistant to the Examiner of Indian Correspondence at a salary of six hundred pounds. With this financial security he sent a marriage proposal to Jane Gryffydh, a woman he met on a walking tour of Wales in 1811 (in spite of a continuing correspondence with another woman, Marianne de St. Croix, whom his friends assumed he would marry). It is not known whether Marianne rejected him, but the circumstances of the proposal are unusual. What is perhaps more unexpected is that Jane accepted him. Their marriage was happy for a while, though after the death of the second of their three daughters in 1826—they also had a son—Jane became an "invalid" (likely a polite way to describe mental illness). A girl who resembled his dead daughter was informally adopted by Peacock during the same year. After this time Peacock and his wife largely lived apart.

Peacock continued his work with the East India Company while also maintaining his literary pursuits. "The Four Ages of Poetry" (1820) inspired Shelley's *Defense of Poetry*, and in 1822 he published another novel, *Maid Marian*, which J.R. Planché adapted into an opera. After 1822 he acted as Shelley's literary executor, and in 1823 he settled with his mother and wife and children to Lower Halliford by the Thames, which was his home for the rest of his life. His East India Company colleagues included the philosopher James Mill and his son John Stuart Mill, and for a number of years he joined them for weekly dinners at the home of Jeremy Bentham (the Utilitarian philosopher). He published the *Misfortunes of Elphin* in 1829 and *Crotchet Castle* in 1831, works influenced by his interest in Welsh poetry and legend. He also wrote reviews on music, literature, opera, and theatre for *The Westminster Review*, *The London Review*, *The Examiner*, and *The Globe and Traveller*.

His literary pursuits tapered off as he became more involved in his position for the East India Company. He was appointed Examiner in 1836, with a salary of two thousand pounds, and he remained in the position until 1856 when he retired and was replaced by John Stuart Mill. As the Company was a trading company under the jurisdiction of the government, his position resembled that of a senior civil servant, and he undertook his duties with care and efficiency. He advocated the use of steamships and suggested that the route to India be shortened by attempting a route through the Euphrates. All of this activity, in addition to family preoccupations, meant that he published nothing between 1838 and 1850. His beloved mother died in 1833 and his wife's health remained delicate until her death in 1851. His son married against his father's wishes and his daughter Mary Ellen (who had been widowed after her first marriage), married George Meredith in 1849, whom she left in 1857 for the artist Henry Wallis. The affair became the basis for Meredith's sonnet cycle *Modern Love*. She died in 1861.

Following his retirement, Peacock turned again to writing. He produced reviews for *Fraser's Magazine* and in 1858, 1860, and 1862 published memoirs of Shelley in the journal, which were written to correct some other biographies, most notably Thomas Jefferson Hogg's *Life of Percy Bysshe Shelley* (1858). The first contribution to *Fraser's* was an essay, "Gastronomy and Civilization," co-authored with his eldest daughter Mary Ellen and published with her initials in 1851.[1] His last novel, *Gryll Grange*, appeared as a serial in *Fraser's* and was published in 1861 when he was seventy-five. He spent his final years in his garden and library and died in 1866 at the age of eighty-one, leaving his estate to his adopted daughter Mary Rosewell. A house fire the previous year which threatened his library had also weakened his already declining health.

---

1 Joukovsky, *Letters of Thomas Love Peacock* 1.xliii. See Anne Mendelson, "The Peacock-Meredith Cookbook Project: Long-Sundered Manuscripts and Unanswered Questions" (*Biblion: The Bulletin of The New York Public Library* 2.1 [1993]: 77–99).

3. Morbidities and the Reading Public: Composition, Publication, and Reception

Peacock's dislike of celebrity and gloom is not simply focused on Byron. His protest about the "systematical 'poisoning' of the 'mind' of the 'Reading Public'" is concerned with the nature of reading and the book trade in the early decades of the nineteenth century. Peacock would likely have envisioned his readership as being small and rather selective. Books were expensive; the cloth industry in Britain was necessary for book production as cotton and linen rags were the source of paper until paper from wood pulp started being used in the 1860s.[1] The price of paper increased during the Napoleonic Wars (1793 to 1815), when the supply of rags imported from France to make paper became unavailable; paper therefore contributed to one half or more of the price of a book.[2] Robert Southey observed in 1805 that "books are now so dear that that they are becoming rather articles of fashionable furniture more than anything else; they who buy them do not read them, and they who read them do not buy them."[3] Treating books as items of consumer fashion is a subject for satire in *Nightmare Abbey,* represented by the character of Mr. Listless. Nevertheless, in the early decades of the nineteenth century, high prices reflected the assumption that books were intended for a selective market. A bestseller in 1810 would sell ten or twenty thousand copies, and these would be purchased by the rich.

An alternative existed in the lending library, which provided the means for the middle classes to have access to books, especially novels.[4] Peacock's friends and publishers, the Hookhams, also ran a circulating library, which Peacock himself used. In a well-known example, Jane Austen makes clear in *Pride and Prejudice* that while Mr. Bennet has his library retreat and Mr. Darcy is maintaining his family tradition of a well-stocked library at Pemberley, the Bennet

---

1   Lee Erickson, *The Economy of Literary Form: English Literature and the Industrialization of Publishing 1800–1850* (Baltimore and London: The Johns Hopkins UP, 1996, 6–7). See also Richard Altick, *The English Common Reader: A Social History of the Mass Reading Public 1800–1900* (Chicago: U of Chicago P, 1957, 260–61) and William St. Clair, *The Reading Nation in the Romantic Period: Cambridge* (Cambridge UP, 2004).

2   Erickson 20.

3   Quoted in Erickson 23.

4   Erickson 24.

sisters get the novels they enjoy from the circulating library.[1] The popularity of the lending library meant that tastes were gradually changing, as people moved from reading poetry to novels. *Nightmare Abbey* was written three years after Sir Walter Scott abandoned poetry for fiction; Byron, whose poems sold in the tens of thousands, died in 1824, after which time poetry began to be produced in gift–book format, and literary annuals and became less of a force than formerly. Novels were typically published in copies of 500 to 1,500, with many copies sold to circulating libraries.[2] At the same time, changes in production like stereotyping (creating plates from molds of set type) and machine-made paper eventually enabled increased book production.

Readers looked to the influence of literary reviews, which were affiliated with publishing houses, including *The Edinburgh Review* (Constable), the *Quarterly Review* (John Murray), *Blackwood's Magazine* (Blackwood), and the *London Magazine* (Taylor and Hessey). The reviews were seen as having enormous power in dictating tastes. During 1817 and 1818 *Blackwood's* published "The Cockney School of Poetry" essays, which attacked Leigh Hunt and his circle, while the disappointment he suffered from a virulent review of his poem *Endymion* in the *Quarterly* in 1818 was wrongly thought to have contributed to John Keats's death in 1821. In his "Essay on Fashionable Literature" Peacock applauds the fact that if in the reviews there is a "greater diffusion of talent," they also contain "much more illiberality and exclusiveness, much more subdivision into petty gangs and factions, much less classicality and very much less philosophy" (see Appendix D, 212–13).

The growth of publishing and reviewing during the opening decades of the nineteenth century contributed to the shaping of a middle-class reading public, which in turn influenced what was produced. As a writer and the friend of publishers, Peacock was aware of the power of the literary market. Yet in 1818 he still retained the belief that writers may hold significant influence on readers. His friend Percy Shelley would say at the end of *A Defence of Poetry*,

---

1   See H.J. Jackson, "What Was Mr. Bennet Doing in his Library, and What Does It Matter?" (*Romantic Libraries*, ed. Ina Ferris, *Romantic Circles* <http://www.rc.umd.edu/praxis/libraries/jackson/jackson.html>).

2   Altick 263–64.

his serious response to Peacock's satirical polemic, "The Four Ages of Poetry," writers and poets are "unacknowledged legislators"; this phrase suggests that in spite of changes in literary tastes, authors still have some control. In 1836 Peacock playfully observes in his essay "The Épicier,"

> Among a people disposed to think, their every-day literature will bear the impress of thought; among a people not so disposed, the absence or negation of thought will be equally conspicuous in their literature. Every variety of mind takes its station, or is ready to do so, at all times in the literary market; the public of the day stamp the currency of fashion on which jumps with their humour. Milton would be forthcoming if he were wanted; but in our time Milton was not wanted, and Walter Scott was. We do not agree with the doctrine implied in Wordsworth's sonnet,
>
> > Milton! Thou shouldn'st be living at this hour:
> > England hath need of thee.
>
> England would have been the better for him, if England would have attended to him, but England would not have attended to him, if she had had him.[1]

In *Nightmare Abbey* Peacock's passion about literature's effect on the public seems to hold out the possibility that, if they are presented with good models, people can think. It is worth remembering that the phrase "Reading Public" appears in Samuel Taylor Coleridge's *The Stateman's Manual* (1816)[2] (see Appendix C, 173–75). Nicholas Joukovsky draws attention to the complexity with which Peacock regarded the term "reading public" by noting that the quotation marks in his protest against the "systematical 'poisoning' of the

---

1   Thomas Love Peacock, "The Épicier" (*The Halliford Edition of the Works of Thomas Love Peacock*. Ed. H.F.B. Brett-Smith and C.E. Jones [London: Constable, 1926], 9.294).

2   The OED suggests that the concept moves from "reading man," a university student whose occupation is reading (the final citation being the *Monthly Magazine* 3 [1797]: 266) to a wider sense of a "reading public" first noted in *Blackwood's Magazine* for January 1831, p. 94. Clearly the term was in use at an earlier date since Coleridge makes use of the phrase in his *Lay Sermons* (1816) and the *Biographia Literaria* (1817). The evolution of the concept of "reading public" reflects the growth of the audience for books in the opening decades of the nineteenth century. See also Q.D. Leavis, *Fiction and the Reading Public* (London: Chatto & Windus, 1965) and Jon Klancher, *The Making of English Reading Audiences, 1790–1832* (Madison: University of Wisconsin Press, 1987).

'mind' of the 'Reading Public'" are allusions to language character-istic of the conservative Tory press.[1] In his letter Peacock adopts the voice of a conservative to parody Tory opinions and rhetoric, but perhaps there is also a sense of ambivalence about using the phrase (not unlike the placement of "scare quotes" around phrases such as "political correctness," implying its limitations and provenance in conservative thought). Peacock questions Coleridge's perspective that writing must be addressed to the few, while also registering his own anxieties about the changing relationship between writer and reader. In his *Biographia Literaria* (1817) Coleridge notoriously calls those using circulating libraries not having *"pass-time"* but *"kill-time,"* and he describes novel-reading as being no better than swinging on a gate or spitting over a bridge.[2] Peacock's objection to Coleridge's claims is conveyed in *Nightmare Abbey* with his satirical portrait of the Coleridgean Mr. Flosky, who suggests, "the great evil is, that there is too much common-place light in our moral and political literature, and light is a great enemy to mystery, and mystery is a great friend to enthusiasm" (76).

As much as his novel can be read as a protest against gloom and obscurity in modern literature, its catalyst seems to have been a celebration of friendship—or rather the absence of friendship. The composition of *Nightmare Abbey* is linked with the departure of Percy and Mary Shelley for Italy on 11 March 1818. They spent the night before attending the first performance in England of Rossini's opera *The Barber of Seville* (1816), which Peacock considered "de-lightful" and which has its own explicit and implicit influences on the novel.[3] When he returned to Marlow he contemplated writing

---

1   Joukovsky, *Letters of Thomas Love Peacock* 1.125n. One of Peacock's many targets for satire in his writings was Tory politics, whose conservative perspective included upholding the authority and order of Church and State and opposition to any widening of parliamen-tary representation. In his day, much like our own, newspapers had particular political allegiances. Peacock is sensitive to the kinds of language that are attached to political thinking. Here the "scare tactics" of the suggestion of poison and of the stress of quotation marks are his attempt to give voice to a conservative perspective so as to gently mock it.
2   Samuel Taylor Coleridge, *Biographia Literaria* (1817), 1.3, 49–50.
3   Marionetta quotes from Rossini's *The Barber of Seville* (1816) in Chapter 5, and Chapter 13 recalls the finale of Act 1. See Margaret McKay, *Peacock's Progress: Aspects of Artistic Develop-ment in the Novels of Thomas Love Peacock* (Stockholm: Almqvist & Wiskell 1992, 37–39); Paulina June Salz, "Peacock's Use of Music in his Novels" (*JEGP* 54 [1955]: 370–79) and Ronald Tetreault, "Shelley at the Opera" (*ELH* 48 [1981]: 144–71).

a novel set in London, but soon changed his mind.[1] By the end of April he wrote to Shelley's friend Thomas Jefferson Hogg: "At present I am writing a comic romance with a title of Nightmare Abbey and amusing myself with the darkness and misanthropy of modern literature, for the lantern jaws of which I shall endeavour to elicit a laugh."[2] It is possible that part of his writing of the novel was to cheer himself; ten days after the Shelleys left he wrote to Hogg—using an unlikely pairing of Wordsworth and Falstaff—that he was "as lonely as a cloud, and as melancholy as a gib cat."[3] His comment suggests that while he may satirize certain Shelleyan perspectives in his novels, Shelley's conversation and company were of inestimable value to him.

He wrote the work very quickly between the end of March and the beginning of June. At the same time he seems to have devised some ostensibly less personal motives for writing; these reasons can be found in a letter to Shelley, written at the end of May 1818, in which he states that his novel is an objection to Byron's *Childe Harold*.[4] It should be noted that this claim—the novel's conception as a protest against Canto Four of *Childe Harold*, published 28 April 1818—is disingenuous, given the fact that by this time he was already well into composition. But this excuse did offer a focus, and Peacock does parody some stanzas from *Childe Harold* in speeches by Mr. Cypress. By 14 June he reported to Shelley that he had completed his novel.[5] Having written about the matter as fiction, in July he then tackled some of the same subjects in his unfinished "An Essay on Fashionable Literature" (see Appendix D, 210-18).

While the novel did not receive much critical attention upon its publication, *Nightmare Abbey* made a second appearance in the 1837. By 1831 it was out of print and in 1835 Thomas Hookham opened negotiations with Richard Bentley to publish *Headlong Hall, Nightmare Abbey*, and *Maid Marian* in his Standard Novels series (this series began in 1831 and ended in 1854, after 126 volumes had appeared, including Mary Shelley's *Frankenstein* and William Godwin's *Caleb Williams*). The Standard Novels were a successful series of cheap

---

1 Joukovsky, *Letters of Thomas Love Peacock* 119 and 120n.
2 Joukovsky, *Letters of Thomas Love Peacock* 1.121–22.
3 Joukovsky, *Letters of Thomas Love Peacock* 1.119 and 120n.
4 Joukovsky, *Letters of Thomas Love Peacock* 1.123.
5 Joukovsky, *Letters of Thomas Love Peacock* 1.126.

reprints at 5 or 6 shillings, about a half or third of their original cost, and about a fifth of the cost of a three-decker novel (three volumes)—the most popular format for printing fiction. The initial print runs of 3,000 copies, with subsequent runs of 1,000 copies, reflect the growth of the book market in the twenty years since the novel's first publication.[1] A sale of the copyright was arranged in December 1836, revised shortly before publication to include *Crotchet Castle*; the sum paid was seventy pounds.[2]

The works appeared in March 1837 as volume 57 of the Standard Novels and were advertised "with Corrections, and a Preface, by the Author."[3] The nature of these corrections is of several orders. Between 1818 and 1837 matters of punctuation had altered sufficiently, following a number of the conventions in accord with what we view as standard usage. The most noticeable is the substitution of the semi-colon for the colon. There are few significant alterations to the novel. A statement about "a little Jew broker" is changed to "A money-dealing Jew" and an extended and vicious attack on the French, which might be more to English tastes three years after the defeat of Napoleon, is in 1837 significantly shortened. Several slightly tangled phrases are smoothed out. The end of the novel also takes on a slightly different flavour, with Scythrop's retreat into wine. A selection of reviews of the 1818 and 1837 editions can be found in Appendix A, 135-52; William S. Ward has traced the contemporary reviews of the novel.[4]

Peacock's critics have remained relatively small in number. The first full-length studies of his life and writings did not appear until the twentieth century, given that he was not the object of a nineteenth-century life and letters. And as James Mulvihill puts it, the standard perspective was to view his fiction as an "eccentric, and inconclusive, *potpourri* of undigested opinion."[5] More recent book-length studies include chapters on the novel, which address the mat-

---

1   Altick 273–74. See Robert L. Patten, "Bentley, Richard (1794–1871)," *Oxford Dictionary of National Biography*, Oxford: Oxford UP, 2004 [http://www.oxforddnb.com/view/article/2171].

2   Joukovsky, *Letters of Thomas Love Peacock* 2.239.

3   Joukovsky, *Letters of Thomas Love Peacock* 2.233.

4   See William S. Ward, "Contemporary Reviews of Thomas Love Peacock: A Supplementary List for the Years 1805–1820" (*Bulletin of Bibliography* 25 [1967]: 35).

5   Mulvihill, *Thomas Love Peacock* iv.

ter of the "Spirit of the Age" on some level. Howard Mills in *Peacock: His Circle and His Age* (1969) considers the novel's use of Shelley and Coleridge and Peacock's tracing of different levels of the fashionable and the creative and his insights into the limitations of his times. In *His Fine Wit: A Study of Thomas Love Peacock* (1970), Carl Dawson examines the works as a critique of tendencies and types that are associated with romanticism before it became recognized as a specific movement, with emphasis on Peacock's talent for comedy. Håkan Kjellin's *Talkative Banquets: A Study in the Peacockian Novels of Talk* (1974) looks at the forms of narrative and a use of dialogue and story. Marilyn Butler's important *Peacock Displayed: A Satirist in His Context* (1979) achieves a detailed contextual reading of literary, historical, and philosophical backgrounds, and traces the intellectual debates in which he was immersed. Her version of Peacock is not as a typical bemused crotchet—as he is so often depicted as being—but as a thoughtful intellectual with a philosophy of life and art that unifies skepticism and humanism. The chapter on *Nightmare Abbey* is particularly helpful for its careful account of Peacock's classical and German influences, which Butler calls an "anatomy of a current intellectual scene" through which certain tendencies in religious introspection are promoted at the expense of Enlightenment reason and the humour of Classical Greece.[1] In the *Novels of Thomas Love Peacock* (1985) Bryan Burns demonstrates that satire gives way to comedy and an exploration of positive qualities in humanity, offering a view of Peacock as a moralist. James Mulvihill's *Thomas Love Peacock* (1987) argues that Peacock is both artist and "observer of his age": here, Peacock's view of the artist is as "an engaged citizen."[2] Mulvihill sees both *Nightmare Abbey* and *Melincourt* as responses to Percy Shelley. In the case of *Nightmare Abbey*, it is a comic corrective of passionate excess, which is more detached in its perspectives than the earlier novel. Margaret McKay in *Peacock's Progress: Aspects of Artistic Development in the Novels of Thomas Love Peacock* (1992) contains chapters on Peacock's narrative technique and style, his satire, and his presentation of clerics and women. She views the novel as literary rather than political. A number of chapters and articles are also available. Robert Polhemus in *Comic Faith* (1980) provides a reading

---

1 Butler, *Peacock Displayed* 113.
2 Mulvihill, *Thomas Love Peacock* iv.

of the novel as offering a religious image of communal experience and loss of egotistical attachment. Gary Dyer has written an excellent contribution on revolutionary enthusiasm, the introduction of "gas light" to satiric tradition (notably by Swift), and contemporary experiments using nitrous oxide. Helpful essays by James Mulvihill, Mark Cunningham, Julia Wright, and Norma Leigh Rudinsky suggest the models for the characters in the novel, while John Colmer has traced the novel's correspondences with William Godwin's *Mandeville*; and Coral Ann Howells and David M. Baulch note references to Coleridge's *Biographia Literaria*. P.J. Salz considers Peacock's use of music in his novels. Full bibliographic citations to these works can be found at the end of this Broadview edition.[1]

It is appropriate (and comic) that his initial "Reading Public" consisted of the inspiration for the figure of Scythrop. When he heard about the novel, Percy Shelley wrote, "I hope that you have given the enemy no quarter. Remember, it is a sacred war."[2] Once he read the novel he suggested,

> I am delighted with *Nightmare Abbey*. I think Scythrop a character admirably conceived and executed, and I know not how to praise sufficiently the lightness, chastity and strength of the language as a whole. It perhaps exceeds all your works in this. I suppose the moral is contained in what Falstaff says—'For God's sake talk like a man of this world;' and yet looking deeper into it, is not the misdirected enthusiasm of Scythrop what J.C. calls the salt of the earth?[3]

Shelley's comment is often quoted; it seems surprising that he should be so delighted with a novel whose main character is a satirical portrait of many of his own opinions. But what is most significant here is Shelley's understanding of the novel's values: the importance of dialogue, and principles of basic, fundamental goodness as antidotes to the poison of "black bile."

---

1   A valuable overview of Peacock's critical reputation can be found in J.P. Donovan, "Thomas Love Peacock," *Literature of the Romantic Period: A Bibliographical Guide*. Ed. Michael O'Neill (Oxford: Clarendon P, 1998), 269–83.

2   Frederick L. Jones, ed. *Letters of Percy Bysshe Shelley* 2 vols. (Oxford: Clarendon P, 1964), 2.27.

3   Jones, *Letters of Percy Bysshe Shelley*, 2.98.

4. *Nightmare Abbey* and the Morbid Anatomy of Black Bile

Peacock uses comic romance to critique the "poisoning" of the reading public; this genre includes conventions of courtship and intrigue and numerous allusions to gothic literature. *Nightmare Abbey* is set in a former abbey "in a highly picturesque state of semidilapidation" on the fens of Lincoln. The abbey's owner, Christopher Glowry, is host to a number of visitors meant to compliment his "atrabilarious temperament" and who enjoy his hospitality (wine) and engage in endless debate. As the novel is a satire, Peacock had in mind specific figures—and, more importantly, their ideas and opinions. These would have been recognizable to his readers among the novel's characters: Mr. Flosky (Coleridge, an enemy of common sense); Mr. Toobad, "the Manichaean Millinarian" (J.F. Newton, a friend of Percy Shelley's who inspired ideas in his poem *Queen Mab* and his vegetarianism); the Reverend Larnyx, a kind of general stereotype of the worldly clergyman who may be based on Thomas Moore; Mr. Asterias, who believes in mermaids, and is likely based on a French scientist Denys de Montfort; Mr. Listless, the fashionable reader (Shelley's friend Sir Lumley Skeffington or perhaps the dandy Beau Brummel); and Mr. Cypress (Byron).[1]

Mr. Glowry's son and heir, Scythrop, has suffered a disappointment in love. He locks himself up in a tower where he reads German tragedies and transcendental philosophy, and develops a "passion for reforming the world." He leaves his solitary pursuits and becomes

---

1   Marilyn Butler wisely reminds readers that Peacock denied representing private characters of specific individuals and cautions against making correspondences that are too specific (*Peacock Displayed* 16–19). A number of critics have attempted such identifications. See Harold Brooks, "A Song from Mr. Cypress" (*Review of English Studies* 38 [1987]: 368–74); Mark Cunningham, "'Fatout! Who Am I?': A Model for the Honourable Mr. Listless in Thomas Love Peacock's *Nightmare Abbey*" (*English Language Notes* 30.1 [1992]: 43–45); James Mulvihill, "A Prototype for Mr. Toobad in Peacock's *Nightmare Abbey*" (*Notes and Queries* 49 [2002]: 470–71); Norma Leigh Rudinsky, "Contemporary Response to the Caricature Asterias in Peacock's *Nightmare Abbey*" (*Notes and Queries.* 24 [1977]: 335–36); "Satire on Sir John Sinclair before Peacock's Asterias in *Nightmare Abbey*" (*Notes and Queries* 23 [1976]: 108–10); "A Second Original of Peacock's Menippean Caricature Asterias in *Nightmare Abbey*: Sir John Sinclair, Bart" (*English Studies: A Journal of English Language and Literature* 56 [1975]: 491–97); and "Source of Asteria's Paean to Science in Peacock's *Nightmare Abbey* (*Notes and Queries* 22 [1975]: 66–68); James Smith, "Peacock's Mr. Asterias and 'Polypodes': A Possible Source" (*Notes and Queries* 51 [2004]: 157); Julia M. Wright, "Peacock's Early Parody of Thomas Moore in *Nightmare Abbey*" (*English Language Notes* 30.4 [1993]: 31–38).

attracted to the charms of the flirtatious Marionetta Celestina O'Carroll, who is visiting with her guardians, the good-humoured Mr. and Mrs. Hilary (Mr. Glowry's sister). However Mr. Glowry has arranged for Scythrop to marry Mr. Toobad's intellectual daughter Celinda, who has fled her father in protest against his authority and the idea of arranged marriage. Ironically, she flees to the tower of the very man she is refusing to marry (she is one of the seven people who has read Scythrop's treatise "Philosophical Gas; or, a Project for a General Illumination of the Human Mind"). She introduces herself as "Stella" (in an allusion to Goethe's melodramatic play of the same name [see Appendix B, 155-59]). Scythrop is unable to choose between Marionetta and Celinda. When the women discover each another's presence, they quickly find husbands among the other guests (Mr. Listless and Mr. Flosky). A sorrowful Scythrop decides the only thing to do is to take the route of Goethe's melancholic young Werther and commit suicide, but circumstances persuade him to follow his father in a love of misanthropy and Madeira.

The true appeal of the work neither lies in the plot nor in its *roman à clef* aspects of a work of fiction with recognizable characters, but in the witty and urbane conversations between characters.[1] These conversations include discussions of "the morbid anatomy of black bile," which captures some of the novel's complexities, as well as its delights. The phrase comes from a passage in Chapter 5 where a selection of recently published books and journals arrives at Nightmare Abbey. Mr. Flosky examines them:

> (*Turning over the leaves.*) "Devilman, a novel." Hm. Hatred—revenge—misanthropy—and quotations from the Bible. Hm. This is the morbid anatomy of black bile—"Paul Jones, a poem." Hm. I see how it is. Paul Jones, an amiable enthusiast—disappointed in his affections—turns pirate from ennui and magnanimity—cuts various masculine throats, wins various feminine hearts—is hanged at the yard-arm! The catastrophe is very awkward, and very unpoetical.—"The Downing-Street Review." Hm. First article—An Ode to the Red Book, by Roderick Sackbut, Esquire. Hm. His own poem reviewed by himself. Hm-m-m. (70–71)

---

1 A roman à clef (French for "novel with a key") is a novel in which actual persons are included under fictitious names, and it is assumed the reader will be able to recognize them despite their disguised identities.

"Devilman" is a satirical allusion to Godwin's *Mandeville: A Tale of the Seventeenth Century* (1817), while "Paul Jones" (the American Revolutionary War naval hero considered a traitor by the British) refers to Byron's *Corsair* (1814)—a poem which sold an amazing 10,000 copies on its day of publication. "Mr. Sackbut" is Poet Laureate Robert Southey, who was associated with the *Quarterly Review* and is satirized writing a poem in tribute to the book containing the names of persons receiving pensions from the State. Like Byron and Shelley, Peacock felt contempt for Southey's growing political conservatism. Surprisingly Mr. Flosky is actually a supporter of black bile—that is, of excessive gloom. He is the character who declares, "Modern literature is a north-east wind—a blight of the human soul. I take credit to myself for having helped to make it so" (72).

This passage reveals a great deal about the state of literature in 1818, and about what was popular in terms of genre: novel, poetry, and review. Clearly the Glowrys have enough money to purchase books (although given Nightmare Abbey's remote location, it is unlikely that a circulating library would have been close at hand). But the passage more significantly reveals Peacock's discontent with modern literature. Peacock has German literature in mind, in particular gothic plays and romances in which the supernatural, terror, heightened emotion, and intrigue of the most unlikely sort are central to the plot. Marilyn Butler calls Scythrop a "thorough-going Germanist": the romances, horror fiction (or *Schauerroman*), and German tragedies that fill his mind with thoughts of secret tribunals and Illuminati create "an ingenious anthology of German literature" as well as a "humorous counter-proposition" of a subject Coleridge treats more seriously in the *Biographia Literaria*.[1] Peacock is playfully drawing on the kinds of literature his friend Percy Shelley reads (excerpts from a selection of these texts are included in Appendix B, 153-67). He is also exploring the potential for self-indulgence and flights from common sense encouraged by writing given to gloom and unwholesome brooding. In this respect Peacock's novel is not that far from Jane Austen's satire of the Gothic in *Northanger Abbey*

---

1   Butler, *Peacock Displayed* 124. See also Baulch, David M. "The 'Perpetual Exercise of an Interminable Quest': The *Biographia Literaria* and the Kantian Revolution" (*Studies in Romanticism* 43 [2004]: 557-81) and "Several Hundred Pages of Promise: The Phantom of the Gothic in Peacock's *Nightmare Abbey* and Coleridge's *Biographia Literaria*" (*Coleridge Bulletin* 25 [2005]:71-77).

(1818) where Catherine Morland confuses what she reads about in works like the *Mysteries of Udolpho* (1794) for reality—while ironically the world around her turns out to be sinister in utterly banal respects. Scythrop "slept with Horrid Mysteries under his pillow, and dreamed of venerable eleutherarchs and ghastly confederates holding midnight conventions in subterranean caves. He passed whole mornings in his study, immersed in gloomy reverie, stalking about the room in his night-cap, which he pulled over his eyes like a cowl, and folding his striped calico dressing-gown about him like the mantle of a conspirator" (57). He is every bit as comical as Catherine Morland in his literary tastes and his reception of what he reads.

But the reference to "black bile" suggests a more serious point than merely poking fun at Scythrop's "gloomy reverie" in his night-cap. Peacock is concerned with the relation between writers and the reading public. The Gothic romance in the early nineteenth century formed a current of popular literature that influenced the character of British writing; it is worth taking a closer look at the phrase "the morbid anatomy of black bile." Associations with the world of disease, the four humours, bile, anatomy, and melancholy are all matters that also pertain to health and to the body. With "the morbid anatomy of black bile," Peacock forges a connection between literature and a nation's well-being; his comic phrase not only parodies the gothic, but also suggests reasons why writing and reading are highly relevant to the health of the body politic. Scythrop Glowry takes Mr. Flosky's perspective too much to heart, as he spends his time in a ruined tower reading romances and German tragedies. In this solitude, "the distempered ideas of metaphysical romance and romantic metaphysics had ample time and space to germinate into a fertile crop of chimeras, which rapidly shot up into vigorous and abundant vegetation." Scythrop's "passion for reforming the world" inspires him to "build castles in the air" and people them "with secret tribunals, and bands of illuminati, who were always the imaginary instruments of his projected regeneration of the human species." Scythrop partakes of an excess of introspection and obscurity:

Scythrop proceeded to meditate on the practicability of reviving a confederation of regenerators. To get a clear view of his own ideas, and to feel the pulse of the wisdom and genius of the age, he wrote and published a treatise, in which his meanings were carefully wrapt up in the monk's hood of transcendental technology, but filled with hints of matter deep and dangerous, which he thought would set the whole nation in a ferment; and he awaited the result in awful expectation, as a miner, who has fired a train, awaits the explosion of a rock. However, he listened and heard nothing; for the explosion, if any ensued, was not sufficiently loud to shake a single leaf of the ivy on the towers of Nightmare Abbey; and some months afterwards he received a letter from his bookseller, informing him that only seven copies had been sold, and concluding with a polite request for the balance.

Scythrop did not despair. "Seven copies," he thought, "have been sold. Seven is a mystical number, and the omen is good. Let me find the seven purchasers of my seven copies, and they shall be the seven golden candlesticks with which I will illuminate the world." (58)

Peacock's satire of secret societies captured in the writings of the Abbé de Barruel, which he knew through Shelley, has been carefully documented by Gary Dyer.[1] If Peacock wishes us to laugh at the fact that the solipsistic Scythrop does find a reader in Celinda (one of the seven people who has purchased his treatise "Philosophical Gas; or, a Project for a General Illumination of the Human Mind"), the joke also points to the importance of the reception of writing by the "Reading Public." If writers need readers, Peacock also believes that works should engage with public discourse rather than simply confirm complaisance and solipsism.

Mr. Listless voices the problem—that fashionable writing is "a very fine mental tonic, which reconciles me to my favorite pursuit of doing nothing, by shewing me that nobody is worth doing any thing for" (88). He suggests that "modern books are very consolatory and congenial to my feelings. There is, as it were, a delightful north-east wind, an intellectual blight, breathing through them; a delicious misanthropy and discontent, that demonstrates the nullity of virtue and energy, and puts me in good humour with myself

---

1 Gary Dyer, "Peacock and the 'Philosophical Gas' of the Illuminati." *Secret Texts: The Literature of Secret Societies*. Eds. Marie Mulvey-Roberts, Hugh Ormsby-Lennon and Michael Foot (New York: AMS, 1995), 188–209.

and my sofa" (72). *Nightmare Abbey* is after all a book written post-Waterloo, a period of disenchantment for those who looked to the French Revolution as a source for political and social change, and considers the perspectives of the Byronic Childe Harold and the so-called "apostasy" of the Lake Poets that encourage "black bile" and inaction.[1] The comments by Mr. Flosky (the man of letters) and Mr. Listless (the reader) convey Peacock's belief that both writing and conversation are more than matters of fashion: they should also be concerned with encouraging virtue, energy, and consideration towards others. At the heart of the novel is his critique of the intellectual misuse of artistic powers, and a firm belief that literary matters do have a political import if writers are able to influence their readers.

With this in mind it is helpful to return to the reference to "Devilman" and its allusion to William Godwin's *Mandeville* (1817), a historical novel set during the time of the English Civil War. It draws upon Charles Brockden Brown's novel *Wieland* (1798) and Joanna Baillie's play *De Monfort* (1800), both of which are concerned with the subject of obsessive forms of jealousy. *Mandeville* is an intense study in the psychology of a jealous character in which Godwin explores how faulty education can have a tragic effect on the development of such an individual. Mandeville lives with his uncle in seclusion in Northern Ireland and is raised to abhor Catholics. He is sent to school at Winchester College, England. Here he meets Clifford, who becomes the object of his obsessive hatred. The events of the novel are played out against the career of Cromwell in the seventeenth century. Its hero's tragic career asks readers to discover a means to freedom that Mandeville is unable to discover. The novel's themes resemble those of another novel published in the same year as *Nightmare Abbey*: *Frankenstein* by Godwin's daughter, Mary Shel-

---

1   The Duke of Wellington's defeat of Napoleon at Waterloo in 1815 was a decisive victory for the British and marked Britain's place of power in Europe. However those with republican sentiments who saw the French Revolution as a sign of political renovation could not be cheered by what Lord Byron calls in Stanza 17 of *Childe Harold's Pilgrimage* Canto 3 "a king-making Victory." His question "but is the world more free?" and bitter response *"prove* before ye praise" in Stanza 19 capture some of this perspective. At the same time the peace led to a depression in agriculture and manufacturing and high levels of unemployment and social tension as the working classes agitated for reform. See Linda Colley, *Britons: Forging the Nation 1707–1837* (New Haven: Yale UP, 1992), especially pages 320–24.

ley.[1] The Shelleys received a copy of *Mandeville* on 1 December 1817 (*Nightmare Abbey* was written between April and June 1818). Several critics have noted that there are similarities between the books, including aspects of setting as well as a father figure whose disappointment in love has driven him to misanthropy. Marilyn Butler suggests "there is much more about Godwin in *Nightmare Abbey* than first meets the eye," though she takes the perspective that is it irritation, not emulation, and that Peacock's novel is an example of negative satire. According to Butler, Peacock "deplores the contemporary Godwin" of determinism and fatalism.[2] In this way, *Mandeville* is part of the general malaise expressed by Mr. Flosky (the writer) echoing Mr. Listless (the fashionable reader): "Modern literature is a north-east wind—a blight of the human soul. I take credit to myself for having helped to make it so" (72). James Mulvihill argues that Flosky "matter-of-factly attributes it to a peevish humor of the age, and thus of a kind with the 'blue devils' that plague the neurotic Mr. Glowry."[3] But Peacock the author must not be conflated with his characters; nor does the author of "Devilman" join the circle at Nightmare Abbey; instead, Peacock focuses on the response of the "Reading Public" assembled there.

Accordingly, Peacock might be more in agreement with Godwin than not. Pamela Clemit argues that Godwin's novel is not so much an abandonment to fatalism as it is an exploration of the complex forces, including interiority, that form character (something Mary Shelley also pursues in *Frankenstein*). In this way, *Mandeville* marks a change in Godwin's thinking, reflecting increasing doubt "about man's rational capacities already registered in his revisions to *Political Justice*."[4] In Peacock's terms, Mandeville suffers from the "morbid anatomy of black bile." Mandeville's isolation and detachment are shared by Scythrop, a comic portrait of the inspired enthusiast who ignores the possibilities for growth that are available through conversation and sociability. Godwin's belief in a need "to stress the pro-

---

1   For discussion of *Mandeville* see Pamela Clemit, *The Godwinian Novel: The Rational Fictions of Godwin, Brockden Brown, Mary Shelley* (Oxford: Clarendon P, 1993), 96–102 and John Colmer, "Godwin's *Mandeville* and Peacock's *Nightmare Abbey*" (*Review of English Studies: A Quarterly Journal of English Literature and the English Language* 21 [1970]: 331–36).
2   Butler, *Peacock Displayed* 120, 122.
3   Mulvihill, *Thomas Love Peacock* 62.
4   Clemit 99.

found internal level at which political reform must begin"[1] is shared by Peacock. However, in *Nightmare Abbey* his critique of excessive interiority is manifested in gently satiric ways, such as in Scythrop's miscalculated suggestion to Marionetta that they "open a vein in the other's arm" and "mix our blood in a bowl, and drink it as a sacrament of love" (in emulation of *Horrid Mysteries*) (62–63), or his desire to give way to self-indulgent isolation in his disappointments at political reform and love.

Mandeville is not the only work by Godwin with which Peacock was familiar. There is also a brief reference to *Caleb Williams* (1794) in Chapter 8 when Mr. Flosky describes "the various ways of getting at secrets ... recommended both theoretically and practically in philosophical novels" (94). Peacock was given a copy of Godwin's *Enquiry Concerning Political Justice* (1793, revised 1796, 1798) by Edward Hookham in 1809.[2] The critical commonplace is that Peacock satirizes Godwin's belief in perfectibility, that is, the capacity for humanity to progress towards physical, mental, or moral perfection, as an impossibility. But Peacock's point of view is more complicated. In his 1836 essay "The Épicier" ("the grocer"), Peacock compares two French novelists: "Pigault le Brun lived in the days of the Rights of Man, Political Justice, and Moral and Intellectual Perfectability. Paul de Kock lives in the days of the march of mechanics, in the days of political economy, in the days of prices-current and percentages, in the days when even to dream like a democrat of the Constituent Assembly, would be held to qualify the dreamer for Bedlam; in short, in the days of the *épicier.*"[3] Peacock makes an allusion here to Godwin with the suggestions that the 1790s were a more "hopeful" era.

A quarter century after 1793 and a far less optimistic epoch, in 1818 Peacock seems to share with Godwin a belief in the importance of removing unhealthy influences and encouraging dialogue. In his *Enquiry Concerning Political Justice* Godwin calls this "the collision of mind with mind":

> The restless activity of intellect will for a time be fertile in paradox and error; but these will be only diurnals, while the truths that oc-

---

1 Clemit 102.
2 Joukovsky, *Letters of Thomas Love Peacock* 1.36.
3 "The Épicier," *Halliford Edition* 9.295.

casionally spring up, like sturdy plants, will defy the rigour of season and climate. In proportion as one reasoner compares his deductions with those of another, the weak places of his argument will be detected, the principles he too hastily adopted will be overthrown, and the judgments, in which his mind was exposed to no sinister influence, will be confirmed. All that is requisite in these discussions is unlimited speculation, and a sufficient variety of systems and opinions.[1]

This suggests a counter to those fertile chimeras that spring up in Scythrop's mind, which he cannot test if he is content to remain in his tower isolated from healthy forms of social interchange. Scythrop's "passion for reforming the world" is a comic version of Mandeville's single-mindedness, as well as a kind of opposite of Godwinian sociability:

[...] conversation accustoms us to hear a variety of sentiments, obliges us to exercise patience and attention, and gives freedom and elasticity to our mental disquisitions. A thinking man, if he will recollect his intellectual history, will find that he has derived inestimable advantage from the stimulus and surprise of colloquial suggestions; and if he review the history of literature, will perceive that minds of great acuteness and ability have commonly existed in a cluster.[2]

It is the "cluster" that comes from conversation that will concern the final section of this introduction.

5. Conversation and Laughter: The Form of the Novel

Peacock's fictions are novels of talk, to the extent that at times they lose their narrative and become predominantly dialogue. There are a number of sources for this: the dialogues of Plato, the recitative of Rossini's operas, eighteenth-century philosophical writings by Hume, Berkeley, and Voltaire, the dialogues of Lucian, Richard Hurd's *Moral and Political Dialogues* (1788), and novels of Robert Bage, especially *Hermsprong* (1796). Peacock admired the satire of

---

1 William Godwin, *Enquiry Concerning Political Justice* (1793), 1.4, Section 1, "Literature."
2 Godwin, *Enquiry*, 4.2, Section 3, "Of Political Associations."

Aristophanes, Petronius, Rabelais, Swift, and Voltaire. But Peacock borrowed widely, and while he has what Carl Dawson calls "a magpie approach to fiction," his writings are "at the same time unmistakably his own."[1] There is a multiplicity of voices in his works, especially when his characters attempt to define and puzzle out what is meant by "lived romanticism."

Peacock resists aligning himself with any single outlook. Lorna Sage argues that "though he needs footnotes, they are footnotes that lead back to the excitement and insecurity of a generation that experimented with life, and are very much worth pursuing. What makes him a truly difficult writer is not his material, but his attitude to it, his mischievous refusal to guide his readers through this maze of conflicting styles of thought."[2] Sage suggests that the "result is that we are forced, for the moment, into a very uncomfortable state of skepticism, an awareness of the ease with which Reason becomes the tool of Prejudice, and 'dialogue' serves to isolate each participant even further in his own lonely conviction."[3] Peacock is aware of the isolating aspects of dialogue when "lonely conviction" rules the day: it is conversation as a concept, rather than particular contexts or styles of thought (no matter how exciting), that is the key to the novel.

Peacock's social milieu was all about conversations, which gave rise to many literary forms of interchange: Coleridge's "Conversation Poems"; the dialogue found in poetry by Wordsworth and Coleridge; the narratives within narratives in *Frankenstein*; the witty exchanges of Jane Austen's *Pride and Prejudice*; Percy Shelley's imagined dialogue with a version of Byron in "Julian and Maddalo." And one might add Shelley's own exchange with Thomas Love Peacock between "The Four Ages of Poetry" and *A Defense of Poetry*. *Nightmare Abbey* offers conversation as a means for overcoming gloom and an overriding sense that other people do not matter. *Nightmare Abbey* foregrounds the importance of conversation as an ideal, rather than becoming overly entwined in its particular content. Regardless of the satirical context, it remains abundantly clear that Scythrop

---

1   Carl Dawson, *His Fine Wit: A Study of Thomas Love Peacock* (London: Routledge and Kegan Paul, 1970), 171, 170.
2   Lorna Sage, ed. "Introduction." *Peacock: The Satirical Novels* (London: Longmans, Green, and Co., 1976), 11–12.
3   Sage 12.

needs to leave his tower, and the visitors to Nightmare Abbey need to escape the manacles of their particular crotchets. Conversation should put ideas in circulation, and correct excessively singular points of view, or perspectives that threaten to keep individuals isolated from sociability.

Scythrop's solipsism is shared in different ways by all of the characters in the novel who represent such singular points of view (or hobby houses and crotchets). In Chapter Eleven Mr. Cypress comes to say farewell to "the moody Mr. Glowry and the mysterious Mr. Scythrop, the sublime Mr. Flosky and the pathetic Mr. Listless." They quickly discover that the one point on which they can agree is the drinking of wine, which they toast from their individual perspectives. The passage is a bravura presentation of a spectrum of lonely conviction, with the attendant declaration by Mr. Asterias that wine "is the only key of conversational truth." As the characters crawl back into the shells of their particular crotchets following a discussion of the spirit of the age, Mr. Hilary offers some advice, which implies a connection between black bile and the body politic:

> To reconcile man, as he is, to the world as it is, to preserve and improve all that is good, and destroy or alleviate all that is evil, in physical and moral nature,—have been the hope and aim of the greatest teachers and ornaments of our species. I will say, too, that the highest wisdom and the highest genius have been invariably accompanied with cheerfulness. We have sufficient proofs on record, that Shakespeare and Socrates were the most festive of companions. But now the little wisdom and genius we have, seem to be entering into a conspiracy against cheerfulness. (113)

Shakespeare and Socrates are not only considered (in Mr. Hilary's mind at least) festive companions, they write in dialogue, again foregrounding the importance of conversation. The conspiracy against cheerfulness is, for Peacock, a more significant threat than anything Scythrop can imagine. And perhaps Peacock implies that rational disputation might not always be the ideal model for communication. In spite of its seeming lack of clear purpose, sometimes an apparently less focused and circuitous form of exchange can bring individuals to a consensus, or perhaps even to adopt new points of view.

Through Mr. Hilary, the group achieves a rare moment of harmony. The Byronic Mr. Cypress presents a solitary song, "There is a fever of the spirit, / The brand of Cain's unresting doom." When those assembled fall into black bile, Mr. Hilary insists that they sing a popular catch, "Seamen three":

> This catch was so well executed by the spirit and science of Mr. Hilary, and the deep tri-une voice of the reverend gentleman, that the whole party, in spite of themselves, caught the contagion, and joined in chorus at the conclusion, each raising a bumper to his lips:
> The bowl goes trim: the moon doth shine:
> And our ballast is old wine. (115)

Conversely, "Mr. Cypress, having his ballast on board, stepped, the same evening, into his bowl, or travelling chariot; and departed to rake seas and rivers, lakes and canals, for the moon of ideal beauty" (116). Here we have a model of sociability based on laughter and chorus, speaking together, and the rejections of solitary individualism in favour of a moment of the carnivalesque of subversive popular humour. The implication is that for all their rarity, such moments are indeed possible.

J.P. Donovan's elegant summary of Peacock's critical reputation explains why he is so often seen as a writer who can only appeal to a limited number of "cultivated" readers:

> From his own day until well into the twentieth century his appeal has typically been accounted for on an implicit (and sometimes explicit) analogy with the old Madeira wine so relished by his characters: this makes him out to be at once pungent and mellow, rather cordial and tonic than intoxicating, improving with age and to be regularly savoured in small quantities, above all an acquired taste for the cultivated palate.[1]

Some contexts can be put around the "Madeira factor." An important point is that this is not the Peacock of 1818.

For all the talking that goes on in *Nightmare Abbey*, Peacock is nowhere under the illusion that dialogue is easily achieved. Equally

---

1 Donovan 269.

often, people do not listen: in Chapter Thirteen, for example, Scythrop, in an attempt to conceal Celinda's presence, tries to drown out his father's voice with a disquisition on the anatomy of the ear. But elsewhere Scythrop listens to his father, including at the end of the novel, where he responds to an observation made by his father that "the fatal time is past," by saying he is qualified to "take a very advanced degree in misanthropy; and there is, therefore, good hope that I may make a figure in the world" (134). If Scythrop still has much to learn, he imagines abandoning his solitude for a skeptical engagement with the world. This implies that he must recognize more of the world than simply the joys of Madeira. Peacock seems to have been far less optimistic in the 1837 revision of his novel which ends with Scythrop pointing to the dining room and calling for Madeira—a retreat merely into wine, rather than towards the communality that wine can offer.

Clearly, *Nightmare Abbey* offers far more than esoteric chitchat and Madeira to savour. It is about the importance of escaping subjectivity and solipsism, and the need to test our ideas and those of others through a process of dialogue. It is a work which fits well into the Broadview Editions series, with its emphasis on social and temporal contexts. Lorna Sage's belief that the novel's necessary footnotes, which "lead back to the excitement and insecurity of a generation that experimented with life, and are very much worth pursuing,"[1] may be tested by readers of the present edition. The appendices give further contexts, including samples of German romanticism, and examples of Peacock's other writings. But one need not agree with Sage that Peacock maintains a "mischievous refusal to guide his readers through this maze of conflicting styles of thought."[2] The format of the Literary Text Series helps us understand that refusal is not the issue. Rather, it is a matter of advocacy for two simultaneous needs: one is to be amused by particular styles of thought and the people who embody them, and the other is to feel affection for these people. Peacock also suggests that consensus and change can only come about through listening to and engaging with others. If this suggests why the novel is well worth reading, it also invites us to consider its place among more canonical fiction. *Nightmare Abbey*

---

1   Sage, 11.
2   Sage, 11–12.

can help us to appreciate the importance of forms of sociability in other literature of the age. Readers might turn to Broadview editions of two other works published in 1818, Jane Austen's *Northanger Abbey* and Mary Shelley's *Frankenstein*, and with the help of a "critic abnormally sensitive to the important movements of the mind and spirit in his age,"[1] perhaps read these works in a new and illuminating manner. At the same time, Peacock might also appeal to readers who care about ideas. Peacock's writings invite those who have the power to read and think to consider the privileges they possess, as well as the responsibilities that accompany such privilege.

---

1   House, 997.

A Note on the Text

Like the much more celebrated case of *Frankenstein* (which has significant variants between its 1818 and 1831 editions), there are two different editions of *Nightmare Abbey*: the first edition of 1818 and a revision prepared for an 1837 volume containing several of Peacock's novels. It is an intention of this edition to give readers a sense of the novel in its original form, while also documenting its subsequent revision by Peacock. The book's publication history offers some insight into the changing nature of the book trade in England during the first half of the nineteenth century. Accordingly, substantive changes to the text made in 1837 are given in the notes.

Nightmare Abbey was published by Peacock's friend Thomas Hookham in 1818 in a one volume duodecimo format, at a price of 6 shillings and 6 pence. It was issued in paper boards of a greenish-brown colour (though some copies have blue-grey boards), uncut edges, white end papers, and paper label on the spine. The text begins on signature B (paginated as page one) and concludes on signature L *verso* (page 218) which is pasted in as a single leaf. A line and "Printed by Jas. Adlard and Sons, 23 Bartholomew Close." are printed in smaller type on the *verso* of the title page at the bottom of the final page. The text is preceded by two leaves (signature A) on which are printed the title page and the quotation from Jonson's *Every Man in His Humour*.

The novel was revised by the author and published with *Headlong Hall,* *Maid Marian*, and *Crochet Castle* as volume 57 of Bentley's Standard Novels in 1837 (Mary Shelley's 1831 version of *Frankenstein* is also part of the series). Opposite to the title page (which includes an engraving of a scene from *Maid Marian*) is a frontispiece by J. Cawse depicting an event in Chapter 12 as the guests at Nightmare Abbey are startled by the apparition of a ghost shrouded in drapery with a bloody turban on its head (identified in Chapter 14 as the servant Crow sleep walking in a sheet and a red nightcap). The revisions are both of a substantive and stylistic nature. Spelling and punctuation are revised according to the standards of the late 1830s, including words ending in "-or" to "-our", "staid" to "stayed," "shew" to "show"; the use of the colon changed to semi-colon; and a number of commas added or deleted. The use of the capital for proper nouns ("Triton" for example) is omitted in 1837. The substantial changes are given in notes within the text and include correction of errors, a slightly less offensive statement about a Jewish money lender, and a shortened and less provocative statement about the French. Peacock also added some additional lines to the end of the novel, by having Scythrop call for Madeira—taking some emphasis off a potentially more political reading of the novel. A cheap reprint of *Headlong Hall* and *Nightmare Abbey* in a one volume, shilling "yellow back" was published by Lock and Ward in 1856 and is of no textual significance.[1]

While 1837 was the choice of copy-text for the Halliford Edition as well as Garnett and Wright, I see the 1818 text as being more significant, both in terms of Peacock's original intentions as well as the text Percy Shelley and Peacock's other readers would have seen. I have retained Peacock's spelling and punctuation to give readers a sense of what reading the text was like in 1818. An obvious misspelling of "technilogy" for "technology" in Chapter 2 (58) has been corrected. While "or" endings for words like "honor" are favoured in the 1818 text (and changed to "our" endings in 1837), a few "our" endings also appear. Peacock did not include accents in Greek quotations. I have used copies of the first edition at Pforzheimer Library, New York Public Library (text formerly in the collection of C.E. Jones), and the Munby Reading Room, University Library, Cambridge University (shelfmark Syn.7.81.37).

Original author notes have been retained in the text and appendices and are identified by asterisks and daggers. Where necessary, editorial explanations of the original author notes are included in square brackets.

---

1 See Brett-Smith, H.F.B. and C.E. Jones, eds. *The Halliford Edition of the Works of Thomas Love Peacock*. 10 vols. (London: Constable, 1924–34), 3.147.

Thomas Love Peacock: A Brief Chronology

[For a detailed chronology of events, readers should consult volume one of Nicholas A. Joukovsky's *The Letters of Thomas Love Peacock*.]

1785   Born 18 October, Weymouth, Dorsetshire, only child of Samuel Peacock and Sarah Love.

1791   Moves with his mother to Chertsey, twenty miles from London, to live near his maternal grandparents.

1792–98 Attends school run by John Harris Wicks at Englefield Green; begins writing poetry circa 1795.

1794   Peacock's father dies.

1800   Employed as a clerk in London and lives with his mother. A poem, "Is History or Biography the more Improving Study," is published in *The Juvenile Library*.

1804   Publishes *The Monks of St. Mark*, a humourous poem.

1805   *Palmyra and other Poems* published. Death of his grandfather Thomas Love at Chertsey.

1806   Summer walking tour of Scotland.

1807   Returns to live in Chertsey. Brief engagement with Fanny Falkner. Begins influential friendship with Edward and Thomas Hookham, who publish his writings (1810–37).

1808–09 Clerk on the H.M.S. *Venerable*, a warship he called a "floating Inferno." Writes prologues and humourous poems.

1809   Excursion along the Thames.

1810   *The Genius of the Thames* published by the Hookhams. Visits Wales, where he meets his future wife. His maternal grandmother dies.

1811–13 Period of financial uncertainty. Works on two farces that are included in *Headlong Hall*.

1812   *The Philosophy of Melancholy* published by the Hookhams, who introduce him to Shelley.

1813   Sees Shelley and meets Thomas Jefferson Hogg and William Godwin. His "grammatico-allegorical ballad" for children, *Sir Hornbook*, published. Visits Wales and travels with Shelley and Harriet Shelley to the Lake District and Scotland.

1814   Begins his unfinished Spenserian romance "Ahrimanes."
        The Hookhams publish *Sir Proteus*, a satirical attack on
        Southey. Shelley elopes with Mary Godwin.
1815   Arrested for debt as the result of an affair with a woman.
        Considers emigrating to Canada. Moves to Marlow near
        Shelley's house at Bishopgate and accepts a stipend from
        Shelley. Boating excursion up the Thames with Shelley
        and Mary. *Headlong Hall* (dated 1816) published by Thomas
        Hookham late in the year.
1816   Second edition of *Headlong Hall*. Suicide of Harriet Shelley;
        Shelley marries Mary Godwin. Works on *Melincourt*.
1817   *Melincourt*, "by the author of *Headlong Hall*," published by
        Thomas Hookham. A children's work, *The Round Table*,
        published. Closely in contact with Shelley who publishes
        Laon and Cythna; Peacock writes *Rhododaphne; or the Thes-
        salian Spirit*.
1818   *Rhododaphne* published by Thomas Hookham. The Shelleys
        leave for Italy. Begins the unfinished essay "On Fashion-
        able Literature." Works on *Maid Marian*. Begins his thirty-
        seven year career with the East India Company. *Nightmare
        Abbey* published by Thomas Hookham.
1820   Marries Jane Gryffyd. Publishes "The Four Ages of Po-
        etry" in *Olliers' Literary Miscellany*.
1821   Trip to Wales. Works on *Maid Marian*. Birth of his daugh-
        ter Mary Ellen.
1822   *Maid Marian* published by Thomas Hookham, which is
        adapted for theatre. Third edition of *Headlong Hall*. Shelley
        dies and Peacock becomes (with Byron) executor of the
        estate, a task which takes much of his time for the next
        several years. Meets Jeremy Bentham.
1823   Birth of his daughter Margaret Love.
1824   Death of Byron.
1825   Birth of his son Edward Gryffydh.
1825–26 Works on *Paper-Money Lyrics*, satiric poems published in
        1837.
1826   Death of his daughter Margaret; her grief over the death
        makes his wife a "nervous invalid." Moves his family to
        Lower Halliford, on the Thames, which is his residence
        for the remainder of his life. Adopts Mary Ann ("May")
        Roswell, who resembles his dead daughter.

1827	Birth of his daughter Rosa Jane. Writes a critical review of Thomas Moore's *The Epicurean*, followed in 1830 by an attack on Moore's *Byron*.
1829	Asked by East India Company to investigate steam navigation. Thomas Hookham publishes *The Misfortunes of Elphin*.
1829–36	Writes opera and other music criticism for *The Globe* and for *The Examiner*.
1830	Writes essays for *The Westminster Review* on Thomas Moore, Thomas Jefferson, and London Bridge. Appointed Senior Assistant Examiner for the East India Company.
1831	Thomas Hookham publishes *Crotchet Castle*.
1833	Death of his mother.
1835	Publishes an essay on Steam Navigation in the *Edinburgh Review* and his essay "French Comic Romances" in *The London Review*. His ideas influenced the East India Company to build ships, his "iron chickens," to his specifications.
1836	Succeeds James Mill as Examiner for the East India Company. Publishes "The Épicier" in *The London Review*.
1837	*Headlong Hall, Nightmare Abbey, Maid Marian, and Crotchet Castle* reprinted as No. LVII in Richard Bentley's Standard Novels. His autobiographical essay "The Abbey House: Recollections of Childhood" published in *Bentley's Miscellany*. *Paper-Money Lyrics* published.
1843	*Sir Hornbook* reprinted.
1844	Birth of his granddaughter Edith Nicholls.
1849	Marriage of his daughter Mary Ellen to writer George Meredith; marriage of his son and his daughter Rosa Jane.
1851	Death of his wife who was ill for many years. Writes "Gastronomy and Civilization" with Mary which is published in *Fraser's Magazine*. Works on an unfinished cookbook, "The Science of Cookery."
1852	Begins a series of essays on drama for *Fraser's Magazine*.
1856	Retires from India House.
1857	Death of his daughter Rosa Jane. Mary Ellen leaves her husband for the painter Henry Wallis.
1858	Writes part one of his "Memoirs of Percy Bysshe Shelley," which appears in *Fraser's Magazine*, and is intended

to "protest against this system of biographical gossip" and publishes several literary reviews.

1860　"Memoirs of Percy Bysshe Shelley," Part II, published in *Fraser's Magazine*.

1861　Death of Mary Ellen. *Gryll Grange* published, after appearing serially in *Fraser's* in 1860. Writes his autobiographical essay "The Last Day of Windsor Forest" and begins several narratives.

1862　Publishes a prose translation of the Italian play that served as a source for Shakespeare's *Twelfth Night*, *Gl'Ingannati, or The Deceived*. Suffers ill health and depressed spirits.

1864　Makes his will and leaves his estate to his adopted daughter.

1866　Dies 23 January at Lower Halliford.

NIGHTMARE ABBEY:

BY

THE AUTHOR OF HEADLONG HALL.[1]

There's a dark lantern of the spirit,
Which none see by but those who bear it,
That makes them in the dark see visions
And hag themselves with apparitions,
Find racks for their own minds, and vaunt
Of their own misery and want.

BUTLER.[2]

LONDON:

PRINTED FOR T. HOOKHAM, JUN.[3] OLD BOND-STREET
AND BALDWIN, CHADOCK, AND JOY,

1818.

---

1 *Headlong Hall*: published 1816, the first of Peacock's satirical novels employing a Socratic dialogue.

2 A composite of several quotations from Samuel Butler's *Hudibras*, a satire in three parts (1663–80): 1.1.5–5–6; 3.3.19–20 and "Upon the Weakness and Misery in Man," 71–72 and 229–31. See letter to Shelley dated 15 September 1818 in which he explains the novel's object "was merely to bring to a sort of philosophical focus a few of the morbidities of modern literature and to let in a little daylight on its atrabilarious complexion" (Joukovsky, *Letters of Thomas Love Peacock* 1.152, 154n.).

3 For information on Thomas Hookham, see Introduction (13).

Matthew. Oh! it's your only fine humour, sir. Your true
melancholy breeds your perfect fine wit, sir. I am melancholy
myself, divers times, sir; and then do I no more but take pen and
paper presently, and overflow you half a score or a dozen of
sonnets at a sitting.
Stephen. Truly, sir, and I love such things out of measure.
Matthew. Why, I pray you, sir, make use of my study; it's at
your service.
Stephen. I thank you, sir, I shall be bold, I warrant you. Have
you a stool there, to be melancholy upon?

BEN JONSON, *Every man in his Humour.*[1]

A.3. S. 1

---

1   The quotation from Jonson's play was supplied by Percy Shelley in a letter dated 24 July
1818 (Frederick L. Jones, ed. *Letters of Percy Bysshe Shelley*. 2 vols. [Oxford: Clarendon P,
1964], 2.27). In his letter of 30 August 1818 to Shelley, Peacock comments, "Your quotation from Jonson is singularly applicable and I shall certainly turn it to account either
in Nightmare Abbey or in a critical essay which I am now writing"; this is probably a
reference to the unfinished "Essay on Fashionable Literature" (Joukovsky, *Letters of Thomas
Love Peacock* 1.145). In his 15 September letter he informs Shelley that "Your extract from
Jonson follows on a separate leaf" from the main epigraph from Butler (Joukovsky, *Letters
of Thomas Love Peacock* 1.152). The epigraphs point to Peacock's satire on melancholy in
the novel.

Ay esleu gazouiller et siffler oye, comme dit le commun proverbe, entre les cygnes, plutoust que d'estre entre tant de gentils poëtes et faconds orateurs mut du tout estimé.

RABELAIS, Prol. L. 5.[1]

CHAPTER I

NIGHTMARE ABBEY, a venerable family-mansion, in a highly picturesque state of semi-dilapidation, pleasantly situated on a strip of dry land between the sea and the fens, at the verge of the county of Lincoln,[2] had the honor to be the seat of Christopher Glowry, Esquire. This gentleman was naturally of an atrabilarious temperament,[3] and much troubled with those phantoms of indigestion which are commonly called *blue devils*.[4] He had been deceived in an early friendship: he had been crossed in love; and had offered his hand, from pique, to a lady, who accepted it from interest, and who, in so doing, violently tore asunder the bonds of a tried and youthful attachment. Her vanity was gratified by being the mistress of a very extensive, if not very lively, establishment; but all the springs of her sympathies were frozen. Riches she possessed, but that which enriches them, the participation of affection, was wanting. All that they could purchase for her became indifferent to her, because that which they could not purchase, and which was more valuable than themselves, she had, for their sake, thrown away. She discovered, when

---

1 François Rabelais (c.1494–c.1553), a physician and satirist whose use of wit, parody, fantasy, and obscenity led to condemnation and censorship of his writings. The passage, from his story of two giants, *Gargantua and Pantagruel* (written 1532–42), is translated as "I have elected to chirrup, and cackle as a Goose among Swans, as the Proverb hath it, rather than be esteemed dumb among so many gentle Poets and eloquent Orators" (from W.F. Smith's translation, quoted by Raymond Wright ed. *Nightmare Abbey and Crochet Castle.* [Harmondsworth: Penguin, 1969], 261).

2 Lincolnshire, in the northeastern coast of the Midlands, is a flat and marshy area. As Scythrop's later comment about "acres of fen" suggests, Peacock seems to be making a joke here.

3 Of or pertaining to black bile; melancholy, hypochondriacal; splenetic, acrimonious (*OED*). See Joukovsky, *Letters of Thomas Love Peacock* 1.152, quoted above (46, n1).

4 Despondency, depression of spirits, hypochondriac melancholy (*OED*).

it was too late, that she had mistaken the means for the end—that riches, rightly used, are instruments of happiness, but are not in themselves happiness. In this wilful blight of her affections, she found them valueless as means: they had been the end to which she had immolated all her affections, and were now the only end that remained to her. She did not confess this to herself as a principle of action, but it operated through the medium of unconscious self-deception, and terminated in inveterate avarice. She laid on external things the blame of her mind's internal disorder, and thus became by degrees an accomplished scold. She often went her daily rounds through a series of deserted apartments, every creature in the house vanishing at the creak of her shoe, much more at the sound of her voice, to which the nature of things affords no simile;[1] for, as far as the voice of woman, when attuned by gentleness and love, transcends all other sounds in harmony, so far does it surpass all others in discord, when stretched into unnatural shrillness by anger and impatience.

Mr. Glowry used to say that his house was no better than a spacious kennel, for every one in it led the life of a dog. Disappointed both in love and in friendship, and looking upon human learning as vanity, he had come to a conclusion that there was but one good thing in the world, videlicet,[2] a good dinner; and this his parsimonious lady seldom suffered him to enjoy: but, one morning, like Sir Leoline in Christabel, "he woke and found his lady dead,"[3] and remained a very consolate widower, with one small child.

This only son and heir Mr. Glowry had christened Scythrop,[4] from the name of a maternal ancestor, who had hanged himself

---

1 A joke about Petrarchan conventions in love poetry.

2 That is to say; namely; to wit: used to introduce an amplification, or more precise or explicit explanation, of a previous statement or word (OED).

3 The line is "rose and found his lady dead" (335). "Christabel" is an unfinished supernatural romance in couplets by Samuel Taylor Coleridge (satirized as Mr. Flosky), published in 1816. A woman praying in the woods for her lover encounters Geraldine; Geraldine claims to have been abducted from her home, as well as being the daughter of Christabel's father's estranged friend. She shares Christabel's bed and bewitches her, thus corrupting innocence with her serpent-like powers. The poem breaks off as Christabel insults her guest in front of her father, Sir Leoline. Peacock defends the poem in his "Essay on Fashionable Literature" (see Appendix D, 210–18).

4 A character related to Peacock's friend Percy Bysshe Shelley. From the Greek ὀκυθρωπος, meaning "a sullen or sad and gloomy countenance." Shelley named the tower at Valsovano (where he wrote The Cenci in 1819) "Scythrop's tower" (David Garnett, ed. The Novels of Thomas Love Peacock [London: Rupert Hart-Davis, 1948], 356).

one rainy day in a fit of *tædium vitæ*,[1] and had been eulogised by a coroner's jury in the comprehensive phrase of *felo de se*;[2] on which account, Mr. Glowry held his memory in high honor, and made a punch-bowl of his skull.[3]

When Scythrop grew up, he was sent, as usual, to a public school, where a little learning was painfully beaten into him, and from thence to the University, where it was carefully taken out of him; and he was sent home like a well-threshed ear of corn, with nothing in his head: having finished his education to the high satisfaction of the master and fellows of his college, who had, in testimony of their approbation, presented him with a silver fish-slice,[4] on which his name figured at the head of a laudatory inscription in some semi-barbarous dialect of Anglo-saxonised Latin.[5]

His fellow-students, however, who drove tandem and random[6] in great perfection, and were connoisseurs in good inns, had taught him to drink deep ere he departed.[7] He had passed much of his time with these choice spirits,[8] and had seen the rays of the midnight lamp tremble on many a lengthening file of empty bottles. He passed his vacations sometimes at Nightmare Abbey, sometimes in London, at the house of his uncle, Mr. Hilary, a very cheerful and elastic gentleman, who had married the sister of the melancholy Mr. Glowry. The company that frequented his house was the gayest of the gay. Scythrop danced with the ladies and drank with the gentlemen, and was pronounced by both a very accomplished charming fellow, and an honor to the University.

1   Weariness of life; extreme ennui or inertia, sometimes regarded as a pathological state (*OED*).
2   One who "deliberately puts an end to his own existence, or commits any unlawful malicious act, the consequence of which is his own death" (Blackstone) (*OED*).
3   Shelley famously drank out of a skull at Eton in order to raise a ghost (White, Newman Ivey. *Shelley*. 2 vols. [London: Secker & Warburg, 1947], 1.41) while Byron drank out of a skull at Newstead Abbey.
4   A fish-carving knife; also, an implement used by cooks for turning fish in the pan (*OED*).
5   A joke about the state of learning in the early nineteenth century at Oxford and Cambridge. Peacock, who did not go to university and was largely self-educated, complains in a letter written in 1812 about his "moral aversion to those doctores sine doctrina, those baccalaurei baculo quam lauro digniores" (doctors without learning and BAs who deserve the rod rather than the laurel), who know "more about cookery than Horace's Art of Poetry" (Joukovsky, *Letters of Thomas Love Peacock* 1.76–77).
6   A joke on "random-tandem" or one behind the other, in single file; originally of a team of two horses (*OED*).
7   Shakespeare's *Hamlet*, 1.2.
8   A pun on drinking and the company Scythrop keeps at university.

At the house of Mr. Hilary, Scythrop first saw the beautiful Miss Emily Girouette.[1] He fell in love; which is nothing new. He was favorably received; which is nothing strange. Mr. Glowry and Mr. Girouette had a meeting on the occasion, and quarrelled about the terms of the bargain; which is neither new nor strange. The lovers were torn asunder, weeping and vowing everlasting constancy; and, in three weeks after this tragical event, the lady was led a smiling bride to the altar, by the Honorable Mr. Lackwit; which is neither strange nor new.

Scythrop received this intelligence at Nightmare Abbey, and was half distracted on the occasion. It was his first disappointment, and preyed deeply on his sensitive spirit. His father, to comfort him, read him a Commentary on Ecclesiastes, which he had himself composed, and which demonstrated incontrovertibly that all is vanity. He insisted particularly on the text, "One man among a thousand have I found, but a woman amongst all those have I not found."[2]

"How could he expect it," said Scythrop, "when the whole thousand were locked up in his seraglio?[3] His experience is no precedent for a free state of society like that in which we live."

"Locked up or at large," said Mr. Glowry, "the result is the same: their minds are always locked up, and vanity and interest keep the key. I speak feelingly, Scythrop."

"I am sorry for it, Sir," said Scythrop. "But how is it that their minds are locked up? The fault is in their artificial education, which studiously models them into mere musical dolls, to be set out for sale in the great toy-shop of society."[4]

"To be sure," said Mr. Glowry, "their education is not so well finished as yours has been: and your idea of a musical doll is good. I bought one myself, but it was confoundedly out of tune. But,

---

1   A character loosely connected with Shelley's cousin Harriet Grove, who was his earliest love. "Girouette" means "weathercock."

2   Ecclesiastes 7.28.

3   Wright identifies this as a reference to a note in Shelley's radical visionary poem *Queen Mab*, Canto 8 (1813): "Solomon kept a thousand concubines, and owned in despair all that was vanity" (261).

4   "Musical dolls" here may be a reference to the "automaton." Throughout the 18th and 19th centuries, European watchmakers and technicians tried to discover the secrets of life. Their attempts included creating automatons and androids, many of which were fakes. The world's first successfully-built biomechanical automaton is considered to be *The Flute Player*, invented by the French engineer Jacques de Vaucanson in 1769.

whatever be the cause, Scythrop, the effect is certainly this: that one is pretty nearly as good as another, as far as any judgment can be formed of them before marriage. It is only after marriage that they shew their true qualities, as I know by bitter experience. Marriage is therefore a lottery, and the less choice and selection a man bestows on his ticket the better: for, if he has incurred considerable pains and expence to obtain a lucky number, and his lucky number proves a blank, he experiences not a simple but a complicated disappointment; the loss of labor and money being superadded to the disappointment of drawing a blank, which, constituting simply and entirely the grievance of him who has chosen his ticket at random, is, from its simplicity, the more endurable." This very excellent reasoning was thrown away upon Scythrop, who retired to his tower as dismal and disconsolate as before.

The tower which Scythrop inhabited stood at the south-eastern angle of the Abbey; and, on the southern side, the foot of the tower opened on a terrace, which was called the garden, though nothing grew on it but ivy, and a few amphibious weeds. The south-western tower, which was ruinous and full of owls, might, with equal propriety, have been called the aviary. This terrace or garden, or terrace-garden, or garden-terrace (the reader may name it *ad libitum*,)[1] took in an oblique view of the open sea, and fronted a long tract of level sea-coast, and a fine monotony of fens and windmills.

The reader will judge from what we have said, that this building was a sort of castellated abbey;[2] and it will probably occur to him to enquire, if it had been one of the strong holds of the ancient church militant.[3] Whether this was the case, or how far it had been indebted to the taste of Mr. Glowry's ancestors for any transmutations from its

---

1 At one's pleasure; to the full extent of one's wishes, as much as one desires (*OED*).

2 Presumably an abbey—a religious institution—which would not look like a castle unless altered to do so. Peacock is satirizing the eighteenth-century fashion for "improving" the houses and grounds of country estates. In *Headlong Hall*, Mr. Marmaduke Milestone is a comic version of the famous landscape designers Sir Uvedale Price, Humphrey Repton, Richard Payne-Knight, and "Capability" Brown; Peacock is poking fun at the claim that humanity is constantly improving.

3 Church militant: the Church on earth considered as warring against the powers of evil. (Sometimes used jocularly in reference to actual warfare or polemics.) Church triumphant: the portion of the church which has overcome the world, and entered into glory. "'He is a monk of the church militant, I think,' answered Locksley; 'and there be more of them abroad'" (Sir Walter Scott, *Ivanhoe* 1819) (*OED*).

original state, are, unfortunately, circumstances not within the pale of our knowledge.

The north-western tower contained the apartments of Mr. Glowry. The moat at its base, and the fens beyond, comprised the whole of his prospect. This moat surrounded the Abbey, and was in immediate contact with the walls on every side but the south.

The north-eastern tower was appropriated to the domestics, whom Mr. Glowry always chose by one of two criterions,—a long face or a dismal name. His butler was Raven; his steward was Crow; his valet was Skellet. Mr. Glowry maintained that the valet was of French extraction, and that his name was Squelette. His grooms were Mattock and Graves. On one occasion, being in want of a footman, he received a letter from a person signing himself Diggory Deathshead, and lost no time in securing this acquisition; but, on Diggory's arrival, Mr. Glowry was horror-struck by the sight of a round ruddy face, and a pair of laughing eyes. Deathshead was always grinning,—not a ghastly smile, but the grin of a comic mask; and disturbed the echoes of the hall with so much unhallowed laughter, that Mr. Glowry gave him his discharge. Diggory, however, had stayed long enough to make conquests of all the old gentleman's maids, and left him a flourishing colony of young Deathsheads to join chorus with the owls, that had before been the exclusive choristers of Nightmare Abbey.

The main body of the building was divided into rooms of state, spacious apartments for feasting, and numerous bed-rooms for visitors, who, however, were few, and far between.

Family interests compelled Mr. Glowry to receive occasional visits from Mr. and Mrs. Hilary, who paid them from the same motive; and, as the lively gentleman on these occasions found few conductors for his exuberant gaiety, he became like a double-charged electric jar,[1] which often exploded in some burst of outrageous merriment, to the signal discomposure of Mr. Glowry's nerves.

Another occasional visitor, much more to Mr. Glowry's taste, was Mr. Flosky,* a very lacrymose and morbid gentleman, of some

---

* A *corruption* of Filosky, quasi Φιλοσκιος, a lover, or sector, of shadows. [This character is based on Samuel Taylor Coleridge.]

---

1 A Leyden jar, an electrical condenser consisting of a cylindrical glass jar lined inside and outside nearly to the top with tin foil, the inner coating being connected at the top with a brass rod which ends in a knob (*OED*).

note in the literary world, but in his own estimation of much more merit than name. The part of his character which recommended him to Mr. Glowry, was his very fine sense of the grim and the tearful. No one could relate a dismal story with so many minutiæ of supererogatory wretchedness. No one could call up a *raw-head* and *bloody-bones*[1] with so many adjuncts and circumstances of ghastliness. Mystery was his mental element. He lived in the midst of that visionary world in which nothing is but what is not.[2] He dreamed with his eyes open, and saw ghosts dancing round him at noontide. He had been in his youth an enthusiast for liberty, and had hailed the dawn of the French Revolution as the promise of a day that was to banish war and slavery, and every form of vice and misery, from the face of the earth.[3] Because all this was not done, he deduced that nothing was done, and from this deduction, according to his system of logic, he drew a conclusion that worse than nothing was done, that the overthrow of the feudal fortresses of tyranny and superstition was the greatest calamity that had ever befallen mankind, and that their only hope now was to rake the rubbish together, and rebuild it without any of those loop-holes by which the light had originally crept in. To qualify himself for a coadjutor in this laudable task, he plunged into the central opacity of Kantian metaphysics,[4] and lay *perdu* several years in transcendental darkness, till the common daylight of common sense became intolerable to his eyes. He called the sun an *ignis fatuus*,[5] and exhorted all who would listen

---

1   The name of a nursery bugbear, usually coupled with bloody-bones. A phrase used, generally in conjunction with Rawhead, as the name of a bug-bear to terrify children. Possibly associated with the apparition of a murdered man supposed to haunt the scene of his murder (*OED*).

2   Shakespeare's *Macbeth*, 1.3.

3   Referring to Coleridge's early radical politics. "Enthusiasm" in this context is a charged term, associated with radical politics. Jon Mee explains that for Coleridge it becomes a concept linked to his objection to the reading public; as an emotion involving a certain loss of self, it should be reserved for the elite and kept away from popular tastes (*Romanticism, Enthusiasm, and Regulation: Poetics and the Policing of Culture in the Romantic Period* [Oxford: Oxford UP, 2003], 131–72).

4   Immanuel Kant (1724–1804), professor of logic and metaphysics at Königsberg, whose best known work *Critique of Pure Reason* (1781) suggests that knowledge comes from the working together of the senses and understanding. Coleridge was interested in Kant, particularly Kant's critique of empirical philosophy.

5   A phosphorescent light that hovers over marshy ground, supposed to be due to the spontaneous combustion of an inflammable gas derived from decaying organic matter, which is popularly called *Will-o'-the-wisp*. Because it seems to recede and vanish, it is thought to

to his friendly voice, which were about as many as called "God save King Richard," to shelter themselves from its delusive radiance in the obscure haunt of Old Philosophy.[1] This word Old had great charms for him. The good old times were always on his lips: meaning the days when polemic theology was in its prime, and rival prelates beat the drum ecclesiastic[2] with Herculean vigour, till the one wound up his series of syllogisms with the very orthodox conclusion of roasting the other.

But the dearest friend of Mr. Glowry, and his most welcome guest, was Mr. Toobad, the Manichæan Millenarian.[3] The twelfth verse of the twelfth chapter of Revelations was always in his mouth: "Woe to the inhabiters of the earth and of the sea, for the devil is come among you, having great wrath, because he knoweth that he hath but a short time." He maintained that the supreme dominion of the world was, for wise purposes, given over for a while to the Evil Principle, and that this precise period of time, commonly called the enlightened age, was the point of his plenitude of power. He used to add that by and by he would be cast down, and a high and happy order of things succeed; but he never omitted the saving clause, "Not in our time:" which last words were always echoed in doleful response by the sympathetic Mr. Glowry.

Another and very frequent visitor was the Reverend Mr. Larynx,[4] the vicar of Claydyke, a village about ten miles distant;—a good natured accommodating divine, who was always most obligingly ready to take a dinner and a bed at the house of any country gentleman in distress for a companion. Nothing came amiss to him,—a game

---

be the work of mischievous spirits who lead travelers astray. Therefore the term is used figuratively to signify a delusive hope, aim, or guiding principle (*OED*).

1   God save King Richard (Shakespeare's *Richard III*, 3.7). Old Philosophy refers to the Scholastic philosophy of the Middle Ages.

2   The pulpit cushion, often vigorously thumped by what are termed "rousing preachers" (*Brewer's Dictionary of Phrase and Fable*). Mentioned in *Hudibras*, 1.1.11–12, and in John Locke's *Two Treatises on Government* (1690).

3   Based on J.F. Newton, a "zodiacal mythologist" and vegetarian who believed that mankind has been in a state of decline since the Golden Age. He influenced Percy Shelley's early radical poem *Queen Mab*. "Manichæanism" is a belief that the world is ruled by good and evil, while a "Millenarian" believes that evil power, in the ascendant, will be replaced by good.

4   Julia Wright suggests that Mr. Larynx is a parody of Irish poet Thomas Moore, who wrote drinking songs, and to whom Peacock objected for his superficial learning ("Peacock's Early Parody of Thomas Moore in *Nightmare Abbey*." *English Language Notes* 30.4 [1993]: 31–38).

at billiards, at chess, at draughts, at backgammon, at piquet, or at all-fours in a tête-à-tête,[1]—or any game on the cards, round, square, or triangular, in a party of any number exceeding two. He would even dance among friends, rather than that a lady, even if she were on the wrong side of thirty, should sit still for want of a partner. For a ride, a walk, or a sail, in the morning,—a song after dinner, a ghost story after supper,—a bottle of port with the squire, or a cup of green tea with his lady,—for all or any of these, or for anything else that was agreeable to any one else, consistently with the dye of his coat, the Reverend Mr. Larynx was at all times equally ready. When at Nightmare Abbey, he would condole with Mr. Glowry,—drink Madeira with Scythrop,[2]—crack jokes with Mr. Hilary,—hand Mrs. Hilary to the piano, take charge of her fan and gloves, and turn over her music with surprising dexterity,—quote Revelations with Mr. Toobad,—and lament the good old times of feudal darkness with the transcendental Mr. Flosky.

CHAPTER II

SHORTLY after the disastrous termination of Scythrop's passion for Miss Emily Girouette, Mr. Glowry found himself, much against his will, involved in a law-suit, which compelled him to dance attendance on the High Court of Chancery.[3] Scythrop was left alone at Nightmare Abbey. He was a burnt child, and dreaded the fire of female eyes. He wandered about the ample pile, or along the garden-terrace, with "his cogitative faculties immersed in cogibundity of cogitation."[4] The terrace terminated at the south-western tower,

---

1   A card-game played by two persons with a pack of 32 cards (the low cards from the two to the six being excluded), in which points are scored on various groups or combinations of cards, and on tricks (*OED*). "All-fours" is a game of cards, played by two; "so named from the four particulars by which it is reckoned, and which, joined in the hand of either of the parties, are said to make all-fours. The all four are high, low, Jack, and the game." Johnson (*OED*).
2   A white wine produced in the island of Madeira. It is of a deep amber tint, full body, and some sweetness, resembling a well-matured full-bodied brown sherry (*OED*).
3   The court of the Lord Chancellor of England, the highest court of judicature next to the House of Lords; but, since the Judicature Act of 1873, a division of the High Court of Justice (*OED*).
4   Garnett identifies this as 1.1 of Henry Carey's 1734 burlesque *Chrononhotonthologos, the most Tragical Tragedy that ever was tragedized by any Company of Tragedies* (362).

which, as we have said, was ruinous and full of owls. Here would Scythrop take his evening seat, on a fallen fragment of mossy stone, with his back resting against the ruined wall,—a thick canopy of ivy, with an owl in it, over his head,—and the Sorrows of Werter in his hand.[1] He had some taste for romance-reading before he went to the university, where, we must confess, in justice to his college, he was cured of the love of reading in all its shapes; and the cure would have been radical, if disappointment in love, and total solitude, had not conspired to bring on a relapse. He began to devour romances and German tragedies, and, by the recommendation of Mr. Flosky, to pore over ponderous tomes of transcendental philosophy, which reconciled him to the labour of studying them by their mystical jargon and necromantic imagery.[2] In the congenial solitude of Nightmare Abbey, the distempered ideas of metaphysical romance and romantic metaphysics had ample time and space to germinate into a fertile harvest[3] of chimæras, which rapidly shot up into vigorous and abundant vegetation.

He now became troubled with the *passion for reforming the world.*★ He built many castles in the air, and peopled them with secret tribunals, and bands of illuminati,[4] who were always the imaginary

---

★ See Forsyth's *Principles of Moral Science.* [Writer Robert Forsyth (1766–1845) published in 1805 a series of essays *Principles of Moral Science* (DNB). Also mentioned in the "Essay on Fashionable Literature." See Appendix D, 210–18.]

---

1 *The Sorrows of Young Werther* (1774), an enormously successful novel in letters written by Johann Wolfgang von Goethe that tells the story of an alienated artist and man of sentiment whose hopeless passion for a woman engaged to someone else leads him to suicide. The novel inspired a cultural phenomenon known as "Wertherism," describing moods of self-indulgent melancholy among young men (who sometimes even wore the yellow breeches and blue coat of the hero). Scythrop is a candidate for Wertherism, and Peacock clearly sees this as being on a continuum with Byronic excess. See Appendix B (160–63).
2 This recalls what we know of Percy Shelley's youthful taste in reading.
3 "harvest": altered to "crop" in 1837.
4 Referring to a celebrated secret society, founded in 1776 at Ingolstadt, in Bavaria by Professor Adam Weishaupt, holding deistic and republican principles, and having an organization akin to freemasonry; hence applied to other thinkers regarded as atheistic or free-thinking, e.g. the French Encyclopædists. But also persons affecting or claiming to possess special knowledge or enlightenment on any subject: often used satirically (*OED*). Peacock heard about the secret society through Percy Shelley's reading of Robert Clifford's 1797–98 translation of the Abbé Barruel's *Memoirs, Illustrating the History of Jacobinism.* Shelley was reading from this in 1814, a time when he was in constant contact with Peacock (Gary Dyer, "Peacock and the 'Philosophical Gas' of the Illuminati." *Secret Texts: The Literature of Secret Societies.* Eds. Marie Mulvey-Roberts, Hugh Ormsby-Lennon, and Michael Foot [New York: AMS, 1995], 192).

instruments of his projected regeneration of the human species. As he intended to institute a perfect republic, he invested himself with absolute sovereignty over these mystical dispensers of liberty. He slept with Horrid Mysteries[1] under his pillow, and dreamed of venerable eleutherarchs[2] and ghastly confederates holding midnight conventions in subterranean caves. He passed whole mornings in his study, immersed in gloomy reverie, stalking about the room in his night-cap, which he pulled over his eyes like a cowl, and folding his striped calico dressing-gown about him like the mantle of a conspirator.

"Action,"—thus he soliloquised,—"is the result of opinion, and to new-model opinion would be to new-model society.[3] Knowledge is power. It is in the hands of a few, who employ it to mislead the many for their own selfish purposes of aggrandisement and appropriation. What if it were in the hands of a few who should employ it to lead the many? What if it were universal, and the multitude were enlightened? No. The many must be always in leading-strings: but let them have wise and honest conductors. A few to think, and many to act: that is the only basis of perfect society. So thought the ancient philosophers: they had their esoterical and exoterical doctrines.[4] So thinks the sublime Kant,[5] who delivers his oracles in language which none but the initiate can comprehend. Such were the views of those secret associations of illuminati, which were the terror of superstition and tyranny, and which,

---

1 A novel entitled *Der Genius*, written by the "Marquis" C.F.A. Grosse and translated from German in 1796 by P. Will.

2 Members of secret societies, and identified by Garnett as from T.J. Hogg's novel *The Memoirs of Prince Alexy Haimatoff* (1813). See T.J. Hogg, *Alexy Haimatoff* (1813): "The Eleutherarch … asked if they had any objection to my being initiated in the mysteries of the Eleutheri" and Percy Shelley, "the Swans and the Eleutherarchs are proofs that you were a little sleepy" (363); he also used the term in his review of the novel for the *Critical Review* 6 (December 1814). See Jones, *Letters of Percy Bysshe Shelley* 1.380 and 1.381n and Appendix B (163–67).

3 Wright points out that this is the theme of Chapter 5 of Godwin's *Political Justice*, "The Voluntary Actions of Men originate in their Opinions" (262).

4 "Esoteric" is associated with the doctrines of Pythagoras, taught only to a select few, and not intelligible to the general body of disciples. In Christian tradition Augustine maintained a distinction between esoteric and exoteric teaching in philosophy and religion. Esoteric wisdom is available only to the few with the ability to understand the wisdom handed down by word of mouth among initiates. Exoteric teachings are capable of being expressed in writing, and were a sufficient guide to the good life for the mass of ordinary folk.

5 See Chapter I (53).

carefully selecting wisdom and genius from the great wilderness of society, as the bee selects honey from the flowers of the thorn and the nettle, bound all human excellence in a chain, which, if it had not been prematurely broken, would have commanded opinion, and regenerated the world."

Scythrop proceeded to meditate on the practicability of reviving a confederation of regenerators. To get a clear view of his own ideas, and to feel the pulse of the wisdom and genius of the age, he wrote and published a treatise, in which his meanings were carefully wrapt up in the monk's hood of transcendental technology, but filled with hints of matter deep and dangerous, which he thought would set the whole nation in a ferment; and he awaited the result in awful expectation, as a miner, who has fired a train, awaits the explosion of a rock. However, he listened and heard nothing; for the explosion, if any ensued, was not sufficiently loud to shake a single leaf of the ivy on the towers of Nightmare Abbey; and some months afterwards he received a letter from his bookseller, informing him that only seven copies had been sold, and concluding with a polite request for the balance.[1]

Scythrop did not despair. "Seven copies," he thought, "have been sold. Seven is a mystical number, and the omen is good. Let me find the seven purchasers of my seven copies, and they shall be the seven golden candlesticks with which I will illuminate the world."

Scythrop had a certain portion of mechanical genius, which his romantic projects tended to develop. He constructed models of cells and recesses, sliding panels and secret passages, that would have baffled the skill of the Parisian police.[2] He took the opportunity of his father's absence to smuggle a dumb carpenter into the Abbey, and between them they gave reality to one of these models in Scythrop's tower. Scythrop foresaw that a great leader of human regeneration

---

1 Revelations 1 and 2. A joke about Shelley's 1812 pamphlet, *Proposals for an Association of those Philanthropists who, convinced of the inadequacy of the moral and political state of Ireland to produce benefits which are nevertheless obtainable, are willing to unite to accomplish its regeneration.*

2 Detective fiction and professional investigation owe much to the work of François Eugène Vidocq. He was instrumental in establishing the first detective bureau in the world, the Parisian Brigade de la Sûreté, in 1812, and opened the world's first private detective agency, Le Bureau des Renseignements, in 1834. The success of these agencies encouraged Robert Peel's metropolitan police in London (1829) and Britain's Scotland Yard to create the Criminal Investigation Department in 1842.

would be involved in fearful dilemmas, and determined, for the benefit of mankind in general, to adopt all possible precautions for the preservation of himself.

The servants, even the women, had been tutored into silence. Profound stillness reigned throughout and around the Abbey, except when the occasional shutting of a door would peal in long reverberations through the galleries, or the heavy tread of the pensive butler would wake the hollow echoes of the hall. Scythrop stalked about like the grand inquisitor, and the servants flitted past him like familiars. In his evening meditations on the terrace, under the ivy of the ruined tower, the only sounds that came to his ear were the rustling of the wind in the ivy—the plaintive voices of the feathered choristers, the owls—the occasional striking of the Abbey-clock,—and the monotonous dash of the sea on its low and level shore. In the mean time he drank Madeira, and laid deep schemes for a thorough repair of the crazy fabric of human nature.

CHAPTER III

Mr. GLOWRY returned from London with the loss of his lawsuit. Justice was with him, but the law was against him. He found Scythrop in a mood most sympathetically tragic, and they vied with each other in enlivening their cups by lamenting the depravity of this degenerate age, and occasionally interspersing divers grim jokes about graves, worms, and epitaphs.[1] Mr. Glowry's friends, whom we have mentioned in the first chapter, availed themselves of his return to pay him a simultaneous visit. At the same time arrived Scythrop's friend and fellow-collegian, the Honorable Mr. Listless.[2] Mr. Glowry had discovered this fashionable young gentleman in London, "stretched on the rack of a too easy chair,"[3] and devoured

---

1 Shakespeare's *Richard II*, 3.2 (one of Shelley's favourite plays).
2 Likely based on Sir Lumley Skeffington, a playwright and schoolmate of Shelley's (see Garnett 365). Shelley consulted Skeffington about the propriety of marrying Mary Godwin following the suicide of Harriet Shelley in 1816 (White, *Shelley*, 1.488 and 724n). Mark Cunningham suggests Listless is based on the dandy Beau Brummel ("'Fatout! Who Am I?': A Model for the Honourable Mr. Listless in Thomas Love Peacock's *Nightmare Abbey*." *English Language Notes* 30.1 [1992]: 43–45).
3 Alexander Pope, *The Dunciad* (1743) 4.1.342.

with a gloomy and misanthropical *nil curo*,[1] and had pressed him so earnestly to take the benefit of the pure country air, at Nightmare Abbey, that Mr. Listless, finding it would give him more trouble to refuse than to comply, summoned his French valet, Fatout,[2] and told him he was going to Lincolnshire. On this simple hint, Fatout went to work, and the imperials were packed,[3] and the post-chariot was at the door, without the Honorable Mr. Listless having said or thought another syllable on the subject.

Mr. and Mrs. Hilary brought with them an orphan niece, a daughter of Mr. Glowry's youngest sister, who had made a runaway love-match with an Irish officer. The lady's fortune disappeared in the first year: love, by a natural consequence, disappeared in the second: the Irishman himself, by a still more natural consequence, disappeared in the third. Mr. Glowry had allowed his sister an annuity, and she had lived in retirement with her only daughter, whom, at her death, which had recently happened, she commended to the care of Mrs. Hilary.

Miss Marionetta Celestina O'Carroll was a very blooming and accomplished young lady.[4] Being a compound of the *Allegro Vivace* of the O'Carrolls, and of the *Andante Doloroso* of the Glowries,[5] she exhibited in her own character all the diversities of an April sky. Her hair was light-brown: her eyes hazel, and sparkling with a mild but fluctuating light: her features regular: her lips full, and of equal size: and her person surpassingly graceful. She was a proficient in music. Her conversation was sprightly, but always on subjects light in their nature and limited in their interest: for moral sympathies, in any general sense, had no place in her mind. She had some coquetry, and more caprice, liking and disliking almost in the same moment; pursuing an object with earnestness, while it seemed unattainable, and rejecting it when in her power, as not worth the trouble of possession.

---

1 Joukovksy connects the phrase with a 14 November 1811 letter to Thomas Forster which begins, "That gloomy and misanthropical nil curo, of which you once complained...." (*Letters of Thomas Love Peacock* 1.66).

2 Fait tout (French) or "do all," which fits the role in which he is placed as a servant of Mr. Listless.

3 A case or trunk for luggage, fitted on, or adapted for, the roof of a coach or carriage. Also the roof or top of a carriage itself (French impériale) (*OED*).

4 Assumed to be based on Harriet Westbrook, Shelley's first wife (Garnett 366).

5 *Allegro* and *vivace* are very brisk, swift, or fast movements; *andante doloroso*: slowly and pathetical.

Whether she was touched with a *penchant* for her cousin Scythrop, or was merely curious to see what effect the tender passion would have on so *outré*[1] a person; she had not been three days in the Abbey, before she threw out all the lures of her beauty and accomplishments to make a prize of his heart. Scythrop proved an easy conquest. The image of Miss Emily Girouette was already sufficiently dimmed by the power of philosophy and the exercise of reason: for to these influences, or to any influence but the true one, are usually ascribed the mental cures performed by the great physician Time. Scythrop's romantic dreams had indeed given him many *pure anticipated cognitions*[2] of combinations of beauty and intelligence, which, he had some misgivings, were not exactly realised in his cousin Marionetta; but, in spite of these misgivings, he soon became distractedly in love; which when the young lady clearly perceived, she altered her tactics, and assumed as much coldness and reserve as she had before shown ardent and ingenuous attachment. Scythrop was confounded at the sudden change; but, instead of falling at her feet and requesting an explanation, he retreated to his tower, muffled himself in his night-cap, seated himself in the president's chair of his imaginary secret tribunal, summoned Marionetta with all terrible formalities, frightened her out of her wits, disclosed himself, and clasped the beautiful penitent to his bosom.

While he was acting this reverie,—in the moment in which the awful president of the secret tribunal was throwing back his cowl and his mantle, and discovering himself to the lovely culprit as her adoring and magnanimous lover, the door of the study opened, and the real Marionetta appeared.

The motives which had led her to the tower were a little penitence, a little concern, a little affection, and a little fear as to what the sudden secession of Scythrop, occasioned by her sudden change of manner, might portend. She had tapped several times unheard, and of course unanswered; and at length, timidly and cautiously opening the door, she discovered him standing up before a black velvet chair, which was mounted on an old oak table, in the act of throwing

---

1   Outré (French): extreme or beyond the bounds of what is considered usual or proper.
2   Garnett (362) identifies this as a phrase from William Drummond's *Academical Questions* (1805), and points out that Peacock and Shelley used this phrase to make fun of both Kantian philosophy and Coleridge himself. For Shelley's use of the phrase, see *Peter Bell the Third* (written 1819) Part 6, stanzas xii–xvi and note (Garnett 366n).

open his striped calico dressing-gown, and flinging away his night-cap,—which is what the French call an imposing attitude.[1]

Each stood a few moments fixed in their respective places,—the lady in astonishment, and the gentleman in confusion. Marionetta was the first to break silence. "For heaven's sake," said she, "my dear Scythrop, what is the matter?"

"For heaven's sake, indeed," said Scythrop, springing from the table; "for your sake, Marionetta, and you are my heaven,—distraction is the matter. I adore you, Marionetta, and your cruelty drives me mad." He threw himself at her knees, devoured her hand with kisses, and breathed a thousand vows in the most passionate language of romance.

Marionetta listened a long time in silence, till her lover had exhausted his eloquence and paused for a reply. She then said, with a very arch look, "I prithee deliver thyself like a man of this world."[2] The levity of this quotation, and of the manner in which it was delivered, jarred so discordantly on the high-wrought enthusiasm of the romantic *innamorato*, that he sprang upon his feet, and beat his forehead with his clenched fists. The young lady was terrified; and, deeming it expedient to sooth him, took one of his hands in hers, placed the other hand on his shoulder, looked up in his face with a winning seriousness, and said, in the tenderest possible tone, "What would you have, Scythrop?"

Scythrop was in heaven again. "What would I have? What but you, Marionetta? You, for the companion of my studies, the partner of my thoughts, the auxiliary of my great designs for the emancipation of mankind."

"I am afraid I should be but a poor auxiliary, Scythrop. What would you have me do?"

"Do as Rosalia does with Carlos, divine Marionetta. Let us each open a vein in the other's arm, mix our blood in a bowl, and drink

---

1 The phrase, associated with monarchy and politics, and used in the context of Scythrop's flirtation with Marionetta, is one of the many jokes in the text. The phrase may be an allusion to a favourite book of Percy Shelley's, C.F. Volney's *The Ruins of Empire and the Law of Nature* (1791), a work that also figures prominently in the education of the creature in *Frankenstein*. In Book 1, Chapter 18, Volney states, "But inaccessible to seduction as well as to fear, the free nation kept silence, and rising universally in arms, assumed an imposing attitude." Peacock repeats the phrase in Chapter 11 of *The Misfortunes of Elphin* (1829) and in Chapter 16 of *Crochet Castle* (1831).
2 Shakespeare's *Henry IV, Part 2*, 5.3: words spoken by Falstaff to Pistol.

it as a sacrament of love.[1] Then we shall see visions of transcendental illumination, and soar on the wings of ideas into the space of pure intelligence."

Marionetta could not reply; she had not so strong a stomach as Rosalia, and turned sick at the proposition. She disengaged herself suddenly from Scythrop, sprang through the door of the tower, and fled with precipitation along the corridors. Scythrop pursued her, crying, "Stop, stop, Marionetta,—my life, my love!" and was gaining rapidly on her flight, when, at an ill-omened corner, where two corridors ended in an angle, at the head of a staircase, he came into sudden and violent contact with Mr. Toobad, and they both plunged together to the foot of the stairs, like two billiard-balls into one pocket. This gave the young lady time to escape, and enclose herself in her chamber; while Mr. Toobad, rising slowly, and rubbing his knees and shoulders, said, "You see, my dear Scythrop, in this little incident, one of the innumerable proofs of the temporary supremacy of the devil; for what but a systematic design and concurrent contrivance of evil could have made the angles of time and place coincide in our unfortunate persons at the head of this accursed staircase?"

"Nothing else, certainly," said Scythrop: "you are perfectly in the right, Mr. Toobad. Evil and mischief, and misery, and confusion, and vanity, and vexation of spirit,[2] and death, and disease, and assassination, and war, and poverty, and pestilence, and famine, and avarice, and selfishness, and rancour, and jealousy, and spleen, and malevolence, and the disappointments of philanthropy, and the faithlessness of friendship, and the crosses of love,—all prove the accuracy of your views, and the truth of your system; and it is not impossible, that the infernal interruption of this fall down stairs may throw a colour of evil on the whole of my future existence."

"My dear boy," said Mr. Toobad, "you have a fine eye for consequences."

So saying, he embraced Scythrop, who retired, with a disconsolate step, to dress for dinner; while Mr. Toobad stalked across the hall, repeating, "Woe to the inhabiters of the earth, and of the sea, for the devil is come among you, having great wrath."[3]

---

1 Alluding to a moment in *Horrid Mysteries* in which Rosalia uses a dagger to open a vein in Carlos' arm and sucks the blood, and invites Carlos to do the same from her arm, saying, "Thus our souls shall be mixed together" (Garnett 368). See Appendix B (153–55).
2 Ecclesiastes 1.14.
3 Revelations 2.12.

CHAPTER IV

THE flight of Marionetta, and the pursuit of Scythrop, had been witnessed by Mr. Glowry, who, in consequence, narrowly observed his son and his niece in the evening; and, concluding from their manner, that there was a better understanding between them than he wished to see, he determined on obtaining, the next morning, from Scythrop, a full and satisfactory explanation. He, therefore, shortly after breakfast, entered Scythrop's tower, with a very grave face, and said, without ceremony or preface, "So, sir, you are in love with your cousin."

Scythrop, with as little hesitation, answered, "Yes, sir."

"That is candid, at least: and she is in love with you."

"I wish she were, sir."

"You know she is, sir."

"Indeed, sir, I do not."

"But you hope she is."

"I do, from my soul."

"Now that is very provoking, Scythrop, and very disappointing: I could not have supposed that you, Scythrop Glowry, of Nightmare Abbey, would have been infatuated with such a dancing, laughing, singing, thoughtless, careless, merry-hearted thing, as Marionetta,— in all respects the reverse of you and me. It is very disappointing, Scythrop. And, do you know, sir, that Marionetta has no fortune?"

"It is the more reason, sir, that her husband should have one."

"The more reason for her; but not for you. My wife had no fortune, and I had no consolation in my calamity. And do you reflect, sir, what an enormous slice this law-suit has cut out of our family estate? we who used to be the greatest landed proprietors in Lincolnshire."

"To be sure, sir, we had more acres of fen than any man on this coast: but what are fens to love? What are dykes and windmills to Marionetta?"

"And what, sir, is love to a windmill? Not grist, I am certain: besides, sir, I have made a choice for you. I have made a choice for you, Scythrop. Beauty, genius, accomplishments, and a great fortune into the bargain. Such a lovely, serious, creature, in a fine state of high dissatisfaction with the world, and every thing in it. Such a delightful surprise I had prepared for you. Sir, I have pledged my honor to the contract—the honor of the Glowries of Nightmare Abbey: and now, sir, what is to be done?"

"Indeed, sir, I cannot say. I claim, on this occasion, that liberty of action which is the co-natal prerogative of every rational being."[1]

"Liberty of action, sir? there is no such thing as liberty of action. We are all slaves and puppets of a blind and unpathetic necessity."[2]

"Very true, sir: but liberty of action, between individuals, consists in their being differently influenced, or modified, by the same universal necessity; so that the results are unconsentaneous,[3] and their respective necessitated volitions clash and fly off in a tangent."

"Your logic is good, sir: but you are aware too, that one individual may be a medium of adhibiting to another a mode or form of necessity, which may have more or less influence in the production of consentaneity; and, therefore, sir, if you do not comply with my wishes in this instance (you have had your own way in every thing else), I shall be under the necessity of disinheriting you, though I shall do it with tears in my eyes." Having said these words, he vanished suddenly, in the dread of Scythrop's logic.

Mr. Glowry immediately sought Mrs. Hilary, and communicated to her his views of the case in point. Mrs. Hilary, as the phrase is, was as fond of Marionetta as if she had been her own child: but—there is always a *but* on these occasions—she could do nothing for her in the way of fortune, as she had two hopeful sons, who were finishing their education at Brazen-nose,[4] and who would not like to encounter any diminution of their prospects when they should be brought out of the house of mental bondage—i.e. the university,—to the land flowing with milk and honey—i.e. the west end of London.

Mrs. Hilary hinted to Marionetta, that propriety, and delicacy, and decorum, and dignity, &c. &c. &c.* would require them to leave

---

* We are not masters of the whole vocabulary. See any Novel by any literary lady. [The reference to women writers is part of Peacock's satire of fashionable literature, as women were not only readers of fiction, but also wrote it.]

---

1 Scythrop is speaking as a Godwinian thinker, who embraces freedom and the belief that the lot of humanity is constantly improving.
2 Mr. Glowry's response to Scythrop echoes classical Stoical philosophy.
3 A form of "consentaneous," done by common consent or concurrent cited in the *OED* as a unique use by Peacock.
4 Reference to Brasenose College, Oxford: brazen means not only brass but hardened in effrontery (*OED*). Peacock is having fun with the name and might be thinking of the brazen age (or brass age), which is the third of the four mythological ages of mankind (between the silver and iron ages). He later uses this term in his essay "The Four Ages of Poetry" (1820).

the Abbey immediately. Marionetta listened in silent submission, for she knew that her inheritance was passive obedience; but, when Scythrop, who had watched the opportunity of Mrs. Hilary's departure, entered, and, without speaking a word, threw himself at her feet in a paroxysm of grief, the young lady, in equal silence and sorrow, threw her arms round his neck and burst into tears. A very tender scene ensued, which the sympathetic susceptibilities of the soft-hearted reader can more accurately imagine than we can delineate. But when Marionetta hinted that she was to leave the Abbey immediately, Scythrop snatched from its repository his ancestor's skull,[1] filled it with Madeira, and, presenting himself before Mr. Glowry, threatened to drink off the contents if Mr. Glowry did not immediately promise that Marionetta should not be taken from the Abbey without her own consent. Mr. Glowry, who took the Madeira to be some deadly brewage, gave the required promise in dismal panic. Scythrop returned to Marionetta with a joyful heart, and drank the Madeira by the way.

Mr. Glowry, during his residence in London, had come to an agreement with his friend Mr. Toobad, that a match between Scythrop and Mr. Toobad's daughter would be a very desirable occurrence. She was finishing her education in a German convent, but Mr. Toobad described her as being fully impressed with the truth of his Ahrimannic★ philosophy, and being altogether as gloomy and antithalian[2] a young lady as Mr. Glowry himself could desire for the future mistress of Nightmare Abbey. She had a great fortune in her

---

★ Ahrimanes, in the Persian mythology, is the evil power, the prince of the kingdom of darkness. He is the rival of Oromazes, the prince of the kingdom of light. These two powers have divided and equal dominion. Sometimes one of the two has a temporary supremacy.—According to Mr. Toobad, the present period would be the reign of Ahrimanes. Lord Byron seems to be of the same opinion, by the use he has made of Ahrimanes in "Manfred;" where the great Alastor, of Κακος Δαιμων, of Persia, is hailed king of the world by the Nemesis of Greece, in concert with three of the Scandinavian Valkyræ, under the name of the Destinies; the astrological spirits of the alchemists of the middle ages; an elemental witch, transplanted from Denmark to the Alps; and a chorus of Dr. Faustus's devils, who come in the last act for a soul. It is difficult to conceive where this heterogeneous mythological company could have originally met, except at a *table d'hôte*, like the six kings in "Candide." [Peacock wrote an unfinished poem in Spenserian stanzas, *Ahrimanes*, which is based upon ideas of J.F. Newton.]

---

1 See note 3, 49.
2 Against comedy or enjoyment.

own right, which was not, as we have seen, without its weight in inducing Mr. Glowry to set his heart upon her as his daughter-in-law that was to be. He was, therefore, very much disturbed by Scythrop's untoward attachment to Marionetta. He condoled on the occasion with Mr. Toobad; who said, that he had been too long accustomed to the intermeddling of the devil in all his affairs, to be astonished at this new trace of his cloven claw; but that he hoped to outwit him yet, for he was sure there could be no comparison between his daughter and Marionetta in the mind of any one who had a proper perception of the fact, that, the world being a great theatre of evil, seriousness and solemnity are the characteristics of wisdom, and laughter and merriment make a human being no better than a baboon. Mr. Glowry comforted himself with this view of the subject, and urged Mr. Toobad to expedite his daughter's return from Germany. Mr. Toobad said, he was in daily expectation of her arrival in London, and would set off immediately to meet her, that he might lose no time in bringing her to Nightmare Abbey. "Then," he added, "we shall see whether Thalia or Melpomene—whether the Allegra or the Penserosa—will carry off the symbol of victory."[1]—"There can be no doubt," said Mr. Glowry, "which way the scale will incline, or Scythrop is no true scion of the venerable stem of the Glowrys."

CHAPTER V

MARIONETTA felt secure of Scythrop's heart; and, notwithstanding the difficulties that surrounded her, she could not debar herself from the pleasure of tormenting her lover, whom she kept in a perpetual fever. Sometimes she would meet him with the most unqualified affection; sometimes with the most chilling indifference; rousing him to anger by artificial coldness,—softening him to love by eloquent tenderness,—or inflaming him to jealousy by coquetting with the Honorable Mr. Listless, who seemed, under her magical influence, to burst into sudden life, like the bud of the evening primrose. Sometimes she would sit by the piano, and listen with

---

[1] The muses of comedy and tragedy; "L'Allegro and Il Penseroso" (1645), companion poems by John Milton about the cheerful man and the contemplative man here feminized to describe Scythrop's two prospective wives.

becoming attention to Scythrop's pathetic remonstrances; but, in the most impassioned part of his oratory, she would convert all his ideas into a chaos, by striking up some Rondo Allegro,[1] and saying "Is it not pretty?" Scythrop would begin to storm; and she would answer him with

"Zitti, zitti, piano, piano,
Non facciamo confusione,"[2]

or some similar *facezia*,[3] till he would start away from her, and enclose himself in his tower, in an agony of agitation, vowing to renounce her, and her whole sex, for ever; and returning to her presence at the summons of the billet, which she never failed to send with many expressions of penitence and promises of amendment. Scythrop's schemes for regenerating the world, and detecting his seven golden candlesticks,[4] went on very slowly in this fever of his spirit.

Things proceeded in this train for several days; and Mr. Glowry began to be uneasy at receiving no intelligence from Mr. Toobad; when, one evening, the latter rushed into the library, where the family and the visitors were assembled, vociferating, "The devil is come among you, having great wrath!" He then drew Mr. Glowry aside into another apartment, and, after remaining some time together, they re-entered the library with faces of great dismay, but did not condescend to explain to any one the cause of their discomfiture.

The next morning, early, Mr. Toobad departed. Mr. Glowry sighed and groaned all day, and said not a word to any one. Scythrop had quarrelled, as usual, with Marionetta, and was enclosed in his tower, in a fit of morbid sensibility. Marionetta was comforting herself at

---

1   A piece of music having one principal subject, to which a return is always made after the introduction of other matter (*OED*).

2   Translated as "Hush, hush, softly, softly/Let us not create confusion." From Rossini, *The Barber of Seville*, Act 2 (1816). See Peacock, "Memoirs of Shelley," II: on the eve of the departure of Percy and Mary Shelley for Italy, Peacock and Leigh and Marianne Hunt (10 March 1818) attended the first performance of an opera by Rossini (*Il Barbiere di Seviglia*) in England. Peacock wrote of his delight in the performance to Thomas Jefferson Hogg; in an article written in 1835 he suggested that "We saw at once that there was a great revolution in dramatic music. Rossini burst on the stage like a torrent, and swept everything before him except Mozart" (Joukovsky, *Letters of Thomas Love Peacock* 1.121, 122n6).

3   Witticism, witty remark (Italian).

4   The reference is to Revelations 1 and 2. See Chapter 2 (58).

the piano, with singing the airs of *Nina pazza per amore*;[1] and the Honorable Mr. Listless was listening to the harmony, as he lay supine on the sofa, with a book in his hand, into which he peeped at intervals. The Reverend Mr. Larynx approached the sofa, and proposed a game at billiards.

THE HONORABLE MR. LISTLESS.

Billiards! Really I should be very happy; but, in my present exhausted state, the exertion is too much for me. I do not know when I have been equal to such an effort. (*He rang the bell for his valet. Fatout entered.*) Fatout! when did I play at billiards last?

FATOUT.

De fourteen December de last year, Monsieur. (*Fatout bowed and retired.*)

THE HONORABLE MR. LISTLESS.

So it was. Seven months ago. You see, Mr. Larynx; you see, sir. My nerves, Miss O'Carroll, my nerves are shattered. I have been advised to try Bath. Some of the faculty recommend Cheltenham. I think of trying both, as the seasons don't clash.[2] The season, you know, Mr. Larynx—the season, Miss O'Carroll—the season is every thing.

MARIONETTA.

And health is something. *N'est-ce pas*, Mr. Larynx?

THE REVEREND MR. LARYNX.

Most assuredly, Miss O'Carroll. For, however reasoners may dispute about the *summum bonum*, none of them will deny that a very good dinner is a very good thing: and what is a good dinner without a good appetite? and whence is a good appetite but from good health? Now, Cheltenham, Mr. Listless, is famous for good appetites.

THE HONORABLE MR. LISTLESS.

The best piece of logic I ever heard, Mr. Larynx; the very best, I assure you. I have thought very seriously of Cheltenham: very seriously and profoundly. I thought of it—let me see—when did I think of it? (*He rang again, and Fatout re-appeared.*) Fatout! when did I think of going to Cheltenham, and did not go?

---

1 A two-act opera by Giovanni Paisiello (1789). Nina is the daughter of a count who has gone mad after her lover has been presumed killed in a duel with a rival. Her intended returns and brings her back to sanity and the lovers marry.

2 Bath and Cheltenham and the seasons: the Bath season was in winter; the Cheltenham season went from the first of June to the first of October.

FATOUT.

De Juillet twenty-von, de last summer, Monsieur. (*Fatout retired.*)

THE HONORABLE MR. LISTLESS.

So it was. An invaluable fellow that, Mr. Larynx—invaluable, Miss O'Carroll.

MARIONETTA.

So I should judge, indeed. He seems to serve you as a walking memory, and to be a living chronicle, not of your actions only, but of your thoughts.

THE HONORABLE MR. LISTLESS.

An excellent definition of the fellow, Miss O'Carroll,—excellent, upon my honour. Ha! ha! he! Heigho! Laughter is pleasant, but the exertion is too much for me.

A parcel was brought in for Mr. Listless: it had been sent express. Fatout was summoned to unpack it; and it proved to contain a new novel, and a new poem, both of which had long been anxiously expected by the whole host of fashionable readers; and the last number of a popular Review, of which the editor and his co-adjutors were in high favour at court, and enjoyed ample pensions[*] for their services to church and state. As Fatout left the room, Mr. Flosky entered, and curiously inspected the literary arrivals.

MR. FLOSKY.

(*Turning over the leaves.*) "Devilman, a novel."[1] Hm. Hatred—revenge—misanthropy—and quotations from the Bible. Hm. This is the morbid anatomy of black bile—"Paul Jones, a poem."[2] Hm. I see how it is. Paul Jones, an amiable enthusiast—disappointed in his

---

[*] "PENSION. Pay given to a slave of state for treason to his country."—*Johnson's Dictionary.* [Garnett points out that Peacock misquotes Johnson's "slave of state" for "state hireling" (375).]

---

1 Godwin's *Mandeville* (1817), which Shelley and Mary Shelley read 1 December 1817 (see above, 30–31). See Jones, *Letters of Percy Bysshe Shelley*, 1.569. John Colmer traces Peacock's debts to the novel in "Godwin's *Mandeville* and Peacock's *Nightmare Abbey*." *Review of English Studies: A Quarterly Journal of English Literature and the English Language* 21 (1970):331–36.

2 Paul Jones or John Paul Jones (1747–92), born in Scotland, he went to America, joined the continental navy, and captured British ships during the American War of Independence. He became a hero of American history and recognized as the "Father of the United States Navy," but was regarded as a pirate in Britain (DNB). Garnett points out that the plot of the poem resembles Byron's *The Corsair* (1814), which sold 10,000 copies on its day of publication (376).

affections—turns pirate from ennui and magnanimity—cuts various masculine throats, wins various feminine hearts—is hanged at
the yard-arm! The catastrophe is very awkward, and very unpoetical.—"The Downing-Street Review."¹ Hm. First article—An Ode
to the Red Book, by Roderick Sackbut, Esquire. Hm. His own
poem reviewed by himself.² Hm-m-m.

(*Mr. Flosky proceeded in silence to look over the other articles of the
Review; Marionetta inspected the novel, and Mr. Listless the poem.*)

THE REVEREND MR. LARYNX.

For a young man of fashion and family, Mr. Listless, you seem to
be of a very studious turn.

THE HONORABLE MR. LISTLESS.

Studious! You are pleased to be facetious, Mr. Larynx. I hope you
do not suspect me of being studious. I have finished my education.
But there are some fashionable books that one must read, because
they are ingredients of the talk of the day: otherwise, I am no fonder
of books than I dare say you yourself are, Mr. Larynx.

THE REVEREND MR. LARYNX.

Why, sir, I cannot say that I am indeed particularly fond of books;
yet neither can I say that I never do read. A tale or a poem, now
and then, to a circle of ladies over their work, is no very heterodox
employment of the vocal energy. And I must say, for myself, that
few men have a more Job-like endurance of the eternally-recurring
questions and answers about pins, needles, threads patterns, hems,
and stitches,³ that interweave themselves, on these occasions, with
the crisis of an adventure, and heighten the distress of a tragedy.

---

1   An invented name for a literary review associated from 1781 with the street in London
    that contains the residence of the Prime Minister, hence a synonym of the Government
    (*OED*).

2   Reference to Robert Southey who became poet laureate in 1813. The poet laureate is
    given a butt of sack (wine). Also a pun on a Renaissance musical instrument, a bass
    trumpet with a slide like that of a trombone for altering the pitch (*OED*). An "Ode to the
    Red Book" is identified by Garnett as *The Red Book of Hergest* (c.1375), an anthology of
    medieval Welsh prose and poetry (376). Wright's suggestion that Roderick is an allusion
    to his narrative poem *Roderick, the last of the Goths* (1814) and that the Red Book is a list of
    those in the royal household (264) seems more likely and continues the joke of Downing
    Street and Sackbut. After 1809 Southey was closely associated with the *Quarterly Review*,
    a conservative journal satirized by Peacock (along with poetry by Southey) in *Melincourt,*
    Chapter 13.

3   "… answers about pins, needles, threads, patterns, hems, and stitches, that interweave …":
    altered to "… answers that interweave …" in 1837.

THE HONORABLE MR. LISTLESS.

And very often make the distress when the author has omitted it.

MARIONETTA.

I shall try your patience some rainy morning, Mr. Larynx: and Mr. Listless shall recommend us the very newest new book, that every body reads.

THE HONORABLE MR. LISTLESS.

You shall receive it, Miss O'Carroll, with all the gloss of novelty; fresh as a ripe green-gage in all the downiness of its bloom. A mail-coach copy from Edinburgh, forwarded express from London.[1]

MR. FLOSKY.

This rage for novelty is the bane of literature. Except my works, and those of my particular friends, nothing is good that is not as old as Jeremy Taylor:[2] and, *entre nous*, the best parts of my friends' books were either written or suggested by myself.[3]

THE HONORABLE MR. LISTLESS.

Sir, I reverence you. But I must say, modern books are very consolatory and congenial to my feelings. There is, as it were, a delightful north-east wind, an intellectual blight, breathing through them; a delicious misanthropy and discontent, that demonstrates the nullity of virtue and energy, and puts me in good humour with myself and my sofa.

MR. FLOSKY.

Very true, sir. Modern literature is a north-east wind—a blight of the human soul. I take credit to myself for having helped to make it so. The way to produce fine fruit is to blight the flower.[4] You call this a paradox. Marry, so be it. Ponder thereon.

---

1   The mail-coach system was introduced in Britain by John Palmer in 1784, and was superseded by the use of the developing railway system in Britain and elsewhere from the middle of the 19th century (*OED*).

2   Jeremy Taylor (1613–67), Chaplain to Laud and Charles I, known for his simplicity of style. His most characteristic works are *The Rule of Exercises for Holy Living* (1650) and *The Rule of Exercises for Holy Dying* (1651). He was a writer of interest to Coleridge.

3   A reference to Coleridge's co-authoring of works with Wordsworth, the *Lyrical Ballads* (1798) and with Southey, *The Devil's Thoughts* (1799) and *Omniana* (1812).

4   "Best way to produce fruit is to blight the flower": Likely a satirical reference to Coleridge's *Statesman's Manual* (1816) in which he advocates that literary culture should be the preserve of an elite from the upper and middle classes who possess the ability to improve society.

The conversation was interrupted by the re-appearance of Mr. Toobad, covered with mud. He just shewed himself at the door, muttered "The devil is come among you!" and vanished. The road which connected Nightmare Abbey with the civilised world was artificially raised above the level of the fens, and ran through them in a straight line as far as the eye could reach, with a ditch on each side, of which the water was rendered invisible by the aquatic vegetation that covered the surface. Into one of these ditches the sudden action of a shy horse, which took fright at a windmill, had precipitated the travelling chariot of Mr. Toobad, who had been reduced to the necessity of scrambling, in dismal plight, through the window. One of the wheels was found to be broken; and Mr. Toobad, leaving the postillion to get the chariot as well as he could to Claydyke, for the purposes of cleaning and repairing, had walked back to Nightmare Abbey, followed by his servant with the imperial, and repeating all the way his favourite quotation from the Revelations.[1]

CHAPTER VI

MR. TOOBAD had found his daughter, Celinda, in London; and, after the first joy of meeting was over, told her he had a husband ready for her. The young lady replied, very gravely, that she should take the liberty to choose for herself. Mr. Toobad said, he saw the devil was determined to interfere with all his projects; but he was resolved on his own part, not to have on his conscience the crime of passive obedience and non-resistance to Lucifer, and therefore she should marry the person he had chosen for her. Miss Toobad replied, *très posément*,[2] she assuredly would not. "Celinda, Celinda," said Mr. Toobad, "you most assuredly shall."—"Have I not a for-tune in my own right, sir?" said Celinda. "The more is the pity," said Mr. Toobad: "but I can find means, miss; I can find means. There are more ways than one of breaking-in obstinate girls." They parted for the night with the expression of opposite resolutions; and, in the morning, the young lady's chamber was found empty, and, what was become of her, Mr. Toobad had no clue to conjec-

---

1   Revelations 12.12.
2   Very calmly (French).

ture. He continued to investigate town and country in search of her, visiting and re-visiting Nightmare Abbey at intervals, to consult with his friend, Mr. Glowry. Mr. Glowry agreed with Mr. Toobad that this was a very flagrant instance of filial disobedience and rebellion; and Mr. Toobad declared, that, when he discovered the fugitive, she should find that "the devil was come unto her, having great wrath."

In the evening, the whole party met, as usual, in the library. Marionetta sat at the harp; the Honorable Mr. Listless sat by her, and turned over her music, though the exertion was almost too much for him. The Reverend Mr. Larynx relieved him occasionally in this delightful labour. Scythrop, tormented by the demon Jealousy, sat in the corner, biting his lips and fingers. Marionetta looked at him every now and then with a smile of most provoking good humour, which he pretended not to see, and which only the more exasperated his troubled spirit. He took down a volume of Dante, and pretended to be deeply interested in the Purgatorio,[1] though he knew not a word he was reading, as Marionetta was well aware, who, tripping across the room, peeped into his book, and said to him—"I see you are in the middle of Purgatory."—"I am in the middle of hell," said Scythrop furiously. "Are you?" said she; "then come across the room, and I will sing you the finale of Don Giovanni."[2]

"Let me alone," said Scythrop. Marionetta looked at him with a deprecating smile, and said, "You unjust, cross creature, you."—"Let me alone," said Scythrop, but much less emphatically than at first, and by no means wishing to be taken at his word. Marionetta left him immediately, and, returning to the harp, said, just loud enough for Scythrop to hear—"Did you ever read Dante, Mr. Listless? Scythrop is reading Dante, and is just now in Purgatory."—"And I," said the Honorable Mr. Listless, "am not reading Dante, and am just now in Paradise;" bowing to Marionetta.

1   Peacock is playing with the three Books of Dante's Inferno: Hell, Purgatory, and Paradise. Coleridge lectured on Dante in 1818 (Garnett 380).

2   Mozart's opera in which Don Juan is pulled down to hell, disappearing in flames; this opera was first performed in London on 12 April 1817 at the King's Theatre. Peacock took Shelley, who was delighted and went several times (Joukovsky, *Letters of Thomas Love Peacock* 1.141n.17 and Richard Holmes, *Shelley: The Pursuit* [London: Weidenfeld & Nicolson, 1974], 408). See Chapter 7 below, 81.

MARIONETTA.

You are very gallant, Mr. Listless, and I dare say you are very fond of reading Dante.

THE HONORABLE MR. LISTLESS.

I don't know how it is, but Dante never came in my way till lately. I never had him in my collection, and, if I had had him, I should not have read him. But I find he is growing fashionable, and I am afraid I must read him some wet morning.[1]

MARIONETTA.

No: read him some evening, by all means. Were you ever in love, Mr. Listless?

THE HONORABLE MR. LISTLESS.

I assure you, Miss O'Carroll, never,—till I came to Nightmare Abbey. I dare say it is very pleasant; but it seems to give so much trouble that I fear the exertion would be too much for me.

MARIONETTA.

Shall I teach you a compendious method of courtship, that will give you no trouble whatever?

THE HONORABLE MR. LISTLESS.

You will confer on me an inexpressible obligation. I am all impatience to learn it.

MARIONETTA.

Sit with your back to the lady, and read Dante, only be sure to begin in the middle, and turn over three or four pages at once—backwards as well as forwards; and she will immediately perceive that you are desperately in love with her—desperately.

(*The Honorable Mr. Listless sitting between Scythrop and Marionetta, and fixing all his attention on the beautiful speaker, did not observe Scythrop, who was doing as she described.*)

THE HONORABLE MR. LISTLESS.

You are pleased to be facetious, Miss O'Carroll. The lady would infallibly conclude that I was the greatest brute in town.

MARIONETTA.

Far from it. She would say, perhaps, some people have odd methods of shewing their affection.

---

1 Garnett notes that H.F. Cary's translation of *The Inferno* appeared in 1805 and the complete translation in 1814 (380).

THE HONORABLE MR. LISTLESS.

But, I should think, with submission—

MR. FLOSKY, (*Joining them from another part of the room.*)

Did I not hear Mr. Listless observe, that Dante is becoming fashionable?

THE HONORABLE MR. LISTLESS.

I did hazard a remark to that effect, Mr. Flosky, though I speak on such subjects with a consciousness of my own nothingness, in the presence of so great a man as Mr. Flosky. I know not what is the colour of Dante's devils, but, as he is certainly becoming fashionable, I conclude they are blue; for the blue devils, as it seems to me, Mr. Flosky, constitute the fundamental feature of fashionable literature.[1]

MR. FLOSKY.

The blue are, indeed, the staple commodity; but, as they will not always be commanded, the black, red, and grey, may be admitted as substitutes. Tea, late dinners,[2] and the French Revolution, have played the devil, Mr. Listless, and brought the devil into play.

Mr. TOOBAD, (*starting up.*)

Having great wrath.

MR. FLOSKY.

This is no play upon words, but the sober sadness of veritable fact.

THE HONORABLE MR. LISTLESS.

Tea, late dinners, and the French Revolution. I cannot exactly see the connexion of ideas.

MR. FLOSKY.

I should be sorry if you could: I pity the man who can see the connexion of his own ideas. Still more do I pity him, the connexion of whose ideas any other person can see. Sir, the great evil is, that there is too much common-place light in our moral and political literature, and light is a great enemy to mystery, and mystery is a great friend to enthusiasm. Now the enthusiasm for abstract truth is an exceedingly fine thing, as long as the truth, which is the object of the enthusiasm, is so completely abstract as to be altogether

---

1   Dante's devils were blue, black, red, and grey. "Blue devils" was an expression for melancholy, as befits the fashionable literature against which Peacock is protesting.

2   Wright notes that during Peacock's life, the hour for dinner among the fashionable moved from early afternoon to mid evening (265).

out of the reach of the human faculties; and, in that sense, I have myself an enthusiasm for truth, but in no other: for the pleasure of metaphysical investigation lies in the means, not in the end; and, if the end could be found, the pleasure of the means would cease. The mind, to be kept in health, must be kept in exercise. The proper exercise of the mind is elaborate reasoning. Analytical reasoning is a base and mechanical process, which takes to pieces and examines, bit by bit, the rude material of knowledge; and extracts therefrom a few hard and obstinate things, called facts, every thing in the shape of which I cordially hate. But synthetical reasoning, setting up as its goal some unattainable abstraction, like an imaginary quantity in algebra, and commencing its course with taking for granted some two assertions which cannot be proved, from the union of these two assumed truths produces a third assumption, and so on in infinite series, to the unspeakable benefit of the human intellect. The beauty of this process is, that at every step it strikes out into two branches, in a compound ratio of ramification; so that you are perfectly sure of losing your way, and keeping your mind in perfect health by the perpetual exercise of an interminable quest: and, for these reasons, I have christened my eldest son Emanuel Kant Flosky.[1]

THE REVEREND MR. LARYNX.

Nothing can be more luminous.

THE HONORABLE MR. LISTLESS.

And what has all that to do with Dante, and the blue devils?

MR. HILARY.

Not much, I should think, with Dante, but a great deal with the blue devils.

Mr. FLOSKY.

It is very certain, and much to be rejoiced at, that our literature is hag-ridden. Tea has shattered our nerves; late dinners make us slaves of indigestion; the French Revolution has made us shrink from the name of philosophy, and has destroyed, in the more refined part of the community, (of which number I am one,) all enthusiasm for political liberty. That part of the *reading public*[2] which shuns the

---

1   Garnett points out that this expands upon a passage in *Melincourt* (381). Emanuel Kant Flosky: Coleridge named his eldest son named Hartley which he mentions in Chapter 10 of the *Biographia Literaria* (1817). His second son was named Berkeley.

2   A phrase associated with Coleridge: "They were found too not in the lower classes of the reading public, but chiefly among young men of strong ability and meditative minds; and

solid food of reason for the light diet of fiction, requires a perpetual adhibition of *sauce piquante* to the palate of its depraved imagination. It lived upon ghosts, goblins, and skeletons, (I and my friend, Mr. Sackbut, served up a few of the best,) till even the devil himself, though magnified to the size of Mount Athos, became too base, common, and popular,[1] for its surfeited appetite. The ghosts have therefore been laid, and the devil has been cast into outer darkness, and now the delight of our spirits is to dwell on all the vices and blackest passions of our nature, tricked out in a masquerade dress of heroism and disappointed benevolence: the whole secret of which lies in forming combinations that contradict all our experience, and affixing the purple shred[2] of some particular virtue to that precise character, in which we should be most certain not to find it in the living world; and making this single virtue not only redeem all the real and manifest vices of the character, but make them actually pass for necessary adjuncts, and indispensable accompaniments and characteristics of the said virtue.

MR. TOOBAD.

That is, because the devil is come among us, and finds it for his interest to destroy all our perceptions of the distinctions of right and wrong.

MARIONETTA.

I do not precisely enter into your meaning, Mr. Flosky, and should be glad if you would make it a little more plain to me.

MR. FLOSKY.

One or two examples will do it, Miss O'Carroll. If I were to take all the mean and sordid qualities of a little Jew broker,[3] and tack on to them, as with a nail, the quality of extreme benevolence, I should have a very decent hero for a modern novel, and should contribute

---

their admiration (inflamed perhaps in some degree by opposition) was distinguished by its intensity, I might almost say, by its *religious* fervour" (*Biographia Literaria*, Chapter 14 [1817]). Joukovsky points out, Peacock is thinking of Coleridge's remarks on the "Reading Public" in *The Statesman's Manual* (1816) (*Letters of Thomas Love Peacock* 1.125n.). See also Chapter 11 below (107) and Appendix C (175–79).

1   "Base, common, and popular": Shakespeare's *Henry V*, 4.1. Spoken by Pistol, one of Falstaff's former tavern-mates, to a disguised King Henry who is interacting with his subjects.

2   Horace, *Ars Poetica*, 151–56.

3   "Little Jew broker": altered to "money-dealing Jew" in 1837; this term refers to a money lender.

my quota to the fashionable method of administering a mass of vice, under a thin and unnatural covering of virtue, like a spider wrapt in a bit of gold leaf, and administered as a wholesome pill. On the same principle, if a man knocks me down, and takes my purse and watch by main force, I turn him to account, and set him forth in a tragedy as a dashing young fellow, disinherited for his romantic generosity, and full of a most amiable hatred of the world in general and his own country in particular, and of a most enlightened and chivalrous affection for himself: then, with the addition of a wild girl to fall in love with him, and a series of adventures in which they break all the Ten Commandments in succession, (always, you will observe, for some sublime motive, which must be carefully analysed in its progress,) I have as amiable a pair of tragic characters as ever issued from that new region of the belles lettres[1] which I have called the Morbid Anatomy of Black Bile, and which is greatly to be admired and rejoiced at, as affording a fine scope for the exhibition of mental power.—

MR. HILARY.

Which is about as well employed as the power of a hot-house would be in forcing up a nettle to the size of an elm. If we go on in this way, we shall have a new art of poetry, of which one of the first rules will be: To remember to forget that there are any such things as sunshine and music in the world.

THE HONORABLE MR. LISTLESS.

It seems to be the case with us at present, or we should not have interrupted Miss O'Carroll's music with this exceedingly dry conversation.

MR. FLOSKY.

I should be most happy if Miss O'Carroll would remind us that there are yet both music and sunshine—

THE HONORABLE MR. LISTLESS.

In the voice and the smile of beauty. May I entreat the favor of—(*turning over the pages of music.*)

---

1 Elegant or polite literature or literary studies. A vaguely used term, formerly taken sometimes in the wide sense of "the humanities," *literæ humaniores*; sometimes in the exact sense in which we now use "literature"; in the latter use it has come down to the present time, but it is now generally applied (when used at all) to the lighter branches of literature or the æsthetics of literary study (*OED*). A subject of interest to Peacock. He was writing an essay on fashionable literature in 1818. See Appendix D (210–18).

All were silent, and Marionetta sung:[1]—

Why are thy looks so blank, grey friar?
Why are thy looks so blue?
    Thou seem'st more pale and lank, grey friar,
    Than thou wast used to do:—
    Say, what has made thee rue?

    Thy form was plump, and a light did shine
    In thy round and ruby face,
    Which showed an outward visible sign
    Of an inward spiritual grace:—
    Say, what has changed thy case?

    Yet will I tell thee true, grey friar,
    I very well can see,
    That, if thy looks are blue, grey friar,
    'Tis all for love of me,—
    'Tis all for love of me.

    But breathe not thy vows to me, grey friar,
    Oh! breathe them not, I pray;
    For ill beseems in a reverend friar,
    The love of a mortal may;[2]
    And I needs must say thee nay.

    But, could'st thou think my heart to move
    With that pale and silent scowl?
    Know, he who would win a maiden's love,
    Whether clad in cap or cowl,
    Must be more of a lark than an owl.

Scythrop immediately replaced Dante on the shelf, and joined the circle round the beautiful singer. Marionetta gave him a smile of approbation that fully restored his complacency, and they continued on the best possible terms during the remainder of the evening. The Honorable Mr. Listless turned over the leaves with double alacrity, saying, "You are severe upon invalids, Miss

---

1   This poem is by Peacock.
2   "May" means "maid."

O'Carroll: to escape your satire, I must try to be sprightly, though the exertion is too much for me."

CHAPTER VII

A NEW visitor arrived at the Abbey, in the person of Mr. Asterias, the ichthyologist.[1] This gentleman had passed his life in seeking the living wonders of the deep through the four quarters of the world: he had a cabinet of stuffed and dried fishes, of shells, sea-weeds, corals, and madrepores, that was the admiration and envy of the Royal Society.[2] He had penetrated into the watery den of the Sepia Octopus,[3] disturbed the conjugal happiness of that turtle-dove of the ocean, and come off victorious in a sanguinary conflict. He had been becalmed in the tropical seas, and had watched, in eager expectation, though unhappily always in vain, to see the colossal polypus[4] rise from the water, and entwine its enormous arms round the masts and the rigging. He maintained the origin of all things from water, and insisted that the polypodes were the first of animated things, and that, from their round bodies and many-shooting arms, the Hindoos had taken their gods, the most ancient of deities. But the chief object of his ambition, the end and aim of his researches, was to discover a Triton and a Mermaid, the existence of which he most potently and implicitly believed, and was prepared to demonstrate, *a priori, a posteriori, a fortiori*,[5] synthetically and analytically, syllogistically and inductively, by arguments deduced both from ac-

---

1   Asterias: a genus of Echinoderms, containing the common five-rayed star-fish, with allied species (*OED*). In "A Second Original of Peacock's Menippean Caricature Asteria's in *Nightmare Abbey*" *English Studies* 56 (1975): 491–97 Norma Leigh Rudinsky notes that Peacock's contemporaries identified the figure as a caricature of the Scottish baronet Sir John Sinclair. Rudinsky has also shown in "Source of Asteria's Paean to Science" *Notes and Queries* 24(1977): 335–36 that Asterias' speeches are translations from French scientist Pierre Denys de Monfort's *Histoire Naturelle des Mollusques* (2 vols, 1801, 1802).

2   The Royal Society of London for the Improving of Natural Knowledge (1662, 1663).

3   Wright points out that these details are from Montfort's *Histoire Naturelle* (265). Noted by Peacock (87).

4   A cuttle-fish, an octopus (*OED*).

5   *A priori* suggests a concept or thing that is knowable in advance, without directly experiencing it; the term is used in the philosophy of Kant to mean independent of any experience; *a posteriori* means knowable only from certain experiences, while *a fortiori* suggests the inference of something weaker from something stronger.

knowledged facts and plausible hypotheses. A report that a mermaid had been seen "sleeking her soft alluring locks"[1] on the sea-coast of Lincolnshire, had brought him in great haste from London, to pay a long-promised and often-postponed visit to his old acquaintance, Mr. Glowry.

Mr. Asterias was accompanied by his son, to whom he had given the name of Aquarius,—flattering himself that he would, in the process of time, become a constellation among the stars of ichthyological science. What charitable female had lent him the mould in which this son was cast, no one pretended to know; and, as he never dropped the most distant allusion to Aquarius's mother, some of the wags of London maintained that he had received the favours of a mermaid, and that the scientific perquisitions which kept him always prowling about the sea-shore, were directed by the less philosophical motive of regaining his lost love.

Mr. Asterias perlustrated the sea-coast for several days, and reaped disappointment, but not despair. One night, shortly after his arrival, he was sitting in one of the windows of the library, looking towards the sea, when his attention was attracted by a figure which was moving near the edge of the surf, and which was dimly visible through the moonless summer-night. Its motions were irregular, like those of a person in a state of indecision. It had extremely long hair, which floated in the wind. Whatever else it might be, it certainly was not a fisherman. It might be a lady; but it was neither Mrs. Hilary nor Miss O'Carroll, for they were both in the library. It might be one of the female servants; but it had too much grace, and too striking an air of habitual liberty, to render it probable. Besides, what should one of the female servants be doing there at this hour, moving to and fro, as it seemed, without any visible purpose? It could scarcely be a stranger; for Claydyke, the nearest village, was ten miles distant; and what female would come ten miles across the fens, for no purpose but to hover over the surf under the walls of Nightmare Abbey? Might it not be a mermaid? It was possibly a mermaid. It was probably a mermaid. It was very probably a mermaid. Nay, what else could it be but a mermaid? It certainly was a mermaid. Mr. Asterias stole out of the library on tiptoe, with his finger on his lips, having beckoned Aquarius to follow him.

---

1   Milton, *Comus* (1634), 882.

The rest of the party was in great surprise at Mr. Asterias's movement, and some of them approached the window to see if the locality would tend to elucidate the mystery. Presently they saw him and Aquarius cautiously stealing along on the other side of the moat, but they saw nothing more; and Mr. Asterias returning, told them, with accents of great disappointment, that he had had a glimpse of a mermaid, but she had eluded him in the darkness, and was gone, he presumed, to sup with some enamoured Triton, in a submarine grotto.

"But, seriously, Mr. Asterias," said the Honorable Mr. Listless, "do you positively believe there are such things as mermaids?"

MR. ASTERIAS.

Most assuredly; and Tritons too.

THE HONORABLE MR. LISTLESS.

What! things that are half human and half fish?

MR. ASTERIAS.

Precisely. They are the Oran-outangs of the sea.[1] But I am persuaded that there are also complete sea men, differing in no respect from us, but that they are stupid, and covered with scales: for, though our organization seems to exclude us essentially from the class of amphibious animals, yet anatomists well know that the *foramen ovale*[2] may remain open in an adult, and that respiration is, in that case, not necessary to life: and how can it be otherwise explained that the Indian divers, employed in the pearl fishery, pass whole hours under the water? and that the famous Swedish gardener, of Troningholm, lived a day and a half under the ice, without being drowned? A Nereid,[3] or mermaid, was taken in the year 1403, in a Dutch lake, and was in every respect like a French woman, except that she did not speak. Towards the end of the seventeenth century, an English ship, a hundred and fifty leagues from land, in the Greenland seas,

---

1   An orangutan is mistaken for a lord in *Melincourt*.

2   A small opening in a fetus between the left and right atria (upper chambers) of the heart. This hole allows blood to bypass the lungs, because they are not used until a baby is born. The foramen ovale normally closes soon after birth.

3   "And in the year 1430 the dikes of Holland being broken down by a violent tempest, the sea overflow'd the meadows, and some maidens of the town of Edam in west Friezland going in a boat to milk their cows, espied a mermaid embarrass'd in the mud, the water being very shallow, they took it into their boat and brought it to Edam, and dress'd it in womans apparel, and taught it to spin. It eat as they did but could never be brought to speak. It was afterwards carried to Harlem, where it liv'd for some years, tho still shewing an inclination to water" (Nathan Bailey, *Universal Etymological Dictionary*, 1736).

discovered a flotilla of sixty or seventy little skiffs, in each of which was a Triton, or sea man: at the approach of the English vessel, the whole of them, seized with simultaneous fear, disappeared, skiffs and all, under the water, as if they had been a human variety of the Nautilus.[1] The illustrious Don Feijoo has preserved an authentic and well-attested story of a young Spaniard, named Francis de la Vega,[2] who, bathing with some of his friends in June 1674, suddenly dived under the sea and rose no more. His friends thought him drowned: they were plebeians and pious Catholics; but a philosopher might very legitimately have drawn the same conclusion.

THE REVEREND MR. LARYNX.

Nothing could be more logical.

MR. ASTERIAS.

Five years afterwards, some fishermen, near Cadiz, found in their nets a Triton, or sea man; they spoke to him in several languages—

THE REVEREND MR. LARYNX.

They were very learned fishermen.

MR. HILARY.

They had the gift of tongues by especial favour of their brother fisherman, Saint Peter.

---

1 *Speculum Regale* (also called the King's Mirror, written in Norway around 1250): "It is reported that the monster called merman is found in the seas of Greenland. This monster is tall and of great size and rises straight out of the water. It appears to have shoulders, neck and head, eyes and mouth, and nose and chin like those of a human being; but above the eyes and the eyebrows it looks more like a man with a peaked helmet on his head. It has shoulders like a man's but no hands. Its body apparently grows narrower from the shoulders down, so that the lower down it has been observed, the more slender it has seemed to be. But no one has ever seen how the lower end is shaped, whether it terminates in a fin like a fish or is pointed like a pole. The form of this prodigy has, therefore, looked much like an icicle. No one has ever observed it closely enough to determine whether its body has scales like a fish or skin like a man. Whenever the monster has shown itself, men have always been sure that a storm would follow. They have also noted how it has turned when about to plunge into the waves and in what direction it has fallen; if it has turned toward the ship and has plunged in that direction, the sailors have felt sure that lives would be lost on that ship; but whenever it has turned away from the vessel and has plunged in that direction, they have felt confident that their lives would be spared, even though they should encounter rough waters and severe storms."

2 Don Feijoo: Feijoo, Benito Jerónimo (1676–1764), Spanish Benedictine scholar and critic, abbot at Oviedo, Asturias. Feijoo led in bringing the Enlightenment to Spain. His writings on philosophy, science, and literature represent the most advanced European thought of his time. His essays were collected in his *Teatro critico universal* (8 vol., 1726–39) and *Cartas eruditas y curiosas* (5 vol., 1742–60). Garnett says his admirers called him "the Spanish Voltaire" (387).

THE HONORABLE MR. LISTLESS.

Is Saint Peter the tutelar saint of Cadiz?[1]

(*None of the company could answer this question, and* MR. ASTERIAS *proceeded.*)

They spoke to him in several languages, but he was as mute as a fish. They handed him over to some holy friars, who exorcised him; but the devil was mute too. After some days, he pronounced the name Lierganes.[2] A monk took him to that village. His mother and brothers recognised and embraced him; but he was as insensible to their caresses as any other fish would have been. He had some scales on his body, which dropped off by degrees; but his skin was as hard and rough as shagreen. He stayed at home nine years, without recovering his speech or his reason: he then disappeared again; and one of his old acquaintance, some years after, saw him pop his head out of the water near the coast of the Asturias. These facts were certified by his brothers, and by Don Gaspardo de la Riba Aguero, Knight of Saint James, who lived near Lierganes, and often had the pleasure of our Triton's company to dinner.—Pliny mentions an embassy of the Olyssiponians to Tiberius, to give him intelligence of a Triton which had been heard playing on its shell in a certain cave; with several other authenticated facts on the subject of Tritons and Nereids.[3]

THE HONORABLE MR. LISTLESS.

You astonish me. I have been much on the sea-shore, in the season, but I do not think I ever saw a mermaid. (*He rang, and summoned Fatout, who made his appearance half-seas over.*) Fatout! did I ever see a mermaid?

FATOUT.

Mermaid! mer-r-m-m-aid! Ah! merry maid! Oui, monsieur! Yes, Sir, very many. I vish dere vas von or two here in de kitchen,—ma foi! Dey be all as melancholic as so many tombstone.

THE HONORABLE MR. LISTLESS.

I mean, Fatout, an odd kind of human fish.

---

1   The patron saints of Cadiz are Saints Servando and Germán (Wright 265). Peter of course was a fisherman and Christ said he would make him a fisher of men.
2   Lierganes is a location in Spain.
3   Pliny 8.3 (Garnett 389); Wright identifies it as 9.4 (265).

FATOUT.

De odd fish! Ah, oui! I understand de phrase: ve have seen nothing else since ve left town, —ma foi!

THE HONORABLE MR. LISTLESS.

You seem to have a cup too much, Sir.

FATOUT.

Non, Monsieur: de cup too little. De fen be very unwholesome, and I drink-a-de ponch vid Raven de butler, to keep out de bad air.

THE HONORABLE MR. LISTLESS.

Fatout! I insist on your being sober.

FATOUT.

Oui, Monsieur; I vil be as sober as de révérendissime père Jean.[1] I should be ver glad of de merry maid; but de butler be de odd fish, and he swim in de bowl de ponch. Ah! ah! I do recollect de leetle-a song:—"About fair maids, and about fair maids, and about my merry maids all." (*Fatout reeled out, singing.*)

THE HONORABLE MR. LISTLESS.

I am overwhelmed: I never saw the rascal in such a condition before. But will you allow me, Mr. Asterias, to inquire into the *cui bono*[2] of all the pains and expense you have incurred to discover a mermaid? The *cui bono*, Sir, is the question I always take the liberty to ask, when I see any one taking much trouble for any object. I am myself a sort of Signor Pococurante,[3] and should like to know if there be any thing better or pleasanter, than the state of existing and doing nothing?

MR. ASTERIAS.

I have made many voyages, Mr. Listless, to remote and barren shores: I have travelled over desert and inhospitable lands: I have defied danger—I have endured fatigue—I have submitted to privation. In the midst of these I have experienced pleasures which I would not at any time have exchanged for that of existing and doing noth-

---

1 Wright identifies as a character in a novel, *Le Compère Matthieu* (1768) by Du Laurens, about which Peacock wrote in his essay "French Comic Romances" (1835) (266). Garnett suggests it is a reference to Rabelais's *Frère Jean des Entommeures*, 1.27 (389).

2 A Latin phrase, properly *cui bono est, fuit*, etc., meaning "to whom [is or was it] for a benefit?" or "who profits (or has profited) by it?" and attributed by Cicero to a certain Lucius Cassius (*Pro Roscio Amer.* xxx). It is popularly taken in English to mean "To what use or good purpose?" (*OED*).

3 A character in Voltaire's *Candide* (1759).

ing. I have known many evils, but I have never known the worst of all, which, as it seems to me, are those which are comprehended in the inexhaustible varieties of *ennui:* spleen, chagrin, vapours, blue devils, time-killing, discontent, misanthropy, and all their interminable train of fretfulness, querulousness, suspicions, jealousies, and fears: which have alike infected society, and the literature of society; and which would make an Arctic ocean of the human mind, if the more humane pursuits of philosophy and science did not keep alive the better feelings and more valuable energies of our nature.

THE HONORABLE MR. LISTLESS.

You are pleased to be severe upon our fashionable belles lettres.

MR. ASTERIAS.

Surely not without reason, when pirates, highwaymen, and other varieties of the extensive genus Marauder,[1] are the only *beau idéal* of the active, as splenetic and railing misanthropy is of the speculative, energy. A gloomy brow and a tragical voice seem to have been, of late, the characteristics of fashionable manners; and a morbid, withering, deadly, antisocial sirocco, loaded with moral and political despair, breathes through all the groves and valleys of the modern Parnassus: while science moves on in the calm dignity of its course, affording to youth delights equally pure and vivid,—to maturity, calm and grateful occupation,—to old age, the most pleasing recollections and inexhaustible materials of agreeable and salutary reflection; and, while its votary enjoys the disinterested pleasure of enlarging the intellect and increasing the comforts of society, he is himself independent of the caprices of human intercourse and the accidents of human fortune. Nature is his great and inexhaustible treasure. His days are always too short for his enjoyment: *ennui* is a stranger to his door. At peace with the world and with his own mind, he suffices to himself, makes all around him happy, and the close of his pleasing and beneficial existence is the evening of a beautiful day.★

★ See Denys Montfort: *Histoire Naturelle des Mollusques; Vues Generales,* 2 vols, 1801, 1802, p. 37, 38. [This is paraphrased from Montfort. Peacock mentions reading Buffon's *Histoire naturelle* in July 1818, at the same time as he is completing the novel (Joukovsky, *Letters of Thomas Love Peacock* 1.135). Joukovsky notes that the edition he used, likely left behind in Marlow by Shelley, also contained Montfort's work (*Letters of Thomas Love Peacock* 1.142n.).]

---

1 A satire on Byron's heroes.

THE HONORABLE MR. LISTLESS.
Really, I should like very well to lead such a life myself, but the exertion would be too much for me. Besides, I have been at college. I contrive to get through my day by sinking the morning in bed, and killing the evening in company, dressing and dining in the intermediate space, and stopping the chinks and crevices of the few vacant moments that remain with a little easy reading. And that amiable discontent and antisociality, which you reprobate in our present parlour-window[1] literature, I find, I do assure you, a very fine mental tonic, which reconciles me to my favorite pursuit of doing nothing, by shewing me that nobody is worth doing any thing for.

MARIONETTA.
But is there not in such compositions a kind of unconscious self-detection, which seems to carry their own antidote with them? For, surely, no one who cordially and truly either hates or despises the world will publish a volume every three months to say so.

MR. FLOSKY.
There is a secret in all this, which I will elucidate with a dusky remark. According to Berkeley, the *esse* of things is *percipi*.[2] They exist as they are perceived. But, leaving for the present, as far as relates to the material world, the materialists, hyloists,[3] and antihyloists, to settle this point among them, which is indeed

> A subtle question raised among
> Those out o' their wits, and those i' the wrong:[4]

for only we transcendentalists are in the right: we may very safely assert that the *esse* of happiness is *percipi*. It exists as it is perceived.

---

1   "parlour-window": altered to "drawing-room-table" in 1837.
2   "To be is to be perceived" or subjective idealism as formulated by Irish philosopher Bishop George Berkeley (1685–1753). Berkeley meant by *esse est percipi* that "nothing but minds and ideas exist." In his conception, to say that an idea "exists" means it is being perceived by some mind. In other words, Berkeley's meaning can be paraphrased as, "to be is to be perceived (ideas) or to be a perceiver. All that is real is a conscious mind or some perception or idea held by such a mind." How, Berkeley asks, could we speak of anything that was other than an idea or mind? The mind exists as it is thought in the mind of God. Berkeley was also known for holding the position that there is no material substance, hence he is also, and prefers to be, called an "immaterialist."
3   One who believes that matter is God. The list represents three perspectives on the material world.
4   Butler, *Hudibras*, 1.2, 703–04.

"It is the mind that maketh well or ill."[1] The elements of pleasure and pain are every where. The degree of happiness that any circumstances or objects can confer on us, depends on the mental disposition with which we approach them. If you consider what is meant by the common phrases, a happy disposition and a discontented temper, you will perceive that the truth for which I am contending is universally admitted.

(*Mr. Flosky suddenly stopped: he found himself unintentionally trespassing within the limits of common sense.*)

MR. HILARY.

It is very true: a happy disposition finds materials of enjoyment every where. In the city, or the country—in society, or in solitude—in the theatre, or the forest—in the hum of the multitude, or in the silence of the mountains, are alike materials of reflection and elements of pleasure. It is one mode of pleasure to listen to the music of "Don Giovanni,"[2] in a theatre glittering with light, and crowded with elegance and beauty: it is another to glide at sunset over the bosom of a lonely lake, where no sound disturbs the silence but the motion of the boat through the waters. A happy disposition derives pleasure from both, a discontented temper from neither, but is always busy in detecting deficiencies, and feeding dissatisfaction with comparisons. The one gathers all the flowers, the other all the nettles, in its path. The one has the faculty of enjoying every thing, the other of enjoying nothing. The one realises all the pleasure of the present good; the other converts it into pain, by pining after something better, which is only better because it is not present, and which, if it were present, would not be enjoyed. These morbid spirits are in life what professed critics are in literature: they see nothing but faults, because they are predetermined to shut their eyes to beauties. The critic does his utmost to blight genius in its infancy: that which rises in spite of him he will not see; and then he complains of the decline of literature. In like manner, these cankers of society complain of human nature and society, when they have wilfully debarred themselves from all the good they contain, and done their utmost to blight their own happiness and that of all around them. Misanthropy is sometimes the

---

1 Spenser, *Faerie Queene*, 6.9, line 30.
2 The opera by Mozart. See Chapter 6 above (74, note 2).

product of disappointed benevolence; but it is more frequently the offspring of overweening and mortified vanity, quarrelling with the world for not being better treated than it deserves.

SCYTHROP (*to Marionetta*).

These remarks are rather uncharitable. There is great good in human nature, but it is at present ill-conditioned. Ardent spirits cannot but be dissatisfied with things as they are; and, according to their views of the probabilities of amelioration, they will rush into the extremes of either hope or despair,—of which the first is enthusiasm, and the second misanthropy: but their sources, in this case, are the same, as the Severn and the Wye run in different directions, and both rise in Plinlimmon. [1]

MARIONETTA.

"And there is salmon in both:"[2] for the resemblance is about as close as that between Macedon and Monmouth.

CHAPTER VIII

MARIONETTA observed, the next day, a remarkable perturbation in Scythrop, for which she could not imagine any probable cause. She was willing to believe, at first, that it had some transient and trifling source, and would pass off in a day or two; but, contrary to this expectation, it daily increased. She was well aware that Scythrop had a strong tendency to the love of mystery, for its own sake; that is to say, he would employ mystery to serve a purpose, but would first choose his purpose by its capability of mystery. He seemed now to have more mystery on his hands than the laws of the system allowed, and to wear his coat of darkness with an air of great discomfort. All her little playful arts lost by degrees much of their power either to irritate or to soothe, and the first perception of her diminished influence produced in her an immediate depression of spirits, and a consequent sadness of demeanour, that rendered her very interesting to Mr. Glowry; who, duly considering the improb-

---

1 The Wye rises in Montgomeryshire on the E. slope of Plinlimmon, close to the source of the Severn, the estuary of which it joins after a widely divergent course. The Severn rises on the N.E. side of Plinlimmon, on the SW border of Montgomeryshire, and flows with a nearly semicircular course of about 210 m. to the Bristol Channel.

2 Shakespeare's *Henry V*, 4.7.

ability of accomplishing his wishes with respect to Miss Toobad, (which improbability naturally increased in the diurnal ratio of that young lady's absence,) began to reconcile himself by degrees to the idea of Marionetta being his daughter.

Marionetta made many ineffectual attempts to extract from Scythrop the secret of his mystery; and, in despair of drawing it from himself, began to form hopes that she might find a clue to it from Mr. Flosky, who was Scythrop's dearest friend, and was more frequently than any other person admitted to his solitary tower. Mr. Flosky, however, had ceased to be visible in a morning. He was engaged in the composition of a dismal ballad;[1] and, Marionetta's uneasiness overcoming her scruples of decorum, she determined to seek him in the apartment which he had chosen for his study. She tapped at the door, and, at the sound "Come in," éntered the apartment. It was noon, and the sun was shining in full splendour, much to the annoyance of Mr. Flosky, who had obviated the inconvenience by closing the shutters, and drawing the window curtains. He was sitting at his table by the light of a solitary candle, with a pen in one hand, and a muffineer in the other, with which he occasionally sprinkled salt on the wick, to make it burn blue.[2] He sate with "his eye in a fine frenzy rolling,"[3] and turned his inspired gaze on Marionetta as if she had been the ghastly ladie of a magical vision;[4] then placed his hand before his eyes, with an appearance of manifest pain—shook his head—withdrew his hand—rubbed his eyes, like a waking man—and said, in a tone of ruefulness most jeremitaylorically[5] pathetic, "To what am I to attribute this very unexpected pleasure, my dear Miss O'Carroll?"

MARIONETTA.

I must apologise for intruding on you, Mr. Flosky; but the interest which I—you—take in my cousin Scythrop—

---

1 An allusion to Coleridge's composition of gothic ballads.
2 A small castor with a perforated top for sprinkling salt, sugar, etc., on muffins (OED); blue flames are thought to indicate the presence of a ghost. See Shakespeare, Richard III, 5.3 (Wright 266).
3 Shakespeare's A Midsummer Night's Dream, 5.1.
4 Reminiscent of "Christabel" and "Kubla Khan," which were published with "The Pains of Sleep" in 1816.
5 A Peacock coinage. The name resembles Jeremy Taylor (1613–67), preacher and divine, who was known for his eloquent prose style and favoured by Coleridge.

MR. FLOSKY.

Pardon me, Miss O'Carroll: I do not take any interest in any person or thing on the face of the earth; which sentiment, if you analyse it, you will find to be the quintessence of the most refined philanthropy.

MARIONETTA.

I will take it for granted that it is so, Mr. Flosky: I am not conversant with metaphysical subtleties, but—

MR. FLOSKY.

Subtleties! my dear Miss O'Carroll. I am sorry to find you participating in the vulgar error of the *reading public*,[1] to whom an unusual collocation of words, involving a juxtaposition of antiperistatical ideas,[2] immediately suggests the notion of hyperoxysophistical paradoxology.[3]

MARIONETTA.

Indeed, Mr. Flosky, it suggests no such notion to me. I have sought you for the purpose of obtaining information.

MR. FLOSKY (*shaking his head*).

No one ever sought me for such a purpose before.

MARIONETTA.

I think, Mr. Flosky—that is, I believe—that is, I fancy—that is, I imagine—

MR. FLOSKY.

The τουτεστι, the *id est*, the *cioè*, the *c'est à dire*, the *that is*, my dear Miss O'Carroll, is not applicable in this case,—if you will permit me to take the liberty of saying so.[4] Think is not synonymous with believe—for belief, in many most important particulars, results from the total absence, the absolute negation of thought, and is thereby the sane and orthodox condition of mind; and thought and belief are both essentially different from fancy, and fancy, again, is distinct from imagination. This distinction between fancy and imagination is one of the most abstruse and important points of metaphysics. I have written seven hundred pages of promise to elu-

---

1   An obsession of Coleridge's; Peacock is thinking of *Biographia Literaria* (1817), Chapter 3 and *Statesman's Manual* (1816). See Chapter 6 (73–80).

2   I.e., heightened by contrast.

3   Paradoxes presented with much sophistry.

4   Peacock is making a joke about Floskey's prolixity and pedantry, in that all of these terms signify the same thing: "that is."

cidate it, which promise I shall keep as faithfully as the bank will its promise to pay.[1]

MARIONETTA.

I assure you, Mr. Flosky, I care no more about metaphysics than I do about the bank; and, if you will condescend to talk to a simple girl in intelligible terms—

MR. FLOSKY.

Say not condescend! Know you not that you talk to the most humble of men, to one who has buckled on the armour of sanctity, and clothed himself with humility as with a garment?

MARIONETTA.

My cousin, Scythrop, has of late had an air of mystery about him, which gives me great uneasiness.

MR. FLOSKY.

That is strange. Nothing is so becoming to a man as an air of mystery. Mystery is the very key-stone of all that is beautiful in poetry, all that is sacred in faith, and all that is recondite in transcendental psychology. I am writing a ballad, which is all mystery: it is "such stuff as dreams are made of,"[2] and is, indeed, stuff made of a dream: for, last night I fell asleep, as usual, over my book, and had a vision of pure reason.[3] I composed five hundred lines in my sleep; so that as I had[4] a dream of a ballad, I am now officiating as my own Peter Quince, and making a ballad of my dream, and it shall be called Bottom's Dream, because it has no bottom.[5]

MARIONETTA.

I see, Mr. Flosky, you think my intrusion unseasonable, and are inclined to punish it, by talking nonsense to me. (*Mr. Flosky gave a start at the word nonsense, which almost overturned the table.*) I assure you, I would not have intruded if I had not been very much interested in the question I wish to ask you.—(*Mr. Flosky listened in sullen dignity.*)—My cousin Scythrop seems to have some secret preying on

---

1   See Coleridge, *Biographia Literaria*, Chapter 13.
2   Shakespeare's *The Tempest*, 4.1.
3   An allusion to the philosopher Kant. See Chapter 1, note 4 (53).
4   "... so that as I had": altered to "so that, having had ..." in 1837.
5   Shakespeare's *A Midsummer Night's Dream*, 4.1. A satirical reference to Coleridge's composition of "Kubla Khan," first published 1816. Peacock repeats the allusion to Bottom's dream as something incommunicable in his review of Moore's *Letters and Journals of Lord Byron* in *The Westminster Review* 12 (1830): 269–304.

his mind.—(*Mr. Flosky was silent.*)—He seems very unhappy— Mr. Flosky.—Perhaps you are acquainted with the cause.—(*Mr. Flosky was still silent.*)—I only wish to know—Mr. Flosky—if it is anything—that could be remedied by anything that any one—of whom I know anything—could do.

MR. FLOSKY (*after a pause*).

There are various ways of getting at secrets. The most approved methods, as recommended both theoretically and practically in philosophical novels,[1] are eaves-dropping at key-holes, picking the locks of chests and desks, peeping into letters, steaming wafers, and insinuating hot wire under sealing wax: none of which methods I hold it lawful to practise.

MARIONETTA.

Surely, Mr. Flosky, you cannot suspect me of wishing to adopt or encourage such base and contemptible arts.

MR. FLOSKY.

Yet are they recommended, and with well-strung reasons, by writers of gravity and note, as simple and easy methods of studying character, and gratifying that laudable curiosity which aims at the knowledge of man.

MARIONETTA.

I am as ignorant of this morality which you do not approve, as of the metaphysics which you do: I should be glad to know, by your means, what is the matter with my cousin: I do not like to see him unhappy, and I suppose there is some reason for it.

MR. FLOSKY.

Now I should rather suppose there is no reason for it. It is the fashion to be unhappy.[2] To have a reason for being so would be exceedingly common-place: to be so without any is the province of genius: the art of being miserable, for misery's sake, has been brought to great perfection in our days; and the ancient Odyssey,[3] which

---

1 A reference to an important incident in William Godwin's *Caleb Williams* (1794). For a satirical reference to Godwin's novel *Mandeville* (1817), see Chapter 5. *Mandeville* is also discussed in the Introduction (see above, 30) and excerpts from the novel are included in Appendix C (171).

2 Peacock is especially thinking of Byron and Canto 4 of *Childe Harold's Pilgrimage*, which he suggests provided a catalyst for writing the novel. See Appendix C (193).

3 Homer's epic, which describes the adventures of Odysseus as he returns to his kingdom of Ithaca following the Trojan War.

held forth a shining example of the endurance of real misfortune, will give place to a modern one, setting out a more instructive picture of querulous impatience under imaginary evils.

MARIONETTA.

Will you oblige me, Mr. Flosky, by giving me a plain answer to a plain question?

MR. FLOSKY.

It is impossible, my dear Miss O'Carroll. I never gave a plain answer to a question in my life.

MARIONETTA.

Do you, or do you not, know what is the matter with my cousin?

MR. FLOSKY.

To say that I do not know, would be to say that I am ignorant of something: and God forbid, that a trancendental metaphysician, who has pure anticipated cognitions of every thing, and carries the whole science of geometry in his head without ever having looked into Euclid,[1] should fall into so empirical an error as to declare himself ignorant of any thing: to say that I do know, would be to pretend to positive and circumstantial knowledge touching present matter of fact, which, when you consider the nature of evidence, and the various lights in which the same thing may be seen—

MARIONETTA.

I see, Mr. Flosky, that either you have no information, or are determined not to impart it; and I beg your pardon for having given you this unnecessary trouble.

MR. FLOSKY.

My dear Miss O'Carroll, it would have given me great pleasure to have said any thing that would have given you pleasure; but, if any person living could have it to say, that they had[2] obtained any information on any subject from Ferdinando Flosky, my transcendental reputation would be ruined for ever.

---

1 Attributed by Wright to Drummond's *Academical Questions* (1805) (358). See Chapter 3.

2 "... have it to say, that they had ...": altered to "... make report of having" in 1837.

CHAPTER IX

SCYTHROP grew every day more reserved, mysterious, and *distrait*; and gradually lengthened the duration of his diurnal seclusions in his tower. Marionetta thought she perceived in all this very manifest symptoms of a warm love cooling.

It was seldom that she found herself alone with him in the morning, and, on these occasions, if she was silent, in the hope of his speaking first, not a syllable would he utter: if she spoke to him indirectly, he assented monosyllabically: if she questioned him, his answers were brief, constrained, and evasive. Still, though her spirits were depressed, her playfulness had not so totally forsaken her, but that it illuminated, at intervals, the gloom of Nightmare Abbey; and, if, on any occasion, she observed in Scythrop tokens of unextinguished or returning passion, her love of tormenting her lover immediately got the better both of her grief and her sympathy, though not of her curiosity, which Scythrop seemed determined not to satisfy. This playfulness, however, was in a great measure artificial, and usually vanished with the irritable Strephon,[1] to whose annoyance it had been exerted. The Genius Loci, the *tutela*[2] of Nightmare Abbey, the spirit of black melancholy, began to set his seal on her pallescent countenance. Scythrop perceived the change, found his tender sympathies awakened, and did his utmost to comfort the afflicted damsel, assuring her that his seeming inattention had only proceeded from his being involved in a profound meditation on a very hopeful scheme for the regeneration of human society. Marionetta called him ungrateful, cruel, cold-hearted, and accompanied her reproaches with many sobs and tears; poor Scythrop growing every moment more soft and submissive,—till, at length, he threw himself at her feet, and declared, that no competition of beauty however dazzling, genius however transcendent, talents however cultivated, or philosophy however enlightened, should ever make him renounce his divine Marionetta.

"Competition!" thought Marionetta, and suddenly, with an air of the most freezing indifference, she said, "You are perfectly at liberty, sir, to do as you please: I beg you will follow your own plans, without any reference to me."

---

1   Strephon and Chloe: archetypal names for lovers; used satirically by Jonathan Swift.
2   "Genius of the place"; *tutela* means the presiding deity or spirit.

Scythrop was confounded. What was become of all her passion and her tears? Still kneeling, he kissed her hand with rueful timidity, and said, in most pathetic accents, "Do you not love me, Marionetta?"

"No," said Marionetta, with a look of cold composure: "No." Scythrop still looked up incredulously. "No, I tell you."

"Oh! very well, madam," said Scythrop, rising, "if that is the case, there are those in the world—"

"To be sure there are, sir;—and do you suppose I do not see through your designs, you ungenerous monster?"

"My designs? Marionetta!"

"Yes, your designs, Scythrop. You have come here to cast me off, and artfully contrive that it should appear to be my doing, and not yours, thinking to quiet your tender conscience with this pitiful stratagem. But do not suppose that you are of so much consequence to me. Do not suppose it. You are of no consequence to me at all. None at all. Therefore, leave me. I renounce you. Leave me. Why do you not leave me?"

Scythrop endeavoured to remonstrate, but without success. She reiterated her injunctions to him to leave her, till, in the simplicity of his spirit, he was preparing to comply. When he had nearly reached the door, Marionetta said, "Farewell." Scythrop looked back. "Farewell, Scythrop," she repeated, "you will never see me again."

"Never see you again, Marionetta?"

"I shall go from hence to-morrow, perhaps to-day; and, before we meet again, one of us will be married, and we might as well be dead, you know, Scythrop."

The sudden change of her voice in the last few words, and the burst of tears that accompanied them, acted like electricity[1] on the tender-hearted youth, and in another instant a complete reconciliation was accomplished without the intervention of words.

There are, indeed, some learned casuists,[2] who maintain that love has no language, and that all the misunderstandings and dissensions

---

1   In early use, the distinctive property of "electric bodies," like amber and glass and their power when excited by friction to attract light bodies placed near them; also, the state of excitation produced in such bodies by friction. Subsequently the name was given to the cause of this phenomenon and of many others which were discovered to be of common origin with it, e.g. the electric spark, lightning, the galvanic current, etc. (*OED*).

2   A theologian (or other person) who studies and resolves cases of conscience or doubtful questions regarding duty and conduct. Often with a sinister connotation (*OED*).

of lovers arise from the fatal habit of employing words on a subject to which words are inapplicable; that love, beginning with looks, that is to say, with the physiognomical expression[1] of congenial mental dispositions, tends, through a regular gradation of signs and symbols of affection, to that consummation which is most devoutly to be wished; and that it neither is necessary that there should be, nor probable that there would be, a single word spoken from first to last between two sympathetic spirits, were it not that the arbitrary institutions of society have raised, at every step of this very simple process, so many complicated impediments and barriers in the shape of settlements and ceremonies, parents and guardians, lawyers, jew-brokers, and parsons; whence many an adventurous knight (who, in order to obtain the conquest of the Hesperian fruit,[2] is obliged to fight his way through all these monsters,) is either repulsed at the onset or vanquished before the achievement of his enterprise: and such a quantity of unnatural talking is rendered inevitably necessary through all the stages of the progression, that the tender and volatile spirit of love often takes flight on the pinions of some of the επεα πτεροεντα, or *winged words*,[3] which are pressed into his service in despite of himself.

At this conjuncture Mr. Glowry entered, and, sitting down near them, said, "I see how it is; and, as we are all sure to be miserable, do what we may, there is no need of taking pains to make one another more so; therefore, with God's blessing and mine, there"—joining their hands as he spoke.

Scythrop was not exactly prepared for this decisive step: but he could only stammer out, "Really, sir, you are too good;" and Mr. Glowry departed to bring Mr. Hilary to ratify the act.

Now, whatever truth there may be in the theory of love and language, of which we have so recently spoken, certain it is, that during Mr. Glowry's absence, which lasted half an hour, not a single word was said by either Scythrop or Marionetta.

---

1 Of or pertaining to the face or form (properly) as an index of character, but often used simply in reference to personal appearance (*OED*).

2 In Greek myth, the Hesperides are the daughters of Night and Darkness who live at the extreme West at the edge of the Ocean and guard a tree that produced golden apples. See note to Burke in Chapter 10 (101, note ★).

3 Attributed to Sappho and to Homer, used in *The Iliad* and *The Odyssey*.

Mr. Glowry returned with Mr. Hilary, who was delighted at the prospect of so advantageous an establishment for his orphan niece, of whom he considered himself in some manner the guardian, and nothing remained, as Mr. Glowry observed, but to fix the day.

Marionetta blushed, and was silent. Scythrop was also silent for a time, and at length hesitatingly said, "My dear sir, your goodness overpowers me; but really you are so precipitate."

Now, this remark, if the young lady had made it, would, whether she thought it or not—for sincerity is a thing of no account on these occasions, nor indeed on any other, according to Mr. Flosky—this remark, if the young lady had made it, would have been perfectly *comme il faut*: but, being made by the young gentleman, it was *toute autre chose*,[1] and was, indeed, in the eyes of his mistress, a most heinous and irremissible offence. Marionetta was angry, very angry, but she concealed her anger, and said, calmly and coldly, "Certainly, you are much too precipitate, Mr. Glowry. I assure you, sir, I have by no means made up my mind; and, indeed, as far as I know it, it inclines the other way: but it will be quite time enough to think of these matter seven years hence." Before surprise permitted reply, the young lady had locked herself up in her own apartment.

"Why, Scythrop," said Mr. Glowry, elongating his face exceedingly, "the devil is come among us, sure enough, as Mr. Toobad observes: I thought you and Marionetta were both of a mind."

"So we are, I believe, sir," said Scythrop, gloomily, and stalked away to his tower.

"Mr. Glowry," said Mr. Hilary, "I do not very well understand all this."

"Whims," brother Hilary, said Mr. Glowry; "some little foolish love quarrel, nothing more. Whims, freaks, April showers. They will be blown over by tomorrow."

"If not," said Mr. Hilary, "these April showers have made us April fools."

"Ah!" said Mr. Glowry, "you are a happy man, and in all your afflictions you can console yourself with a joke, let it be ever so bad, provided you crack it yourself. I should be very happy to laugh with you, if it would give you any satisfaction; but, really, at present, my heart is so sad, that I find it impossible to levy a contribution on my muscles."

---

1 "Comme il faut": as it is necessary; "toute autre chose": quite another thing (French).

CHAPTER X

ON the evening on which Mr. Asterias had caught a glimpse of a female figure on the sea-shore, which he had translated into the visual sign of his interior cognition[1] of a mermaid, Scythrop, retiring to his tower, found his study pre-occupied. A stranger, muffled in a cloak, was sitting at his table. Scythrop paused in surprise. The stranger rose at his entrance, and looked at him intently a few minutes, in silence. The eyes of the stranger alone were visible. All the rest of the figure was muffled and mantled in the folds of a black cloak, which was raised, by the right hand, to the level of the eyes. This scrutiny being completed, the stranger, dropping the cloak, said, "I see, by your physiognomy, that you may be trusted;" and revealed to the astonished Scythrop a female form and countenance of dazzling grace and beauty, with long flowing hair of raven blackness, and large black eyes of almost oppressive brilliancy: which strikingly contrasted with a complexion of snowy whiteness.[2] Her dress was extremely elegant, but had an appearance of foreign fashion, as if both the lady and her mantua-maker were of "a far countree."

> "I guess 'twas frightful there to see
> A lady so richly clad as she,
> Beautiful exceedingly."[3]

For, if it be terrible to one young lady to find another under a tree at midnight, it must, *a fortiori*,[4] be much more terrible to a young gentleman to find a young lady in his study at that hour. If the logical consecutiveness of this conclusion be not manifest to my readers, I am sorry for their dulness, and must refer them, for more ample elucidation, to a treatise which Mr. Flosky intends to write, on the Categories of Relation,[5] which comprehend Substance and Accident, Cause and Effect, Action and Re-action.

---

1 See Chapter 3 (61, note 2).
2 Celinda is often assumed to be based on Mary Shelley (although she was fair and blue eyed).
3 Coleridge, "Christabel" (1818), Part I, lines 66–68.
4 Even more so (Latin).
5 Peacock is using terminology from Kant here.

Scythrop, therefore, either was or ought to have been frightened: at all events, he was astonished; and astonishment, though not in itself fear, is nevertheless a good stage towards it, and is, indeed, as it were, the half-way house between respect and terror, according to Mr. Burke's graduated scale of the sublime.*

"You are surprised," said the lady; "yet why should you be surprised? If you had met me in a drawing-room, and I had been introduced to you by an old woman, it would have been a matter of course: can the division of two or three walls, and the absence of an unimportant personage, make the same object essentially different in the perception of a philosopher?"

"Certainly not," said Scythrop; "but when any class of objects has habitually presented itself to our perceptions, in invariable conjunction with particular relations, then, on the sudden appearance of one object of the class, divested of those accompaniments, the essential difference of the relation is, by an involuntary process, transferred to

---

* There must be some mistake in this, for the whole honorable band of gentlemen-pensioners has resolved unanimously, that Mr. Burke was a very sublime person, particularly after he had prostituted his own soul, and betrayed his country and mankind, for *1200l.* a year: yet he does not appear to have been a very terrible personage, and certainly possessed no portion of human respect, ["… possessed no portion of human respect": altered to "went off with a very small" in 1837] though he contrived to excite, in a great degree, the astonishment of all honest men. Our immaculate laureate (who gives us to understand that, if he had not been purified by holy matrimony into a mystical type, he would have died a virgin,) is another sublime gentleman of the same genus: he very much astonished some persons when he sold his birth-right for a pot of sack: but not even his *Sosia* has a grain of respect for him, though, doubtless, he thinks his name very terrible to the enemy, when he flourishes his criticopoeticopolitical tomahawk, and sets up his Indian yell for the blood of his old friends: but, at best, he is a mere political scarecrow, a man of straw, ridiculous to all who know of what material he is made; and to none more so, than to those who have stuffed him, and set him up, as the Priapus of the garden of the golden apples of corruption. [See Burke's *Philosophical Inquiry into the Origin of our Idea of the Sublime and Beautiful* (1757). Edmund Burke is being contrasted with Robert Southey. While Burke was criticized for receiving a pension of 1200 pounds from the Civil List for his services to the government, Southey is seen as betraying his beliefs to become poet laureate. Priapus is the son of Aphrodite and Dionysius, is the god of fertility whose symbol is the phallus. In Italy he was the god of gardens, where statues of him as a misshapen figure with a huge phallus was placed to ward off thieves and birds. The golden apples of the Hesperides grew on a tree of wisdom. Sosia is a name for a person who closely resembles another (from Plautus' *Amphitryon*). Garnett suggests Peacock means Southey's earlier self as an author of republican poems (403), while Wright suggests it is his brother-in-law Coleridge or Wordsworth, with whom he promoted the Tory interest in the Westmoreland election of 1818 (268).]

the object itself, which thus offers itself to our perceptions with all the strangeness of novelty."

"You are a philosopher," said the lady, "and a lover of liberty. You are the author of a treatise, called 'Philosophical Gas;[1] or, a Project for a General Illumination of the Human Mind.'"

·"I am," said Scythrop, delighted at this first blossom of his renown.

"I am a stranger in this country," said the lady; "I have been but a few days in it, yet I find myself immediately under the necessity of seeking refuge from an atrocious persecution. I had no friend to whom I could apply, and, in the midst of my difficulties, accident threw your pamphlet in my way. I saw that I had, at least, one kin-dred mind in this nation, and determined to apply to you."

"And what would you have me do?" said Scythrop, more and more amazed, and not a little perplexed.

"I would have you," said the young lady, "assist me in finding some place of retreat, where I can remain concealed from the in-defatigable search that is being made for me. I have been so nearly caught once or twice already, that I cannot confide any longer in my own ingenuity."

Doubtless, thought Scythrop, this is one of my golden candle-sticks.[2] "I have constructed," said he, "in this tower, an entrance to a small suite of unknown apartments in the main building, which I defy any creature living to detect. If you would like to remain there a day or two, till I can find you a more suitable concealment, you may rely on the honor of a transcendental eleutherarch."[3]

"I rely on myself," said the lady. "I act as I please, go where I please, and let the world say what it will. I am rich enough to set it at defiance. It is the tyrant of the poor and the feeble, but the slave of those who are above the reach of its injury."

---

1 Gary Dyer in "Peacock and the 'Philosophical Gas' of the Illuminati" (188–209) points out that Peacock is creating a critique of radical enthusiasm with reference to Jonathan Swift's *Tale of a Tub* (1704) and the introduction of gas lighting due to Murdoch 1792–1808 (*OED*). An occult principle supposed by Van Helmont to be contained in all bodies, and regarded by him as an ultra-rarefied condition of water (1662) The *OED* traces the modern meaning of gas dating from 1779.

2 See Chapters 2 (58) and 5 (68): the reference is to Revelations 1 and 2.

3 See Chapter 2 (57). transcendental eleutherarch: The chief of an (imaginary) secret society called "the Eleutheri" and a word associated with the Shelley Peacock circle.

Scythrop ventured to enquire the name of his fair *protégée*. "What is a name?" said the lady: "any name will serve the purpose of distinction. Call me Stella. [1]—I see, by your looks," she added, "that you think all this very strange. When you know me better, your surprise will cease. I submit not to be an accomplice in my sex's slavery. I am, like yourself, a lover of freedom, and I carry my theory into practice. *They alone are subject to blind authority who have no reliance on their own strength.*"[2]

Stella took possession of the recondite apartments. Scythrop intended to find her another asylum, but from day to day he postponed his intention, and by degrees forgot it. The young lady reminded him of it from day to day, till she also forgot it. Scythrop was anxious to learn her history; but she would add nothing to what she had already communicated, that she was shunning an atrocious persecution. Scythrop thought of Lord C. and the Alien Act, and said, "As you will not tell your name, I suppose it is in the green-bag."[3] Stella, not understanding what he meant, was silent; and Scythrop, translating silence into acquiescence, concluded that he as sheltering an *illuminée*,[4] whom Lord S. suspected of an intention to take the Tower, and set fire to the Bank: exploits, at least, as likely to be accomplished by the hands and eyes of a young beauty, as by a drunken cobbler and doctor, armed with a pamphlet and an old stocking.

Stella, in her conversations with Scythrop, displayed a highly cultivated and energetic mind, full of impassioned schemes of liberty,[5] and impatience of masculine usurpation. She had a lively sense of all the oppressions that are done under the sun;[6] and the vivid pictures which her imagination presented to her of the numberless scenes

---

1 From Goethe's *Stella*, translated in 1798 by Hookham and Carpenter. Garnett points out that the play, about a man with several lovers, resembles the situation of Percy, Harriet and Mary (406).

2 Mary Wollstonecraft, *A Vindication of the Rights of Woman* (1792), Chapter 5, Section 4.

3 Lord Castlereagh and Lord Sidmouth. The Alien Act (1816) gave the government power to deport those suspected of being aliens. The green bag (a brief case) was used by the Attorney General (see Percy Shelley's *Swellfoot the Tyrant* [1820]). The cobbler and doctor were Thomas Preston and Dr. James Watson, arrested after a riot in the City of London (December 1816). The Bank of England and the Tower of London are two symbols of government.

4 One of the Illuminati. See Chapter 2 (56).

5 Perhaps a reference to Mary Wollstonecraft's *Vindication of the Rights of Woman* (1792).

6 Ecclesiastes 4.1. In his 29 November 1818 letter to Shelley, Peacock mentions writing a comic romance (*Maid Marian*), "the vehicle of much oblique satire on all the oppressions

of injustice and misery which are being acted at every moment in every part of the inhabited world, gave an habitual seriousness to her physiognomy, that made it seem as if a smile had never once hovered on her lips. She was intimately conversant with the German language and literature; and Scythrop listened with delight to her repetitions of her favorite passages from Schiller and Göethe,[1] and to her encomiums on the sublime Spartacus Weishaupt,[2] the immortal founder of the sect of the Illuminati. Scythrop found that his soul had a greater capacity of love than the image of Marionetta had filled. The form of Stella took possession of every vacant corner of the cavity, and by degrees displaced that of Marionetta from many of the outworks of the citadel, though the latter still held possession of the *keep*. He judged, from his new friend calling herself Stella, that, if it were not her real name, she was an admirer of the principles of the German play from which she had taken it,[3] and took an opportunity of leading the conversation to that subject: but, to his great surprise, the lady spoke very ardently of the singleness and exclusiveness of love, and declared that the reign of affection was one and indivisible; that it might be transferred, but could not be participated. "If I ever love," said she, "I shall do so without limit or restriction. I shall hold all difficulties light, all sacrifices cheap, all obstacles gossamer. But, for love so total, I shall claim a return as absolute. I will have no rival: whether more or less favoured will be of little moment. I will be neither first nor second—I will be alone. The heart which I shall possess I will possess entirely, or entirely renounce."

Scythrop did not dare to mention the name of Marionetta: he trembled lest some unlucky accident should reveal it to Stella, though he scarcely knew what result to wish or anticipate, and lived in the double fever of a perpetual dilemma. He could not dissemble to himself that he was in love, at the same time, with two damsels of

---

that are done under the sun" (Joukovsky, *Letters of Thomas Love Peacock* 1.156). Joukovsky mentions that Shelley used the quotation in his preface to *Laon and Cythna* (1817) and Peacock used it again in *Gryll Grange* (1860–61) (*Letters of Thomas Love Peacock* 1.159n).

1   German dramatists favoured by Percy Shelley; Goethe's play *Stella* likely would be included in her favourite passages. See Appendix B (155–159).

2   Adam Weishaupt, who founded the secret society of Illuminati in 1176 at Ingoldstadt. See Chapter 2 (56, note 4).

3   Identified by Garnett as Goethe's *Stella*. The hero Ferdinand becomes involved with "three incomparable beings, made miserable by me—wretched without me!" (404). See Appendix B (155–59).

minds and habits as remote as the Antipodes. The scale of predilection always inclined to the fair one who happened to be present, but the absent was never effectually outweighed, though the degrees of exaltation and depression varied according to accidental variations in the outward and visible signs of the inward and spiritual graces of his respective charmers. Passing and re-passing several times a day from the company of the one to that of the other, he was like a shuttlecock between two battledores,[1] changing its direction as rapidly as the oscillations of a pendulum, receiving many a hard knock on the cork of a sensitive heart, and flying from point to point on the feathers of a super-sublimated head. This was an awful state of things. He had now as much mystery about him as any romantic transcendentalist or transcendental romancer could desire. He had his esoterical and his exoterical love.[2] He could not endure the thought of losing either of them, but he trembled when he imagined the possibility that some fatal discovery might deprive him of both. The old proverb concerning two strings to a bow gave him some gleams of comfort: but that concerning two stools occurred to him more frequently, and covered his forehead with a cold perspiration.[3] With Stella, he could indulge freely in all his romantic and philosophical visions. He could build castles in the air, and she would pile towers and turrets on the imaginary edifices. With Marionetta, it was otherwise: she knew nothing of the world and society beyond the sphere of her own experience. Her life was all music and sunshine, and she wondered what any one could see to complain of in such a pleasant state of things. She loved Scythrop, she hardly knew why: indeed, she was not always sure that she loved him at all: she felt her fondness increase or diminish in an inverse ratio to his. When she had manoeuvred him into a fever of passionate love, she often felt, and always assumed indifference: if she found that her coldness was contagious, and that Scythrop either was, or pretended to be, as indifferent as herself, she would become doubly kind, and raise him again to that elevation from which she had

---

1   An early form of badminton played with a flat wooden paddle and a shuttlecock.

2   See Chapter 2 (57). Scythrop is using his interests in philosophy to distinguish between the more cerebral Celinda and the coquettish Marionetta.

3   Two means of accomplishing his object; if one fails, he can try the other. The allusion is to the custom of the British bowmen carrying a reserve string in case of accident. It is the opposite of "Between two stools you come to the ground" (*Brewer's Dictionary of Phrase and Fable*).

previously thrown him down. Thus, when his love was flowing, hers was ebbing: when his was ebbing, hers was flowing. Now and then there were moments of level tide, when reciprocal affection seemed to promise imperturbable harmony: but Scythrop could scarcely resign his spirit to the pleasing illusion, before the pinnace[1] of the lover's affections was caught in some eddy of the lady's caprice, and he was whirled away from the shore of his hopes, without rudder or compass, into an ocean of mists and storms. It resulted, from this system of conduct, that all that passed between Scythrop and Marionetta consisted in making and unmaking love. He had no opportunity to take measure of her understanding by conversation on general subjects, and on his favorite designs; and, being left, in this respect, to the exercise of indefinite conjecture, he took it for granted, as most lovers would do in similar circumstances, that she had great natural talents, which she wasted at present on trifles: but coquetry would end with marriage, and leave room for philosophy to exert its influence on her mind. Stella had no coquetry, no disguise: she was an enthusiast in subjects of general interest; and her conduct to Scythrop was always uniform, or rather shewed a regular progression of partiality, which seemed fast ripening into love.

CHAPTER XI

SCYTHROP, attending one day the summons to dinner, found in the drawing-room his friend Mr. Cypress, the poet,[2] whom he had known at college, and who was a great favourite of Mr. Glowry. Mr. Cypress said, he was on the point of leaving England, but could not think of doing so without a farewell look at Nightmare Abbey and his respected friends, the moody Mr. Glowry and the mysterious Mr. Scythrop, the sublime Mr. Flosky and the pathetic Mr. Listless; to all of whom, and the morbid hospitality of the melancholy dwelling, in

---

1 A light boat propelled by sails or oars.
2 A figure based on Byron, who went to Cambridge. Shelley met Byron in 1816 when Byron left England following the failure of his marriage. Peacock suggested his novel was written against the histrionics of Byron's *Childe Harold*, Canto IV (published 28 April 1818 just as Peacock is writing *Nightmare Abbey*). He commented in a letter of 30 May addressed to Shelley, "I think it necessary to 'make a stand' against the 'encroachments' of black bile. The fourth canto of Childe Harold is really too bad" (Joukovsky, *Letters of Thomas Love Peacock* 1.123). See Introduction (9) and Appendix C (193–98).

which they were then assembled, he assured them he should always look back with as much affection as his lacerated spirit could feel for any thing. The sympathetic condolence of their respective replies was cut short by Raven's announcement of "dinner on table."

The conversation that took place when the wine was in circulation, and the ladies were withdrawn, we shall report with our usual scrupulous fidelity.

MR. GLOWRY.

You are leaving England, Mr. Cypress. There is a delightful melancholy in saying farewell to an old acquaintance, when the chances are twenty to one against ever meeting again. A smiling bumper to a sad parting, and let us all be unhappy together.

MR. CYPRESS (*filling a bumper*).

This is the only social habit that the disappointed spirit never unlearns.

THE REVEREND MR. LARYNX (*filling*).

It is the only piece of academical learning that the finished educatee retains.

MR. FLOSKY (*filling*).

It is the only objective fact which the sceptic can realise.

SCYTHROP (*filling*).

It is the only styptic for a bleeding heart.

THE HONORABLE MR. LISTLESS (*filling*).

It is the only trouble that is very well worth taking.

MR. ASTERIAS (*filling*).

It is the only key of conversational truth.

MR. TOOBAD (*filling*).

It is the only antidote to the great wrath of the devil.

MR. HILARY (*filling*).

It is the only symbol of perfect life. The inscription HIC NON BIBITUR will suit nothing but a tomb-stone.[1]

MR. GLOWRY.

You will see many fine old ruins, Mr. Cypress, crumbling pillars, and mossy walls—many a one-legged Venus and headless Minerva—many a Neptune buried in sand—many a Jupiter turned topsy-turvy—many a perforated Bacchus doing duty as a water-

---

1   The toasts are in character with each of the figures. "Hic non bibitur" means "here there is no drinking" (Rabelais, *Gargantua and Pantagruel*, Book 1, Chapter 1).

pipe[1]—many reminiscences of the ancient world, which I hope was better worth living in than the modern; though, for myself, I care not a straw more for one than the other, and would not go twenty miles to see any thing that either could shew.

MR. CYPRESS.

It is something to seek, Mr. Glowry. The mind is restless, and must persist in seeking, though to find is to be disappointed. Do you feel no aspirations towards the countries of Socrates and Cicero?[2] no wish to wander among the venerable remains of the greatness that has past for ever?

MR. GLOWRY.

Not a grain.

SCYTHROP.

It is, indeed, much the same as if a lover should dig up the buried form of his mistress, and gaze upon relics which are any thing but herself, to wander among a few mouldy ruins, that are only imperfect indexes to lost volumes of glory, and meet at every step the more melancholy ruins of human nature—a degenerate race of stupid and shrivelled slaves, grovelling in the lowest depths of servility and superstition.[3]

THE HONORABLE MR. LISTLESS.

It is the fashion to go abroad. I have thought of it myself, but am hardly equal to the exertion. To be sure, a little eccentricity and originality are allowable in some cases; and the most eccentric and original of characters[4] is an Englishman who stays at home.

SCYTHROP.

I should have no pleasure in visiting countries that are past all hope of regeneration. There is great hope of our own; and it seems to me that an Englishman, who, either by his station in society, or by his genius, or (as in your instance, Mr. Cypress,) by both, has the power of essentially serving his country in its arduous struggle with its domestic enemies, yet forsakes his country,[5] which is still so

---

1   A statue being used as a fountain.
2   The countries of Socrates and Cicero are Greece and Italy.
3   Garnett cites a letter Shelley wrote to Peacock from Milan on 20 April 1818 (409).
4   "… of characters": altered to "… of all characters" in 1837.
5   Wright cites the same letter cited in note 3 (268–69). Peacock might also be thinking of Byron and his travels, depicted in the four cantos of *Childe Harold's Pilgrimage*, as well at the fact that Percy and Mary Shelley had recently left England for Italy.

rich in hope, to dwell in others which are only fertile in the ruins of memory, does what none of those ancients, whose fragmentary memorials you venerate, would have done in similar circumstances.
MR. CYPRESS.

Sir, I have quarrelled with my wife; and a man who has quarrelled with his wife is absolved from all duty to his country. I have written an ode to tell the people as much, and they may take it as they list.[1]
SCYTHROP.

Do you suppose, if Brutus had quarrelled with his wife, he would have given it to Cassius as a reason[2] for having nothing to do with his enterprise?[3] Or would Cassius have been satisfied with such an excuse?
MR. FLOSKY.

Brutus was a senator; so is our dear friend: but the cases are different. Brutus had some hope of political good: Mr. Cypress has none.[4] How should he, after what we have seen in France?
SCYTHROP.

A Frenchman is a monstrous compound of monkey, spaniel, and tiger: the most parasitical, the most servile, and the most cruel, of all animals in human shape. He is born in harness, ready saddled, bitted, and bridled, for any tyrant to ride. He will fawn under his rider one moment, and throw him and kick him to death the next: but another adventurer springs on his back, and by dint of whip and spur, on he goes as before, dipping his handkerchief in blood or in otto of roses with the same polite *empressement*, and cutting a throat or an orange with the same grinning *nonchalance*. France is no precedent for the hopes and prospects of enlightened, feeling, and generous nations.[5]

---

1 This is a reference to Byron's quarrel with Annabella Milbanke, which led to the break up of his marriage and Byron's exile from England in 1816. The ode may be Byron's "Fare Thee Well."

2 "… to Cassius as a reason": altered to "… as a reason to Cassius" in 1837.

3 Marcus Junius Brutus (c.85–42 BCE) was, under the influence of Cassius, the primary assassin of Julius Caesar.

4 Cassius persuaded Brutus that the murder of Caesar was in the name of patriotism and would restore the republic. Byron was a member of the House of Lords and made several speeches before he gave up his potentially promising political career.

5 A metaphorical treatment of the French Revolution. The passage was abbreviated and accordingly toned down in 1837 to meet with the tenor of the times: "A Frenchman is born in harness, ready saddled, bitted, and bridled, for any tyrant to ride. He will fawn under his rider one moment, and throw him and kick him to death the next; but another adventurer

MR. CYPRESS.

I have no hope for myself or for others. Our life is a false nature: it is not in the harmony of things: it is an all-blasting upas, whose root is earth, and whose leaves are the skies which rain their poison-dews upon mankind. We wither from our youth: we gasp with unslaked thirst for unattainable good: lured from the first to the last by phantoms—love, fame, ambition, avarice—all idle, and all ill—one meteor of many names, that vanishes in the smoke of death.*

MR. FLOSKY.

A most delightful speech, Mr. Cypress. A most amiable and instructive philosophy. You have only to impress its truth on the minds of all living men, and life will then, indeed, be the desert and the solitude; and I must do you, myself, and our mutual friends, the justice to observe, that, let society only give fair play at one and the same time, as I flatter myself it is inclined to do, to your system of morals, and my system of metaphysics, and Scythrop's system of politics, and Mr. Listless's system of manners, and Mr. Toobad's system of religion; and the result will be as fine a mental chaos as even the immortal Kant himself could ever have hoped to see; in the prospect of which I rejoice.

MR. HILARY.

"Certainly, ancient, it is not a thing to rejoice at:"[1] I am one of those who cannot see the good that is to result from all this mystifying and blue-devilling of society. The contrast it presents to the cheerful and solid wisdom of antiquity, is too forcible not to strike any one who has the least knowledge of classical literature. To represent vice and misery as the necessary accompaniments of genius, is as mischievous as it is false, and the feeling is as unclassical as the language in which it is usually expressed.

MR. TOOBAD.

It is our calamity. The devil has come among us, and has begun by taking possession of all the cleverest fellows. Yet, forsooth, this is the enlightened age. Marry, how? Did our ancestors go peeping about with dark lanterns; and do we walk at our ease in broad sun-

---

* Childe Harold: Canto 4. cxxiv. cxxvi.

---

springs on his back, and by dint of whip and spur on he goes as before. We may, without much vanity, hope better of ourselves."

1 Shakespeare's *Henry V*, 3.6.

shine? Where is the manifestation of our light? By what symptoms do you recognise it? What are its signs, its tokens, its symptoms, its symbols, its categories, its conditions? What is it, and why? How, where, when, is it to be seen, felt, and understood? What do we see by it which our ancestors saw not, and which at the same time is worth seeing? We see a hundred men hanged, where they saw one. We see five hundred transported, where they saw one. We see five thousand in the workhouse, when they saw one. We see scores of Bible Societies, where they saw none. We see paper, where they saw gold. We see men in stays, where they saw men in armour. We see painted faces, where they saw healthy ones. We see children perishing in manufactories, where they saw them flourishing in the fields. We see prisons, where they saw castles. We see masters, where they saw representatives.[1] In short, they saw true men, where we see false knaves. They saw Milton, and we see Mr. Sackbut.[2]

MR. FLOSKY.

"The false knave, sir, is my honest friend:[3] therefore, I beseech you, let him be countenanced. God forbid but a knave should have some countenance at his friend's request."

MR. TOOBAD.

"Good men and true" was their common term, like the καλος κάγαθος[4] of the Athenians. It is so long since men have been either good or true, that it is to be questioned which is most obsolete, the fact or the phraseology.

MR. CYPRESS.

There is no worth nor beauty but in the mind's idea. Love sows the wind and reaps the whirlwind.* Confusion, thrice confounded, is the portion of him, who rests, even for an instant, on that most brittle of reeds—the affection of a human being. The sum of our social destiny is to inflict or to endure.†

---

*   Childe Harold: Canto 4, cxxiii.
†   Ib. Canto 3. lxxi.

---

1   Heirs of great families, considered the leaders of the nobility (Garnett 412).
2   Signs of things getting worse. See Wordsworth's sonnet "England in 1802": "Milton thou shouldst be living at this hour." Peacock includes a similar passage in his essay "The Épicier" (1836).
3   Shakespeare's 2 Henry IV, 5.1.
4   Greek phrase: "beautiful and good" fair and good (Garnett 412).

MR. HILARY.

Rather to bear and forbear, Mr. Cypress,—a maxim which you perhaps despise. Ideal beauty is not the mind's creation: it is real beauty, refined and purified in the mind's alembic, from the alloy which always more or less accompanies it in our mixed and imperfect nature. But still the gold exists in a very ample degree. To expect too much, is a disease in the expectant, for which human nature is not responsible; and, in the common name of humanity, I protest against these false and mischievous ravings. To rail against humanity for not being abstract perfection, and against human love for not realising all the splendid visions of the poets of chivalry, is to rail at the summer for not being all sunshine, and at the rose for not being always in bloom.

MR. CYPRESS.

Human love! Love is not an inhabitant of the earth. We worship him as the Athenians did their Unknown God: but broken hearts are the martyrs of his faith, and the eye shall never see the form which Phantasy paints, and which Passion pursues through paths of delusive beauty; among flowers, whose odours are agonies; and trees, whose gums are poison.*

MR. HILARY.

You talk like a Rosicrucian,[1] who will love nothing but a sylph, who does not believe in the existence of a sylph, and who yet quarrels with the whole universe for not containing a sylph.

MR. CYPRESS.

The mind is diseased of its own beauty, and fevers into false creation. The forms which the sculptor's soul has seized, exist only in himself.†

MR. FLOSKY.

Permit me to discept. They are the mediums of common forms combined and arranged into a common standard. The ideal beauty of the Helen of Zeuxis was the combined medium of the real beauty of the virgins of Crotona.[2]

---

* Childe Harold: Canto 4, cxxi, cxxxvi.
† Childe Harold: Canto 4, cxxii.

---

1 Someone who has secret and magical knowledge, a member of the society founded by Christian Rosenkreuz in 1484. Also mentioned by Pope in *The Rape of the Lock* (1712, 1714).
2 From Cicero's *De Inventione*, Book 2: When Zeuxis painted a portrait of Helen he chose five women from Crotona because he did not think that he could find all the component parts of perfect beauty in a single person.

MR. HILARY.

But to make ideal beauty the shadow in the water, and, like the dog in the fable, to throw away the substance in catching at the shadow, is scarcely the characteristic of wisdom, whatever it may be of genius. To reconcile man, as he is, to the world as it is, to preserve and improve all that is good, and destroy or alleviate all that is evil, in physical and moral nature,—have been the hope and aim of the greatest teachers and ornaments of our species. I will say, too, that the highest wisdom and the highest genius have been invariably accompanied with cheerfulness. We have sufficient proofs on record, that Shakespeare and Socrates were the most festive of companions. But now the little wisdom and genius we have, seem to be entering into a conspiracy against cheerfulness.

MR. TOOBAD.

How can we be cheerful with the devil among us?

THE HONORABLE MR. LISTLESS:

How can we be cheerful when our nerves are shattered?

MR. FLOSKY.

How can we be cheerful, when we are surrounded by a *reading public*,[1] that is growing too wise for its betters?

SCYTHROP.

How can we be cheerful when our great general designs are crossed every moment by our little particular passions?

MR. CYPRESS.

How can we be cheerful in the midst of disappointment and despair?

MR. GLOWRY.

Let us all be unhappy together.

MR. HILARY.

Let us sing a catch.

MR. GLOWRY.

No: a nice tragical ballad. The Norfolk Tragedy to the tune of the hundredth Psalm.[2]

MR. HILARY.

I say a catch.

---

1 See Chapter 4 (64–67) above.

2 Or "The Babes in the Wood," a ballad about two children who get lost and die; Old Hundredth: "Praise God from whom all blessings flow," sung to the tune *Old Hundredth* from the Genevan Psalter.

MR. GLOWRY.

I say no. A song from Mr. Cypress.

ALL.

A song from Mr. Cypress.

MR. CYPRESS *sung:*[1]

There is a fever of the spirit,
The brand of Cain's unresting doom,
Which in the lone dark souls that bear it
Glows like the lamp in Tullia's tomb:[2]
Unlike that lamp, its subtle fire
Burns, blasts, consumes its cell, the heart,
Till, one by one, hope, joy, desire,
Like dreams of shadowy smoke depart.

When hope, love, life itself, are only
Dust—spectral memories—dead and cold—
The unfed fire burns bright and lonely,
Like that undying lamp of old:
And by that drear illumination,
Till time its clay-built home has rent,
Thought broods on feeling's desolation—
The soul is its own monument.

MR. GLOWRY.

Admirable. Let us all be unhappy together.[3]

MR. HILARY.

Now, I say again, a catch.

THE REVEREND MR. LARYNX.

I am for you.

MR. HILARY.

"Seamen three."

---

1   A parody of Byron's poetry, composed by Peacock. See Harold Brooks, "A Song from Mr. Cypress." *Review of English Studies* 38 (1987): 368–74.

2   A lamp said to have been burning when the tomb of Cicero's daughter was opened in the sixteenth century.

3   An echo perhaps of a 25 December 1801 verse letter "To 'a friend'" that presents a satire of a political debate which ends with the line, "'So let's all, my good friends, be unhappy together!'" noted by Joukovsky, *Letters of Thomas Love Peacock* 1.18–19.

THE REVEREND MR. LARYNX.
Agreed. I'll be Harry Gill, with the voice of three.[1] Begin.
MR. HILARY AND THE REVEREND MR. LARYNX.

> Seamen three! What men be ye?
> Gotham's three wise men we be.
> Whither in your bowl so free?
> To rake the moon from out the sea.
> The bowl goes trim. The moon doth shine.
> And our ballast is old wine.
> And your ballast is old wine.

> Who art thou, so fast adrift?
> I am he they call Old Care.
> Here on-board we will thee lift.
> No: I may not enter there.
> Wherefore so? 'Tis Jove's decree,
> In a bowl Care may not be.
> In a bowl Care may not be.

> Fear ye not the waves that roll?
> No: in charmed bowl we swim.
> What the charm that floats the bowl?
> Water may not pass the brim.
> The bowl goes trim. The moon doth shine.
> And our ballast is old wine;
> And your ballast is old wine.

This catch was so well executed by the spirit and science of Mr. Hilary, and the deep tri-une voice of the reverend gentleman, that the whole party, in spite of themselves, caught the contagion, and joined in chorus at the conclusion, each raising a bumper to his lips:

> The bowl goes trim: the moon doth shine:
> And our ballast is old wine.

---

1   Wordsworth's lyrical ballad "Goody Blake and Harry Gill," line 20 (1798). Seaman Three: Julia Wright suggests that the poem alludes to Thomas Moore's translation of the Odes of Anacreon and his own celebrations of wine ("Peacock's Early Parody of Thomas Moore in *Nightmare Abbey*," 31–38).

Mr. Cypress, having his ballast on board, stepped, the same evening, into his bowl, or travelling chariot; and departed to rake seas and rivers, lakes and canals,[1] for the moon of ideal beauty.

CHAPTER XII

IT was the custom of the Honorable Mr. Listless, on adjourning from the bottle to the ladies, to retire for a few moments to make a second toilette, that he might present himself in becoming taste. Fatout, attending as usual, appeared with a countenance of great dismay, and informed his master that he had just ascertained that the Abbey was haunted.[2] Mr. Hilary's *gentlewoman*, for whom Fatout had lately conceived a *tendresse*, had been, as she expressed it, "fritted out of her seventeen senses" the preceding night, as she was retiring to her bed-chamber, by a ghastly figure, which she had met stalking along one of the galleries, wrapped in a white shroud, with a bloody turban on its head. She had fainted away with fear; and, when she recovered, she found herself in the dark, and the figure was gone. "*Sacre—cochon—bleu!*"[3] exclaimed Fatout, giving very deliberate emphasis to every portion of his terrible oath,—"I vould not meet de *revenant*,[4] de ghost—*non*—not for all de *bowl-de-ponch* in de vorld."

"Fatout," said the Honorable Mr. Listless, "did I ever see a ghost?"

"*Jamais*, monsieur, never."

"Then I hope I never shall, for, in the present shattered state of my nerves, I am afraid it would be too much for me. There—loosen the lace of my stays a little, for really this plebeian practice of eating—Not too loose—consider my shape. That will do. And I desire that you bring me no more stories of ghosts; for, though I do not believe in such things, yet, when one is awake in the night, one is apt, if one thinks of them, to have fancies that give one a kind of a chill, particularly if one opens one's eyes suddenly on one's

---

1 Byron was living in Venice in 1818 and had published *Childe Harold*, Canto 4, which has a famous passage about Venice. See Appendix C (193–98).
2 Byron's home Newstead Abbey was said to have several ghosts.
3 Holy swinish god (French).
4 Ghost (French).

dressing-gown, hanging in the moonlight, between the bed and the window."

The Honorable Mr. Listless, though he had prohibited Fatout from bringing him any more stories of ghosts, could not help thinking of that which Fatout had already brought; and, as it was uppermost in his mind, when he descended to the tea and coffee cups, and the rest of the company in the library, he almost involuntarily asked Mr. Flosky, whom he looked up to as a most oraculous personage, whether any story of any ghost that had ever appeared to any one, was entitled to any degree of belief?

MR. FLOSKY.

By far the greater number, to a very great degree.[1]

THE HONORABLE MR. LISTLESS.

Really, that is very alarming.

MR. FLOSKY.

Sunt geminæ somni portæ.[2] There are two gates through which ghosts find their way to the upper air: fraud and self-delusion. In the latter case, a ghost is a *deceptio visûs*, an ocular spectrum, an idea with the force of a sensation. I have seen many ghosts myself. I dare say there are few in this company who have not seen a ghost.

THE HONORABLE MR. LISTLESS.

I am happy to say, I never have, for one.

THE REVEREND MR. LARYNX.

We have such high authority for ghosts, that it is rank scepticism to disbelieve them. Job saw a ghost,[3] which came for the express purpose of asking a question, and did not wait for an answer.

THE HONORABLE MR. LISTLESS.

Because Job was too frightened to give one.

THE REVEREND MR. LARYNX.

Spectres appeared to the Egyptians during the darkness with which Moses covered Egypt. The witch of Endor raised the ghost of Samuel. Moses and Elias appeared on Mount Tabor.[4] An evil spirit

---

1   Garnett mentions Coleridge's proposed course of lectures for 1818 in which Lecture 12 was to have Dreams and Apparitions as its subject (416).
2   "These are the twin gates of sleep" (Virgil, *Aeneid*, 6.893).
3   "Then a spirit passed before my face; the hair of my flesh stood up" (Job 4.15).
4   For Moses and the Egyptians see Exodus 10. In the Bible, I Samuel 28, the witch of Endor was said to have called up the ghost of the prophet Samuel at the command of King Saul.

was sent into the army of Sennacherib,[1] and exterminated it in a single night.

MR. TOOBAD.

Saying, The devil is come among you, having great wrath.

MR. FLOSKY.

Saint Macarius[2] interrogated a skull, which was found in the desert, and made it relate, in presence of several witnesses, what was going forward in hell. Saint Martin, of Tours,[3] being jealous of a pretended martyr, who was the rival saint of his neighbourhood, called up his ghost, and made him confess that he was damned. Saint Germain,[4] being on his travels, turned out of an inn a large party of ghosts, who had every night taken possession of the *table d'hôte*, and consumed a copious supper.

MR. HILARY.

Jolly ghosts, and no doubt all friars. A similar party took possession of the cellar of M. Swebach, the painter,[5] in Paris, drank his wine, and threw the empty bottles at his head.

THE REVEREND MR. LARYNX.

An atrocious act.

The ghost angrily predicted Saul's downfall. The reference to Moses and Elias is to Matthew 17.1–13 and Mark 9.2–13.

1 "The Destruction of Sennacherib," poem by Byron published in 1815. See 2 Kings 19:20–34.

2 Macarius the Great (Macarius of Egypt), monk (c.300–90). A native of Upper Egypt, he founded a monastery in the desert of Scetis c.330.

3 Saint Martin of Tours (c.316–397), monk bishop. One of the most popular saints of the Middle Ages.

4 Saint Germain of Paris (c.500–76): "On a time he was harboured in a place where every night the table was made ready for to eat after supper, when men had supped, and he was much amarvelled thereof, and demanded of the host of the house wherefore they made ready for to eat after supper. And the host said to him, that it was for his neighbours, which would come and drink one after the other. And that night Saint Germain established him to wake for to see what it was. It was not long after that there came thither a great multitude of devils, and came to the table in guise of men and women. And when the holy man saw them, he commanded them that they should not go away, and after he sent for to wake the neighbours on all sides, in such wise that every body was found in his bed, and in their houses, and made the people to come and see if they knew any of them, but they said nay. And then he showed them that they were devils, whereof the people were much abashed because the devils had mocked them so. And then Saint Germain conjured that they never after returned thither no came more there" (Jacobus de Voragine, *The Golden Legend or Lives of the Saints*, trans. William Caxton [1483]).

5 M. Swebach: James Swebach, a Flemish painter (1768–1824) also known as Desfontaines (Garnett 417). He was known for his military scenes.

MR. FLOSKY.

Pausanias[1] relates, that the neighing of horses and the tumult of combatants were heard every night on the field of Marathon: that those who went purposely to hear these sounds suffered severely for their curiosity: but those who heard them by accident passed with impunity.

THE REVEREND MR. LARYNX.

I once saw a ghost myself, in my study: which is the last place where any one but a ghost would look for me. I had not been into it for three months, and was going to consult Tillotson,[2] when, on opening the door, I saw a venerable figure in a flannel dressing-gown, sitting in my arm-chair, and reading my Jeremy Taylor. It vanished in a moment, and so did I; and what it was or what it wanted I have never been able to ascertain.

MR. FLOSKY.

It was an idea with the force of a sensation.[3] It is seldom that ghosts appeal to two senses at once: but, when I was in Devon-shire, the following story was well attested to me. A young woman, whose lover was at sea, returning one evening over some solitary fields, saw her lover sitting on a stile over which she was to pass. Her first emotions were surprise and joy, but there was a paleness and seriousness in his face that made them give place to alarm. She advanced towards him, and he said to her, in a solemn voice, "The eye that hath seen me shall see me no more. Thine eye is upon me, but I am not."[4] And with these words he vanished; and on that very day and hour, as it afterwards appeared, he had perished by shipwreck.

The whole party now drew round in a circle, and each related some ghostly anecdote, heedless of the flight of time, till, in a pause of the conversation, they heard the hollow tongue of midnight sounding twelve.[5]

---

1 Pausanias, *Itinerary of Greece*, 1.32–4 (Garnett 418).
2 John Tillotson (1630–94), Archbishop of Canterbury, whose sermons were considered a model and often reprinted.
3 Wright cites Part 1 of Peacock's *Memoirs of Shelley* (1858): "Coleridge has written much and learnedly on the subject of ideas with the force of sensations, of which he found many examples in himself" (270).
4 See Job 7.8
5 Shakespeare's *A Midsummer Night's Dream*, 5.1: "The iron tongue of midnight hath told twelve."

MR. HILARY.

All these anecdotes admit of solution on psychological principles. It is more easy for a soldier, a philosopher, or even a saint, to be frightened at his own shadow, than for a dead man to come out of his grave. Medical writers cite a thousand singular examples of the force of imagination. Persons of feeble, nervous, melancholy, temperament, exhausted by fever, by labour, or by spare diet, will readily conjure up, in the magic ring of their own phantasy, spectres, gorgons, chimæras, and all the objects of their hatred and their love. We are most of us like Don Quixote, to whom a windmill was a giant, and Dulcinea[1] a magnificent princess: all more or less the dupes of our own imagination, though we do not all go so far as to see ghosts, or to fancy ourselves pipkins and teapots.[2]

MR. FLOSKY.

I can safely say I have seen too many ghosts myself to believe in their external existence.[3] I have seen all kinds of ghosts: black spirits and white, red spirits and grey. Some in the shapes of venerable old men, who have met me in my rambles at noon: some of beautiful young women,[4] who have peeped through my curtains at midnight.

THE HONORABLE MR. LISTLESS.

And have proved, I doubt not, "palpable to feeling as to sight."[5]

MR. FLOSKY.

By no means, sir. You reflect upon my purity. Myself and my friends, particularly my friend Mr. Sackbut, are famous for our purity.[6] No, sir, genuine untangible ghosts. I live in a world of ghosts. I see a ghost at this moment.

Mr. Flosky fixed his eyes on a door at the farther end of the library. The company looked in the same direction. The door silently

---

1 The name given by Don Quixote to his mistress in Cervantes' romance; hence, a mistress, sweetheart, lady of one's devotion. (*OED*).
2 Alexander Pope, *Rape of the Lock* (1712, 1714), Canto 4, 49–51.
3 Garnett explains that C.R. Leslie, in *Autobiographical Reflections* (Vol. 1 [1860]), says that Sir James Mackintosh quoted this as Coleridge's answer to a question in one of his Shakespeare lectures (419). See also *The Friend*, Vol. 1 (Wright 270).
4 I.e., venerable old men (Ancient Mariner) and beautiful young women (Christabel and Geraldine).
5 Shakespeare's *Macbeth*, 2.1 (misquoted).
6 Wright refers to Coleridge's *Biographia Literaria* (1817), Chapter 3 for his praise of Southey (270). See Appendix C (175–79).

opened, and a ghastly figure, shrouded in white drapery, with the semblance of a bloody turban on its head, entered, and stalked slowly up the apartment. Mr. Flosky, familiar as he was with ghosts, was not prepared for this apparition, and made the best of his way out at the opposite door. Mrs. Hilary and Marionetta followed, screaming. The Honorable Mr. Listless, by two turns of his body, rolled first off the sofa and then under it. The Reverend Mr. Larynx leaped up and fled with so much precipitation, that he overturned the table on the foot of Mr. Glowry. Mr. Glowry roared with pain in the ear of Mr. Toobad. Mr. Toobad's alarm so bewildered his senses, that, missing the door, he threw up one of the windows, jumped out in his panic, and plunged over head and ears in the moat. Mr. Asterias and his son, who were on the watch for their mermaid, were attracted by the splashing, threw a net over him, and dragged him to land.

Scythrop and Mr. Hilary meanwhile had hastened to his assistance, and, on arriving at the edge of the moat, followed by several servants with ropes and torches, found Mr. Asterias and Aquarius busy in endeavouring to extricate Mr. Toobad from the net, who was entangled in the meshes, and floundering with rage. Scythrop was lost in amazement; but Mr. Hilary saw, at one view, all the circumstances of the adventure, and burst into an immoderate fit of laughter; on recovering from which, he said to Mr. Asterias, "You have caught an odd fish, indeed." Mr. Toobad was highly exasperated at this unseasonable pleasantry; but Mr. Hilary softened his anger, by producing a knife, and cutting the Gordian knot[1] of his reticular envelopement. "You see," said Mr. Toobad, "you see, gentlemen, in my unfortunate person, proof upon proof of the present dominion of the devil in the affairs of this world; and I have no doubt but that the apparition of this night was Apollyon[2] himself in disguise, sent for the express purpose of terrifying me into this complication of misadventures. The devil is come among you, having great wrath, because he knoweth that he hath but a short time."

---

1   A drastic action taken to solve a difficulty. An intricate knot tied by Gordius, king of Gordium in Phrygia. The oracle declared that whoever should loosen it should rule Asia; Alexander the Great overcame the difficulty by cutting through the knot with his sword (*OED*).
2   Apollyon the Destroyer, a name given to the devil.

CHAPTER XIII

Mr. GLOWRY was much surprised, on occasionally visiting Scythrop's tower, to find the door always locked, and to be kept sometimes waiting many minutes for admission: during which he invariably heard a heavy rolling sound, like that of a ponderous mangle, or of a waggon, or of a weighing-bridge,[1] or of theatrical thunder.

He took little notice of this for some time: at length his curiosity was excited, and, one day, instead of knocking at the door, as usual, the instant he reached it, he applied his ear to the key-hole, and like Bottom, in the Midsummer Night's Dream, "spied a voice,"[2] which he guessed to be of the feminine gender, and knew to be not Scythrop's, whose deeper tones he distinguished at intervals. Having attempted in vain to catch a syllable of the discourse, he knocked violently at the door, and roared for immediate admission. The voices ceased, the accustomed rolling sound was heard, the door opened, and Scythrop was discovered alone. Mr. Glowry looked round to every corner of the apartment, and then said, "Where is the lady?"

"The lady, sir?" said Scythrop.

"Yes, sir, the lady."

"Sir, I do not understand you."

"You don't, sir?"

"No, indeed, sir. There is no lady here."

"But, sir, this is not the only apartment in the tower, and I make no doubt there is a lady up-stairs."

"You are welcome to search, sir."

"Yes, and, while I am searching, she will slip out from some lurking-place, and make her escape."

"You may lock this door, sir, and take the key with you."

"But there is the terrace-door: she has escaped by the terrace."

"The terrace, sir, has no other outlet, and the walls are too high for a lady to jump down."

"Well, sir, give me the key."

Mr. Glowry took the key, searched every nook of the tower, and returned.

---

1 "… or of a waggon, or of a weighing-bridge": altered to "… waggon on a weighing-bridge" in 1837.

2 Shakespeare's *A Midsummer Night's Dream*, 5.1.

"You are a fox, Scythrop, you are an exceedingly cunning fox, with that demure visage of yours. What was that lumbering sound I heard before you opened the door?"

"Sound, sir?"

"Yes, sir, sound."

"My dear sir, I am not aware of any sound, except my great table, which I moved on rising to let you in."

"The table!—let me see that. No, sir; not a tenth part heavy enough, not a tenth part."

"But, sir, you do not consider the laws of acoustics:[1] a whisper becomes a peal of thunder in the focus of reverberation. Allow me to explain this: Sounds striking on concave surfaces are reflected from them, and, and, after reflection, converge to points which are the foci of these surfaces. It follows, therefore, that the ear may be so placed in one, that it shall hear a sound better than when situated nearer to the point of the first impulse: again, in the case of two concave surfaces placed opposite to each other—"

"Nonsense, sir. Don't tell me of foci. Pray, sir, will concave surfaces produce two voices when nobody speaks? I heard two voices, and one was feminine; feminine, sir: what say you to that?"

"Oh! sir, I perceive your mistake: I am writing a tragedy, and was acting over a scene to myself. To convince you, I will give you a specimen: but you must first understand the plot. It is a tragedy on the German model.[2] The Great Mogul is in exile, and has taken lodgings at Kensington, with his only daughter, the Princess Rantrorina, who takes in needle-work, and keeps a day-school. *The Princess is discovered hemming a set of shirts for the parson of the parish: they are to be marked with a large R. Enter to her the Great Mogul. A pause, during which they look at each other expressively. The Princess changes colour several times. The Mogul takes snuff in great agitation. Several grains are heard to fall on the stage. His heart is seen to beat through his upper benjamin.*—THE MOGUL, (*with a mournful look at his left shoe,*) "My shoe-string is broken."—THE PRINCESS, (*after an interval*

---

1   Peacock is accurate that a concave surface can collect acoustic energy; but the energy collected cannot be greater than that emitted by a source. Thanks to Dr. Thomas Steele, Department of Physics, University of Saskatchewan.

2   Wordsworth, Preface to *Lyrical Ballads* (1802) and its reference to "frantic novels, sickly and stupid German tragedies, and deluges of idle and extravagant stories in verse" that have taken over the popular imagination and were favoured by the young Percy Shelley.

of melancholy reflection,) "I know it."—THE MOGUL, "My second shoe-string! The first broke when I lost my empire: the second has broken to-day. When will my poor heart break?"—THE PRINCESS, "Shoe-strings, hearts, and empires! Mysterious sympathy!"

"Nonsense, sir," interrupted Mr. Glowry. "That is not at all like the voice I heard."

"But, sir," said Scythrop, "a key-hole may be so constructed as to act like an acoustic tube, and an acoustic tube, sir, will modify sound in a very remarkable manner. Consider the construction of the ear, and the nature and causes of sound. The external part of the ear is a cartilaginous funnel."[1]

"It wo'n't do, Scythrop. There is a girl concealed in this tower, and find her I will. There are such things as sliding panels and secret closets."—He sounded round the room with his cane, but detected no hollowness.—"I have heard, sir," he continued, "that, during my absence, two years ago, you had a dumb carpenter closeted with you day after day. I did not dream that you were laying contrivances for carrying on secret intrigues. Young men will have their way: I had my way when I was a young man: but, sir, when your cousin Marionetta—"

Scythrop now saw that the affair was growing serious. To have clapped his hand upon his father's mouth, to have entreated him to be silent, would, in the first place, not have made him so; and, in the second, would have shown a dread of being overheard by somebody. His only resource, therefore, was to try to drown Mr. Glowry's voice; and, having no other subject, he continued his description of the ear, raising his voice continually as Mr. Glowry raised his.

"When your cousin Marionetta," said Mr. Glowry, "whom you profess to love—whom you profess to love, sir—"

"The internal canal of the ear," said Scythrop, "is partly bony and partly cartilaginous. This internal canal is—"[2]

"Is actually in the house, sir; and, when you are so shortly to be—as I expect—"

"Closed at the further end by the *membrana tympani*—"

"Joined together in holy matrimony—"

"Under which is carried a branch of the fifth pair of nerves—"

---

1   Identified by Wright as being from Drummond's *Academical Questions*, 112–13 (271).
2   I.e., parts of the ear.

"I say, sir, when you are so shortly to be married to your cousin Marionetta—"

"The *cavitas tympani*—"

A loud noise was heard behind the book-case, which, to the astonishment of Mr. Glowry, opened in the middle, and the massy compartments, with all their weight of books, receding from each other, in the manner of a theatrical scene, with a heavy rolling sound, (which Mr. Glowry immediately recognised to be the same which had excited his curiosity,) disclosed an interior apartment, in the entrance of which stood the beautiful Stella; who, stepping forward, exclaimed, "Married! Is he going to be married? The profligate!"

"Really, madam," said Mr. Glowry, "I do not know what he is going to do, or what I am going to do, or what any one is going to do; for all this is incomprehensible."

"I can explain it all," said Scythrop, "in a most satisfactory manner, if you will but have the goodness to leave us alone."

"Pray, sir, to which act of the tragedy of the Great Mogul does this incident belong?"

"I entreat you, my dear sir, leave us alone."

Stella threw herself into a chair, and burst into a tempest of tears. Scythrop sat down by her, and took her hand. She snatched her hand away, and turned her back upon him. He rose, sat down on the other side, and took her other hand. She snatched it away, and turned from him again. Scythrop continued entreating Mr. Glowry to leave them alone; but the old gentleman was obstinate, and would not go.

"I suppose, after all," said Mr. Glowry, maliciously, "it is only a phænomenon in acoustics, and this young lady is a reflection of sound from concave surfaces."

Some one tapped at the door: Mr. Glowry opened it, and Mr. Hilary entered. He had been seeking Mr. Glowry, and had traced him to Scythrop's tower. He stood a few moments in silent surprise, and then addressed himself to Mr. Glowry for an explanation.

"The explanation," said Mr. Glowry, "is very satisfactory. The Great Mogul has taken lodgings at Kensington, and the external part of the ear is a cartilaginous funnel."

"Mr. Glowry, that is no explanation."

"Mr. Hilary, it is all I know about the matter."

"Sir, this pleasantry is very unseasonable. I perceive that my niece is sported with in a most unjustifiable manner; and I shall see if she will be more successful in obtaining an intelligible answer." And he departed in search of Marionetta.

Scythrop was now in a hopeful predicament. Mr. Hilary made a hue and cry in the Abbey, and summoned his wife and Marionetta to Scythrop's apartment. The ladies, not knowing what was the matter, hastened in great consternation. Mr. Toobad saw them sweeping along the corridor; and, judging from their manner that the devil had manifested his wrath in some new shape, followed from pure curiosity.

Scythrop, meanwhile, vainly endeavoured to get rid of Mr. Glowry, and to pacify Stella. The latter attempted to escape from the tower, declaring she would leave the Abbey immediately, and he should never see her or hear of her more. Scythrop held her hand, and detained her by force, till Mr. Hilary re-appeared with Mrs. Hilary and Marionetta. Marionetta, seeing Scythrop grasping the hand of a strange beauty, fainted away in the arms of her aunt. Scythrop flew to her assistance; and Stella, with redoubled anger, sprang towards the door, but was intercepted in her intended flight by being caught in the arms of Mr. Toobad, who exclaimed—"Celinda!"

"Papa!" said the young lady, disconsolately.

"The devil is come among you," said Mr. Toobad: "how came my daughter here?"

"Your daughter!" exclaimed Mr. Glowry.

"Your daughter!" exclaimed Scythrop, and Mr. and Mrs. Hilary.

"Yes," said Mr. Toobad, "my daughter Celinda."

Marionetta opened her eyes, and fixed them on Celinda. Celinda, in return, fixed hers on Marionetta. They were at remote points of the apartment. Scythrop was equidistant from both of them, central and motionless, like Mahomet's coffin.[1]

"Mr. Glowry," said Mr. Toobad, "can you tell by what means my daughter came here?"

"I know no more," said Mr. Glowry, "than the Great Mogul."

---

1   It is said that Mahomet's coffin, in the Hadgira of Medina, is suspended in mid-air without any support. Many explanations have been given of this phenomenon. The one most generally received is that the coffin is of iron, placed midway between two magnets. Burckhardt visited the sacred enclosure, and found the ingenuity of science useless in this case, as the coffin is not suspended at all (*Brewer's Dictionary of Phrase and Fable*).

"Mr. Scythrop," said Mr. Toobad, "how came my daughter here?"

"I did not know, Sir, that the lady was your daughter."

"But how came she here?"

"By spontaneous locomotion," said Scythrop, sullenly.

"Celinda," said Mr. Toobad, "what does all this mean?"

"I really do not know, Sir."

"This is most unaccountable. When I told you in London that I had chosen a husband for you, you thought proper to run away from him; and now, to all appearance, you have run away to him."

"How, Sir! was that your choice?"

"Precisely; and, if he is yours too, we shall be both of a mind, for the first time in our lives."

"He is not my choice, Sir. This lady has a prior claim: I renounce him."

"And I renounce him," said Marionetta.

Scythrop knew not what to do. He could not attempt to conciliate the one without irreparably offending the other; and he was so fond of both, that the idea of depriving himself for ever of the society of either was intolerable to him: he, therefore, retreated into his strong hold, mystery; maintained an impenetrable silence; and contented himself with stealing occasionally a deprecating glance at each of the objects of his idolatry. Mr. Toobad and Mr. Hilary, in the mean time, were each insisting on an explanation from Mr. Glowry, who, they thought, had been playing a double game on this occasion. Mr. Glowry was vainly endeavouring to persuade them of his innocence in the whole transaction. Mrs. Hilary was endeavouring to mediate between her husband and brother. The Honorable Mr. Listless, the Reverend Mr. Larynx, Mr. Flosky, Mr. Asterias, and Aquarius, were attracted by the tumult to the scene of action, and were appealed to severally and conjointly by the respective disputants. Multitudinous questions and answers, *en masse*, composed a *charivari*, to which the genius of Rossini alone could have given a suitable accompaniment;[1] and which was only terminated by Mrs. Hilary and Mr. Toobad retreating with the captive damsels. The

---

1   A serenade of "rough music," with kettles, pans, tea-trays, and the like, used in France, in mockery and derision of incongruous or unpopular marriages, and of unpopular persons generally; hence a confused, discordant medley of sounds; a babel of noise (*OED*). For Rossini, see Chapter 5 (68, note 2).

whole party followed, with the exception of Scythrop, who threw himself into his arm-chair, crossed his left foot over his right knee, placed the hollow of his left hand on the interior ancle of his left leg, rested his right elbow on the elbow of the chair, placed the ball of his right thumb against his right temple, curved the forefinger along the upper part of his forehead, rested the point of the middle finger on the bridge of his nose, and the points of the two others on the lower part of the palm, fixed his eyes intently on the veins in the back of his left hand, and sat, in this position, like the immoveable Theseus,[1] who, as is well known to many who have not been at college, and to some few who have, *sedet, æternumque sedebit*.★ We hope the admirers of the *minutiæ* in poetry and romance will appreciate this accurate description of a pensive attitude.

CHAPTER XIV

SCYTHROP was still in this position, when Raven entered to announce that dinner was on table.

"I cannot come," said Scythrop.

Raven sighed. "Something is the matter," said Raven: "but man is born to trouble."[2]

"Leave me," said Scythrop: "go, and croak elsewhere."

"Thus it is," said Raven. "Five-and-twenty years have I lived in Nightmare Abbey, and now all the reward of my affection is—Go, and croak elsewhere. I have danced you on my knee, and fed you with marrow."

"Good Raven," said Scythrop, "I entreat you to leave me."

"Shall I bring your dinner here?" said Raven. "A boiled fowl and a glass of madeira are prescribed by the faculty in cases of low spirits.[3] But you had better join the party: it is very much reduced already."

"Reduced! how?"

★   Sits, and will sit for ever. [Virgil *Aeneid*, Book 6, 617.]

---

1   Said by Plutarch to be steadfast in his power

2   "For affliction does not come from the dust, nor does trouble sprout from the ground;/ But man is born to trouble as the sparks fly upward." (Job 5.6–7).

3   Madeira is a fortified wine used as a tonic to exhilarate the spirits. Faculty: of the medical profession (in popular language "The Faculty") (*OED*).

"The Honorable Mr. Listless is gone. He declared that, what with family quarrels in the morning, and ghosts at night, he could get neither sleep nor peace; and that the agitation was too much for his nerves: though Mr. Glowry assured him that the ghost was only poor Crow walking in his sleep, and that the shroud and bloody turban were a sheet and a red nightcap."

"Well, sir?"

"The Reverend Mr. Larynx has been called off on duty, to marry or bury (I don't know which) some unfortunate person or persons at Claydyke: but man is born to trouble."

"Is that all?"

"No. Mr. Toobad is gone too, and a strange lady with him."

"Gone!"

"Gone. And Mr. and Mrs. Hilary, and Miss O'Carroll: they are all gone. There is nobody left but Mr. Asterias and his son, and they are going to-night."

"Then I have lost them both."

"Wo'n't you come to dinner?"

"No."

"Shall I bring your dinner here?"

"Yes."

"What will you have?"

"A pint of port and a pistol."*

"A pistol!"

"And a pint of port. I will make my exit like Werter.[1] Go. Stay. Did Miss O'Carroll say any thing?"

"No."

"Did Miss Toobad say any thing?"

"The strange lady? No."

"Did either of them cry?"

"No."

"What did they do?"

"Nothing."

---

*. See the Sorrows of Werter: Letter 93.

---

1 Goethe's hero decides to commit suicide and sends his servant to borrow pistols, and then asks him to bring a bottle of wine. Garnett notes a similar moment in *Stella* when the hero Ferdinand who has involved himself with three women snatches a pistol and says, "Here it must end!" (428). See Appendix B (155–59).

"What did Mr. Toobad say?"

"He said, fifty times over, the devil was come among us."

"And they are gone?"

"Yes; and the dinner is getting cold. There is a time for every thing under the sun. You may as well dine first, and be miserable afterwards."

"True, Raven. There is something in that. I will take your advice: therefore, bring me—"

"The port and the pistol?"

"No; the boiled fowl and madeira."

Scythrop had dined, and was sipping his madeira alone, immersed in melancholy musing, when Mr. Glowry entered, followed by Raven, who, having placed an additional glass and set a chair for Mr. Glowry, withdrew. Mr. Glowry sat down opposite Scythrop. After a pause, during which each filled and drank in silence, Mr. Glowry said, "So, sir, you have played your cards well. I proposed Miss Toobad to you: you refused her. Mr. Toobad proposed you to her: she refused you. You fell in love with Marionetta, and were going to poison yourself, because, from pure fatherly regard to your temporal interests, I withheld my consent. When, at length, I offered you my consent, you told me I was too precipitate. And, after all, I find you and Miss Toobad living together in the same tower, and behaving in every respect like two plighted lovers. Now, sir, if there be any rational solution of all this absurdity, I shall be very much obliged to you for a small glimmering of information."

"The solution, sir, is of little moment; but I will leave it in writing for your satisfaction. The crisis of my fate is come: the world is a stage, and my direction is *exit*."[1]

"Do not talk so, sir;—do not talk so, Scythrop. What would you have?"

"I would have my love."

"And pray, sir, who is your love?"

"Celinda—Marionetta—either—both."

"Both! That may do very well in a German tragedy;[2] and the Great Mogul might have found it very feasible in his lodgings at

---

1   A variation on the melancholy Jacques' speech from Shakespeare's *As You Like It* (2.7), "All the world's a stage,/And all men and women merely players;/They have their exits and their entrances."

2   Wright suggests this might refer to *Stella* (271).

Kensington: but it will not do in Lincolnshire. Will you have Miss Toobad?"

"Yes."

"And renounce Marionetta?"

"No."

"But you must renounce one."

"I cannot."

"And you cannot have both. What is to be done?"

"I must shoot myself."

"Do'n't talk so, Scythrop. Be rational, my dear Scythrop. Consider, and make a cool calm choice, and I will exert myself in your behalf."

"Why should I choose, sir? Both have renounced *me*: I have no hope of either."

"Tell me, which you will have, and I will plead your cause irresistibly."

"Well, sir—I will have—no, sir, I cannot renounce either. I cannot choose either. I am doomed to be the victim of eternal disappointments; and I have no resource but a pistol."

"Scythrop—Scythrop;—if one of them should come to you—what then?"

"That, sir, might alter the case: but that cannot be."

"It can be, Scythrop: it will be: I promise you it will be. Have but a little patience—but a week's patience; and it shall be."

"A week, sir, is an age: but, to oblige you, as a last act of filial duty, I will live another week. It is now Thursday evening, twenty-five minutes past seven. At this hour and minute, on Thursday next, love and fate shall smile on me, or I will drink my last pint of port in this world."

Mr. Glowry ordered his travelling chariot, and departed from the Abbey.

CHAPTER XV

THE day after Mr. Glowry's departure was one of incessant rain, and Scythrop repented of the promise he had given. The next day was one of bright sunshine: he sat on the terrace, read a tragedy of

Sophocles,[1] and was not sorry, when Raven announced dinner, to find himself alive. On the third evening, the wind blew, and the rain beat, and the owl flapped against his windows; and he put a new flint in his pistol. On the fourth day, the sun shone again; and he locked the pistol up in a drawer, where he left it undisturbed, till the morning of the eventful Thursday, when he ascended the turret with a telescope, and spied anxiously along the road that crossed the fens from Claydyke: but nothing appeared on it. He watched in this manner from ten A.M. till Raven summoned him to dinner at five; when he stationed Crow at the telescope, and descended to his own funeral-feast. He left open the communications between the tower and turret, and called aloud, at intervals, to Crow—"Crow, Crow, is any thing coming?"[2] Crow answered, "The wind blows, and the windmills turn, but I see nothing coming:" and, at every answer, Scythrop found the necessity of raising his spirits with a bumper. After dinner, he gave Raven his watch to set by the Abbey-clock. Raven brought it. Scythrop placed it on the table, and Raven departed. Scythrop called again to Crow; and Crow, who had fallen asleep, answered mechanically, "I see nothing coming." Scythrop laid his pistol between his watch and his bottle. The hour-hand passed the VII.—the minute-hand moved on;—it was within three minutes of the appointed time. Scythrop called again to Crow: Crow answered as before. Scythrop rang the bell: Raven appeared.

"Raven," said Scythrop, "the clock is too fast."

"No, indeed," said Raven, who knew nothing of Scythrop's intentions; "if any thing, it is too slow."

"Villain!" said Scythrop, pointing the pistol at him, "it is too fast."

"Yes—yes—too fast, I meant," said Raven, in manifest fear.

"How much too fast?" said Scythrop.

"As much as you please," said Raven.

---

1 Sophocles (496–406 BCE), a favourite of Percy Shelley who read *Oedipus Tyrannus* in August 1817 when living at Marlow and was carrying a copy of the play when he drowned in 1822.

2 Crow, crow ...: "Anne, ma soeur Anne, ne vois-tu rien venir?" et la soeur Anne lui répondait, "Je ne vois rien que le soleil qui poudroie et l'herbe qui verdoie." From the Charles Perrault (1628-1703) tale *Barbe Bleue* or "Blue Beard." (1697). The refrain is between Bluebeard's wife to her sister as she waits for her brothers to arrive and rescue her from death: "Anne, my sister Anne, do you see anything coming?" And sister Anne answered, "I see nothing but a cloud of dust in the sun, and the green grass."

"How much, I say?" said Scythrop, pointing the pistol again.

"An hour, a full hour, sir," said the terrified butler.

"Put back my watch," said Scythrop.

Raven, with trembling hand, was putting back the watch, when the rattle of wheels was heard in the court, and Scythrop springing down the stairs by three steps together, was at the door in sufficient time to have handed either of the young ladies from the carriage, if she had happened to be in it: but Mr. Glowry was alone.

"I rejoice to see you," said Mr. Glowry; "I was fearful of being too late, for I waited to the last moment in the hope of accomplishing my promise: but all my endeavours have been vain, as these letters will shew."

Scythrop impatiently broke the seals. The contents were these:—

"Almost a stranger in England, I fled from parental tyranny, and the dread of an arbitrary marriage, to the protection of a stranger and a philosopher, whom I expected to find something better than, or at least something different from, the rest of his worthless species. Could I, after what has occurred, have expected nothing more from you than the common-place impertinence of sending your father to treat with me, and with mine, for me? I should be a little moved in your favor, if I could believe you capable of carrying into effect the resolutions which your father says you have taken, in the event of my proving inflexible: though I doubt not, you will execute them, as far as relates to the pint of wine, twice over, at least. I wish you much happiness with Miss O'Carroll. I shall always cherish a grateful recollection of Nightmare Abbey, for having been the means of introducing me to a true transcendentalist; and, though he is a little older than myself, which is all one in Germany, I shall very soon have the pleasure of subscribing myself

CELINDA FLOSKY."[1]

"I hope, my dear cousin, that you will not be angry with me, but that you will always think of me as a sincere friend, who will always

---

1   Wright (271) notes that in his edition of *Nightmare Abbey* (1891) Richard Garnett points out he hopes Celinda knows of the existence of Emanuel Kant Flosky (see Chapter 6, 77, note 1).

feel interested in your welfare; I am sure you love Miss Toobad much better than me, and I wish you much happiness with her. Mr. Listless assures me that people do not kill themselves for love now-a-days, though it is still the fashion to talk about it. I shall, in a very short time, change my name and situation, and shall always be happy to see you in Berkeley Square, when, to the unalterable designation of your affectionate cousin, I shall subjoin the signature of
MARIONETTA LISTLESS."

Scythrop tore both the letters to atoms, and railed in good set terms against the fickleness of women.

"Calm yourself, my dear Scythrop," said Mr. Glowry; "there are yet maidens in England."

"Very true, sir," said Scythrop.

"And the next time," said Mr. Glowry, "have but one string to your bow."

"Very good advice, sir," said Scythrop.

"And, besides," said Mr. Glowry, "the fatal time is past, for it is now almost eight."

"Then that villain, Raven," said Scythrop, "deceived me when he said that the clock was too fast: but, as you observe very justly, the time has gone by, and I have just reflected, that these repeated crosses in love qualify me to take a very advanced degree in misanthropy; and there is, therefore, good hope that I may make a figure in the world."[1]

THE END.

---

1   Revised ending 1837, following the last sentence:
"But I shall ring for the rascal Raven, and admonish him."
"Raven appeared. Scythrop looked at him very fiercely two or three minutes; and Raven, still remembering the pistol, stood quaking in mute apprehension, till Scythrop, pointing significantly towards the dining-room, said, 'Bring some Madeira.'"

Appendix A: The Reception of Nightmare Abbey

[*Nightmare Abbey* received little critical attention in the year of its publication (1818), or the year of its reissue (1837). Shelley's enthusiastic reception has been mentioned (see Introduction, p. 24). Certainly some of his readers appreciated the work. Writer Mary Mitford observed in a letter, "I have been laughing at *Nightmare Abbey*, the pleasantest of all Mr. Peacock's works, whether in verse or prose, *Rhododaphne* and *Melincourt* included. I have not met with a more cheerful or amiable piece of *raillerie*. The chief objects of his attack are misanthropical poetry and transcendental metaphysics (deuce take Mr. Peacock for putting me [to] such hard words) in the person of Lord Byron and my poor dear friend Mr. Coleridge—the last in particular fares most lamentably."[1] James Mulvihill notes that the novel is mentioned in a list of new publications in *Blackwood's Magazine* for November 1818, followed by a neutral review in the 12 December issue of the *Literary Gazette*, while the only sustained review appeared in the *Monthly Review*.[2] When the novel was republished in 1837 for Bentley's Standard Novel Series, three reviews appeared. Two are reprinted below; a short notice also appeared in *The Guide*, 22 April 1837, page 5.[3]]

1. The *Monthly Review* 90 (November 1819): 327–29

We cannot offer kinder advice to the reader in this dreary month of November, than by recommending him to read this very entertaining novel. The gloomy philosophy and metaphysical poetry of the present day are exposed with so humorous and masterly a hand, and the characters of those who, as Hudibras has it,

---

1   Quoted in James Mulvihill, *Thomas Love Peacock,* Boston: G.K. Hall, 1987, 58–59.
2   Mulvihill 58.
3   See *Halliford Edition* 3.183–84 and Ward, "Contemporary Reviews of Thomas Love Peacock: A Supplementary List for the Years 1805–1820." *Bulletin of Bibliography* 25 (1967): 35. Another review, not included in this selection, appeared in *The Literary Journal, and General Miscellany* 1 (5 December 1818) 573–74.

"Find racks for their own minds, and vaunt
Of their own misery and want,"[1]

are painted with so much wit and spirit, that he must be splenetic indeed whose muscles will not relax at the drollery of the exhibition. That author deserves well of his country who, in times like the present, can excite a laugh in which mankind may join without malice, and indulge without compunction. In the gradation of literary dignities which we would recommend, this writer should receive the rank that he has merited. While, therefore, we remember the pleasure which we experienced from his two former works, *Headlong Hall*, and *Melincourt*,★ let us, for the additional proof of his genius, now award to him equal honour with a Bashaw of *three* tales.[2]

We may just introduce our readers to two or three of the principal personages of the story, in order to give them a *taste* of the author's piquant mode of writing, without diminishing their interest in its progress if they afterward peruse the whole. [...]

2. *The Literary Gazette* 99 (12 December 1818), 787–88

The author of this work, and of several similar productions, is, we understand, a Mr. Peacock. It would be difficult to say what his books are, for they are neither romances, novels, tales, nor treatises, but a mixture of all these combined. They display a sort of caricature of modern characters and incidents; executed with greater license than nature, and with more humour than wit.

The contrivance is to group together a number either of persons, whose originals are easily recognized in the literary or political world, or of individuals who are made the representatives of some fashionable folly or doctrine; and from their collision to elicit a laugh at the actors or at their opinions. Thus in Nightmare Abbey, its proprietor, Christopher Glowry, Esq. is a gentleman of highly atrabilarious temperament, and a prey to gloom and blue

---

★   See vol. lxxii. p. 330, and vol. lxxxiii. p. 322.

---

1   Composite from Samuel Butler's *Hudibras* that Peacock uses as an epigraph for *Nightmare Abbey*.
2   An early variant for pasha, the Turkish word for high official (*OED*).

devils; his only son, Scythrop, is a transcendentalist, filled with a grand plan for rendering mankind perfectly happy. At the ancient mansion, which gives the name to the publication, assemble as visitors, Mr. Hilary, a gay and lively relative, with his niece Marionetta O'Carroll, a blooming coquette; Mr. Flosky, a morbid personage of some note in literature, and a disciple of Kant (we suppose aimed at Mr. Coleridge;) a Mr. Toobad, "the Manichaan Millenarian," who is constantly asserting the predominancy of the evil principle; the Rev. Mr. Larynx, an accommodating divine, "always most obligingly ready to take a dinner and a bed at the house of any country gentleman in distress for a companion." To these are afterwards added the Hon. Mr. Listless, a dandy, with a disposition suitable to his name; Mr. Asterias, (quasi that worthy baronet Sir J. Sinclair) a believer in, and hunter after Mermaids; Mr. Cypress, a Lord Byron bard; Miss Toobad, the daughter of the Manichaan, herself a philosopher of the independent school; and one or two others of less notoriety.

The principal parts of the volume are occupied with conversations, in which these parties figure, generally in a whimsical and amusing manner. Scythrop becomes attached to Marionetta and Miss Toobad, and is so enamoured of both, that he knows not to which to give the palm. After some curious adventures an eclaircissement ensues, and both ladies renounce a lover who finds it so difficult to make up his mind.

There are several pretty little poems introduced, of which we select a song by Mr. Cypress, who maintains that "having quarrelled with his wife, he is absolved from all duty to his country." [...]

Upon the whole, we think this little volume cannot fail to be read with pleasure throughout, and with the delightful adjunct of several hearty laughs in turning over its most farcical pages.

3. *The Tickler; or, Monthly Compendium of Good Things: Ancient and Modern Literature* 1.1 (1 December 1818): 8–9

The volume just published under this whimsical title, is by the author of those excellent works, Melincourt and Headlong Hall. The style is much the same; it is therefore scarcely necessary to add, that whoever takes up Nightmare Abbey, in the hope of finding a novel of *exquisite horror*, and *terrific mystery*, will be disappointed. It is, in fact, a spirited satire upon the popular follies of the age, in which leading topics and varied opinions are discussed, in the form of dialogue, by the *dramatis personæ*.

To derive entertainment from this performance, the reader should himself possess a strong turn for satire; a quick perception for the ridiculous; good sense to smile at folly, when justly, even though severely lashed; and good nature not to be offended, if by chance he should discern some features of resemblance to himself. Thus, according to the taste of the reader, may Nightmare Abbey prove either a *bonne bouche* or a bitter morsel. The dialogues are all good in their way. The turn that is sometimes given to them is irresistibly comic, particularly in the person of Mr. Toobad. The incident, or rather accident in which that personage is subsequently implicated, when Mr. Asterias and his son are watching for a *Mermaid*, is quite too much for gravity. Some neat cuts are dealt with a sharp fine-tempered blade to those who "rear their heads on high," in all "the pomp of woe;"[1] but we fear they are invulnerable to shame, as a Rhinoceros to a bullet, or as Achilles was to an arrow, without even excepting the heel. [...]

4. *The European Magazine, and London Review* 75 (March 1819): 254–55

In the modern day, when satire so readily assumes the garb of truth, and truth that of satire, it becomes a matter of much nice difficulty to determine between the rival claims. The author of "Nightmare Abbey," however, has kindly spared our falling into any error as to his intention. He has relieved us from all the trouble of deciphering his meaning, or discovering the object he has in view. He is intelligible at first sight; and though this may possess charms for the more common observer, with us it is his greatest failing. We confess we like the misty haze of obscurity; and feel no inconsiderable gratification when smoking our piece of glass to assist our visual organs. The professed object of this volume is, to satirize the philosophy, as it is termed, of the day; or, in other words, to place in the most ridiculous light, by the association of the most opposite and outré characters, that morbidness of soul, and moody melancholy of mind, which

---

1 Mathilda Betham *Lay of Marie* (1816) and Lord Byron, "Inscription on the Monument of a Newfoundland Dog" (1808).

too much prevails in the present school both of prose and poetry. Satire has, in all ages, been found the most powerful instrument that can be laid to the root of folly or vice. The language of friendship may warn, and public censure intimidate, but satire can alone deter future aberrations. Still it is not every pen that is qualified for the task. The proverbialist well forewarned us, "*non omnia possumus omnes.*"[1] It requires, indeed, a more than common strength to wield the weapon of satire, and the most cautious discrimination where to deal the blow. We do not mean to say, that the author of "Nightmare Abbey" has wholly failed in the attempt, but we certainly do think he has fallen far short of actual success. The author who studies to please in a work of fiction, must create a probable reality. He must invest his characters in a dress which we have either seen or heard of before. Their actions and ideas must correspond, in some degree, with actual life. These requisites the author of "Nightmare Abbey" has, in a great measure, neglected. Most of his characters are absurd in the extreme; and their pursuits too monstrous to excite interest. An Ichthyologist, and a Mermaid-wooer, are surely incurable lunatics. However, to preserve consistency, they rant and rave in true Bedlamite style; and though Mr. Asterias is made in his first introduction to utter some sensible sentences, yet, of course, they are only meant to be taken as the offspring of lucid intervals. Marionetta is well cast and natural, though her subsequent coquetry ill gratifies the expectations one is led to form of her at first sight. Mr. Cypress is evidently the personifier of Lord Byron, in which character we think the author has displayed a bad and vitiated taste. We are confident that our readers will coincide in our assertion when they learn, that even the domestic misfortunes of the noble Lord are caricatured—*we loathe and detest such total want of feeling and delicacy*; and though that event may be a hydra-headed topic for a village *coterie*, it should never form an incident in the page of literature. M. D'Israeli, in his late most entertaining work, intitled "The Literary Character," most appositely remarks, "Every class of men in society have their peculiar sorrows or enjoyments, as they have their habits and their characteristics. In the history of men of genius, we may often open the secret story of their minds; they have above others, the privilege of communicating their own feelings; and it is their

---

[1] None of us is able to do all things. Virgil, *Eclogues* 8.63.

talent to interest us, whether with their pen they talk of themselves, or paint others."[1] But we add, this privilege is exclusively their own; it is their birthright, and cannot ever be deemed as a ball which may be bandied about at the discretion of others. Were it otherwise, such a licence would become a most grievous evil; for inasmuch as the literary man increased in reputation, by so much the more would public curiosity pry into his domestic life, and search out the happiness or misery inseparable from it. Should the author of "Nightmare Abbey" again indulge his vein of satire, we trust our foregoing remarks will have their due influence with him; and that he will scrupulously avoid his present error, which will prejudice him materially in the estimation of his readers, and perhaps cause no very charitable imputations to be affixed to his conduct.

5. From James Spedding,[2] *Edinburgh Review* 68 (January 1839): 439–52

There was an officer attached to one of the ancient regal establishments whose business it was to appear before the king every morning, and gravely remind him that he was mortal. How long this office was endured, and what was the fate of the person who first held it, we are not informed. It probably soon sunk into a sinecure, its active duties being discharged in deputy by a death's head, till the times of change came when, among other bulwarks of that constitution, it was swept away altogether. But though names change and salaries cease, wants remain. Courts still stood in need of some such monitor; and in the person of the king's jester the old office was revived in an improved form, and with additional duties. The jester was licensed to utter other and newer truths than that one, so long as he did not seem to be uttering them in earnest; and the king could listen patiently to speeches by which his own follies were anatomized, so long as it was understood that the speaker, not himself, was the fool. The profession of the jester was simply to make sport for the great; but his real use was to tell unwelcome

---

1   Isaac Disraeli, *The Literary Character, Illustrated by the History of Men of Genius, Drawn from Their Own Feelings and Confessions.* (London: John Murray, 1818), 11.
2   James Spedding (1808–81), literary editor and biographer who was editor of the works of Francis Bacon.

truths; his privilege to tell them without offence; and his great art and faculty (supposing him duly qualified for his office) was one in which no lover of truth should omit to exercise himself,—that of detecting secret resemblances between things most distant, and, in common estimations, most unlike; and of searching the substance of popular judgments, by turning the seamy side outward. It was a sad day for kings when that divine right passed from them of hearing reason only from the lips of fools. It came, however, at its appointed time. Truths of the most uncourtly kind found their way to court unbidden and undisguised; and the jester's office became obsolete. But though in courts it is now perhaps a little needed, there are many places in which it might, we think, be revived with great advantage. The immunity which passed from the Crown was divided among the public. Every man's house became his castle. Every man's peculiar set, creed, system, or party became a kind of court, in which he might live surrounded by the echoes of his own thoughts, and flattered by a convincing uniformity of sentiment, as secure as kings were once from the intrusion of unwelcome censures. But this is a security which a man who duly distrusts his own skill or courage in self-dissection can hardly wish to enjoy; though if he distrusts likewise his resolution to court annoyances because they are wholesome, which he might exclude because they are disagreeable, he will wish it broken as inoffensively as possible; and with as few of those shocks and mortifications from which correction, in whatever form it comes, can never wholly be free. It is for this purpose that, if it were possible to restore dead fashions to life, we would revive the office of jester. It is by the squandering glances of the fool that the wise man's folly is anatomized with least discomfort. From the professed fool he may receive the reproof without feeling the humiliation of it; and the medicine will not work the worse, but the better, for being administered under the disguise of indulgence or recreation. It would be well, indeed, if every man could keep a licensed jester, who, whether in thought or action, has too much his own way. All coteries, literary, political, or fashionable, which enjoy the dangerous privilege of leading the tastes and opinions of the little circle which is their world, ought certainly to keep one as part of their establishment. The House of Commons, being at once the most powerful body on the earth, and the most intolerant of criticism, stands especially in need of an officer who may speak out at random without fear of Newgate.[1] Every philosopher who has a system, every theologian who heads a sect, every projector who gathers a company, every interest that can command a party, would do wisely to retain a privileged jester. The difficulty is to find a becoming disguise under which the exercise of such a privilege would be pleasant or even endurable. The motley and the coxcomb are obsolete. They belonged to the "free and holiday-rejoicing" youth of England, and have no mirth in them for us. To the nineteenth century, in which every hour must have its end to attain, and its account to render, and every soul must be restlessly bent on providing wares for the market, or seeking a market for its wares (which is what we now mean by "doing well"), the foolishness of fools is only folly. A modern Jacques, desirous of a fool's license to speak his mind, and of procuring from the infected world a patient reception of his cleansing medicines, must find some other passport into its self-included and self-applauding circles,—some other stalking-horse than professional foolery under which to shoot his wit.[2] But in one form or other the heart of man will have its holiday; and whichever of the pursuits of the day has in it most of relaxation and amusement and least of conscious object, whichever is most popular yet least prized—the favourite that has no friend—will supply a suitable mask under which freedom of speech may still be carried on. This, in our day, is unquestionably the novel. It is over novels in three volumes that the mind of this generation relaxes itself from its severer pursuits, into that state of dreamy inadvertency which is the best condition for the alternative treatment which we recommend. It is a maxim that "the mind is brought to anything better, and with more sweetness and happiness, if that whereunto you pretend be not first in the intention but *tanquam aliud agendo*,"[3]—and certainly the mind of a modern novel reader, forgetting its graver purposes in a pleasurable anxiety for the marriage of the hero and heroine,—purified by terror and pity,—perpetual pity for their crosses, and occasional terror for their fate,—may be brought by the way to imbibe many strange and salutary lessons, which, if formally ad-

---

1   In the first half of the 19th century Newgate Prison was London's chief prison and was where prisoners were held before execution.

2   Jacques, the melancholy lord in Shakespeare's *As You Like It* who gives the famous speech "All the world's a stage" in 2.7.

3   From Francis Bacon, *The Advancement of Learning* (1605).

dressed to it, would have been rejected at once as tedious, mischievous, or unprofitable. The truth of this has in practice been largely
recognised. Politics, religion, criticism, metaphysics, have all used this
introduction to the heart of the public; and the disguise is at least
equally well-fitted for the purposes of that philosophy, the function
of which is to detect the sore places in favourite creeds, doctrines, or
fashions, by the test of half-earnest ridicule; to insinuate the vanity
of popular judgments which are too popular to be openly assailed
with success; to steal on men's minds some suspicion of the frauds,
and corruptions, and inanities, and absurdities, which pass current in
the world under the protection of names too sacred to be called in
question without impiety.

The author of the works which we are about to review is in
many respects eminently qualified for this office; in which he has
for some years been labouring with great skill and assiduity. His
influence, indeed, does not seem as yet to have been considerable. The popularity of his works has been just sufficient to make
them scarce; which implies that they are highly esteemed, but by
a limited circle of readers. In fact, an early popularity was not to
be expected for them; and it may be doubted whether they will
ever attain a place in our circulating literature. Their rare excellence in some qualities carries them too high above the taste of
ordinary readers; while their serious deficiency in some others will
prevent them from obtaining a permanent value in the estimation
of a better class. The refined beauty of the composition, pure as
daylight from the flaring colours by which vulgar tastes are attracted, "as wholesome as sweet, and by very much more handsome
than fine,"[1] is of itself sufficient to keep them on the upper shelves
of circulating libraries; while certain shallows and questionable regions in the author's philosophy will make them uninteresting to
many deeper judges.

For our own parts, however, we are not so easily deterred. Good
books are not so plentiful that we can afford to throw them away
because they are not better; and though fully prepared to be just
judges in public, we must take the liberty to be familiar in private,
and keep a copy of these questionable volumes within reach of our
easier chair. In truth we much doubt the wisdom of living only

---

1 Shakespeare's *Hamlet*, 2.2.

in the company of such as are perfect. It is to go out of the world before our time; to deal with the children of the world as if they were no wiser in their generation than ourselves. Doubtless, mental and moral obliquities are to be censured wherever we meet them, and if possible amended. Yet it cannot be denied that they help to perform much necessary service, which could not be done so well without them. The economy of the world requires characters and talents adapted to various offices, low as well as high; and it is vain to deny that the lower offices will be most readily undertaken and most efficiently discharged by minds which are defective in some of the higher attributes. There is work to be done in the state which a man may be too good to qualify himself for without in some degree contracting the circle of his goodness; and there is work to be done in the province of knowledge and literature to which the deepest and largest and best balanced intellects cannot address themselves with eager interest or undivided attention. We must have spies as well as soldiers, hangmen and informers as well as magistrates and lawgivers, advocates as well as judges, antiquaries as well as historians, critics as well as poets, pullers down as well as builders up, scoffers to scourge falsehood as well as philosophers to worship truth. There is a place as well as a time for all things, and a hand for every work that is done under the sun.[1]

Whether, indeed, these works are so necessary as to justify us in *educating* workmen to excel in them, we are happily not concerned to enquire. There is no danger of a scarcity. When we have done all we can to extend education and raise the tone of public feeling, and train all men to the noblest functions of which they are capable, there will still be more than enough of coarse grain and tortuous growth, who abilities will not rise higher, and who will really, in performing these necessary works, be cultivating their talents to the best advantage. Being there, the only question is how they shall be dealt with; whether they shall be acknowledged, as good after their kind, or cast out as unworthy of our better company; praised for being faithful over a few things, or condemned because so few have been entrusted to them. For ourselves we have no hesitation in preferring the humaner alternative. It is our favourite belief that there is in every man and in every thing a germ of good, which, if

---

1   An allusion to *Ecclesiastes* 3.1.

judiciously educed and fostered, may be made gradually to prevail over the surrounding bad, and convert it more and more into its own likeness. But this must be done by favour and encouragement. It is not by whipping the faults, but by expressing a just sympathy with the virtues that the final predominance of the better nature is to be brought about. And if it is for their interest that this treatment should be adopted, it will be our own fault if we do not turn it to advantage for ourselves. The labours of men who are pursuing anything with an earnest desire to find it, can never be positively worthless. They are sure to make out something which is worth knowing; the possession of which can only be injurious when improperly applied, or valued at more than its real worth; the pursuit of which can only become mischievous or unprofitable when it involves the sacrifice, or interferes with the attainment, of something better. Wealth, distinction, power, though not worth living for, are well worth having while we live. A fragment of truth is a good thing, as far as it goes. Wit does not lose its value as wit, when it mistakes itself for wisdom. The things themselves are of sterling worth; they lose the value which they have only by arrogating a value which they have not; and it is our own fault if we cannot restore them to their proper place, and make that good for us by regarding it in its true character, which is bad where we find it only because it affects a higher.

It is not to be denied that this faculty is called into unusual activity by the works before us. The reader must bring with him his own philosophy, moral, religious, and political. The feast is ample and various, but every man must help and digest for himself. Indeed the very aim and idea of them requires that it should be so. That the author should come before us, not as a teacher, but as a questioner of what others teach, is of the essence of his privilege. For this purpose something of waywardness and levity;—some apparent looseness, inconsistency, or absurd liberty; some daring claim to allowance and indulgence too extravagant to be meant or taken in earnest,—is as necessary to him as motley to the jester, or bluntness and oddity of manners to the humorist. It is the pretext and excuse for his raillery; the illusion (more or less discerned, but willingly submitted to) which disarms resentment, and makes censure and earnest opposition seem ridiculous and out of place; which enables us, in the words of Jacques,—

"To weed our better judgments
Of all opinion that grows rank in them.
That he is wise."[1]

He must not mean all he says, or he could not say all he means. It is for us to find out for ourselves how much is to be taken in earnest. He appears not as a judge, but as an advocate; licensed to espouse either side, and to defend it by bad evidence as well as good; by sophistry where sound arguments are not forthcoming; and by improvements on the truth where the simple truth will not serve his turn. It is for his opponent to argue the question on the opposite side; and for us the judges to bear a wary eye and catch the truth which is struck forth from the collision of the two. The motto which he has prefixed to his earliest work gives us the key to all—

"All philosophers who find
Some favorite system to their mind;
In every point to make it fit,
Will force all nature to submit."[2]

He is the disturber-general of favourite systems; the self-retained advocate of nature against all philosophers who affect to discern her secrets.
[...]
The impartiality with which he quits himself in this warfare is marvelous, and scarcely explicable unless on the supposition that he has within a deeper and more substantial faith to repose on than any which he allows to appear. Naked skepticism,—blank privation of faith and hope,—can never be really impartial; it is an uncertain succession of fleeting partialities; vain, querulous, discontented, full of quarrel and unquietness, full of spite and favouritism, full, above all, of itself. Not so with our author. He stands, among the disputing opinions of the time, a disengaged and disinterested looker-on; among them, but not of them; showing neither malice nor favour, but a certain sympathy, companionable rather than brotherly, with all; with natural glee cheering on the combatants to their discomfiture,

---

1   Shakespeare's *As You Like It*, 2.7.
2   Epigraph to *Headlong Hall*, Jonathan Swift, "Cadenus and Vanessa" (1713).

and as each rides his hobby boldly to the destruction prepared for him, regarding them all alike with the same smile of half compassionate amusement. Of all the philosophies which are encouraged to expose themselves in these pages, we have endeavoured in vain to conjecture which enjoys the largest, or which the smallest share of his sympathy. Could we find one constantly associated with more agreeable personal qualities, or with more brilliant conversation, or with sounder argument than any other;—were there any which he seemed to handle with peculiar tenderness, or in the showing up of which he appeared to take peculiar pleasure; we might suspect that we had discovered the secret of his preference or aversion. But no such clue is offered to us. The instances of the kind which we have been able to detect serve only, when rightly understood, to baffle us more completely. It might certainly seem that his respect for the good old time of roast-beef and quarter-staff, and his contempt for the "march of intellect," have a tough of earnestness about them;—that of all the theories of human life, that which maintains the superiority, in all that concerns man's real welfare, of the twelfth century to the nineteenth, has most of his secret sympathy; and, that that which is advocated in broken Scotch by certain imaginary members of our own fraternity, and which may be called the politico-economical theory, is most to his personal distaste;—that of all characters his favourite is the worldly man who boldly proclaims and acquiesces in his infirmity; his aversion, the worldly man whose weakness is disguised by himself under the affectation of something better, or protected from the censure of society by the sanctity of his profession or his order.[1] But, rightly considered, these apparent sympathies and antipathies are not to be taken as an index to his real feelings. It is not their greater or less conformity to his own tastes, but their greater or less acceptance in the world, by which he is repelled or attracted. We see in them only the working of a scepticism truly impartial and insatiable, which, after knocking down all the opinions which are current in the world, proceeds to set up an opinion made up of all that is *not* current in the world, that when that falls too, the desolation may be complete. Hence his tenderness to the twelfth century.[2] The

---

1   A reference to Utilitarian theory and Peacock's friendships with Jeremy Bentham and James Mill and his son John Stuart Mill. Peacock satirizes utilitarianism in his novels.
2   A reference to Peacock's comic romance of the twelfth century, *Maid Marian* (1822).

worshippers of the twelfth century are a race extinct. It is a fallen image, to insult which would be to flatter not to oppose the dogmatists of the time. That which has no friends he can treat with tenderness; that which others have thrown aside as false, his vocation requires or his genius moves him to seek some truth in. Our own philosophy, on the contrary, is of a newer fashion. It draws the largest audience; therefore the largest variety of folly, pretension, and credulity, as well as of their opposites. It is the article which best meets the wants of the time, and is therefore most puffed, hawked, and counterfeited. It provides him, we need not care to confess, with a great deal of legitimate work; nor do we desire to exclude him from our precincts. The light shafts which he employs cannot hurt us where we are sound; and where they do touch us, we are not above profiting by the hint. We will not fall into the common error of taking, what we see to be good physic in our neighbour's case, to be poison in our own. His apparent predilections with regard to personal character are to be explained in the same way. Some predilection for something, it was necessary to feel or feign. Otherwise, his fictions would have wanted warmth and a body. They would have wanted that reference to something positive, without which his world of negations could not have been made palpable; that standard of substance, without which the emptiness of the surrounding shadows could not have been explained. Being obliged to represent some character or other as an object of sympathy, he naturally fixes on that with which no one professes to sympathize. Projects for the diffusion of knowledge, the suppression of vice, the advancement of science, the regeneration of philosophy, or the purification of politics, are entertained as amusing vanities; but a genuine devotion to good eating and drinking, neither disguised or excused, but studiously indulged, and boldly professed, as the natural occupation of a sound mind in a sound body, is a quality on which his eye pauses with an enjoyment almost akin to love. Not that he really esteems it (we know nothing of him, but imagine him a temperate man, with a thorough contempt for made dishes), but because it is his calling and his delight thus audaciously to reverse the opinion of the world; and to make all the idols for the worship of which mean quarrel, appear hollow and ridiculous in the presence of that which they agree in despising. On the same principle it may be observed that the desire of Dinner is, in these novels, the one touch of nature that makes the whole world kin; the one thing good for man all the days of this vain life which he spendeth as a shadow, on which all philosophers agree,—the one thing which abides with him of his labour. All conflicting theories shake hands at the sound of the dinner-bell. All controversies, however divergent, where the disputants are growing ever hotter and wider asunder as they proceed, strangely converge and meet in the common centre of the dinner table. [...]

Assuming the legitimacy of his general design, the praise of great skill in the execution will hardly be denied him. He shows a free delight and a prevailing thirst for excellence in his art, which places him, in our estimation, decidedly among men of *genius*, properly so called; men, that is, whose minds are moved and controlled by an inner spirit, working restlessly towards some end of its own, in the simple attainment of which, independently of any use to be made of it, and in that alone, it finds satisfaction. Hence his rare accomplishment in the use of his weapons, which he wields with a grace, a dexterity, and (excepting a few cases, in which, not content with public conduct and opinions, he undertakes, not very happily, to interpret motives and exhibit personal qualities) with a gay good-humour which takes away all offence from his raillery, and secures for him a free toleration in the exercise of his privilege. The spirit of frolic exaggeration in which the characters are conceived,—each a walking epitome of all that is absurd in himself,—the ludicrous felicity of self-exposure with which they are made to talk and act,—and the tone of decided though refined caricature which runs through the whole, unite to set grave remonstrance fairly at defiance. And while the imagination is thus forced into the current of his humour, the taste is charmed by a refinement of manners, and by a classical purity and reserved grace of style, which carries all sense of coarseness or vulgarity clean away; and the understanding is attracted and exercised by the sterling quality of the wit, the brilliancy, fullness, and solidity of the dialogue, the keenness of observation, the sharpness and intelligence, if not the delicacy or philosophical depth, of satire; and a certain roguish familiarity with the deceitfulness of human nature, from which we may derive many useful hints, to be improved at pleasure. Add to this, that although he dwells more habitually among doubts and negations than we believe to be good for any man, he is not without positive impulses,—generous and earnest, so far as they go,—which impart a uniformly healthy tone to his writings. There are many things both good and bad which he does not recognise; but the good which he does recognise is really good; the bad really bad. Explicit faith of his own he seems to have none; the creeds, systems, and theories of other men he treats alike as toys to play with; his humour, though pure, is shallow: his irony covers little or none of that latent reverence and sympathy,—rarely awakens within that "sweet recoil of love and pity,"[1]—which gives to irony its deepest meaning, and makes it in many minds the purest, if not the only natural language of tender and profound emotion; his general survey of life has something of coldness and hardness, so that much good seed falls in vain and withers on the surface. But his nature bears no weeds, and the natural products of the soil are healthy and hardy. Inhumanity, oppression, cant, and false pretensions of all kinds are hated with a just hatred; mirth, sunshine, and good fellowship are relished with a hearty relish; simplicity, unassuming goodness, and the pure face of nature never fail to touch him with natural delight. It is most pleasant and encouraging to observe these better qualities gradually prevailing and exercising in each successive production a larger influence. The humour seems to run deeper; the ridicule is informed with a juster appreciation of the meaning of the thing ridiculed; the disputants are more in earnest, and less like scoffers in disguise; there is more of natural warmth and life in the characters; and, altogether, there is a humaner spirit over his later works, and a kindlier sympathy with his subject.

[...]

Here, then, we must take our leave of this disturber of the peace of coteries, whom we do not hesitate to recommend to general acceptance as a most witty, shrewd, and entertaining companion. But we cannot thus commend him, without recording our strong protest against a blemish which, we are sorry to say, grievously taints his speculations on the personal politics of the day. We allude to the cant doctrine, that when a man, who in the glow of youth and hope has chiefly signalized himself by an impassioned proclamation of the *rights* of men, turns in his maturer ages to warn them of their *duties*,—such change can only be considered as an act of deliberate apostacy from the truth, in consideration of value received. This we call cant; and we would almost stake the justice of the entire censure upon his own answer to a plain question—Did he, when he spoke of Edmund Burke as having "prostituted his soul, and betrayed his

---

1   Coleridge, "Christabel" 2.674.

own country and mankind for L.1200 a-year,"[1] really believe that he was speaking the truth? Had it, in fact, ever occurred to him to consider whether the thing he was saying was true or false? He could surely give but one answer. That Burke was wrong—that his feelings being too much a-head of his judgment, all facts came before him through a fiery medium of pity or indignation, or religious love—and that his understanding working on data thus distorted, led him to unreasonable conclusions,—any man with a mind differently constituted from Burke's, may easily believe. But that his adoption of those conclusions can only be regarded as an act of deliberate and venal falsehood, is a monstrous proposition, which the man who can truly believe, must have a narrower understanding and a shallower heart than we can believe our author to possess. No—he has in this instance, and in some others, (which, lest our censure should preserve the allusions from becoming unintelligible, we pass by silently) allowed himself to adopt a species of cant, familiar and excusable amongst schoolboys, but as much to be hated in a grown man as any of the many cants which are so successfully held up in these volumes to the scorn they deserve.

6. *The Examiner* (28 May 1837): 341

We cannot imagine a pleasanter pocket novel than this. Mr. Peacock is one of the few writers of his class who can stand the test of republication. His stories relish with age.

One prevailing idea—and that an admirable one—is the characteristic of nearly all Mr. Peacock's novels, which form, we think, the most brilliant exception imaginable to the rule that "second parts are failures," or that a second presentation of an idea is an infelicitous one. *Headlong Hall*, *Nightmare Abbey*, and *Crotchet Castle*, are, severally, only the new setting of one idea, that

> "All philosophers who find
> Some favourite system to their mind,
> In every point to make it fit,
> Will force all nature to submit—"[2]

---

1 When Burke retired from Parliament, it was arranged that he should get £1,200 a year from the Civil List. See Peacock's note in Chapter 10 of *Nightmare Abbey* (101).
2 See note 2, 146.

Or, in plain prose, that any one opinion carried to excess, and supported after the general fashion of poor mortals, becomes ridiculous, and involves its supporters in its worst absurdities.

Precisely as the "philosophers" in the rhymes we have quoted are to their observer, so are Messrs. Escot, Forster, and the compeers of the *Hall*, to Mr. Jenkison—Messrs. Cypress and Toobad of the *Abbey* to Mr. Hilary—and Messrs. Mac Quedy and Toogood of the *Castle* to the Rev. Dr. Folliott. Yet, throughout all, there is such versatility of illustration, variety of character, and brilliancy of wit, that we should desire nothing better than an eternal succession of these *positions* of the author (evidently the "sensible man" of his own book in every case), with his ever-varying confluence of grotesque and sparkling characters around him at once, like the gay arrangement of a kaleidoscope. Mr. Peacock evidently feels that in the *coup d'oeil* of each group lies the real merit of the novel, and accordingly it is very careless in the little bit of story he contributes—somewhat sarcastically as regards the reader. The tales are all remarkably short, and more like the famous little books of Ferney[1] than any thing else—but full of genuinely liberal and ameliorating spirit, which is always perceivable above the "follies shot flying."

We must quote one passage from a short by most characteristic preface attached to this edition—

[...]

We must confess a wish in conclusion that, in place of *Maid Marian*—charming things as are in it, sweet old songs, and exquisite bits of rural scenery—the author had substituted *The Misfortunes of Elphin*, that racy little book. The oration in behalf of the embankment is fresh on our minds, the war of Dinas Vohr sounds in our ears as happy and logical as ever, and the Praise of the Buffalo makes us think of "Meade and Ypocrasse."[2] But all Mr. Peacock's lyrics are clever and characteristic to the highest degree. Even the names of his personages are felicitous beyond those of any other author's we remember.

---

1   House to which Voltaire retired in old age and wrote a number of works.
2   Novel based on Welsh legend set in the time of King Arthur published in 1829. "The War-Song of Dinas Vawr" is an original poem Peacock included in the novel.

Appendix B: German Literature

[Marilyn Butler calls Scythrop a "thorough-going Germanist": the romances, horror fiction (or *Schauerroman*), and German tragedies that fill his mind with thoughts of secret tribunals and Illuminati create "an ingenious anthology of German literature" as well as a "humorous counter-proposition" of a subject Coleridge treats more seriously in the *Biographia Literaria*.[1] The Marquis Grosse's *Genius* was translated into English by Peter Will for the Minerva Press in 1796 with the title of *Horrid Mysteries*. This is the book Scythrop keeps under his pillow and emulates as he stalks about like a Gothic villain. The episode included echoes his proposal to Marionetta for pledging their troth: Celinda's pseudonym "Stella" is an allusion to Goethe's play, while Scythrop's plan to commit suicide draws upon Goethe's *Sorrows of Young Werther* (1774). The phrase "venerable eleutherarchs" derives from *Memoirs of Prince Alexy Haimatoff* (1813), written by Shelley's friend Thomas Jefferson Hogg. While Peacock is thinking of Shelley as the author of two novels, *Zastrozzi* (1810) and *St. Irvyne* (1811), he is also drawing on a more general interest in gothic writings, whose adherents include Byron and Coleridge, and which influenced the ghost-telling contest in 1816 which resulted in the writing of Mary Shelley's *Frankenstein* (1818).]

1. From Karl Grosse, "The Marquis of Grosse" (1796)[2]

[...] "Eternal powers!" she exclaimed, with the highest degree of enthusiasm, "to you I am going to devote this victim." She was no more the fond girl she had been, but quite a different person. I scarcely could think that she was the same Rosalia. She seemed to rush between the Godhead and humanity to sacrifice the latter to the former. Like an inexorable judge, she had raised the dagger to destroy the devoted victim with one blow. What a greatness of look, what a sublime majesty in every feature, did she display! "Rise,

---

1 Butler, *Peacock Displayed* 124.
2 Source: *Horrid Mysteries: A Story Translated from the German of The Marquis of Grosse by Peter Will* (London: Folio Press, 1968), 68–69.

Carlos, and kneel down before me!" I obeyed her stern command. "Hear my imprecation!" "I hear, Rosalia." "Swear as I do." "Here is my hand." "Swear that no other being shall intrude between us; that no living being, not even a thought, shall tear our bond asunder; that we will be united for ever, and keep firm to the society who gave us leave to love each other; that neither of us shall attempt to alienate the other from it." "I swear." "That each of us shall prosecute the faithless part with nameless tortures, and vent the most unrelenting revenge even on the half withered bones of the perfidious wretch; that the burning resentment of the avenger shall not be appeased till every thing that renews the memory of the traitor shall be extirpated along with every vestige of his love and his posterity." "I swear."

"And if the reprobate should escape the resentment of the avenger, may then the marrow in his bones dry up, may cankered poison corrode his heart, burning thirst parch his tongue in the midst of water, and an insatiable hunger torment him in the lap of plenty! Even in love's paradise, may infernal glory excruciate his heart and blast his hopes; may he be miserable amid the smiles of pleasure, and become a picture of woe unutterable to humankind. Swear Carlos?" "I swear."

"So do I then consecrate thee to be my faithful husband. May heaven be propitious to our union. Ye invisible powers be witness to our mutual oath!" So saying, she strained me to her heart, and imprinted the bridal kiss on my trembling lips. The voice of my desires was silent in that solemn moment; the stillness of the grave swayed all around us, and even the waving leaves of the trees ceased to rustle. I pressed my heavenly wife speechless to my bosom, and her large blue eye, animated with a soft fire, repeated the oath her lips had uttered.

Her hand was still armed with the dagger. She bared my arm, and opened a vein, sucking the blood which flowed from the orifice in large drops; and then wounded her arm in return, bidding me to imbibe the roseate stream, and exclaimed, "thus our souls shall be mixed together!" However, she dropped suddenly fainting into my arms, exhausted by the loss of blood. I started up, seized with terror, bound up her wound with my handkerchief, and with difficulty restored her to the use of her senses. But I was also seized with a sudden fainting fit, having neglected my wound; my eyes grew dim, and my senses fled. Rosalia called out for assistance. Some females appeared, and led me to the castle, where I laid down, and instantly fell asleep. [...]

2. From Johann Wolfgang von Goethe, *Stella: A Play for Lovers* (1774)[1]

ACT V

SCENE—STELLA'S *apartment by moonlight*

Stel [*alone—holds the picture of* FERDINAND, *and is preparing to take it out of the frame*]. Deep shades of night surround me! Conduct me! Lead me! I know not where I step! I must go; ah, where! where! And am I banished from this place of my own creation? Must I no longer wander where the sacred moon illumines the top of my tall trees? whose deep shade shelters the grave of my sweet child; from the place destined for my own grave, which I have so often and so devoutly washed with my tears; where my free spirit hoped again to hover after death, and recall past pleasure. From you must I be driven, banished! But I am grown callus, heaven be praised; I begin to lose all sensation! My mind is confused. Banished! I cannot comprehend the idea. I shall lose myself again. Now! my eyes are dim! Farewell! farewell! Never to see you more! Cold death is in the thought! You must be gone, Stella! [*She seizes the portrait.*] But you! should I leave you behind! [*She begins to take out the nails*]. Oh! that I could pour out my life in tears, and sleep a sleep of death! I am—I ever must be miserable! [*She turns the picture to the light of the moon.*] O Ferdinand! when you first approached me, how my heart sprang towards you. Were you not touched with my unsuspecting confidence in your faith and virtue? When I received you into my heart, did you not feel what a sanctuary what opened to you? and you did not start from me—fly me! How was it that you could in cruel sport root up my life, my innocence, my happiness, and throw them so carelessly, so thoughtlessly, away? Oh honour! generosity! My youth! my golden days! And you hid such deep deceit in your soul. Your wife! Your daughter! My heart was open and pure as the

---

1 Source: Johann Wolfgang von Goethe. *Stella: A Play for Lovers* (1774); trans. London: Printed for Hookham and Carpenter, 1798; rpt. George Canning, George Ellis, and John Hookham Frere. *Parodies and Other Burlesque Pieces With the Whole Poetry of the Anti-Jacobin*. Ed. by Henry Morley (London: G. Routledge, 1890), 441–46.

fairest morning of spring. Everything smiled around me. Where am I! [*Contemplating the picture.*] So noble! so seducing! That look it was which ruined me! I hate thee! No! no destroyer! Me! Me! You! Me! [*She makes a point at the picture with the knife as if she would cut it.*] Ferdinand! [*She turns away, lets fall the knife, and bursts into a flood of tears.*] Oh! my dear, dear, dear Ferdinand! It is in vain! in vain!

Enter SERVANT

Ser. My lady, according to your orders, the horses are brought to the back gate of the garden. Your trunks are packed up. You won't forget to take money—

Stel. Take that picture! [*The* SERVANT *takes up the knife, cuts the picture out of the frame, and rolls it up.*] Here is money.

Ser. But why?

Stel. [*after standing a few moments and looking round her*]. Come!
[*Exit.*]

Scene changes to the Hall.

Fer. [*alone*]. Peace, peace! This conflict is agony—despair and horror seize me again! Cold and deadly lies all the prospect before me, as if the world were now nothing, as if I had been guilty of nothing. And they? Oh! am I not more wretched than they are? What is to be done? Here! there! whichever way I look, the scene is more cruel! more and more horrible! [*Striking his forehead.*] To what am I reduced? No man can give me aid or counsel. The past and future equally perplex me! And these women, these three lovely and incomparable beings, made miserable by my means, wretched without me! Still more wretched with me! If I could pour out my heart in tears and lamentations, could implore forgiveness, throw myself at their feet, and by partaking of their sorrows, again feel a ray of comfort! But where are they? Stella, prostrate on the earth, turns her dying eyes to heaven, and exclaims—"Of what had I, an opening flower, been guilty, that in Thy wrath thou shouldest cut me off? unfortunate as I am, of what had I been guilty that Thou shouldest bring this monster to me?" And Cecilia! my wife! horror, endless horror! What blessings are assembled round me, only to make me wretched. Husband! father! lover! The noblest, tenderest, best of women thine! Canst thou comprehend this ineffable happiness? but 'tis this which rends thy soul, each demands an undivided heart, and I—but it is unfathomable. The will be wretched! Stella! Stella! all thy hopes are blasted. Oh! what have I robbed thee of? Thy peaceful days! the bloom of thy youth! And am I so cold, so calm! [*He snatches a pistol and instantly loads it.*] Ay! this is well! here it must end!

    CECILIA *enters*

Cec. My dear—Ha! [*starting with alarm at the sight of the pistols; then recovering herself, she says with composure*]. Are those for your journey? [*He lays down the pistols.*] My dear friend, you seem more calm; may I say one word to you?

Fer. What do you wish, Cecilia? What do you wish, my dear wife?

Cec. Call me not so till I have done speaking. We are now grievously involved. Can nothing be done by which we may be extricated? I have suffered much, and my misfortunes have taught me to take strong measures. Do you understand me, Ferdinand?

Fer. I hear.

Cec. Consider well what I say. I am but a wife, a troublesome, complaining wife; but firm resolution is in my soul, Ferdinand. It is my purpose, my determined purpose, to leave you!

Fer. [*ironically*]. You are brief, Cecilia!

Cec. Do you think it impossible to quit those we love with deliberation?

Fer. Cecilia!

Cec. I do not reproach you; and think not that I make too great a sacrifice. In your absence I was absorbed by grief. I was lost in vain lamentations. I find you again, and your presence inspires me with new strength. Ferdinand, my love for you is not selfish. 'Tis not the passion of a mistress; it is the affection of a wife who can resign her happiness for yours.

Fer. Never! never!

Cec. Are you angry?

Fer. You distress me!

Cec. I wish you to be happy. I have my daughters, and in you I have a friend. We will part without being disunited; I will live at a distance from you, but I shall know that you are happy. I will be a confidential friend; you shall impart to me your joys and sorrows. Your letters will be all my existence, and mine will be to you as friendly visitors. You need not, therefore, retire with Stella to a remote corner of the world. We shall love one another, take an interest in each other, and so, Ferdinand, give me your hand upon it.

Fer. As raillery this is too much, as serious it is inconceivable. Be it as it will, my best friend, cold reasoning will not extricate us. What you say is generous and noble, but you deceive yourself. The heart accepts not these imaginary consolations. No, Cecilia—my wife—no, no! You are mine, I am yours. Why should I say more? I am yours, or—

Cec. But Stella! [FERDINAND *starts up and walks wildly backwards and forwards.*] Which of us is deceived? Which of us, from cold reasoning, endeavours to find a momentary consolation? Yes, yes, men know themselves!

Fer. Depend not too much upon your calmness!—the unhappy Stella will weep and linger out her life far from me and you. Think not of her, think not of me!

Cec. Yes, I am convinced that in her solitude the thought of our reunion would be a solace to her angelic mind. Cruel reproaches now embitter her moments. And she would suppose me far more unhappy than I should be were I to leave you, for she would judge by herself. She would not live in peace, the angel would not live at all if she thought her happiness were a robbery. It were better for her—

Fer. Let her retire to a cloister.

Cec. By why should she be immured? Of what has she been guilty, that in her most blooming years, with all her rising hopes before her, she should be sent to waste her days in loneliness and despair? Separated from every object that is dear to her, from the man she so passionately loves, from the man who so—Is it not true, Ferdinand, you love her?

Fer. [*starts back*]. Ha! what mean you? Are you an evil spirit in the form of my wife? Why do you seek to turn me thus at pleasure? Why do you rend what is already torn? Am I not distracted enough? Leave me, consign me to my fate! And heaven have pity on you!

[*He throws himself into a chair.*]

Cec. [*goes to him and takes his hand*]. There was once a count [FERDINAND *would spring from her, she holds him*], a German count, who from a sense of religious duty, left his wife and country to go to the Holy Land. He traveled through many kingdoms, and was at length taken captive. His slavery excited the compassion of his master's daughter, she loosened his chains, they escaped together; she accompanied him through the perils of war as his page. Crowned with victory, he returned to his noble wife. But he dear girl (*for he thought humanely*) did not desert. His high-born consort hastened to meet him, and thought all her faith and love rewarded by folding him again in her arms. And when the knight proudly threw himself from his horse upon his native soil, and the spoils were laid at her feet—"My wife," said he, "the greatest prize is still behind." A gentle damsel appeared veiled ámidst the crown; he took her by the hand and presented her to his wife, saying, "Here is my deliverer, she freed me from captivity, she made the winds propitious, she attended upon me, fought by me, nursed me. What do I not owe her? Here she is, do you reward her." The generous wife embraced her, wept upon her neck, and cried, "Take all that I can give. Let him be yours; he of right belongs to you, he of right, too, belongs to me; let us not part, let us all remain together." Then falling into her husband's arms, "We are yours," she exclaimed. "We are both yours," they cried with one voice; "we are yours forever!" And heaven smiled propitious on their love, the holy vicar pronounced his benediction over them, and they had but one dwelling, one grave.

Fer. Great God! Thou who sendest angels to us in our extremities, grant us strength to support their presence! O my wife!

   [*He sinks with his face on the table*]

Cec. [*opens a door and calls*]. Stella!

   [STELLA *enters, looks wildly at the pistols, at* CECILIA *and* FER-DINAND. *Then clasping* CECILIA *in her arms*—]

Stel. Father of mercies! what is this?

   [FERDINAND *starts up, and is running distractedly from them;* CE-CILIA *holds him.*]

Cec. Divide with me that heart, Stella, the whole of which belongs to you. You have saved my husband—saved him from himself, and you restore him to me again.

Fer. [*approaches* STELLA]. My Stella!

Stel. I comprehend it not.

Cec. You will know all—even now your heart explains it!

Stel. [*falling on Ferdinand's neck*]. And may I trust that heart!

Cec. Do you thank me for arresting the fugitive?

Stel. [*taking* CECILIA *in her arms*]. O Cecilia!

Fer. [*embracing both*]. Mine! mine!

Stel. [*taking hold of his hands and hanging upon him*]. I am thine.

Cec. We are both thine!

3. From Johann Wolfgang von Goethe, *The Sorrows of Young Werther* (1774)[1]

[AFTER dinner he had his trunk packed up, destroyed a great many papers, and went out to discharge some trifling debts. He returned home; and then went out again, notwithstanding the rain, first to the Count's garden, and then farther into the country. He returned when night came on, and began to write again.]

—MY dear friend, I have for the last time seen the mountains, the forests, and the sky. Adieu!—My dearest mother, forgive me: my friend, I entreat you to comfort her. God bless you!—I have settled all my affairs; farewell! We shall see one another when we are more happy.

I have but ill requited you, Albert; and you forgive me.—I have disturbed the peace of your family; I have occasioned a want of confidence between you. Adieu! I am going to put an end to all this. May my death remove every obstacle to your happiness! Albert, Albert, make that angel happy; and may the benediction of Heaven be upon you!

[HE finished the settling of his papers; tore and burned a great many, others he sealed up and directed to his friend. They contained loose thoughts and maxims, some of which I have seen. At ten o'clock he ordered his fire to be made up, and a pint of wine to be brought to him, and then dismissed his servant; who, with the rest of the family, lay in another part of the house. The servant lay down in his cloaths, that he might be sooner ready the next morning, his master having told him that the post-horses would be at the door before six o'clock.]

Werter, in continuation, to Charlotte.

PAST eleven o'clock. All is silent round me, and my soul is calm!—I render thanks to thee, O God! that thou grantest to me in these last moments warmth and vigour.

I draw near to the window, my dear friend, and through clouds which are driven rapidly along by impetuous winds, I see some stars. Heavenly bodies! you will not fall: the Eternal supports both you and me! I have also seen the greater bear—favourite of all the

---

1   Source: Johann Wolfgang von Goethe, *The Sorrows of Werter. A German Story. A New Edition.* [trans. Daniel Malthus]. (London: J. Dodsley, Paul-Mall, 1789), 211–19.

constellations; for when I left you in the evening it used to shine opposite your door. How often have I looked at it with rapture! how often raised my hands towards it, and made it a witness of my felicity! And still—Oh! Charlotte! what is there which does not bring your image before me? Do you not surround me on all sides; and have I not, like a child, collected together all the little things which you have made sacred by your touch?

The profile, which was so dear to me, I return to you, Charlotte; and I pray you to have a regard for it. Thousands of kisses have I imprinted on it, and a thousand times have I addressed myself to it as I went out and came in.

I have wrote a note to your father, to beg he will protect my remains. At the corner of the church-yard, which looks towards the fields, there are two lime-trees; it is there I wish to rest: this is in your father's power, and he will wish to do it for his friend. Join your entreaties to mine. Perhaps pious Christians will not chuse that their bodies should be interred near the corpse of an unhappy wretch like me. Ah! let me then be hid in some remote valley; or by the side of the highway, that the Priest and the Levite,[1] when they pass my tomb, may lift their eyes to Heaven, and render thanks to the Lord, whilst the Samaritan gives a tear to my fate.

Charlotte! I do not shudder now that I hold in my hand the fatal instrument of my death. You present it to me, and I do not draw back. All, all is now finished;—this is the accomplishment of all my hopes; thus all my vows are fulfilled!

Why had I not the satisfaction to die for you, Charlotte, to sacrifice myself for you?—And could I restore peace and happiness to your bosom, with what resolution, with what pleasure should I meet my fate! But to a chosen few only it is given to shed their blood for those who are dear to them, and augment their happiness by the sacrifice.

I wish, Charlotte, to be buried in the cloaths I now wear: you have touched them, and they are sacred. I have asked this favour too of your father.—My soul hovers over my grave.—My pockets are not to be searched.—The knot of pink ribband, which you wore on your bosom the first time I saw you, surrounded by your children— (Dear children! I think I see them playing round you; give them a

---

1 Used somewhat contemptuously for a clergyman (*OED*).

thousand kisses, and tell them the fate of their unfortunate friend. Ah! at that first moment, how strongly was I attracted to you! how unable ever since to loose myself from you!)—This knot of ribband is to be buried with me; you gave it me on my birth-day.—Be at peace; let me entreat you, be at peace!—

They are loaded—the clock strikes twelve—I go—Charlotte! Charlotte! Farewell! Farewell!

[ONE of the neighbours saw the flash, and heard report of the pistol; but everything remaining quiet, he thought no more of it.]

At six in the morning, his servant went into the room with a candle. He found his master stretched on the floor, and weltering in his blood: he took him up in his arms, and spoke to him, but received no answer. Some small symptoms of life still appearing, the servant ran to fetch a surgeon, and then went to Albert's. Charlotte heard the gate-bell ring; an universal tremor seized her: she waked her husband, and both got up. The servant, all in tears, told them the dreadful event.—Charlotte fell senseless at Albert's feet.

When the surgeon came to the unfortunate Werter, he was still lying on the floor, and his pulse beat: but the ball going in above his eye, had pierced through the skull. However, a vein was opened in his arm; the blood came, and he still continued to breathe.

It was supposed, by the blood round his chair, that he committed this rash action, as he was sitting at his bureau; that he afterwards fell on the floor—He was found lying on his back, near the window. He was dressed in a blue frock and buff waistcoat, and had boots on.[1] Every body in the house and in the neighbourhood, and in short people from all parts of the town, ran to see him. Albert came in: Werter was laid on his bed, his head was bound up, and the paleness of death was on his face. There were still some signs of life; but every moment they expected him to expire. He had drank only one glass of wine. Emilia Galoti was lying open on his bureau.[2]

I will say nothing of Albert's great distress, nor of the situation of Charlotte.—

---

1   Werter's blue coat and yellow waistcoat became a fad among some fashionable men.
2   A tragedy by Gotthold Lessing (1729–81) that tells the story of a virtuous young woman from the upper middle class who because of her beauty and some entanglements with a nobleman who lacks moral scruples, falls into disgrace and has her father kill her to preserve her purity and virtue.

The old Steward, as soon as he heard of this event, hurried to the house: he embraced his dying friend, and wept bitterly. His eldest boys soon followed him on foot; they threw themselves on their knees by the side of Werter's bed, in the utmost despair, and kissed his hands and face. The eldest, who was his favourite, held him in his arms till he expired; and even then he was taken away by force. At twelve Werter breathed his last. The Steward, by his presence and his precautions, prevented any disturbance amongst the populace; and in the night the body of Werter was buried in the place he had himself chosen. The Steward and his sons followed him to the grave. Albert was not able to do it. Charlotte's life was despaired of. The body was carried by labourers, and no priest attended.][1]

4. From Thomas Jefferson Hogg, *Memoirs of Prince Alexy Haimatoff* (1813)[2]

I rose in the morning harassed and feverish; the conversation of Bruhle in some degree calmed me. After breakfast, he said, that if I would accompany him to the university, he would introduce me to the most wonderful man I had ever seen. I readily consented; it may possibly be the very stranger, whose gaze made so powerful an impression upon my mind, at least it will throw some light upon this obscure subject. I felt desirous to satisfy myself at once, by relating the whole business to Bruhle; but just as I was about to do so, I experienced a strange reluctance. I make no doubt that I should in time have conquered this unwillingness, if I had seen no other channel through which I could derive the wished-for information; but as I trusted all would now so soon be cleared up, I did not apply to Bruhle.

At the university I was shown into a small apartment; Bruhle promised to return in a few minutes: I remained alone in anxious expectation, mingled with awe, which the memory of the adventure of the preceding night inspired. In about an hour my companion returned, and told me to follow him. I obeyed, and we entered a library, where the mysterious being, who had produced so powerful an effect on my imagination, was seated at a table, strewed with

---

1   Because he was a suicide, there would not be a religious service.
2   Source: Thomas Jefferson Hogg. *Memoirs of Prince Alexy Haimatoff.* (London: Printed for T. Hookham, Jun. and E.T. Hookham, 1813. London: The Folio Society, 1952), 113–17.

books and papers. Bruhle introduced him to me as the principal of the university, and as the Eleutherach.[1] I bowed to him with the profound respect which was due to his venerable appearance. He ordered me to be seated. A boy, of about ten years of age, was construing the first Aenid of Virgil: he continued his task. The Eleutherach made several observations to me, in Italian, on the mistakes of his little pupil; he told me what were the most usual blunders of school boys in translating any passage, what expressions they were the latest in comprehending, and what in general escaped the notice even of me: he explained the reasons in the most novel and acute manner, and illustrated several of the most unintelligible principles of the human mind. I was astonished at his penetration.

When he had dismissed the boy, he drew his chair towards mine, and said, "From what your friend Bruhle has told me, and from my own observation, I am induced to believe that you are a young man of talents. Your talents have convinced you, that man is by nature free. Liberty should have been as generally diffused as the light of the sun, as the air of heaven: liberty is as essential to the happiness of man, as light and air to his existence. You are a witness to the encroachment of man upon natural liberty, the birthright of his fellow-creatures, and to the consequent misery. Your head and your heart, doubtless, conspire in instructing you, that it is your duty to promote the happiness of your associates in this world. And how is this important duty to be best performed? Surely, by restoring to every man his natural rights; by banishing oppression; by breaking the bonds, and shaking off the yoke of slavery. We have formed ourselves into a society to attain this great end, as far as it can be effected by united talents, by ardent zeal, by strenuous, unceasing expectations."

He had hardly finished, when I exclaimed, "O excellent sages! O amiable institution! O great and good men! how happy I should be if I were ever permitted to become a member of your society! If it be possible, make me one now, even this very moment." The Eleutherarch smiled at my impatience. "You are very enthusiastic, young man," he said; "I fear it will cool your ardour, if I inform you, that a long noviciate, no less than three years preparation, is necessary, previous to your admission." "If human life were sufficiently long, I would rather undergo a probation of a thousand years, than be

---

1   The *OED* credits Hogg with the first use in English of the term.

excluded from such an association." "You promise fair," he answered; "I give you three days to determine."

We then returned home. My mind was made up; I waited the termination of the three days with impatience. At the appointed time Bruhle conducted me to the university; the Eleutherarch asked if I had resolved to submit to the necessary initiation. I answered in the affirmative; he then informed me that he had consulted with his brethren upon the propriety of shortening the term of my probation, and that they had determined, that, in consideration of my ardent zeal in the cause, of the extraordinary diligence which they were persuaded I should use, and of the high character which Bruhle had given me, my term should be contracted to one year; a favour which had never been granted to any one. I expressed my gratitude for the high compliment which was paid to me, and requested that my initiation might commence as soon as possible.

In a week I was informed my career should commence. My curiosity was excessive; but, as Bruhle was not permitted to satisfy it, even by the slightest hint, I was obliged to wait with patience. At the expiration of that period I received a note, requesting me to attend the university in the evening. I obeyed the summons most willingly. The hall was crowded with members of the society; the major part consisted of young men; the remainder were the venerable sages whom I had seen before, and a few old men, to whom I was a stranger. The Eleutherarch was not present. We walked about the room, conversing upon miscellaneous subjects in different languages. I overheard many men talking in a language, of which I was entirely ignorant, and dissimilar in sound to any language I had ever heard.

In about half an hour the Eleutherarch entered, attended by two old men. The men formed into different classes, and prostrated themselves in various attitudes. The Eleutherarch knelt down also upon a sort of rostrum; he pronounced some words in a language to which I was a stranger: he rose, and the others did so likewise. He then addressed himself in the same language to the whole company, and, as I was afterwards informed, asked them, if they had any objections to my being initiated into the mysteries of the Eleutheri. The whole assembly expressed their assent. The Eleutherarch said, "I confirm your approbation." He then asked, if they objected to the term of my initiation being shortened to one year instead of three. The younger part of the assembly appearing dissatisfied, he beckoned to Bruhle, who came forwards, and spoke very fluently, and for a long time, but in the language in which they seemed to be accustomed to debate. When he was silent, the assembly applauded him, and expressed their assent as before. The Eleutherarch replied, "I confirm your approbation."

Bruhle advanced, and presented to me a long and solemn oath in Latin, that I would submit to all the trials which were required of me. I read it over with attention, and asked if it was possible to omit that part of the ceremony? He answered, that it was absolutely necessary, and asked if I was willing to swear? I hesitated for a few minutes, and at last replied, "I am." Every man immediately drew forth a sword, which had been concealed under his gown. The Eleutherarch commanded me to kneel; I obeyed, and the men, crowding round me, as many as were able, touched my body with their drawn swords, which they held in that manner whilst the Eleutherarch read the oath in a slow, distinct voice, and I repeated it after him. When I had concluded, the Eleutheri clashed their swords together several times. The Eleutherarch spoke for about half an hour in the unknown language, and the younger men departed. The Eleutherarch and about twenty old men remained with Bruhle and myself.

We walked about the hall until supper was introduced. During that temperate meal we conversed upon historical subjects. I was charmed with the brilliancy of the observations, the beauty of the language, the depth of the remarks, and above all, with the pure spirit of liberty breathed by these profound philosophers. The Eleutherarch alone was silent, but his silence was only the prelude to the most overwhelming eloquence. He arose; we listened with mute attention; he commenced a discourse to prove, that the soul was material, and that death was complete annihilation, an eternal sleep. So subtile were his arguments, so ingeniously arranged, and pressed with such irresistible and relentless force, that notwithstanding my repugnance to that gloomy, that detestable doctrine, I was compelled to assent, as was reluctantly convinced of what I shuddered to believe.

When he had concluded he left the table, and, scowling upon me, beckoned me to follow him. We quitted the hall; he took a lighted torch in his hand, and proceeded along the cloisters to the cathedral, which we entered. The cold damp, like an icy hand, pressed upon my forehead; this shook the arguments I had just heard to the foundation. My guide remained silent; I heard no sound by the echo of our footsteps reverberating through the long-drawn aisles. When we reached the middle of the church, just beneath the lofty central tower, I perceived a corpse, wrapped in grave-clothes, extended upon a bier; the red light of the torch gleamed horribly upon the pale cheeks of the departed. The Eleutherarch fixed his eyes upon me, and riveted me to the earth. "Take this dagger in your right hand, this skull in your left," said he, drawing a dagger and a skull from under his gown, and presenting them to me: "young man, you must watch this corpse to-night." He then departed with the torch.

I was petrified with horror; I was in total darkness; strange thoughts benumbed my brain; strange visions flitted before my eyes; I mused upon my situation. [...]

Appendix C: Literary Contexts

[The documents in this appendix are examples of contemporary works that Peacock had in mind when writing *Nightmare Abbey*. If his reading of Canto 4 of Byron's *Childe Harold's Pilgrimage* was the supposed catalyst for his satire, in other respects the two writers shared a critical sensibility. Byron's Dedication to *Don Juan*, which is contemporary to the novel, would not have been known by Peacock; however, at the same time it contains a sense of protest against contemporary literature similar to Peacock. As his novel might be said to form a portrait of the "spirit of the age," two excerpts from William Hazlitt's 1825 collection of essays are also included.]

1. From William Godwin, *An Enquiry Concerning Political Justice* (1793)[1]

[Peacock was given a copy of *Political Justice* by Edward Hookham in 1809.[2] The selection here offers a defence of political groups as being conducive to education and rational discussion; it is a counter to government legislation outlawing such groups as potentially might pose a threat of political revolution. At the same time the chapter contextualizes Peacock's satire of Scythrop's obsession with secret societies as opposed to the more salutary atmosphere of enlightened discussion promoted by his father. I have silently emended the long "s" from the text and omitted the marginal gloss.]

Volume 1, Book 4, Chapter 2: Of Political Associations

[...] But, though association, in the received sense of that term, must be granted to be an instrument of a very dangerous nature, it should be remembered that unreserved communication in a smaller circle, and especially among persons who are already awakened to the pursuit of truth, is of unquestionable advantage. There is at present in the world a cold reserve that keeps man at a distance from man.

---

1   Source: William Godwin, *An Enquiry Concerning Political Justice.* (London, 1793; rev. 1796; rev. 1798).

2   Joukovsky, *Letters of Thomas Love Peacock.* 1.36.

There is an art in the practice of which individuals communicate for ever, without any one telling his neighbour what estimate he should form of his attainments and character, how they ought to be employed, and how to be improved. There is a sort of domestic tactics, the object of which is to instruct us to elude curiosity, and to keep up the tenour of conversation, without the disclosure either of our feelings or our opinions. The philanthropist has no object more deeply at heart than the annihilation of this duplicity and reserve. No man can have much kindness for his species, who does not habituate himself to consider upon each successive occasion of social intercourse how that occasion may be most beneficently improved. Among the topics to which he will be anxious to awaken attention, politics will occupy a principal share.

Books have by their very nature but a limited operation; though, on account of their permanence, their methodical disquisition, and their easiness of access, they are entitled to the foremost place. But their efficacy ought not to engross our confidence. The number of those by whom reading is neglected is exceedingly great. Books to those by whom they are read have a sort of constitutional coldness. We review the arguments of an "insolent innovator" with sullenness, and are unwilling to stretch our minds to take in all their force. It is with difficulty that we obtain the courage of striking into untrodden paths, and questioning tenets that have been generally received. But conversation accustoms us to hear a variety of sentiments, obliges us to exercise patience and attention, and gives freedom and elasticity to our mental disquisitions. A thinking man, if he will recollect his intellectual history, will find that he has derived inestimable advantage from the stimulus and surprise of colloquial suggestions; and, if he review the history of literature, will perceive that minds of great acuteness and ability have commonly existed in a cluster.

It follows that the promoting of the best interests of mankind eminently depends upon the freedom of social communication. Let us imagine to ourselves a number of individuals, who, having first stored their minds with reading and reflection, proceed afterwards in candid and unreserved conversation to compare their ideas, to suggest their doubts, to remove their difficulties, and to cultivate a collected and striking manner of delivering their sentiments. Let us suppose these men, prepared by mutual intercourse, to go forth to the world, to explain with succinctness and simplicity, and in a manner well calculated to arrest attention, the true principles of society. Let us suppose their hearers instigated in their turn to repeat these truths to their companions. We shall then have an idea of knowledge as perpetually gaining ground, unaccompanied with peril in the means of its diffusion. Reason will spread itself, and not a brute and unintelligent sympathy.

Discussion perhaps never exists with so much vigour and utility as in the conversation of two persons. It may be carried on with advantage in small and friendly societies. Does the fewness of their numbers imply the rarity of their existence? Far otherwise: the time perhaps will come when such institutions will be universal. Shew to mankind by a few examples the advantages of political discussion undebauched by political enmity and vehemence, and the beauty of the spectacle will soon render the example contagious. Every man will commune with his neighbour. Every man will be eager to tell and to hear what the interest of all requires them to know. The bolts and fortifications of the temple of truth will be removed. The craggy steep of science, which it was before difficult to ascend, will be levelled with the plain. Knowledge will be accessible to all. Wisdom will be the inheritance of man, from which none will be excluded but by their own heedlessness and prodigality. If these ideas cannot completely be realised, till the inequality of conditions and the tyranny of government are rendered somewhat less oppressive, this affords no reason against the setting afloat so generous a system. The improvement of individuals and the melioration of political institutions are destined mutually to produce and reproduce each other. Truth, and above all political truth, is not hard of acquisition, but from the superciliousness of its professors. It has been slow and tedious of improvement, because the study of it has been relegated to doctors and civilians. It has produced little effect upon the practice of mankind, because it has not been allowed a plain and direct appeal to their understandings. Remove these obstacles, render it the common property, bring it into daily use, and you may reasonably promise yourself consequences of the most inestimable value. [...]

2. From William Godwin, *Mandeville: A Tale of the Seventeenth Century in England* (1817)[1]

[*Mandeville* is parodied in Chapter 5 as "'Devilman, a novel.' Hm. Hatred—revenge—misanthropy—and quotations from the Bible" (70). In Godwin's novel, the first person narrator has lost his father in an Irish uprising and is raised by his melancholy uncle Audley Mandeville. The narrator is taught by an anti-Catholic tutor and goes to Winchester in 1650 where he meets Clifford, whom he comes to envy and hate. Clifford becomes a kind of double for the narrator, who scars his face and therefore sets his mark on the narrator. Peacock seems to incorporate some parallels with the work in his novel.]

Volume 1, Chapter 3

[...] The dwelling-place of my uncle was an old and spacious mansion, the foundation of which was a rock, against which the waves of the sea for ever beat, and by their incessant and ineffectual rage were worked into a foam, that widely spread itself in every direction. The sound of the dashing waters was eternal, and seemed calculated to inspire sobriety, and almost gloom, into the soul of every one who dwelt within the reach of its influence. The situation of this dwelling, on that side of the island which is most accessible to an enemy, had induced its original architect to construct it in such a manner, as might best enable it to resist an invader, though its fortifications had since fallen into decay. It was a small part of the edifice only that was inhabited in my time. Several magnificent galleries, and a number of spacious apartments, were wholly neglected, and suffered to remain in a woful state of dilapidation. Indeed it was one wing only that was now tenanted, and that imperfectly; the centre and the other wing had long been resigned to the owls and the bitterns. The door which formed the main entrance of the building was never opened; and the master and all that belonged to him were accustomed to pass by an obscure postern only. The court-yard exhibited a striking scene of desolation. The scythe and spade were never admitted to violate its savage character. It was overgrown with tall and rank grass of a peculiar species, intermingled with elder trees, nettles, and briars.

---

1 Source: William Godwin, *Mandeville: A Tale of the Seventeenth Century in England*. 3 vols. (Edinburgh: Archibald Constable and Co., and London: Longman, Hurst, Rees, Orme & Brown, 1817), 1.47–50, 1.103–4.

The dwelling which I have thus described was surrounded on three sides by the sea; it was only by the north-west that I could reach what I may call my native country. The whole situation was eminently insalubrious. Though the rock on which our habitation was placed was, for the most part, of a perpendicular acclivity, yet we had to the west a long bank of sand, and in different directions various portions of bog and marshy ground, sending up an endless succession of vapours, I had almost said steams, whose effect holds unmitigated war with healthful animal life. The tide also threw up vast quantities of sargassos[1] and weeds, the corruption of which was supposed to contribute eminently to the same effect. For a great part of the year we were further involved in thick fogs and mists, to such a degree as often to render the use of candles necessary even at noon-day.

Volume 1, Chapter 4

My uncle had felt much regard for my father,—as much as was compatible with the peculiar turn his mind had taken; which was to dwell for ever on one event, to consider that in relation to himself as the only reality, and scarcely to bestow so much regard on every thing that existed in the world beside, as an ordinary human would bestow upon the shadows of a magic lanthorn.[2] Years rolled over the head of this unfortunate man in vain. While he was young, the amiable object of his early love was all that interested him on earth; and, as he grew older, habit produced upon him the same effect, which had at first been the child of passion. He loved his sadness, for it had become a part of himself. All his motions had for so long a time been languid, that, if he had been excited in any instance to make them otherwise, he would scarcely have recognized his own identity. He found a nameless pleasure in the appendages and forms of melancholy, so great, that he would as soon have consented to cut off his right hand, as to part with them. In reality he rather vegetated than lived; and he had persisted so long in this passive mode of existence, that there was not nerve and spring enough left in him, to enable him to sustain any other.

---

1   A type of seaweed, with the figurative meaning of "a confused or stagnant mass" (*OED*).
2   A "magic lantern" is an optical device that uses slides to display a magnified image on a white screen or wall in a darkened room (*OED*).

3. From Samuel Taylor Coleridge, *The Statesman's Manual, a Lay Sermon Addressed to the Higher Classes of Society* (1816)[1]

[In discussing *Nightmare Abbey* in his 30 May letter to Percy Bysshe Shelley, Peacock mentions a "systematic 'poisoning' of the 'mind' of the 'Reading Public.'"[2] Joukovsky glosses "Reading Public," a phrase Mr. Flosky uses in Chapters 6 and 11, as a reference to a passage in *The Statesman's Manual*. He previously satirized the passage in a speech by Moley Mystic in Chapter 31 of *Melincourt*.[3] But his satire is as much a sense of impatience for a man whose talents he respects; his "Essay on Fashionable Literature" (see Appendix D) includes a spirited defense of Coleridge's poems "Christabel" and "Kubla Khan" (1816). The text used here includes capitalizations and italicizations which echo Peacock's own satire of such contemporary conventions.]

[...] When I named this Essay a Sermon, I sought to prepare the inquirers after it for the absence of all the usual softenings suggested by worldly prudence, of all compromise between truth and courtesy. But not even as a Sermon would I have addressed the present Discourse to a promiscuous audience; and for this reason I likewise announced it in the title-page as exclusively *ad clerum*; i.e., (in the old and wide sense of the word) to men of *clerkly* acquirements, of whatever profession. I would that the greater part of our publications could be thus *directed*, each to its appropriate class of Readers. But this cannot be! For among other odd burs and kecksies,[4] the misgrowth of our luxuriant activity, we have now a READING PUBLIC★—as strange a phrase, methinks, as ever forced a splenetic

---

★ Some participle passive in the diminutive form, ERUDITULORUM NATIO for instance, might seem at first sight a fuller and more exact designation; but the superior force and humor of the former become evident whenever the phrase occurs as a step or stair in a *climax* of irony. By way of example take the following sentences, transcribed from a work *demonstrating* that the New Testament was intended exclusively for the primitive converts from Judaism, was accommodated to their prejudices, and is of no authority, as a rule of faith; for Christians in general. "The READING PUBLIC in this ENLIGHTENED

---

1 Source: Samuel Taylor Coleridge, *The Statesman's Manual, a Lay Sermon Addressed to the Higher Classes of Society* (London: Printed for Gale and Fenner, Pater-Noster Row, 1816).
2 Joukovsky, *Letters of Thomas Love Peacock* 1.123.
3 Joukovsky, *Letters of Thomas Love Peacock* 1.125n.
4 A hollow plant-stem (*OED*).

smile on the staid countenance of Meditation; and yet no fiction! For our Readers have, in good truth, multiplied exceedingly, and have waxed proud. It would require the intrepid accuracy of a Colquhoun to venture at the precise number of that vast company only, whose heads and hearts are dieted at the two public *ordinaries* of Literature, the circulating libraries and the periodical press. But what is the result? Does the inward man thrive on this regimen?

AGE, and THINKING NATION, by its favourable reception of LIBERAL IDEAS, has long demonstrated the benign influence of that PROFOUND PHILOSOPHY which has already emancipated us from so many absurd prejudices held in superstitious awe by our deluded forefathers. But the *Dark Age* yielded at length to the dawning light of Reason and Common-Sense at the glorious, though imperfect, Revolution. THE PEOPLE can be no longer duped or scared out of their *imprescriptible and inalienable* RIGHT to judge and decide for themselves on all important questions of Government and Religion. The *scholastic jargon* of jarring articles and metaphysical creeds may continue for a time to deform our Church-establishment; and like the grotesque figures in the nitches of our old gothic cathedrals may serve to remind the nation of its former barbarism; but the *universal suffrage* of a FREE AND ENLIGHTENED PUBLIC," &c. &c.!

Among the Revolutions worthy of notice, the change in the nature of the introductory sentences and prefatory matter in serious Books is not the least striking. The same gross flattery which disgusts us in the dedications to individuals in the elder writers, is now transferred to the Nation at large, or the READING PUBLIC: while the Jeremiads of our old Moralists, and their angry denunciations concerning the ignorance, immorality, and irreligion of the *People*, appear (mutatis mutandis, and with an appeal to the worst passions, envy, discontent, scorn, vindictiveness, &c.) in the shape of bitter libels on Ministers, Parliament, the Clergy: in short, on the State and Church, and all persons employed in them. Likewise, I would point out to the Reader's attention the marvellous predominance at present of the *words*, Idea and Demonstration. Every talker now a days has an *Idea*; aye, and he will demonstrate it too! A few days ago, I heard one of the READING PUBLIC, a thinking and independent smuggler, *euphonize* the latter word with much significance, in a tirade against the planners of the late African expedition:—"*As to Algiers, any man that has half an IDEA in his skull, must know, that is had been long ago dey-monstered, I should say, dey-monstrified, &c.*" But, the phrase, which occasioned this note, brings to my mind the mistake of a lethargic Dutch traveller, who returning highly gratified from a showman's caravan, which he had been tempted to enter by the words, THE LEARNED PIG, gilt on the pannels, met another caravan of a similar shape with THE READING FLY on it, in letters of the same size and splendour. "Why, dis is voonders above voonders!" exclaims the Dutchman, takes his seat as first comer, and soon fatigued by waiting, and by the very hush and intensity of his expectation, gives way to his constitutional somnulence, from which he is roused by the supposed showman at Hounslow, with a "*In what name, Sir! was your place taken? Are you booked all the way for Reading?*"—Now a Reading Public is (to my mind) more marvellous still, and in the third tier of "Voonders above Voonders." [Coleridge's note.] "Eruditulorum natio" means "thinking nation" (Latin). In the latter eighteenth century a "Learned Pig" and a "Wonderful Intelligent Goose" appeared in London. Wordsworth's description of Bartholomew Fair in *The Prelude*: "All moveables of wonder, from all parts, /Are here—Albinos, painted Indians, Dwarfs, / The Horse of knowledge, and the learned Pig," (7.706-8).

Alas! if the average health of the consumers may be judged of by the articles of largest consumption; if the secretions may be conjectured from the ingredients of the dishes that are found best suited to their palates; from all that I have seen, either of the banquet or the guests, I shall utter my *Profaccia* with a desponding sigh. From a popular philosophy and a philosophic populace, Good Sense deliver us!

4. From Samuel Taylor Coleridge, *Biographia Literaria* (1817)[1]

[Coral Ann Howells has traced similarities between comments by Mr. Flosky and passages from Coleridge's "Critique on Bertram," a tragedy by C.R. Maturin which becomes Chapter 23 of the *Biographia*.[2] Excerpted here are examples of Coleridge's discussion of critics and the reading public; these also form part of both Peacock's critique of Coleridge and of his "Essay on Fashionable Literature."]

Chapter III

[...] To anonymous critics in reviews, magazines, and news-journals of various name and rank, and to satirists with or without a name, in verse or prose, or in verse-text aided by prose-comment, I do seriously believe and profess, that I owe full two thirds of whatever reputation and publicity I happen to possess. For when the name of an individual has occurred so frequently, in so many works, for so great a length of time, the readers of these works (which with a shelf or two of BEAUTIES ELEGANT EXTRACTS and ANAS,[3] form nine-tenths of the reading of the reading public*) cannot but

---

* For as to the devotees of the circulating libraries, I dare not compliment their *pass-time*, or rather *kill-time*, with the name of *reading*. Call it rather a sort of beggarly day-dreaming, during which the mind of the dreamer furnishes for itself nothing but laziness and a little mawkish sensibility; while the whole *materiel* and imagery of the doze is supplied *ab extra* by a sort of mental *camera obscura* manufactured at the printing office, which *pro tempore* fixes, reflects and transmits the moving phantasms of one man's delirium, so as to people

---

1 Source: Samuel Taylor Coleridge, *Biographia Literaria*. 2 vols. (London: Rest Fenner, 1817).
2 "*Biographia Literaria* and *Nightmare Abbey*." (*Notes and Queries* 16 [1969]: 50–51).
3 Coleridge is referring to the fashion of creating excerpts of literature in a volume and meant to serve as models for writing or as set pieces for recitation; his allusion here is to Vicesimus Knox's *Elegant Extracts: or, useful and entertaining Pieces of Poetry, Selected for the Improvement of Young Persons: being similar in Design to Elegant Extracts in Prose*. 2 vols (London: C. Robinson; Weybridge: S. Hamilton, 1809).

be familiar with the name, without distinctly remembering whether it was introduced for an eulogy or for censure. And this becomes the more likely, if (as I believe) the habit of perusing periodical works may be properly added to Averrhoe's* catalogue of ANTI-MNEMONICS, or weakeners of the memory.[1] But where this has not been the case, yet the reader will be apt to suspect, that there must be something more than usually strong and extensive in a reputation, that could either require or stand so merciless and long-continued a cannonading. Without any feeling of *anger* therefore (for which indeed, on my own account, I have no pretext) I may yet be allowed to express some degree of *surprize*, that after having run the critical gauntlet for a certain class of faults which I *had*, nothing having come before the judgement-seat in the interim, I should, year after year, quarter after quarter, month after month (not to mention sundry petty periodicals of still quicker revolution, "or weekly or diurnal") have been for at least 17 years consecutively, dragged forth by them into the foremost ranks of the *proscribed*, and forced to abide the brunt of abuse, for faults directly opposite, and which I certainly had not. How shall I explain this?

the barrenness of an hundred other brains afflicted with the same trance or suspension of all common sense and all definite purpose. We should therefore transfer this species of *amusement*, (if indeed those can be said to retire *a musis*, who were never in their company, or relaxation be attributable to those, whose bows are never bent) from the genus, *reading*, to that comprehensive class characterized by the power of reconciling the two contrary yet co-existing propensities of human nature, namely; indulgence of sloth, and hatred of vacancy. In addition to novels and tales of chivalry in prose or rhyme, (by which last I mean neither rhythm nor metre) this genus comprizes as its species, gaming, swinging, or swaying on a chair or gate; spitting over a bridge; smoking; snuff-taking; tete a tete quarrels after dinner between husband and wife; conning word by word all the advertisements of the daily advertizer in a public house on a rainy day, &c. &c. &c.

* Ex. gr. *Pediculos e capillis excerptos in arenam jacere incontusos*; eating of unripe fruit; gazing on the clouds, and (in genere) on moveable things suspended in the air; riding among a multitude of camels; frequent laughter; listening to a series of jests and humourous anecdotes, as when (so to modernise the learned Saracen's meaning) one man's droll story of an Irishman inevitably occasions another's droll story of a Scotchman, which again by the same sort of conjunction disjunctive leads to some *etourderie* of a Welchman, and that again to some sly hit of a Yorkshireman; the habit of reading tomb-stones in church-yards, &c. By the bye, this catalogue strange as it may appear, is not insusceptible of a sound pcychological commentary.

1 Arabian Aristotelian philosopher, born in Cordova, 1126; died in Morocco, 1198; who Coleridge confuses for Burhan al-Din, al-Zarnuji (see *Biographia Literaria*, ed. James Engell and W. Jackson Bate. [Princeton: Princeton UP and London: Routledge & Kegan Paul, 1983], 1.49n).

Whatever may have been the case with others, I certainly cannot attribute this persecution to personal dislike, or to envy, or to feelings of vindictive animosity. Not to the former, for, with the exception of a very few who are my intimate friends, and were so before they were known as authors, I have had little other acquaintance with literary characters, than what may be implied in an accidental introduction, or casual meeting in a mixt company. And, as far as words and looks can be trusted, I must believe that, even in these instances, I had excited no unfriendly disposition.* Neither

---

* Some years ago, a gentleman, the chief writer and conductor of a celebrated review, distinguished by its hostility to Mr. Southey, spent a day or two at Keswick. That he was, without diminution on this account, treated with every hospitable attention by Mr. Southey and myself, I trust I need not say. But one thing I may venture to notice; that at no period of my life do I remember to have received so many, and such high coloured compliments in so short a space of time. He was likewise circumstantially informed by what series of accidents it had happened, that Mr. Wordsworth, Mr. Southey, and I had become neighbours; and how utterly unfounded was the supposition, that we considered ourselves, as belonging to any common school, but that of good sense confirmed by the long-established models of the best times of Greece, Rome, Italy, and England; and still more groundless the notion, that Mr. Southey (for as to myself I have published so little, and that little, of so little importance, as to make it almost ludicrous to mention my name at all) could have been concerned in the formation of a poetic sect with Mr. Wordsworth, when so many of his works had been published not only previously to any acquaintance between them; but before Mr. Wordsworth himself had written any thing but in a diction ornate, and uniformly sustained; when too the slightest examination will make it evident, that between those and the after writings of Mr. Southey, there exists no other difference than that of a progressive degree of excellence from progressive developement of power, and progressive facility from habit and increase of experience. Yet among the first articles which this man wrote after his return from Keswick, we were characterized as "the School of whining and hypochondriacal poets that haunt the Lakes." In reply to a letter from the same gentleman, in which he had asked me, whether I was in earnest in preferring the style of Hooker to that of Dr. Johnson; and Jeremy Taylor to Burke; I stated, somewhat at large, the comparative excellences and defects which characterized our best prose writers, from the reformation, to the first half of Charles 2nd; and that of those who had flourished during the present reign, and the preceding one. About twelve months afterwards, a review appeared on the same subject, in the concluding paragraph of which the reviewer asserts, that his chief motive for entering into the discussion was to separate a rational and qualified admiration of our elder writers, from the indiscriminate enthusiasm of a recent school, who praised what they did not understand, and caracatured what they were unable to imitate. And, that no doubt might be left concerning the persons alluded to, the writer annexes the names of Miss BAILIE, W. SOUTHEY, WORDSWORTH and COLERIDGE. For that which follows, I have only ear-say evidence; but yet such as demands my belief; viz. that on being questioned concerning this apparently wanton attack, more especially with reference to Miss Bailie, the writer had stated as his motives, that this lady when at Edinburgh had declined a proposal of introducing him to her; that Mr. Southey had written against him; and Mr. Wordsworth had talked contemptuously of

by letter, or in conversation, have I ever had dispute or controversy beyond the common social interchange of opinions. Nay, where I had reason to suppose my convictions fundamentally different, it has been my habit, and I may add, the impulse of my nature, to assign the grounds of my belief, rather than the belief itself; and not to express dissent, till I could establish some points of complete sympathy, some grounds common to both sides, from which to commence its explanation.

Still less can I place these attacks to the charge of envy. The few pages, which I have published, are of too distant a date; and the extent of their sale a proof too conclusive against their having been popular at any time; to render probable, I had almost said possible, the excitement of envy on *their* account; and the man who should envy me on any *other*, verily he must be *envy-mad!*

Lastly, with as little semblance of reason, could I suspect any animosity towards me from vindictive feelings as the cause. I have before said, that my acquaintance with literary men has been limited and distant; and that I have had neither dispute nor controversy. From my first entrance into life, I have, with few and short intervals, lived either abroad or in retirement. My different essays on subjects of national interest, published at different times, first in the Morning Post and then in the Courier, with my courses of lectures on the principles of criticism as applied to Shakespeare and Milton, constitute my whole publicity; the only occasions on which I *could* offend any member of the republic of letters.[1] With one solitary exception in which my words were first misstated and then wantonly applied to an individual, I could never learn, that I had excited the displeasure of any among my literary contemporaries. Having

---

him; but that as to *Coleridge* he had noticed him merely because the names of Southey and Wordsworth and Coleridge always went together. But if it were worth while to mix together, as ingredients, half the anecdotes which I either myself know to be true, or which I have received from men incapable of intentional falsehood, concerning the characters, qualifications, and motives of our anonymous critics, whose decisions are oracles for our reading public; I might safely borrow the words of the apocryphal Daniel; *"Give me leave, O SOVEREIGN PUBLIC, and I shall slay this dragon without sword or staff."* For the compound would be as the *"Pitch, and fat, and hair, which Daniel took, and did seethe them together, and made lumps thereof, and put into the dragon's mouth, and so the dragon burst in sunder; and Daniel said LO; THESE ARE THE GODS YE WORSHIP."*

---

1   Newspapers to which Coleridge contributed material between 1797 and 1814.

announced my intention to give a course of lectures on the characteristic merits and defects of English poetry in its different æras;
first, from Chaucer to Milton; second, from Dryden inclusive to
Thomson; and third, from Cowper to the present day; I changed my
plan, and confined my disquisition to the two former æras, that I
might furnish no possible pretext for the unthinking to misconstrue,
or the malignant to misapply my words, and having stamped their
own meaning on them, to pass them as current coin in the marts of
garrulity or detraction.[1]

★★★★

Poets and Philosophers, rendered diffident by their very number,
addressed themselves to "*learned* readers;" then, aimed to conciliate the graces of "the *candid* reader;" till, the critic still rising as the
author sunk, the amateurs of literature collectively were erected into
a municipality of judges, and addressed as the THE TOWN! And
now finally, all men being supposed able to read, and all readers able
to judge, the multitudinous PUBLIC, shaped into personal unity
by the magic of abstraction, sits nominal despot on the throne of
criticism. But, alas! as in other despotisms, it but echoes the decisions
of its invisible ministers, whose intellectual claims to the guardi-
anship of the muses seem, for the greater part, analogous to the
physical qualifications which adapt their oriental brethren for the
superintendance of the Harem. Thus it is said, that St. Nepomuc
was installed the guardian of bridges because he had fallen over one,
and sunk out of sight; thus, too, St. Cecilia is said to have been first
propitiated by musicians, because having failed in her own attempts,
she had taken a dislike to the art, and all its successful professors.[2]
But I shall probably have occasion hereafter to deliver my convictions more at large concerning this state of things, and its influences
on taste, genius and morality.

5. Percy Bysshe Shelley, "Hymn to Intellectual Beauty" (1817)[3]

[The poem was written in Geneva during the summer the Shelleys
spent with Byron, while Byron was composing Canto 3 of *Childe*

---

1   Coleridge delivered public lectures on Shakespeare in 1808 and 1811–12.
2   St. John of Nepomuc of Bohemia (1330–93) was ordered drowned; St. Cecilia is associated
    with music and the organ.
3   Source: *The Examiner*. No. 473 (19 January 1817), 41.

Harold's Pilgrimage (1816) and Mary Shelley was composing *Frankenstein* (1818). The poem portrays Shelley not only as a "votary of romance," but also suggests similarity between his more esoteric ideas and those of Scythrop.]

ORIGINAL POETRY

[The following Ode, originally announced under the signature of the *Elfin Knight*, we have since found to be from the pen of the author, whose name was mentioned among others a week or two back in an article entitled "Young Poets." The reader will think with us, that it is alone sufficient to justify what was there observed;— but we shall say more on this subject in a review of the book we mentioned:—]

HYMN TO INTELLECTUAL BEAUTY

I

The awful shadow of some unseen Power
Floats tho' unseen among us,—visiting
This various world with as inconstant wing
As summer winds that creep from flower to flower.—
Like moonbeams that behind some piny mountain shower,
It visits with inconstant glance
Each human heart and countenance;
Like hues and harmonies of evening,—
Like clouds in starlight widely spread,—
Like memory of music fled,—
Like aught that for its grace may be
Dear, and yet dearer for its mystery.

2

Spirit of Beauty, that doth consecrate
With thine own hues all thou dost shine upon
Of human thought or form,—where art thou gone?
Why dost thou pass away and leave our state,
This dim vast vale of tears, vacant and desolate?
Ask why the sunlight not forever
Weaves rainbows o'er yon mountain-river,

Why aught should fail and fade that once is shewn,
Why fear and dream and death and birth
Cast on the daylight of this earth
Such gloom,—why man has such a scope
For love and hate, despondency and hope?

3

No voice from some sublimer world hath ever
To sage or poet these responses given—
Therefore the names of Demon, Ghost, and Heaven,
Remain the records of their vain endeavour,
Frail spells—whose uttered charm might not avail to sever,
From all we hear and all we see,
Doubt, chance, and mutability.
Thy light alone—like mist o'er the mountains driven,
Or music by the night-wind sent,
Thro' strings of some still instrument,
Or moonlight on a midnight stream,
Gives grace and truth to life's unquiet dream.

4

Love, Hope, and Self-esteem, like clouds, depart
And come, for some uncertain moments lent.
Man were immortal, and omnipotent,
Didst thou, unknown and awful as thou art,
Keep with thy glorious train firm state within his heart.
Thou messenger of sympathies,
That wax and wane in lovers' eyes—
Thou—that to human thought art nourishment,
Like darkness to a dying flame!
Depart not as thy shadow came,
Depart not—lest the grave should be,
Like life and fear, a dark reality.

5

While yet a boy I sought for ghosts, and sped
Thro many a listening chamber, cave and ruin,
And starlight wood, with fearful steps pursuing
Hopes of high talk with the departed dead.

I called on poisonous names with which our youth is fed,
I was not heard— I saw them not—
When musing deeply on the lot
Of life, at that sweet time when winds are wooing
All vital things that wake to bring
News of birds and blossoming,—
Sudden, thy shadow fell on me;
I shrieked, and clasped my hands in extacy!

6

I vowed that I would dedicate my powers
To thee and thine—have I not kept the vow?
With beating heart and streaming eyes, even now
I call the phantoms of a thousand hours
Each from his voiceless grave: they have in visioned bowers
Of studious zeal or loves delight
Outwatched with me the envious night—
They know that never joy illumed my brow
Unlinked with hope that thou wouldst free
This world from its dark slavery,
That thou, O awful Loveliness,
Wouldst give whate'er these words cannot express.

7

The day becomes more solemn and serene
When noon is past—there is a harmony
In autumn, and a lustre in its sky,
Which thro' the summer is not heard or seen,
As if it could not be, as if it had not been!
Thus let thy power, which like the truth
Of nature on my passive youth
Descended, to my onward life supply
Its calm—to one who worships thee,
And every form containing thee,
Whom, Spirit fair, thy spells did bind
To fear himself, and love all human kind.

PERCY B. SHELLEY

6. From Percy Bysshe Shelley, Author's Preface to *The Revolt of Islam; A Poem, in Twelve Cantos* (1818)[1]

[First published as *Laon and Cythna; or, The Revolution of the Golden City: A Vision of the Nineteenth Century* in December 1817, Peacock helped Shelley with revisions to the poem when the publisher withdrew it fearing prosecution for its description of incest and critique of religion. It was reissued in 1818 under the title *The Revolt of Islam*. The poem presents Shelley's imaginative and idealised recasting of the French Revolution that views its failure as providing instruction for those with revolutionary aspirations. The Preface gives a sense of Shelley's politics in 1818.]

PREFACE

The Poem which I now present to the world, is an attempt from which I scarcely dare to expect success, and in which a writer of established fame might fail without disgrace. It is an experiment on the temper of the public mind, as to how far a thirst for a happier condition of moral and political society survives, among the enlightened and refined, the tempests which have shaken the age in which we live. I have sought to enlist the harmony of metrical language, the etherial combinations of the fancy, the rapid and subtle transitions of human passion, all those elements which essentially compose a Poem, in the cause of a liberal and comprehensive morality, and in the view of kindling within the bosoms of my readers, a virtuous enthusiasm for those doctrines of liberty and justice, that faith and hope in something good, which neither violence, nor misrepresentation, nor prejudice, can ever totally extinguish among mankind.

For this purpose I have chosen a story of human passion in its most universal character, diversified with moving and romantic adventures, and appealing, in contempt of all artificial opinions or institutions, to the common sympathies of every human breast. I have made no attempt to recommend the motives which I would substitute for those at present governing mankind by methodical and systematic argument. I would only awaken the feelings, so that

---

1   Source: Percy Bysshe Shelley, *The Revolt of Islam; A Poem, in Twelve Cantos* (London: Printed for C. and J. Ollier, Welbeck-Street, 1818), v–xv, xvii–xix.

the reader should see the beauty of true virtue, and be incited to those enquiries which have led to my moral and political creed, and that of some of the sublimest intellects in the world. The Poem therefore, (with the exception of the first Canto, which is purely introductory), is narrative, not didactic. It is a succession of pictures illustrating the growth and progress of individual mind aspiring after excellence, and devoted to the love of mankind; its influence in refining and making pure the most daring and uncommon impulses of the imagination, the understanding, and the senses; its impatience at "all the oppressions which are done under the sun;"[1] its tendency to awaken public hope and to enlighten and improve mankind; the rapid effects of the application of that tendency; the awakening of an immense nation from their slavery and degradation to a true sense of moral dignity and freedom; the bloodless dethronement of their oppressors, and the unveiling of the religious frauds by which they had been deluded into submission; the tranquillity of successful patriotism, and the universal toleration and benevolence of true philanthropy; the treachery and barbarity of hired soldiers; vice not the object of punishment and hatred, but kindness and pity; the faithlessness of tyrants; the confederacy of the Rulers of the World, and the restoration of the expelled Dynasty by foreign arms; the massacre and extermination of the Patriots, and the victory of established power; the consequences of legitimate despotism, civil war, famine, plague, superstition, and an utter extinction of the domestic affections; the judicial murder of the advocates of Liberty; the temporary triumph of oppression, that secure earnest of its final and inevitable fall; the transient nature of ignorance and error, and the eternity of genius and virtue. Such is the series of delineations of which the Poem consists. And if the lofty passions with which it has been my scope to distinguish this story, shall not excite in the reader a generous impulse, an ardent thirst for excellence, an interest profound and strong, such as belongs to no meaner desires—let not the failure be imputed to a natural unfitness for human sympathy in these sublime and animating themes. It is the business of the Poet to communicate to others the pleasure and the enthusiasm arising out of those images and feelings, in the vivid presence of which within his own mind, consists at once his inspiration and his reward.

---

1   Ecclesiastes 4.1.

The panic which, like an epidemic transport, seized upon all classes of men during the excesses consequent upon the French Revolution, is gradually giving place to sanity. It has ceased to be believed, that whole generations of mankind ought to consign themselves to a hopeless inheritance of ignorance and misery, because a nation of men who had been dupes and slaves for centuries, were incapable of conducting themselves with the wisdom and tranquillity of freemen so soon as some of their fetters were partially loosened. That their conduct could not have been marked by any other characters than ferocity and thoughtlessness, is the historical fact from which liberty derives all its recommendations, and falshood the worst features of its deformity. There is a reflux in the tide of human things which bears the shipwrecked hopes of men into a secure haven, after the storms are past. Methinks, those who now live have survived an age of despair.

The French Revolution may be considered as one of those manifestations of a general state of feeling among civilized mankind, produced by a defect of correspondence between the knowledge existing in society and the improvement or gradual abolition of political institutions. The year 1788 may be assumed as the epoch of one of the most important crises produced by this feeling. The sympathies connected with that event extended to every bosom. The most generous and amiable natures were those which participated the most extensively in these sympathies. But such a degree of unmingled good was expected, as it was impossible to realise. If the Revolution had been in every respect prosperous, then misrule and superstition would lose half their claims to our abhorrence, as fetters which the captive can unlock with the slightest motion of his fingers, and which do not eat with poisonous rust into the soul. The revulsion occasioned by the atrocities of the demagogues and the re-establishment of successive tyrannies in France was terrible, and felt in the remotest corner of the civilized world. Could they listen to the plea of reason who had groaned under the calamities of a social state, according to the provisions of which, one man riots in luxury whilst another famishes for want of bread? Can he who the day before was a trampled slave, suddenly become liberal-minded, forbearing, and independent? This is the consequence of the habits of a state of society to be produced by resolute perseverance and indefatigable hope, and long-suffering and long believing courage, and the systematic efforts of generations of men of intellect and virtue. Such is the lesson which experience teaches now. But on the first reverses of hope in the progress of French liberty, the sanguine eagerness for good overleapt the solution of these questions, and for a time extinguished itself in the unexpectedness of their result. Thus many of the most ardent and tender-hearted of the worshippers of public good, have been morally ruined by what a partial glimpse of the events they deplored, appeared to shew as the melancholy desolation of all their cherished hopes. Hence gloom and misanthropy have become the characteristics of the age in which we live, the solace of a disappointment that unconsciously finds relief only in the wilful exaggeration of its own despair. This influence has tainted the literature of the age with the hopelessness of the minds from which it flows. Metaphysics,* and enquiries into moral and political science, have become little else than vain attempts to revive exploded superstitions, or sophisms like those† of Mr. Malthus, calculated to lull the oppressors of mankind into a security of everlasting triumph. Our works of fiction and poetry have been overshadowed by the same infectious gloom. But mankind appear to me to be emerging from their trance. I am aware, methinks, of a slow, gradual, silent change. In that belief I have composed the following Poem.

★★★

There is an education peculiarly fitted for a Poet, without which, genius and sensibility can hardly fill the circle of their capacities. No education indeed can entitle to this appellation a dull and unobservant mind, or one, though neither dull nor unobservant, in which the channels of communication between thought and expression have been obstructed or closed. How far it is my fortune to belong to either of the latter classes, I cannot know. I aspire to be something better. The circumstances of my accidental education have been favourable to this ambition. I have been familiar from boyhood with,

---

* I ought to except Sir W. Drummond's "Academical Questions;" a volume of very acute and powerful metaphysical criticism.

† It is remarkable, as a symptom of the revival of public hope, that Mr. Malthus has assigned, in the later editions of his work, an indefinite dominion to moral restraint over the principle of population. This concession answers all the inferences from his doctrine unfavourable to human improvement, and reduces the "ESSAY ON POPULATION," to a commentary illustrative of the unanswerableness of "POLITICAL JUSTICE." [Thomas Malthus (1766–1834), author of *An Essay on the Principle of Population* (1798).]

mountains and lakes, and the sea, and the solitude of forests: Danger which sports upon the brink of precipices, has been my playmate. I have trodden the glaciers of the Alps, and lived under the eye of Mont Blanc. I have been a wanderer among distant fields. I have sailed down mighty rivers, and seen the sun rise and set, and the stars come forth, whilst I have sailed night and day down a rapid stream among mountains. I have seen populous cities, and have watched the passions which rise and spread, and sink and change amongst assembled multitudes of men. I have seen the theatre of the more visible ravages of tyranny and war, cities and villages reduced to scattered groups of black and roofless houses, and the naked inhabitants sitting famished upon their desolated thresholds. I have conversed with living men of genius. The poetry of antient Greece and Rome, and modern Italy, and our own country, has been to me like external nature, a passion and an enjoyment. Such are the sources from which the materials for the imagery of my Poem have been drawn. I have considered Poetry in its most comprehensive sense, and have read the Poets and the Historians, and the Metaphysicians* whose writings have been accessible to me, and have looked upon the beautiful and majestic scenery of the earth as common sources of those elements which it is the province of the Poet to embody and combine. Yet the experience and the feelings to which I refer, do not in themselves constitute men Poets, but only prepare them to be the auditors of those who are. How far I shall be found to possess that more essential attribute of Poetry, the power of awakening in others sensations like those which animate my own bosom, is that which, to speak sincerely, I know not; and which with an acquiescent and contented spirit, I expect to be taught by the effect which I shall produce upon those whom I now address.

7. From George Gordon, Lord Byron, *The Corsair, A Tale* (1814)[1]

[Peacock's Mr. Cypress was readily recognized as a Byronic poet, and Byron's poem *The Corsair*, which sold 10,000 copies on its first

---

* In this sense there may be such a thing as perfectibility in works of fiction, nothwithstanding the concession often made by the advocates of human improvement, that perfectibility is a term applicable only to science.

---

1 Source: George Gordon, Lord Byron. *The Corsair, A Tale* (London: John Murray, 1814).

day of publication, is parodied as "Paul Jones. A Poem" in Chapter 5
of *Nightmare Abbey*. Byron's poem tells the story of Conrad, a pirate
who loves and is loved by Medora. He engages in battle with the
Turkish Pacha and is wounded and made prisoner; before his capture, however, he rescues a slave in the Pacha's harem named Gulnare.
Gulnare falls in love with Conrad, kills the Pacha, and frees Conrad.
They escape and return to the pirate's island where Medora has died
from grief, thinking Conrad is dead. Conrad disappears and is never
seen again. I have omitted the early nineteenth-century convention
of the running quotation mark from passages of dialogue.]

From Canto the First

I
"O'er the glad waters of the dark blue sea,
Our thoughts as boundless, and our souls as free,
Far as the breeze can bear, the billows foam,
Survey our empire, and behold our home!
These are our realms, no limits to their sway—
Our flag the sceptre all who meet obey.
Ours the wild life in tumult still to range
From toil to rest, and joy in every change.
Oh, who can tell? not thou, luxurious slave!
Whose soul would sicken o'er the heaving wave;
Not thou, vain lord of wantonness and ease!
Whom slumber soothes not—pleasure cannot please—
Oh, who can tell, save he whose heart hath tried,
And danc'd in triumph o'er the waters wide,
The exulting sense—the pulse's maddening play,
That thrills the wanderer of that trackless way?
That for itself can woo the approaching fight,
And turn what some deem danger to delight;
That seeks what cravens shun with more than zeal,
And where the feebler faint—can only feel—
Feel—to the rising bosom's inmost core,
Its hope awaken and its spirit soar?
No dread of death—if with us die our foes—
Save that it seems even duller than repose:
Come when it will—we snatch the life of life—
When lost—what recks it—by disease or strife?

Let him who crawls enamoured of decay,
Cling to his couch, and sicken years away;
Heave his thick breath; and shake his palsied head;
Ours—the fresh turf, and not the feverish bed.
While gasp by gasp he faulters forth his soul,
Ours with one pang—one bound—escapes controul.
His corse may boast it's urn and narrow cave,
And they who loath'd his life may gild his grave:
Ours are the tears, though few, sincerely shed,
When Ocean shrouds and sepulchres our dead.
For us, even banquets fond regret supply
In the red cup that crowns our memory;
And the brief epitaph in danger's day,
When those who win at length divide the prey,
And cry, Remembrance saddening o'er each brow,
How had the brave who fell exulted *now!*"

★★★

XII

None are all evil—clinging round his heart,
One softer feeling would not yet depart;
Oft could he sneer at others as beguil'd
By passions worthy of a fool or child—
Yet 'gainst that passion vainly still he strove,
And even in him it asks the name of Love!
Yes, it was love—unchangeable—unchanged—
Felt but for one from whom he never ranged;
Though fairest captives daily met his eye,
He shunn'd, nor sought, but coldly pass'd them by;
Though many a beauty droop'd in prison'd bower,
None ever sooth'd his most unguarded hour.
Yes—it was Love—if thoughts of tenderness,
Tried in temptation, strengthen'd by distress,
Unmoved by absence, firm in every clime,
And yet—Oh more than all!—untired by time—
Which nor defeated hope, nor baffled wile,
Could render sullen were she ne'er to smile,
Nor rage could fire, nor sickness fret to vent
On her one murmur of his discontent—
Which still would meet with joy, with calmness part,

Lest that his look of grief should reach her heart;
Which nought remov'd—nor menaced to remove—
If there be love in mortals—this was love!
He was a villain—aye—reproaches shower
On him—but not the passion, nor its power,
Which only proved, all other virtues gone,
Not guilt itself could quench this loveliest one!

From Canto the Second

XI

In the high chamber of his highest tower,
Sate Conrad, fetter'd in the Pacha's power.
His palace perish'd in the flame—this fort
Contain'd at once his captive and his court.
Not much could Conrad of his sentence blame,
His foe, if vanquish'd, had but shared the same:—
Alone he sate—in solitude had scann'd
His guilty bosom, but that breast he mann'd:
One thought alone he could not—dared not meet—
"Oh, how these tidings will Medora greet?"
Then—only then—his clanking hands he rais'd,
And strain'd with rage the chain on which he gazed;
But soon he found—or feign'd—or dream'd relief,
And smil'd in self-derision of his grief,
"And now come torture when it will—or may—
More need of rest to nerve me for the day!"
This said, with langour to his mat he crept,
And, whatso'er his visions, quickly slept.
[The Corsair is rescued by Gulnare.]

★★★

XIII

She gazed in wonder, "can he calmly sleep,
While other eyes his fall or ravage weep?
And mine in restlessness are wandering here—
What sudden spell hath made this man so dear?
True—'tis to him my life, and more, I owe,
And me and mine he spared from worse than woe:
'Tis late to think—but soft—his slumber breaks—
How heavily he sighs!—he starts—awakes!"

He raised his head—and dazzled with the light,
His eye seem'd dubious if it saw aright:
He moved his hand—the grating of his chain
Too harshly told him that he liv'd again.
"What is that form? if not a shape of air,
Methinks, my jailor's face shows wond'rous fair!"
"Pirate! thou know'st me not, but I am one,
Grateful for deeds thou hast too rarely done;
Look on me—and remember her, thy hand
Snatch'd from the flames, and thy more fearful band.
I come through darkness—and I scarce know why—
Yet not to hurt—I would not see thee die."

★★★

XIV
"Corsair! thy doom is named—but I have power
To soothe the Pacha in his weaker hour.
Thee would I spare—nay more—would save thee now,
But this—time—hope—nor even thy strength allow;
But all I can,—I will: at least, delay
The sentence that remits thee scarce a day.
More now were ruin—even thyself were loth
The vain attempt should bring but doom to both."

"Yes!—loth indeed:—my soul is nerv'd to all,
Or fall'n too low to fear a further fall:
Tempt not thyself with peril—me with hope,
Of flight from foes with whom I could not cope;
Unfit to vanquish—shall I meanly fly,
The one of all my band that would not die?—
Yet there is one—to whom my memory clings,
'Till to these eyes her own wild softness springs.
My sole resources in the path I trod
Were these—my bark—my sword—my love—my God!
The last I left in youth—he leaves me now—
And Man but works his will to lay me low.
I have no thought to mock his throne with prayer
Wrung from the coward crouching of despair,
It is enough—I breathe—and I can bear.

My sword is shaken from the worthless hand
That might have better kept so true a brand;
My bark is sunk or captive—but my love—
For her in sooth my voice would mount above:
Oh! she is all that still to earth can bind—
And this will break a heart so more than kind,
And blight a form—till thine appeared, Gulnare!
Mine eye ne'er ask'd if others were as fair?"

"Thou lov'st another then?—but what to me
Is this—'tis nothing—nothing e'er can be:
But yet—thou lov'st—and—Oh! I envy those
Whose hearts on hearts as faithful can repose,
Who never feel the void—the wandering thought
That sighs o'er visions—such as mine hath wrought."

"Lady—methought thy love was his, for whom
This arm redeem'd thee from a fiery tomb."

"My love stern Seyd's! Oh—No—No—not my love—
Yet much this heart, that strives no more, once strove
To meet his passion—but it would not be.
I felt—I feel—love dwells with—with the free.
I am a slave, a favoured slave at best,
To share his splendour, and seem very blest!
Oft must my soul the question undergo,
Of—[']Dost thou love?' and burn to answer, 'No!'
Oh! hard it is that fondness to sustain,
And struggle not to feel averse in vain;
But harder still the heart's recoil to bear,
And hide from one—perhaps another there.
He takes the hand I give not—nor withhold—
Its pulse nor check'd—nor quicken'd—calmly cold:
And when he quits—it drops a lifeless weight
From one I never loved enough to hate.
No warmth these lips return by his imprest,
And chilled remembrance shudders o'er the rest.
Yes—had I ever proved that passion's zeal,
The change to hatred were at least to feel:

But still—he goes unmourn'd—returns unsought—
And oft when present—absent from my thought.
Or when reflection comes, and come it must—
I fear that henceforth 'twill but bring disgust;
I am his slave—but, in despite of pride,
'Twere worse than bondage to become his bride.
Oh! that this dotage of his breast would cease!
Or seek another and give mine release,
But yesterday—I could have said, to peace!
Yes—if unwonted fondness now I feign,
Remember—captive! 'tis to break thy chain.
Repay the life that to thy hand I owe;
To give thee back to all endear'd below,
Who share such love as I can never know.
Farewell—morn breaks—and I must now away:
'Twill cost me dear—but dread no death to-day!"

8. From George Gordon, Lord Byron, *Childe Harold's Pilgrimage*, Canto the Fourth (1818)[1]

[Peacock's reading of the fourth canto of *Childe Harold's Pilgrimage* might be said to have served as the catalyst for the writing of the novel (see Introduction, 21). In his dedication to his friend John Hobhouse, Byron suggests, "With regard to the conduct of the last canto, there will be found less of the pilgrim than in any of the preceding, and that little slightly, if at all, separated from the author speaking in his own person" (vii).]

I

I stood in Venice, on the Bridge of Sighs;[2]
A Palace and a prison on each hand:
I saw from out the wave her structures rise
As from the stroke of the enchanter's wand:
A thousand years their cloudy wings expand
Around me, and a dying Glory smiles

---

1   Source: George Gordon, Lord Byron. *Childe Harold's Pilgrimage*, Canto the Fourth. (London: John Murray, 1818).
2   The Bridge of Sighs links the Prison of St. Mark and the Palace of the Doges. The wingéd Lion is the lion of St. Mark who is patron saint of Venice.

O'er the far times, when many a subject land
Look'd to the winged Lion's marble piles,
Where Venice sate in state, thron'd on her hundred isles!

II

She looks a sea Cybele, fresh from the ocean,[1]
Rising with her tiara of proud towers
At airy distance, with majestic motion,
A ruler of the waters and their powers:
And such she was;—her daughters had their dowers
From spoils of nations, and the exhaustless East
Pour'd in her lap all gems in sparkling showers.
In purple was she robed, and of her feast
Monarchs partook, and deem'd their dignity increas'd.

III

In Venice Tasso's echoes are no more,[2]
And silent rows the songless gondolier;
Her palaces are crumbling to the shore,
And music meets not always now the ear:
Those days are gone—but Beauty still is here.
States fall, arts fade—but Nature doth not die,
Nor yet forget how Venice once was dear,
The pleasant place of all festivity,
The revel of the earth, the masque of Italy!

IV

But unto us she hath a spell beyond
Her name in story, and her long array
Of mighty shadows, whose dim forms despond
Above the dogeless city's vanish'd sway;
Ours is a trophy which will not decay
With the Rialto; Shylock and the Moor,
And Pierre, can not be swept or worn away—

---

1 Cybele: the mother of the gods, who is often depicted wearing a crown.
2 During the early nineteenth century a few gondoliers chanted stanzas from Tasso's six-teenth-century epic *Gerusalemme Liberata*.

The keystones of the arch! though all were o'er,
For us repeopled were the solitary shore.[1]

V

The beings of the mind are not of clay;
Essentially immortal, they create
And multiply in us a brighter ray
And more beloved existence: that which Fate
Prohibits to dull life, in this our state
Of mortal bondage, by these spirits supplied
First exiles, then replaces what we hate;
Watering the heart whose early flowers have died,
And with a fresher growth replenishing the void.

VI

Such is the refuge of our youth and age,
The first from Hope, the last from Vacancy;
And this worn feeling peoples many a page,
And, may be, that which grows beneath mine eye:
Yet there are things whose strong reality
Outshines our fairy-land; in shape and hues
More beautiful than our fantastic sky,
And the strange constellations which the Muse
O'er her wild universe is skilful to diffuse:

VII

I saw or dreamed of such,—but let them go,—
They came like truth, and disappeared like dreams;
And whatsoe'er they were—are now but so:
I could replace them if I would, still teems
My mind with many a form which aptly seems
Such as I sought for, and at moments found;
Let these too go—for waking Reason deems
Such over-weening phantasies unsound,
And other voices speak, and other sights surround.

---

1   Napoleon deposed Venice's last doge in 1797. Characters from Shakespeare's *The Merchant of Venice* and *Othello*; Pierre is from Thomas Otway's tragedy *Venice Preserved* (1682).

VIII

I've taught me other tongues—and in strange eyes
Have made me not a stranger; to the mind
Which is itself, no changes bring surprise;
Nor is it harsh to make, nor hard to find
A country with—ay, or without mankind;
Yet was I born where men are proud to be,
Not without cause; and should I leave behind
The inviolate island of the sage and free,
And seek me out a home by a remoter sea,

IX

Perhaps I loved it well: and should I lay
My ashes in a soil which is not mine,
My spirit shall resume it—if we may
Unbodied choose a sanctuary. I twine
My hopes of being remembered in my line
With my land's language: if too fond and far
These aspirations in their scope incline,—
If my fame should be, as my fortunes are,
Of hasty growth and blight, and dull Oblivion bar

X

My name from out the temple where the dead
Are honoured by the nations—let it be—
And light the laurels on a loftier head!
And be the Spartan's epitaph on me—
"Sparta hath many a worthier son than he."[1]
Meantime I seek no sympathies, nor need;
The thorns which I have reaped are of the tree
I planted,—they have torn me,—and I bleed:
I should have known what fruit would spring from such a seed.

★★★

---

1   From Plutarch's *Sayings of Spartan Women*: "Some Amphipolitans came to Sparta and visited Archileonis, the mother of Brasidas, after her son's death. She asked if her son had
died nobly, in a manner worthy of Sparta. As they heaped praise on him and declared that
in his exploits he was the best of all the Spartans, she said, 'Strangers, my son was indeed
noble and brave, but Sparta has many better men than he.'"

XXI

Existence may be borne, and the deep root
Of life and sufferance make its firm abode
In bare and desolated bosoms: mute
The camel labours with the heaviest load,
And the wolf dies in silence,—not bestow'd
In vain should such example be; if they,
Things of ignoble or of savage mood,
Endure and shrink not, we of nobler clay
May temper it to bear,—it is but for a day.

XXII

All suffering doth destroy, or is destroy'd,
Even by the sufferer; and, in each event
Ends:—Some, with hope replenish'd and rebuoy'd,
Return to whence they came—with like intent,
And weave their web again; some, bow'd and bent,
Wax gray and ghastly, withering ere their time,
And perish with the reed on which they leant;
Some seek devotion, toil, war, good or crime,
According as their souls were formed to sink or climb:

XXIII

But ever and anon of griefs subdued
There comes a token like a scorpion's sting,
Scarce seen, but with fresh bitterness imbued;
And slight withal may be the things which bring
Back on the heart the weight which it would fling
Aside for ever: it may be a sound—
A tone of music, summer's eve—or spring,
A flower—the wind—the ocean—which shall wound,
Striking the electric chain wherewith we are darkly bound;[1]

XXIV

And how and why we know not, nor can trace
Home to its cloud this lightning of the mind,

---

1   Chiefly with reference to the swiftness of electricity, or to the thrilling effect of the
electric shock (*OED*).

But feel the shock renew'd, nor can efface
The blight and blackening which it leaves behind,
Which out of things familiar, undesigned,
When least we deem of such, calls up to view
The spectres whom no exorcism can bind,
The cold—the changed—perchance the dead—anew,
The mourn'd, the loved, the lost—too many!—yet how few!

XXV

But my soul wanders; I demand it back
To meditate amongst decay, and stand
A ruin amidst ruins; there to track
Fall'n states and buried greatness, o'er a land
Which *was* the mightiest in its old command,
And *is* the loveliest, and must ever be
The master-mould of Nature's heavenly hand;
Wherein were cast the heroic and the free,
The beautiful, the brave—the lords of earth and sea,

★★★

CXXIV

We wither from our youth, we gasp away—
Sick—sick; unfound the boon—unslaked the thirst,
Though to the last, in verge of our decay,
Some phantom lures, such as we sought at first—
But all too late,—so are we doubly curst.
Love, fame, ambition, avarice—'tis the same,
Each idle—and all ill—and none the worst—
For all are meteors with a different name,
And Death the sable smoke where vanishes the flame. [...]

9. George Gordon, Lord Byron, Dedication to *Don Juan* (1833)[1]

[Byron began writing the poem in July 1818; Cantos One and Two
were published in July 1819. Byron added to the poem, publishing it
in instalments of two or three cantos until March 1824, the month
before his death. The Dedication, written in 1818 and therefore con-

---

1 Source: *The Poetical Works of Lord Byron*. 17 vols. (London: John Murray, 1833), 15.101–8.

temporary with *Nightmare Abbey*, was withheld and did not appear until 1833. It is included by way of providing a literary/political commentary; it might also explain why after reading *Nightmare Abbey*, Byron asked that Peacock be presented with a rosebud, which Peacock mounted in an oval gold locket.[1]]

From DEDICATION

I

Bob Southey! You're a poet — Poet-laureate,[2]
And representative of all the race;
Although 'tis true that you turn'd out a Tory at
Last,—yours has lately been a common case,—
And now, my Epic Renegade! what are ye at?
With all the Lakers,[3] in and out of place?
A nest of tuneful persons, to my eye
Like "four and twenty Blackbirds in a pye;

II

"Which pye being open'd they began to sing"
(This old song and new simile holds good),
"A dainty dish to set before the King,"
Or Regent, who admires such kind of food;[4] —
And Coleridge, too, has lately taken wing,
But like a hawk encumber'd with his hood,—
Explaining metaphysics to the nation—
I wish he would explain his Explanation.[5]

III

You, Bob! are rather insolent, you know,
At being disappointed in your wish
To supersede all warblers here below,

---

1 Garnett 354.
2 Robert Southey (1774–1843) was appointed Poet Laureate after the death of Henry James Pye in 1813.
3 A term popularized by the *Edinburgh Review* to describe Wordsworth, Coleridge, and Southey who lived in the Lake District.
4 When mental illness made George III incapable of rule, the Regency Act of February 1811 made the Prince of Wales Regent; the Prince was quite overweight and often depicted as a glutton in political cartoons.
5 Likely the *Biographia Literaria*, published in 1817.

And be the only Blackbird in the dish;
And then you overstrain yourself, or so,
And tumble downward like the flying fish
Gasping on deck, because you soar too high, Bob,
And fall, for lack of moisture, quite a-dry, Bob![1]

IV

And Wordsworth, in a rather long "Excursion"[2]
(I think the quarto holds five hundred pages),
Has given a sample from the vasty version
Of his new system to perplex the sages;
'Tis poetry—at least by his assertion,
And may appear so when the dog-star rages—
And he who understands it would be able
To add a story to the Tower of Babel.

V

You—Gentlemen! by dint of long seclusion
From better company, have kept your own
At Keswick,[3] and, through still continued fusion
Of one another's minds, at last have grown
To deem as a most logical conclusion,
That Poesy has wreaths for you alone:
There is a narrowness in such a notion,
Which makes me wish you'd change your lakes for ocean.

VI

I would not imitate the petty thought,
Nor coin my self-love to so base a vice,
For all the glory your conversion brought,
Since gold alone should not have been its price.
You have your salary; was't for that you wrought?
And Wordsworth has his place in the Excise.[4]

---

1 Slang for coition without emission; hence, sterile.
2 Long serious poem published in 1814.
3 A town in the Lake District where Southey lived.
4 References to Wordsworth's conservatism. The Earl of Lonsdale, a Tory, helped Wordsworth receive the sinecure of Distributor of Stamps for the county of Westmoreland.
   Wordsworth dedicated *The Excursion* (1814) to him.

You're shabby fellows—true—but poets still,
And duly seated on the immortal hill.[1]

VII

Your bays may hide the baldness of your brows—
Perhaps some virtuous blushes;—let them go—
To you I envy neither fruit nor boughs—
And for the fame you would engross below,
The field is universal, and allows
Scope to all such as feel the inherent glow:
Scott, Rogers, Campbell, Moore, and Crabbe,[2] will try
'Gainst you the question with posterity.

★★★

XVI

Where shall I turn me not to *view* its bonds,
For I will never *feel* them;—Italy!
Thy late reviving Roman soul desponds
Beneath the lie this State-thing breathed o'er thee—
Thy clanking chain, and Erin's yet green wounds,
Have voices—tongues to cry aloud for me.
Europe has slaves—allies—kings—armies still,
And Southey lives to sing them very ill.

XVII

Meantime—Sir Laureate—I proceed to dedicate,
In honest simple verse, this song to you.
And, if in flattering strains I do not predicate,

---

1 A mountain in central Greece associated with the Nine Muses and therefore the meta-phorical home of poets.
2 Sir Walter Scott (1771–1832), Scottish novelist and poet, who collected ballads, wrote narrative poetry, and a series of regional and the historical novels. Samuel Rogers (1763–1855), author of *The Pleasures of Memory* (1792); Thomas Campbell (1777–1844), author of *The Pleasures of Hope* (1799) and *Gertrude of Wyoming* (1809); Thomas Moore (1779–1852), Irish poet and friend of Byron, author of *Irish Melodies* (1808–34) and the long poem *Lalla Rookh* (1817); and George Crabbe (1754–1832), author of *The Village* (1783), *The Borough* (1810), and *Tales* (1812).

'Tis that I still retain my "buff and blue;"*
My politics as yet are all to educate:
Apostasy's so fashionable, too,
To keep *one* creed's a task grown quite Herculean;
Is it not so, my Tory, ultra-Julian?[1]
Venice, September 16, 1818.

10. From William Hazlitt, *The Spirit of the Age* (1825)[2]

[Although not published until 1825, Hazlitt's collection of essays about contemporary writers and thinkers shares Peacock's sense both of critique and of celebration of the characteristics of his times.]

From "Mr. Coleridge"

The present is an age of talkers, and not of doers; and the reason is, that the world is growing old. We are so far advanced in the Arts and Sciences, that we live in retrospect, and doat on past atchievements. The accumulation of knowledge has been so great, that we are lost in wonder at the height it has reached, instead of attempting to climb or add to it; while the variety of objects distracts and dazzles the looker-on. What *niche* remains unoccupied? What path untried? What is the use of doing anything, unless we could do better than all those who have gone before us? What hope is there of this? We are like those who have been to see some noble monument of art, who are content to admire without thinking of rivalling it; or like guests after a feast, who praise the hospitality of the donor "and thank the bounteous Pan"[3]—perhaps carrying away some trifling fragments; or like the spectators of a mighty battle, who still hear its sound afar off, and the clashing of armour and the neighing of the war-horse and the shout of victory is in their ears, like the rushing of innumerable waters!

---

* "Mr. Fox and the Whig Club of his time adopted an uniform of blue and buff."

---

1 Julian the Apostate, Roman emperor (361–63), who abandoned Christianity for worship of the pagan gods.
2 Source: William Hazlitt. *The Spirit of the Age: or Contemporary Portraits.* (London: H. Colburn, 1825), 61–63, 73–74, 76–79, 167–70.
3 John Milton (1608–74), *Comus*, (1634): "In wanton dance they praise the bounteous Pan,/ And thank the gods amiss" (176–77).

Mr. Coleridge has "a mind reflecting ages past:"[1] his voice is like the echo of the congregated roar of the "dark rearward and abyss"[2] of thought. He who has seen a mouldering tower by the side of a chrystal lake, hid by the mist, but glittering in the wave below, may conceive the dim, gleaming, uncertain intelligence of his eye: he who has marked the evening clouds uprolled (a world of vapours), has seen the picture of his mind, unearthly, unsubstantial, with gorgeous tints and ever-varying forms—

"That which was now a horse, even with a thought
The rack dislimns, and makes it indistinct
As water is in water."[3]

Our author's mind is (as he himself might express it) *tangential*. There is no subject on which he has not touched, none on which he has rested. With an understanding fertile, subtle, expansive, "quick, forgetive, apprehensive,"[4] beyond all living precedent, few traces of it will perhaps remain. He lends himself to all impressions alike; he gives up his mind and liberty of thought to none. He is a general lover of art and science, and wedded to no one in particular. He pursues knowledge as a mistress, with outstretched hands and winged speed; but as he is about to embrace her, his Daphne turns—alas! not to a laurel! Hardly a speculation has been left on record from the earliest time, but it is loosely folded up in Mr. Coleridge's memory, like a rich, but somewhat tattered piece of tapestry: we might add (with more seeming than real extravagance), that scarce a thought can pass through the mind of man, but its sound has at some time or other passed over his head with rustling pinions. On whatever question or author you speak, he is prepared to take up the theme with advantage—from Peter Abelard down to Thomas Moore, from the subtlest metaphysics to the politics of the *Courier*. There is no man of genius, in whose praise he descants, but the critic seems to stand

---

1 See Willliam Hazlitt, "Shakespeare's Genius" (1818): "He had 'a mind reflecting ages past' and present:—all the people that ever lived are there. There was no respect of persons with him. His genius shone equally on the evil and on the good, on the wise and the foolish, the monarch and the beggar."
2 Shakespeare's *The Tempest*, 1.2: "What seest thou else/In the dark backward and abysm of time?"
3 Shakespeare's *Antony and Cleopatra*, 4.14.
4 Shakesepeare's *2 Henry IV*, 4.3: "apprehensive, quick, forgetive, full of nimble fiery and delectable shapes."

above the author, and "what in him is weak, to strengthen, what is low, to raise and support:"[1] nor is there any work of genius that does not come out of his hands like an Illuminated Missal, sparkling even in its defects. If Mr. Coleridge had not been the most impressive talker of his age, he would probably have been the finest writer; but he lays down his pen to make sure of an auditor, and mortgages the admiration of posterity for the stare of an idler. If he had not been a poet, he would have been a powerful logician; if he had not dipped his wing in the Unitarian controversy, he might have soared to the very summit of fancy. But in writing verse, he is trying to subject the Muse to *transcendental* theories: in his abstract reasoning, he misses his way by strewing it with flowers. All that he has done of moment, he had done twenty years ago: since then, he may be said to have lived on the sound of his own voice. Mr. Coleridge is too rich in intellectual wealth, to need to task himself to any drudgery: he has only to draw the sliders of his imagination, and a thousand subjects expand before him, startling him with their brilliancy, or losing themselves in endless obscurity—

"And by the force of blear illusion,
They draw him on to his confusion."[2]

What is the little he could add to the stock, compared with the countless stores that lie about him, that he should stoop to pick up a name, or to polish an idle fancy? He walks abroad in the majesty of an universal understanding, eyeing the "rich strond,"[3] or golden sky above him, and "goes sounding on his way,"[4] in eloquent accents, uncompelled and free!

★★★

---

1 John Milton, *Paradise Lost* (1667): "What in me is dark/Illumine, what is low raise and support" (1.22–23).
2 John Milton, *Comus* (1634): "Of power to cheat the eye with blear illusion" (155) and Shakespeare's *Macbeth*, 3.5: "As by the strength of their illusion/Shall draw him on to his confusion."
3 Edmund Spenser, *The Faerie Queene* (1590): III.IV, epigraph: "Bold Marinell of Britomart,/ Is throwne on the Rich strond:/Faire Florimell of Arthur is Long followed, but not fond."
4 Chaucer, "General Prologue" to *The Canterbury Tales* (1387), describing The Clerk of Ox-enford: "Sownynge in moral vertu was his speche,/And gladly wolde he lerne and gladly

Alas! "Frailty, thy name is, *Genius!*"[1]—What is become of all this mighty heap of hope, of thought, of learning, and humanity? It has ended in swallowing doses of oblivion and in writing paragraphs in the *Courier.*—Such, and so little is the mind of man![2]

It was not to be supposed that Mr. Coleridge could keep on at the rate he set off; he could not realize all he knew or thought, and less could not fix his desultory ambition; other stimulants supplied the place, and kept up the intoxicating dream, the fever and the madness of his early impressions. Liberty (the philosopher's and the poet's bride) had fallen a victim, meanwhile, to the murderous practices of the hag, Legitimacy. Proscribed by court-hirelings, too romantic for the herd of vulgar politicians, our enthusiast stood at bay, and at last turned on the pivot of a subtle casuistry to the *unclean side*: but his discursive reason would not let him trammel himself into a poet-laureate or stamp-distributor,[3] and he stopped, ere he had quite passed that well-known "bourne from whence no traveller returns"[4]—and so has sunk into torpid, uneasy repose, tantalized by useless resources, haunted by vain imaginings, his lips idly moving, but his heart forever still, or, as the shattered chords vibrate of themselves, making melancholy music to the ear of memory! Such is the fate of genius in an age, when in the unequal contest with sovereign wrong, every man is ground to powder who is not either a born slave, or who does not willingly and at once offer up the yearnings of humanity and the dictates of reason as a welcome sacrifice to besotted prejudice and loathsome power.

★★★

No two persons can be conceived more opposite in character or genius than the subject of the present and of the preceding sketch. Mr. Godwin, with less natural capacity, and with fewer acquired

---

teche" (307–08). See William Hazlitt, "My First Acquaintance with Poets," first published in the *The Liberal*, April 1823: "The scholar in Chaucer is described as going—'Sounding on his way.' So Coleridge went on his."

1 A variation on "Frailty, thy name is woman," from Shakespeare's *Hamlet*, 1.2.
2 An allusion to Coleridge's addiction to opium.
3 In 1813 Southey became poet-laureate and Wordsworth the Distributer of Stamps for Westmoreland.
4 Shakespeare's *Hamlet*, 3.1.

advantages, by concentrating his mind on some given object, and doing what he had to do with all his might, has accomplished much, and will leave more than one monument of a powerful intellect behind him; Mr. Coleridge, by dissipating his, and dallying with every subject by turns, has done little or nothing to justify to the world or to posterity, the high opinion which all who have ever heard him converse, or known him intimately, with one accord entertain of him. Mr. Godwin's faculties have kept house, and plied their task in the work-shop of the brain, diligently and effectually: Mr. Coleridge's have gossipped away their time, and gadded about from house to house, as if life's business were to melt the hours in listless talk. Mr. Godwin is intent a subject, only as it concerns himself and his reputation; he works it out as a matter of duty, and discards from his mind whatever does not forward his main object as impertinent and vain. Mr. Coleridge, on the other hand, delights in nothing but episodes and digressions, neglects whatever he undertakes to perform, and can act only on spontaneous impulses, without object or method. "He cannot be constrained by mastery."[1] While he should be occupied with a given pursuit, he is thinking of a thousand other things; a thousand tastes, a thousand objects tempt him, and distract his mind, which keeps open house, and entertains all comers; and after being fatigued and amused with morning calls from idle visitors, finds the day consumed and its business unconcluded. Mr. Godwin, on the contrary, is somewhat exclusive and unsocial in his habits of mind, entertains no company but what he gives his whole time and attention to, and wisely writes over the doors of his understanding, his fancy, and his senses—"No admittance except on business." He has none of that fastidious refinement and false delicacy, which might lead him to balance between the endless variety of modern attainments. He does not throw away his life (nor a single half-hour of it) in adjusting the claims of different accomplishments, and in choosing between them or making himself master of them all. He sets about his task, (whatever it may be) and goes through it with spirit and fortitude. He has the happiness to think an author the greatest character in the world, and himself the greatest author in it. Mr. Coleridge, in writing an harmonious stanza, would stop to con-

---

1   Geoffrey Chaucer, "The Franklin's Tale" *The Canterbury Tales* (1387–1400): "Love wol nat been constreyned by maistrye."

sider whether there was not more grace and beauty in a *Pas de trois*, and would not proceed till he had resolved this question by a chain of metaphysical reasoning without end. Not so Mr. Godwin. That is best to him, which he can do best. He does not waste himself in vain aspirations and effeminate sympathies. He is blind, deaf, insensible to all but the trump of Fame. Plays, operas, painting, music, ball-rooms, wealth, fashion, titles, lords, ladies, touch him not—all these are no more to him than to the magician in his cell, and he writes on to the end of the chapter, through good report and evil report. *Pingo in eternitatem*—is his motto.[1] He neither envies nor admires what others are, but is contented to be what he is, and strives to do the utmost he can. Mr. Coleridge has flirted with the Muses as with a set of mistresses: Mr. Godwin has been married twice, to Reason and to Fancy, and has to boast no short-lived progeny by each. So to speak, he has *valves* belonging to his mind, to regulate the quantity of gas admitted into it, so that like the bare, unsightly, but well-compacted steam-vessel, it cuts its liquid way, and arrives at its promised end: while Mr. Coleridge's bark, "taught with the little nautilus to sail,"[2] the sport of every breath, dancing to every wave,

"Youth at its prow, and Pleasure at its helm,"[3]

flutters its gaudy pennons in the air, glitters in the sun, but we wait in vain to hear of its arrival in the destined harbour. Mr. Godwin, with less variety and vividness, with less subtlety and susceptibility both of thought and feeling, has had firmer nerves, a more determined purpose, a more comprehensive grasp of his subject, and the results are as we find them. Each has met with his reward: for justice has, after all, been done to the pretensions of each; and we must, in all cases, use means to ends!

From "Lord Byron"

Intensity is the great and prominent distinction of Lord Byron's writings. He seldom gets beyond force of style, nor has he produced

---

1   Joshua Reynolds, *Seven Discourses on Art* (1770), Discourse 3. "I am painting an eternity."
2   Alexander Pope, *Essay on Man*, Epistle 3 (1733), line 177.
3   Thomas Gray, "The Bard," II.2, Line 12. Quoted in Chapter one of Coleridge's *Biographia Literaria*.

any regular work or masterly whole. He does not prepare any plan beforehand, nor revise and retouch what he has written with polished accuracy. His only object seems to be to stimulate himself and his readers for the moment—to keep both alive, to drive away *ennui*, to substitute a feverish and irritable state of excitement for listless indolence or even calm enjoyment. For this purpose he pitches on any subject at random without much thought or delicacy—he is only impatient to begin—and takes care to adorn and enrich it as he proceeds with "thoughts that breathe and words that burn."[1] He composes (as he himself has said) whether he is in the bath, in his study, or on horseback—he writes as habitually as others talk or think—and whether we have the inspiration of the Muse or not, we always find the spirit of the man of genius breathing from his verse. He grapples with his subject, and moves, penetrates, and animates it by the electric force of his own feelings. He is often monotonous, extravagant, offensive; but he is never dull, or tedious, but when he writes prose. Lord Byron does not exhibit a new view of nature, or raise insignificant objects into importance by the romantic associations with which he surrounds them; but generally (at least) takes common-place thoughts and events, and endeavours to express them in stronger and statelier language than others. His poetry stands like a Martello tower by the side of his subject. He does not, like Mr. Wordsworth, lift poetry from the ground, or create a sentiment out of nothing. He does not describe a daisy or a periwinkle, but the cedar or the cypress: not "poor men's cottages, but princes' palaces."[2] His Childe Harold contains a lofty and impassioned review of the great events of history, of the mighty objects left as wrecks of time, but he dwells chiefly on what is familiar to the mind of every school-boy; has brought out few new traits of feeling or thought; and has done no more than justice to the reader's preconceptions by the sustained force and brilliancy of his style and imagery.

Lord Byron's earlier productions, *Lara*, the *Corsair*, &c. were wild and gloomy romances, put into rapid and shining verse. They discover the madness of poetry, together with the inspiration: sullen, moody, capricious, fierce, inexorable, gloating on beauty, thirsting for revenge, hurrying from the extremes of pleasure to pain, but with

---

1 Thomas Gray, "The Progress of Poesy" III.3, line 4.
2 Shakespeare's *The Merchant of Venice*, 1.2.

nothing permanent, nothing healthy or natural. The gaudy decorations and the morbid sentiments remind one of flowers strewed over the face of death! In his *Childe Harold* (as has been just observed) he assumes a lofty and philosophic tone, and "reasons high of providence, fore-knowledge, will, and fate."[1] He takes the highest points in the history of the world, and comments on them from a more commanding eminence: he shews us the crumbling monuments of time, he invokes the great names, the mighty spirit of antiquity. The universe is changed into a stately mausoleum:—in solemn measures he chaunts a hymn to fame. Lord Byron has strength and elevation enough to fill up the moulds of our classical and time-hallowed recollections, and to rekindle the earliest aspirations of the mind after greatness and true glory with a pen of fire. The names of Tasso, of Ariosto, of Dante, of Cincinnatus, of Cæsar, of Scipio, lose nothing of their pomp or their lustre in his hands, and when he begins and continues a strain of panegyric on such subjects, we indeed sit down with him to a banquet of rich praise, brooding over imperishable glories,

"Till Contemplation has her fill."[2]

Lord Byron seems to cast himself indignantly from "this bank and shoal of time,"[3] or the frail tottering bark that bears up modern reputation, into the huge sea of ancient renown, and to revel there with untired, outspread plume. Even this in him is spleen—his contempt of his contemporaries makes him turn back to the lustrous past, or project himself forward to the dim future! [...]

---

1   John Milton, *Paradise Lost* (1667), Book 2, lines 558–59: "and reason'd high/Of providence, foreknowledge, will, and fate."
2   John Dyer, "Grongar Hill" (1716), line 26.
3   Shakespeare's *Macbeth*, 1.7.

Appendix D: Peacock's Critical and Autobiographical Writings

[The documents here include a range of works, including the uncompleted "Essay on Fashionable Literature," which echoes many of the critical positions Peacock explores in *Nightmare Abbey*. Two years later he explored similar themes in his best known critical work, "The Four Ages of Poetry," which inspired Percy Shelley's *Defense of Poesy* by way of a response. Peacock's critical attitudes are maintained in his essay on French comedy. Excerpts from his own memoirs, his 1837 Introduction, as well as his 1860 memoirs of Shelley provide further insight into Peacock's literary attitudes about the role of literature in society.]

1. From "An Essay on Fashionable Literature" (1818)[1]

I. The fashionable metropolitan winter, which begins in spring and ends in autumn, is the season of happy re-union to those ornamental varieties of the human species who live to be amused for the benefit of social order. It is the period of the general muster, the levy *en masse* of gentleman in stays and ladies in short petticoats against their arch enemy Time. It is the season of operas and exhibitions, of routs and concerts, of dinners at midnight and suppers at sunrise. But these are the arms with which they assail the enemy in battalion: there are others with which in moments of morning solitude they are compelled to encounter him single-handed: and one of these weapons is the reading of light and easy books which command attention without the labour of application, and amuse the idleness of fancy without disturbing the sleep of understanding.

II. This species of literature, which aims only to amuse and must be very careful not to instruct, had never so many purveyors as at

---

1 Source: *The Halliford Edition of the Works of Thomas Love Peacock*, Ed. H.F.B. Brett-Smith and C.E. Jones, Volume 8, (London: Constable and Co, 1934), 261–91. The essay was left unfinished, and, in editing the manuscript, the Halliford editors numbered the paragraphs, and placed cancellations in brackets.

present: for there never was any state of society in which there were so many idle persons as there are at present in England, and it happens that these idle persons are for the most part so circumstanced that they can do nothing if they would, and in the next place that they are united in the links of a common interest which, being based in delusion, makes them even more averse than the well-dressed vulgar always are from the free exercise of reason and the bold investigation of truth.

III. That the faculty of amusing should be the only passport of a literary work into the hands of general readers is not very surprising, more especially when we consider that the English is the most thinking people in the universe: but that the faculty of amusing should be as transient as the gloss of a new coat does seem at first view a little singular: for though all fashionable people read (gentlemen who have been at college excepted), yet as the soul of fashion is novelty, the books and the dress of the season go out of date together; and to be amused this year by that which amused others twelve months ago would be to plead guilty to the heinous charge of having lived out of the world.

IV. The stream of new books, therefore, floats over the parlour window, the boudoir sofa, and the drawing-room table to furnish a ready answer to the question of Mr. Donothing as to what Mrs. Dolittle and her daughters are reading, and having served this purpose, and that of putting the monster Time to a temporary death, flows peacefully on towards the pool of Lethe.

V. The nature of this lighter literature, and the changes which it has undergone with the fashions of the last twenty years, deserve consideration for many reasons, and afford a subject of speculation which may be amusing, and I would add instructive, were I not fearful of terrifying my readers at the outset. As every age has its own character, manners, and amusements, which are influenced even in their lightest forms by the fundamental features of the time, the moral and political character of the age or nation may be read by an attentive observer even in its lightest literature, how remote soever *prima facie*[1] from morals and politics.

---

1 At first sight; on the face of it (Latin).

VI. The newspaper of the day, the favorite magazine of the month, the review of the quarter, the tour, the novel, and the poem which are most recent in date and most fashionable in name, furnish forth the morning table of the literary dilettante. The spring tide of metropolitan favor floats these intellectual *deliciae* into every minor town and village in the kingdom, where they circle through their little day in the eddies of reading societies.

VII. It may be questioned how far the favor of fashionable readers is a criterion of literary merit. It is certain that no work attracts any great share of general attention, which does not possess considerable originality and great power to interest and amuse. But originality will sometimes attract notice for a little space, as Mr. Romeo Coates attracted some three or four audiences by the mere fore of excessive absurdity: and the records of the Minerva Press will shew that a considerable number of readers can be both interested and amused by works completely expurgated of all the higher qualities of mind. And without dragging reluctant dullness back to-day, let us only consider the names of Monk Lewis and of Kotzebue, from what acclamations of popular applause they have sunk in a few years into comparative oblivion, and we shall see that condition of fashionable author differs very little in stability from that of a political demagogue.[1]

★★★

IX. Periodical publications form a very prominent feature in this transitory literature:—To any one who will compare the Reviews and Magazines of the present day with those of thirty years ago, it must be obvious that there is a much greater diffusion of general talent through them all, and more instances of great individual talent in the present than at the former period: and at the same time it must

---

1   Robert "Romeo" Coates (1772–1848) was an actor known for playing Shakespeare's Romeo and during the death scene he would take out his handkerchief, dust the stage, place his hat on the handkerchief, and pose in an attitude for death (DNB). The Minerva Press was a publishing house known for its gothic novels; August Von Kotzebue (1761–1819), playwright whose best-known play in England was Elizabeth Inchbald's adaptation, *Lover's Vows*, which figures in the plot of Jane Austen's *Mansfield Park* (1814); Matthew Lewis was author of the notorious novel *The Monk* (1796) which features rape, incest, and matricide.

be equally obvious that there is much less literary honesty, much more illiberality and exclusiveness, much more subdivision into petty gangs and factions, much less classicality and very much less philosophy. The stream of knowledge seems spread over a wider superficies, but what it has gained in breadth it has lost in depth. There is more dictionary learning, more scientific smattering, more of that kind of knowledge which is calculated for shew in general society, to produce a brilliant impression on the passing hour of literature, and less, far less, of that solid and laborious research which builds up in the silence of the closet, and in the disregard of perishable fashions of mind, the strong and permanent structure of history and philosophy.

XII. The *country gentlemen*★ appear to be in the habit of considering reviews as the joint productions of a body of men who meet at a sort of green board, where all new literary productions are laid before them for impartial consideration, and the merits of each having been fairly canvassed, some aged and enlightened censor records the opinion of the council and promulgates its definitive judgment to the world. The solitary quack becomes a medical board. The solitary play-frequenter becomes a committee of amateurs of the drama. The elector of Old Sarum is a respectable body of constituents.[1] This is an all-pervading quackery. Plurality is its essence. The mysterious *we* of the invisible assassin converts his poisoned dagger into a host of legitimate broadswords. Nothing, however, can be more remote from the facts. Of the ten or twelve articles which compose the *Edinburgh Review*, one is manufactured on the spot, another comes from Aberdeen, another from Islington, another from Herefordshire, another from the coast of Devon, another from bonny Dundee, *etc., etc., etc.*, without any one of the contributors even knowing the names of his brethren, or having any communication with any one but the editor. The only point of union among them is respect for the magic circle drawn by the compasses of faction and nationality, within which the dullness and ignorance is secure of favor, and without which genius and knowledge are equally certain of neglect or persecution.

★ A generic term applied by courtesy to the profoundly ignorant of all classes.

---

1 The "rotten borough," where until the 1832 Reform Bill only 31 people had the vote but were entitled to elect a Member of Parliament.

★★★

XIV. The monthly publications are so numerous that the most indefatigable reader of desultory literature could not get through the whole of their contents in a month: a very happy circumstance no doubt for that not innumerous class of persons who make the reading of reviews and magazines the sole business of their lives.

XV. All these have their own little exclusive circles of favor and faction, and it is very amusing to trace in any one of them half a dozen favored names circling in the preeminence of glory in that little circle, and scarcely named or known out of it. Glory, it is said, is like a circle in the water, that grows feebler and feebler as it recedes from the center and expands with a wider circumference: but the glory of these little idols of little literary factions is like the many circles produced by the simultaneous splashing of a multitude of equalized pebbles, which each throws out for a few inches its own little series of concentric circles, limiting and limited by the small rings of its brother pebbles, [while in the midst of all this petty splashing in the pool of public favor Scott or Byron plunges a ponderous fragment in the center and effaces them all with its eddy: but the disturbing power ceases: the splashings recommence, and the pebbles dance with joy in the rings of their self-created fame.]

★★★

XVII. In these publications, the mutual flattery of "learned correspondents" to their own "inescapable miscellany" carries the "Tickle me, Mr. Hayley"[1] principle to a surprising extent.

★★★

XX. Sir William Drummond complains that philosophy is neglected at the universities from an exclusive respect for classical literature.[2] I wish the reason were so good. Philosophy is discouraged from fear

---

1   William Hayley (1745–1820), poet and biographer. The comment might refer to his cultivation of talented people and tendency to praise while controlling their personal and professional lives (See DNB).
2   Sir William Drummond (1770?–1828), classical scholar and diplomatist whose 1805 *Academical Questions*, a summary of systems of philosophy included a dismissal of Kant and influenced Peacock and Percy Shelley (see DNB and Marilyn Butler, *Peacock Displayed: A Satirist in His Context.* [London: Routledge, 1979], 38).

of itself, not from love of the classics. There would be too much philosophy in the latter for the purposes of public education, were it not happily neutralized by the very ingenious process of academical chemistry which separates reason from grammar, taste from prosody, philosophy from philology, and absorbs all perception of the charms of the former in tedium and disgust at the drudgery of the latter. Classical literature, thus disarmed of all power to shake the dominion of venerable mystery and hoary imposture, is used merely as a stepping-stone to church preferment, and there, God knows,

> Small skill in Latin and still less in Greek
> Is more than adequate to all we seek.—[1]

XXI. If periodical criticism were honestly and conscientiously conducted, it might be a question how far it has been beneficial or injurious to literature: but being, as it is, merely a fraudulent and exclusive tool of party and partiality, that it is highly detrimental to it none but a trading critic will deny. The success of a new work is made to depend, in a great measure, not on the degree of its intrinsic merit, but on the degree of interest the publisher may have with the periodical press. Works of weight and utility, indeed, aided by the great counterpoise Time, break through these flimsy obstacles; but on the light and transient literature of the day its effect is almost omnipotent. Personal or political alliance being the only passports to critical notice, the independence and high thinking, that keeps an individual aloof from all the petty subdivisions of faction, makes every several gang his foe: and of this the *late* Mr. Wordsworth is a striking example.[2]

★★★

XXIV. In orthodox families that have the advantage of being acquainted with such a phaenomenon as a reading parson (which is fortunately as rare as the Atropos Belladonna—a hunting parson, on the other hand, a much more innocent variety, being as com-

---

1 From William Cowper's poem "Tirocinium; or, a Review for Schools" (1784).
2 Wordworth's social and religious poem *The Excursion* (1814) which inspired a review which begins "This will never do" and Mary Shelley to observe in her journal "He is a slave" (Butler, *Peacock Displayed* 70).

mon as the Solanum Nigrumm—)[1] or any tolerably literate variety of political and theological orthodoxy—the reading of the young ladies is very much influenced by his advice. He is careful not to prohibit, unless in extreme cases—Voltaire, for example—who is by many well-meaning grown ladies and gentlemen in leading-strings considered little better than a devil incarnate. He is careful not to prohibit, for prohibition is usually accompanied with longing for forbidden fruit—it is much more easy to exclude by silence, and pre-occupy by counter-recommendation. Young ladies read only for amusement: the best recommendation a work of fancy can have is that it should inculcate no opinions at all, but implicitly acquiesce in all the assumptions of worldly wisdom. The next best is that it should be well-seasoned with *petitiones principii*[2] in favor of things as they are.

XXV. Fancy indeed treads on dangerous ground when she trespasses on the land of opinion—the soil is too slippery for her glass slippers, and the atmosphere too heavy for her filmy wings. But she is a degenerate spirit if she be contented within the limits of her own empire, and keep the mind continually gazing upon phantasms without pointing to more important realities. Her province is to awaken the mind, not to enchain it. Poetry precedes philosophy, but true poetry prepares its path.—See Forsyth.—[3]

XXVI. Cervantes—Rabelais—Swift—Voltaire—Fielding—have led fancy against opinion with a success that no other names can parallel. Works of mere amusement, that teach nothing, may have an accidental and transient success, but cannot of course have influence on their own times, and will certainly not pass to posterity.[4] Mr. Scott's

---

1   Deadly Nightshade, a poisonous plant and Black Nightshade, which is used as a herbal medicine.
2   Translated as "begging the question" and referring to circular argument.
3   Robert Forsyth's *Principles of Moral Science* (1805) which Peacock first read in 1809 and whose chapter on revolution influences his portrait of Scythrop's "passion for reforming the world" in *Nightmare Abbey* (Butler, *Peacock Displayed* 129).
4   Miguel de Cervantes (1547–1616), Spanish novelist known for *Don Quixote* (1605, 1615); François Rabelais (c.1494–c.1553), French physician and satirist known for his *Gargantua* (1534) and *Pantagruel* (1532); Jonathan Swift (1667–1745), Anglo-Irish satirist who wrote *Gulliver's Travels* (1726); Voltaire, the pen name for François-Marie Arouet (1694–1778), French satirist and moralist associated with the Enlightenment and author of *Candide*

success has been attributed in a great measure to his keeping clear of opinion. [But he is far from being a writer who teaches nothing. On the contrary, he communicates great and valuable information. He is a painter of manners. He is the historian of a peculiar and remote class of our own countrymen, who within a few years have completely passed away. He offers materials to the philosopher in depicted, with the truth of life, the features of human nature in a peculiar state of society, before comparatively little known.]

★★★

XXIX. Reviews have been published in this country seventy years: eight hundred and forty months: and if we reckon only on an average four numbers to a month, we shall find that in that period three thousand three hundred and sixty numbers have been published:* three thousand three hundred and sixty numbers, two hundred thousand pages, of sheer criticism, every page of which is now in existence. What a treasury of information! What a repertory of excellent jokes to be cracked on an unhappy author and his unfavoured publications! So it would seem. Yet on examination these excellent jokes reduce themselves to some half-dozen, which have been repeated through every number of every review of the bulk of periodical criticism to the present day (and were stale in the first instance), without apparently losing any portion of what Miss Edgeworth would call the raciness of their humour.[1] They were borrowed in the first instance from Pope, who himself took one or two of them at second hand. They have an everlasting gloss, like the three coats in the *Tale of a Tub*.[2]

---

* This excludes magazines.

(1759) and English novelist Henry Fielding (1707–54) are satirical writers who are contrasted with Peacock's contemporary Sir Walter Scott (1771–1832), who wrote romantic narrative poems and historical novels.

1 Maria Edgeworth (1768–1849) was deeply admired by Sir Walter Scott and wrote novels with an historical setting or about English society as well as lessons and stories for children. The reference is to a passage from *Tales of Fashionable Life*, 3 vols. (London, 1809), 1.136.

2 Jonathan Swift's satire *A Tale of a Tub* (1704) includes an allegory of three sons who each receive a legacy of a coat, symbolizing the Roman Catholic, Anglican and Dissenting Churches.

XXX. One of these is the profundity of the Bathos. There is in the lowest deep a lower still, and the author in question (be he who he may) has plunged lower than any one before him. Another is that that work in question is a narcotic, and sets the unfortunate critic to sleep. A third is that it is unintelligible, and that true no-meaning puzzles more than wit. A fourth, that the author is insane. It cannot be denied that this super-excellent wit which can bear so much repetition without palling, for there is not any number of any review which does not contain them all at least once, and sometimes six or seven times: but taking them only at an average of one in a number, they have been repeated six or seven times: but taking them only at an average of one in a number, they have been repeated three thousand three hundred and sixty times in seventy years, and so far it is demonstrated that they are three thousand three hundred and sixty times better than the best joke in Joseph Miller, whose brightest recorded repartees will not bear a second repetition.[1]

★★★

[An extended discussion of "Christabel" follows.]

[XXXII.] I blush for an age of literature in which any one can require an explanation of so plain a sentence; still more for an age in which any one can come forward and tell the public that, in the groveling stupidity of his intellect, he cannot understand what is intelligible to a child, and that for this very declaration he shall be held an oracle. Truly this is like what Locke tells us of Egypt, where complete and incurable idiocy is a title to divine honors.

2. From "The Four Ages of Poetry" (1820)[2]

[...] The descriptive poetry of the present day has been called by its cultivators a return to nature. Nothing is more impertinent than this pretension. Poetry cannot travel out of the regions of its birth, the uncultivated lands of semi-civilized men. Mr. Wordsworth, the great

---

1 Joseph Miller (1684–1738), a comedian, whose name was affixed to the first joke-book, *Joe Miller's jests, or the Wit's Vade-mecum* (1739) compiled by John Mottley.
2 Source: *The Halliford Edition of the Works of Thomas Love Peacock*, Ed. H.F.B. Brett-Smith and C.E. Jones, Volume 8 (London: Constable and Co, 1934), 18–25.

leader of the returners to nature, cannot describe a scene under his own eyes without putting into it the shadow of a Danish boy or the living ghost of Lucy Gray, or some similar phantastical parturition of the moods of his own mind.[1]

In the origin and perfection of poetry, all the associations of life were composed of poetical materials. With us it is decidedly the reverse. We know too that there are no Dryads in Hyde-park nor Naiads in the Regent's-canal.[2] But barbaric manners and supernatural interventions are essential to poetry. Either in the scene, or in the time, or in both, it must be remote from our ordinary perceptions. While the historian and the philosopher are advancing in, and accelerating, the progress of knowledge, the poet is wallowing in the rubbish of departed ignorance, and raking up the ashes of dead savages to find gewgaws and rattles for the grown babies of the age. Mr. Scott digs up the poachers and cattle-stealers of the ancient border. Lord Byron cruizes for thieves and pirates on the shores of the Morea[3] and among the Greek Islands. Mr. Southey wades through ponderous volumes of travels and old chronicles, from which he carefully selects all that is false, useless, and absurd, as being essentially poetical; and when he has a commonplace book full of monstrosities, strings them into an epic. Mr. Wordsworth picks up village legends from old women and sextons; and Mr. Coleridge, to the valuable information acquired from similar sources, superadds the dreams of crazy theologians and the mysticisms of German metaphysics, and favours the world with visions in verse, in which the quadruple elements of sexton, old woman, Jeremy Taylor, and Emanuel Kant, are harmonized into a delicious poetical compound. Mr. Moore presents us with a Persian, and Mr. Campbell with a Pennsylvanian tale, both formed on the same principle as Mr. Southey's epics, by extracting from a perfunctory and desultory perusal of a collection of voyages and travels, all that useful investigation would not seek for and that common sense would reject.[4]

---

1   "Lucy Gray" and "A Fragment" appeared in the second edition of Wordsworth's *Lyrical Ballads* (1800).

2   The Serpentine is a lake constructed in London's Hyde Park in 1730 and Regent's Canal was opened in 1801.

3   The Morea is the Peloponnese peninsula in southern Greece. A reference to Byron's poems *The Giaour*, (1813), *The Bride of Abydos* (1813), and *The Corsair* (1814).

4   The works satirized here include Wordsworth and Coleridge's *Lyrical Ballads* (1798, 1800), Thomas Campbell's *Gertrude of Wyoming* (1809), Thomas Moore's *Lalla Rookh* (1817), and

These disjointed relics of tradition and fragments of second-hand observation, being woven into a tissue of verse, constructed on what Mr. Coleridge calls a new principle (that is, no principle at all), compose a modern-antique compound of frippery and barbarism, in which the puling sentimentality of the present time is grafted on the misrepresented ruggedness of the past into a heterogeneous congeries of unamalgamating manners, sufficient to impose on the common readers of poetry, over whose understandings the poet of this class possesses that commanding advantage, which, in all circumstances and conditions of life, a man who knows something, however little, always possesses over one who knows nothing.

A poet in our times is a semi-barbarian in a civilized community. He lives in the days that are past. His ideas, thoughts, feelings, associations, are all with barbarous manners, obsolete customs, and exploded superstitions. The march of his intellect is like that of a crab, backward. The brighter the light diffused around him by the progress of reason, the thicket is the darkness of antiquated barbarism, in which he buries himself like a mole, to throw up the barren hillocks of his Cimmerian labours.[1] The philosophic mental tranquility which looks round with an equal eye on all external things, collects a store of ideas, discriminates their relative value, assigns to all their proper place, and from the materials of useful knowledge thus collected, appreciated, and arranged, forms new combinations that impress the stamp of their power and utility on the real business of life, is diametrically the reverse of that frame of mind which poetry inspires, or from which poetry can emanate. The highest inspirations of poetry are resolvable into three ingredients: the rant of unregulated passion, the whining of exaggerated feeling, and the cant of factitious sentiment: and can therefore serve only to ripen a splendid lunatic like Alexander,[2] a puling driveller like Werter, or a morbid dreamer like Wordsworth. It can never make a philosopher, nor a statesman, nor in any class of life an useful or rational man. It cannot claim the slightest share in any one of the comforts and

---

Southey's narratives including *Thalaba the Destroyer* (1801), *Madoc* (1805), *The Curse of Kehama* (1810), and *Roderick, the Last of the Goths* (1814).

1 Cimmerians are a people fabled by the ancients to live in perpetual darkness and mentioned in Homer's *Odyssey*.

2 Alexander the Great (356-323 BC) who conquered most of the world as it was known to the Greeks.

utilities of life of which we have witnessed so many and so rapid advances. But though not useful, it may be said it is highly ornamental, and deserves to be cultivated for the pleasure it yields. Even if this be granted, it does not follow that a writer of poetry in the present state of society is not a waster of his own time, and a robber of that of others. Poetry is not one of those arts which, like painting, require repetition and multiplication, in order to be diffused among society. There are more good poems already existing than are sufficient to employ that portion of life which any mere reader and recipient of poetical impressions should devote to them, and these having been produced in poetical times, are far superior in all the characteristics of poetry to the artificial reconstructions of a few morbid ascetics in unpoetical times. To read the promiscuous rubbish of the present time to the exclusion of the select treasures of the past, is to substitute the worse for the better variety of the same mode of enjoyment.

But in whatever degree poetry is cultivated, it must necessarily be to the neglect of some branch of useful study: and it is a lamentable spectacle to see minds, capable of better things, running to seed in the specious indolence of these empty aimless mockeries of intellectual exertion. Poetry was the mental rattle that awakened the attention of intellect in the infancy of civil society: but for the maturity of mind to make a serious business of the playthings of its childhood, is as absurd as for a full-grown man to rub his gums with coral, and cry to be charmed to sleep by the jingle of silver bells.

★★★

Now when we consider that it is not the thinking and studious, and scientific and philosophical part of the community, not to those whose minds are bent on the pursuit and promotion of permanently useful ends and aims, that poets must address their minstrelsy, but to that much larger portion of the reading public, whose minds are not awakened to the desire of valuable knowledge, and who are indifferent to any thing beyond being charmed, moved, excited, affected, and exalted: charmed by harmony, moved by sentiment, excited by passion, affected by pathos, and exalted by sublimity: harmony, which is language on the rack of Procrustes;[1]

---

1   A host who stretched or mutilated his guests to adjust them to the length of his bed.

sentiment, which is canting egotism in the mask of refined feeling; passion, which is the commotion of a weak and selfish mind; pathos, which is the whining of an unmanly spirit; and sublimity, which is the inflation of an empty head: when we consider that the great and permanent interests of human society become more and more the main spring of intellectual pursuit; that in proportion as they become so, the subordinacy of the ornamental to the useful will be more and more seen and acknowledged; and that therefore the progress of useful art and science, and of moral and political knowledge, will continue more and more to withdraw attention from frivolous and unconducive, to solid and conducive studies: that therefore the poetical audience will not only continually diminish in the proportion of its number to that of the rest of the reading public, but will also sink lower and lower in the comparison of intellectual acquirement: when we consider that the poet must still please his audience, and must therefore continue to sink to their level, while the rest of the community is rising above it: we may easily conceive that the day is not distant, when the degraded state of every species of poetry will be as generally recognized as that of dramatic poetry has long been: and this not from any decrease either of intellectual power, or intellectual acquisition, but because intellectual power and intellectual acquisition have turned themselves into other and better channels, and have abandoned the cultivation and the fate of poetry to the degenerate fry of modern rhymesters, and their olympic judges, the magazine critics, who continue to debate and promulgate oracles about poetry, as if it were still what it was in the Homeric age,[1] the all-in-all of intellectual progression, and as if there were no such things in existence as mathematicians, astronomers, chemists, moralists, metaphysicians, historians, politicians, and political economists, who have built into the upper air of intelligence a pyramid, from the summit of which they see the modern Parnassus far beneath them, and, knowing how small a place it occupies in the comprehensiveness of their prospect, smile at the little ambition and the circumscribed perceptions with which the drivellers and mountebanks upon it are contending for the poetical palm and the critical chair.

---

1   The age in which Homer's *The Odyssey* and *The Iliad* depict before the Fall of Troy in the twelfth century BCE. Homer lived in the eighth century BCE.

3. From "French Comic Romances" (1835)[1]

In respect of presenting or embodying opinion, there are two very distinct classes of comic fictions: one in which the characters are abstractions or embodied classifications, and the implied or embodied opinions the main matter of the work; another, in which the characters are individuals, and the events and the action those of actual life—the opinions, however prominent they may be made, being merely incidental. To the first of these classes belong the fictions of Aristophanes, Petronius Arbiter, Rabelais, Swift, and Voltaire;[2] to the latter, those of Henry Fielding, his Jonathan Wild perhaps excepted, which is a felicitous compound of both classes; for Jonathan and his gang are at once abstractions and individuals. Jonathan is at once king of the thieves and the type of an arch whig.[3]

★★★

It would be, we think, an interesting and amusing inquiry to trace the progress of French comic fiction, in its bearing on opinion, from the twelfth century to the Revolution; and to show how much this unpretending branch of literature has, by its universal diffusion through so many ages in France, contributed to directing the stream of opinion against the mass of delusions and abuses which it was the object of those who were honest in the cause of the Reformation, and in the causes of the several changes which have succeeded it to the present time, to dissipate and destroy. If, as has frequently happened, the selfishness and dishonesty of many of the instru-

---

1 Source: Art. III. "French Comic Romances." (*The London Review* 2 [1835]: 70–2. rpt. [London: Simpkin, Marshall and Co., Stationers'-Hall Court; Edinburgh: W. Tait, Liverpool: Wilmer, 1836]).

2 Writers known for their satire: Aristophanes (c. 448–380 BCE), Athenian dramatist who wrote satirical comedies; Petronius Arbiter (d AD 65); Latin satirical writer whose *Satyricon* is a picaresque novel containing much parody; François Rabelais (c. 1494–c. 1553), French physician and satirist known for his *Gargantua* (1534) and *Pantagruel* (1532); Jonathan Swift (1667–1745), Anglo-Irish satirist who wrote *Gulliver's Travels* (1726); and Voltaire, the pen name for François-Marie Arouet (1694–1778), French satirist and moralist associated with the Enlightenment and author of *Candide* (1759).

3 Jonathan Wild (c. 1682–1725), famous London criminal who led a gang of thieves while posing as a policeman. Following his disgrace he became synonymous with hypocrisy and corruption. Wild was the subject of a number of literary treatments but Peacock alludes to Henry Fielding's *The History of the Life of the Late Mr. Jonathan Wild the Great* (1743), in which Wild stands in for the Whig politician and Prime Minister Robert Walpole.

ments has converted the triumph of a good cause into a source of greater iniquities than the triumph overthrew; if use and abuse have been sometimes swept away together, and the evils of abuse have returned, while the benefits of use have been irretrievably lost; if the overthrow of religious tyranny has been made the pretext for public robbery; if the downfall of one species of state-delusion has been made the stepping-stone to the rise of a new variety of political quackery; if the quieting of civil discord has been made the basis of military despotism;* if what has been even ultimately gained in the direct object proposed, has been counterbalanced by losses in collateral matters, not sufficiently attended to in the heat of the main pursuit—(a debtor and creditor account well worthy the making out, if the requisite quantity of leisure, knowledge, and honesty could be brought to bear upon it); if the principles which were honestly pursued have been stigmatized as the necessary causes of effects which did not belong to them, and which were never contemplated by those by whom those principles were embraced; and if those who were honest in the cause have been amongst the first victims of their own triumph, perverted from its legitimate results;—we shall find, nevertheless, in the first place, that every successive triumph, however perverted in its immediate consequences, has been a step permanently gained in advance of the objects of the first authors of the Reformation—freedom of conscience and freedom of inquiry; and we shall find, in the second place, not only that comic fiction has contributed largely to this result, but that among the most illustrious authors of comic fiction are some of the most illustrious specimens of political honesty and heroic self-devotion. We are here speaking, however, solely of the authors of the highest order of comic fiction—that which limits itself, in the exposure of abuses, to turning up into full daylight their intrinsic absurdities—not that which makes ridiculous things not really so, by throwing over them a fool's coat which does not belong to them, or setting upon them, as honest Bottom has it, an ass's head of its own.

Ridicule, in the first case, the honest development of the ridiculous *ab intrà*, is very justly denominated the test of truth: but ridicule,

---

* Lepidi atque Antonii arma in Augustum cessere: qui *cuncta, discordiis civilibus fessa,* nominee principis, sub *imperio* accepit. Tacitus, Ann. I. *Weariness of civil discord* founded the despotisms of Augustus, Cromwell, and Napoleon.

in the second case, the dishonest superinduction of the ridiculous *ab extrà*,[1] is the test of nothing but the knavery of the inventor. In the first case, the ridicule is never sought; it always appears, as in the comic tales of Voltaire, to force itself up obviously and spontaneously: in the second case, the most prominent feature of the exhibition is the predetermination to be caustic and comical. To writers of the latter class most truly applies the axiom—*homines derisores civitatem perdunt*.[2] But an intense love of truth, and a clear apprehension of truth, are both essential to comic writing of the first class. An intense love of truth may exist without the faculty of detecting it; and a clear apprehension of truth may co-exist with a determination to pervert it. The union of both is rare; and still more rare is the combination of both with that peculiar 'composite of natural capacity and superinduced habit,' which constitutes what is usually denominated comic genius.

4. "Preface," Headlong Hall, Nightmare Abbey, Maid Marian, and Crotchet Castle (for the Standard Novels Series, No. 57)[3]

ALL these little publications appeared originally without prefaces. I left them to speak for themselves; and I thought I might very fitly preserve my own impersonality, having never intruded on the personality of others, nor taken any liberties but with public conduct and public opinions. But an old friend assures me, that to publish a book without a preface is like entering a drawing-room without making a bow. In deference to this opinion, though I am not quite clear of its soundness, I make my prefatory bow at this eleventh hour.

"Headlong Hall" was written in 1815; "Nightmare Abbey," in 1817; "Maid Marian," with the exception of the last three chapters, in 1818; "Crotchet Castle," in 1830. I am desirous to note the intervals, because, at each of those periods, things were true, in great matters and in small, which are true no longer. "Headlong Hall" begins with the Holyhead Mail, and "Crotchet Castle" ends with a rotten borough. The Holyhead mail no longer keeps the same hours, nor

---

1 From within and from without (*OED*).
2 *homines derisores civitatem perdunt* (Latin): men's mockery destroys communities.
3 Source: "Preface." *Headlong Hall, Nightmare Abbey, Maid Marian, and Crotchet Castle*. Standard Novels, No. 57. (London: Bentley, 1837), v–vii.

stops at the Capel Cerig Inn, which the progress of improvement has thrown out of the road; and the rotten boroughs of 1830 have ceased to exist, though there are some very pretty pocket properties, which are their worthy successors. But the classes of tastes, feelings, and opinions, which were successively brought into play in these little tales, remain substantially the same. Perfectibilians, deterio-rationists, statu-quo-ites, phrenologists, transcendentalists, political economists, theorists in all sciences, projectors in all arts, morbid visionaries, romantic enthusiasts, lovers of music, lovers of the pic-turesque, and lovers of good dinners, march, and will march for ever, *pari passu*[1] with the march of mechanics, which some facetiously call the march of intellect. The fastidious in old wine are a race that does not decay. Literary violators of the confidences of private life still gain a disreputable livelihood and an unenviable notoriety. Match-makers from interest, and the disappointed in love and in friendship, are varieties of which specimens are extant. The great principle of the Right of Might is as flourishing now as in the days of Maid Marian: the array of false pretensions, moral, political, and literary, is as imposing as ever: the rulers of the world still feel things in their effects, and never foresee them in their causes; and politi-cal mountebanks continue, and will continue, to puff nostrums and practise legerdemain under the eyes of the multitude; following, like the "learned friend" of Crotchet Castle, a course as tortuous as that of a river, but in a reverse process; beginning by being dark and deep, and ending by being transparent.

THE AUTHOR OF "HEADLONG HALL."

March 4. 1837.

5. "Recollections of Childhood: The Abbey House." *Bentley's Miscellany* I (1837): 187–90[2]

I PASSED many of my earliest days in a country town, on whose immediate outskirts stood an ancient mansion, bearing the name of the Abbey House.[3] This mansion has long since vanished from the

---

1   *Pari passu* (Latin): side by side.
2   Source: *The Halliford Edition of the Works of Thomas Love Peacock*, Ed. H.F.B. Brett-Smith and C.E. Jones, Volume 8, (London: Constable and Co, 1934), 29–36.
3   In Chertsey, Surrey.

face of the earth; but many of my pleasantest youthful recollections are associated with it, and in my mind's eye I can still see it as it stood, with its amiable, simple-mannered, old English inhabitants.

The house derived its name from standing near, though not actually on, the site of one of those rich old abbeys, whose demesnes the pure devotion of Henry the Eighth transferred from their former occupants (who foolishly imagined they had a right to them, though they lacked the might which is its essence,) to the members of his convenient parliamentary chorus, who helped him run down his Scotch octave of wives. Of the abbey itself a very small portion remained: a gateway, and a piece of a wall which formed part of the enclosure of an orchard, wherein a curious series of fish-ponds, connected by sluices, was fed from a contiguous stream with a perpetual circulation of fresh water,—a sort of piscatorial panopticon,[1] where all approved varieties of fresh-water fish had been classified, each in its own pond, and kept in good order, clean and fat, for the mortification of the flesh of the monastic brotherhood on fast-days.

The road which led to the Abbey House terminated as a carriage-road with the house itself. Beyond it, a footpath over meadows conducted across a ferry to a village about a mile distant. A large clump of old walnut-trees stood on the opposite side of the road to a pair of massy iron gates, which gave entrance to a circular gravel road, encompassing a large smooth lawn, with a sun-dial in the centre, and bordered on both sides with tall thick evergreens and flowering shrubs, interspersed in the seasons with hollyhocks, sunflowers, and other gigantic blossoms, such as are splendid in distance. Within, immediately opposite the gates, a broad flight of stone steps led to a ponderous portal, and to a large antique hall, laid with a chequered pavement of black and white marble. On the left side of the entrance was the porter's chair, consisting of a cushioned seat, occupying the depth of a capacious recess resembling a niche for a full-sized statue, a well-stuffed body of black leather glittering with gold-headed nails. On the right of this hall was the great staircase; on the left, a passage to a wing appropriated to the domestics.

---

1 A panopticon is a circular prison with cells arranged around a central well, from which inmates can be observed at all times. The design was first proposed by Jeremy Bentham (1748–1832) in 1787 (*OED*). Peacock knew Bentham, with whom he had weekly dinners, through his East India Company colleagues James Mill and John Stuart Mill (see Introduction, 15).

Facing the portal, a door opened into an inner hall, in the centre of which was a billiard table. On the right of this hall was a library; on the left a parlour, which was the common sitting-room; and facing the middle door was a glazed door, opening on the broad flight of stone steps which led into the gardens.

The gardens were in the old style: a large square lawn occupied an ample space in the centre, separated by broad walks from belts of trees and shrubs on each side; and in front were two advancing groves, with a long wide vista between them, looking to the open country, from which the grounds were separated by a terraced wall over a deep sunken dyke. One of the groves we called the green grove, and the other the dark grove. The first had a pleasant glade, with sloping banks covered with flowery turf; the other was a mass of trees, too closely canopied with foliage for grass to grow beneath them.

The family[1] consisted of a gentleman and his wife, with two daughters and a son. The eldest daughter was on the confines of womanhood, the youngest was little more than a child; the son was between them. I do not know his exact age, but I was seven or eight, and he was two or three years more. The family lived, from taste, in a very retired manner; but to the few whom they received they were eminently hospitable. I was perhaps the foremost among these few; for Charles, who was my schoolfellow, was never happy in our holidays unless I was with him. A frequent guest was an elderly male relation, much respected by the family,—but no favourite of Charles, over whom he was disposed to assume greater authority than Charles was willing to acknowledge.

The mother and daughter had all the solid qualities which were considered female virtues in the dark ages. Our enlightened age has, wisely no doubt, discarded many of them, and substituted show for solidity. The dark ages preferred the natural blossom, and the fruit that follows it; the enlightened age prefers the artificial double-blossom, which falls and leaves nothing. But the double blossom is brilliant while it lasts; and where there is so much light, there ought to be something to glitter in it.

---

1   The family in the Abbey House was named Barwell and had connections with East India House. See Felix Fenton, *Thomas Love Peacock*. (London: George Allen & Unwin, 1973), 29, 30, 291.

These ladies had the faculty of staying at home; and this was a principal among the antique faculties that upheld the rural mansions of the middling gentry. Ask Brighton, Cheltenham, *et id genus omne*,[1] what has become of that faculty. And ask the ploughshare what has become of the rural mansions.

They never, I think, went out of their own grounds but to church, or to take their regular daily airing in the old family-carriage. The young lady was an adept at preserving: she had one room, in a corner of the hall, between the front and the great staircase, entirely surrounded with shelves in compartments, stowed with classified sweetmeats, jellies, and preserved fruits, the work of her own sweet hands. These wee distinguished ornaments of the supper-table; for the family dined early, and maintained the old fashion of supper. A child would not easily forget the bountiful and beautiful array of fruits, natural and preserved, and the ample variety of preparations of milk, cream, and custard, by which they were accompanied. The supper-table had matter for all tastes. I remember what was most to mine.

The young lady performed on the harpsichord. Over what a gulph of time this name alone looks back! What a stride from that harpsichord to one of Broadwood's last grand-pianos![2] And yet with what pleasure, as I stood by the corner of the instrument, I listened to it, or rather to her! I would give much to know that the worldly lot of this gentle and amiable creature had been a happy one. She often gently remonstrated with me for putting her harpsichord out of tune by playing the bells upon it; but I was never in a serious scrape with her except once. I had insisted on taking from the nursery-maid the handle of the little girl's garden-carriage, with which I set off at full speed; and had not run many yards before I overturned the carriage, and rolled out the little girl. The child cried like Alice Fell, and would not be pacified.[3] Luckily she ran to her sister, who let me off with an admonition, and the exaction of a promise never to meddle again with the child's carriage.

---

1 And of all that kind (Latin).
2 A British company founded by John Broadwood that originally made harpsichords (until 1793) and is thought by some to have been the most important piano manufacturer of the 18th and early 19th centuries.
3 "Alice Fell; or Poverty" (1801), a poem by William Wordsworth that tells the story of an orphan who loses her cloak when it becomes entangled in a carriage wheel. The poem is mentioned in Chapter 3 of *Melincourt*.

Charles was fond of romances. The Mysteries of Udolpho,[1] and all the ghost and goblin stories of the day, were his familiar reading. I cared little about them at the time; but he amused me by narrating their grimmest passages. He was very anxious that the Abbey House should be haunted; but it had no strange sights or sounds, and no plausible tradition to hang a ghost on. I had very nearly accommodated him with what he wanted. The garden-front of the house was covered with jasmine, and it was a pure delight to stand in the summer twilight on the top of the stone steps inhaling the fragrance of the multitudinous blossoms. One evening, as I was standing on these steps alone, I saw something like the white head-dress of a tall figure advance from the right-hand grove,—the dark grove, as we called it,—and, after a brief interval, recede. This, at any rate, looked awful. Presently it appeared again, and again vanished. On which I jumped to my conclusion, and flew into the parlour with the announcement that there was a ghost in the dark grove. The whole family sallied forth to see the phenomenon. The appearances and disappearances continued. All conjectured what it could be, but none could divine. In a minute or two all the servants were in the hall. They all tried their skill, and all were equally unable to solve the riddle. At last, the master of the house leading the way, we marched in a body to the spot, and unravelled the mystery. It was a large bunch of flowers on top of a tall lily, waving in the wind at the edge of the grove, and disappearing at intervals behind the stem of a tree. My ghost, and the compact phalanx in which we sallied against it, were long the subject of merriment. It was a cruel disappointment to Charles, who was obliged to abandon all hopes of having the house haunted.

One day Charles was in disgrace with his elderly relation, who had exerted sufficient authority to make him captive in his chamber. He was prohibited from seeing anyone but me; and, of course, a most urgent messenger was sent to me express. I found him in his chamber, sitting by the fire, with a pile of ghostly tales, and an accumulation of lead, which he was casting into dumps in a mould. Dumps, the inexperienced reader must know, are flat circles of lead,—sort of petty quoits,—with which schoolboys amused themselves half

---

1   *The Mysteries of Udolpho*, by Ann Radcliffe (1764–1823), was first printed in 1794. See, Chapter VI of *Northanger Abbey* by Jane Austen (published posthumously in 1818), for Catherine Morland's similar literary tastes.

a century ago, and perhaps do so still, unless the march of mind has marched off with such vanities.[1] No doubt, in the "astounding progress of intellect," the time will arrive when boys will play at philosophers instead of playing at soldiers,—will fight with wooden arguments instead of wooden swords,—and pitch leaden syllogisms instead of leaden dumps. Charles was before the dawn of this new light. He had cast several hundred dumps, and was still at work. The quibble did not occur to me at the time; but, in after years, I never heard of a man in the dumps without thinking of my schoolfellow. His position was sufficiently melancholy. His chamber was at the end of a long corridor. He was determined not to make any submission, and his captivity was likely to last till the end of his holidays. Ghost-stories, and lead for dumps, were his stores and provisions for standing the siege of ennui: I think, with the aid of his sister, I had some share in making his peace; but, such is the association of ideas, that, when I first read in Lord Byron's Don Juan,

"I pass my evenings in my long galleries solely,
And that's the reason I'm so melancholy,"[2]

the lines immediately conjured up the image of poor Charles in the midst of his dumps and specters at the end of his long gallery.

6. From "Memoirs of Percy Bysshe Shelley" (1860)[3]

At Bracknell, Shelley was surrounded by a numerous society, all in a great measure of his own opinions in relation to religion and politics, and the larger portion of them in relation to vegetable diet. But they wore their rue with a difference. Every one of them adopting some of the articles of the faith of their general church, had each nevertheless some predominant crotchet of his or her own, which left a number of open questions for earnest and not always temperate discussion. I was sometimes irreverent enough to laugh at the fervour with which opinions utterly unconducive to any practical

---

1   The sport of throwing the quoit or of playing with quoits; in one modern form the quoit is aimed at a pin stuck in the ground, and is intended to fall with the ring surrounding this, or to cut into the ground as near to it as possible.
2   *Don Juan*, Canto 5, stanza 58, lines 463–64 (1820).
3   Source: "Memoirs of Percy Bysshe Shelley." Part II. (*Fraser's Magazine* 61 [1860]: 92–109).

result were battled for as matters of the highest importance to the well-being of mankind; Harriet Shelley was always ready to laugh with me, and we thereby both lost caste with some of the more hot-headed of the party. Mr. Hogg was not there during my visit, but he knew the whole of the persons there assembled, and has given some account of them under their initials, which for all public purposes are as well as their names.

The person among them best worth remembering was the gentleman whom Mr. Hogg calls J.F.N.,[1] of whom he relates some anecdotes.

★★★

He saw the Zodiac in everything. I was walking with him one day on a common near Bracknell. When we came on a public-house which had the sign of the Horse-shoes. They were four on the sign, and he immediately determined that this number had been handed down from remote antiquity as representative of the compartments of the Zodiac. He stepped into the public-house, and said to the landlord, 'Your sign is the Horse-shoes?'—'Yes, sir,' 'This sign has always four Horse-shoes?'—'Why mostly, sir.' 'Not always?'—'I think I have seen three.' 'I cannot divide the Zodiac into three. But it is mostly four. Do you know why it is mostly four?'—'Why, sir, I suppose because a horse has four legs.' He bounced out in great indignation, and as soon as I joined him, he said to me, 'Did you ever see such a fool?'

★★★

He might well have said, after first seeing Mary Wollstonecraft Godwin, *'Ut vidi! ut perii!'*[2] Nothing that I ever read in tale of history could present a more striking image of a sudden, violent, irresistible, uncontrollable passion, than that under which I found him labouring when, at his request, I went up from the country to call on him

---

1   J.F. Newton, whom Mulvihill calls a "Peacockian crotcheteer" (*Thomas Love Peacock* 5). He believed that human failings were a result of use of meat and alcohol and he connected his theories with the Zodiac. He influenced Shelley to become a vegetarian and his *Return to Nature, or a Defence of Vegetable Regimen* (1811) helped to influence Shelley's early poem *Queen Mab* (1813). A version of Newton appears as Mr. Toobad in the novel.

2   Virgil, *Eclogues*, Book 8, line 38: "How I saw you! how I perished [for love of you]!"

in London. Between his old feelings towards Harriet, *from whom he was not then separated,* and his new passion for Mary, he showed in his looks, in his gestures, in his speech, the state of a mind "suffering, like a little kingdom, the nature of an insurrection."[1] His eyes were bloodshot, his hair and dress disordered. He caught up a bottle of laudanum, and said: 'I never part from this.'* He added: 'I am always repeating to myself your lines from Sophocles:

> Man's happiest lot is not to be:
> And when we tread life's thorny steep,
> Most blest are they, who earliest free
> Descend to death's eternal sleep.'

I believe that up to this time he had never traveled without pistols for defence, nor without laudanum as a refuge from intolerable pain. His physical suffering was often very severe; and this last letter must have been written under the anticipation that it might become incurable, and unendurable to a degree from which he wished to be permanently provided with the means of escape.

★★★

Few are now living who remember Harriet Shelley. I remember her well, and will describe her to the best of my recollection. She had a good figure, light, active, and graceful. Her features were regular

---

* In a letter to Mr. Trelawny, dated June 18th, 1822, Shelley says: 'You of course enter into society at Leghorn. Should you meet with any scientific person capable of preparing the *Prussic Acid, or Essential Oil of Bitter Almonds,* I should regard it as a great kindness if you could procure me a small quality. It requires the greatest caution in preparation, and ought to be highly concentrated. I would give any price for this medicine. You remember we talked of it the other night, and we both expressed a wish to possess it. My wish was serious, and sprung form the desire of needless suffering. I need not tell you I have no intention of suicide at present; but I confess it would be a comfort to me to hold in my possession that golden key to the chamber of perpetual rest. The *Prussic Acid* is used in medicine in infinitely minute doses; but that preparation is weak, and has not the concentration necessary to medicine all ills infallibly. A single drop even less, is a dose, and it acts by paralysis.' (*Trelawny,* pp. 100, 101). [The reference is to Edward John Trelawny (1792–1881), writer and adventurer, whose *Recollections of the Last Days of Shelley and Byron* (1858) formed a catalyst for the review.]

---

1 Shakespeare's *Julius Caesar* 2.1.

and well proportioned. Her hair was light brown, and dressed with taste and simplicity. In her dress she was truly *simplex munditiis*.[1] Her complexion was beautifully transparent; the tint of the blush rose shining through the lily. The tone of her voice was pleasant; her speech the essence of frankness and cordiality; her spirits always cheerful; her laugh spontaneous, hearty, and joyous. She was well educated. She read agreeably and intelligently. She wrote only letters, but she wrote them well. Her manners were good; and her whole aspect and demeanour such manifest emanations of pure and truthful nature, that to be once in her company was to know her thoroughly. She was fond of her husband, and accommodated herself in every way to his tastes. If they mixed in society, she adorned it; if they lived in retirement, she was satisfied; if they travelled, she enjoyed the change of scene.

That Shelley's second wife was intellectually better suited to him than his first, no one who knew them both will deny; and that a man, who lived so totally out of the ordinary world and in a world of ideas, needed such an ever-present sympathy more than the general run of men, must also be admitted; but Southey, who did not want an intellectual wife, and was contented with his own, may well have thought that Shelley had no equal reason to seek no change.

★★★

I must add, that in the expression of these differences, there was not a shadow of anger. They were discussed with freedom and calmness; with the good temper and good feeling which never forsook him in conversations with his friends. There was an evident anxiety for acquiescence, but a quiet and gentle toleration of dissent. A personal discussion, however interesting to himself, was carried on with the same calmness as if it related to the most abstract question in metaphysics.

Indeed, one of the great charms of intercourse with him was the perfect good humour and openness to conviction with which he responded to opinions opposed to his own. I have known eminent men, who were no doubt very instructive as lecturers to people

---

1 Simple, in neat attire; neat, not gaudy. See Ben Jonson's "Simplex Munditiis" (1–2): "Still to be neat, still to be drest,/As you were going to a feast."

who like being lectured; which I never did; but with whom conversation was impossible. To oppose their dogmas, even to question them, was to throw their temper off its balance. When once this infirmity showed itself in any of my friends, I was always careful not to provoke a second ebullition. I submitted to the preachment, and was glad when it was over.

★★★

So perished Percy Bysshe Shelley, in the flower of his age, and not perhaps even yet in the full flower of his genius; a genius unsurpassed in the description and imagination of scenes of beauty and grandeur; in the expression of impassioned love of ideal beauty; in the illustration of deep feeling by congenial imagery; and in the infinite variety of harmonious versification. What was, in my opinion, deficient in his poetry was, as I have already said, the want of reality in the characters with which he peopled his splendid scenes, and to which he addressed or imparted the utterance of his impassioned feelings. He was advancing, I think, to the attainment of this reality. It would have given his poetry the only element of truth which it wanted; though at the same time, the more clear development of what men were would have lowered his estimate of what they might be, and dimmed his enthusiastic prospect of the future destiny of the world. I can conceive him, if he had lived to the present time, passing his days like Volney,[1] looking on the world from his windows without taking part in its turmoils; and perhaps like the same, or some other great apostle of liberty (for I cannot at this moment verify the quotation), desiring that nothing should be inscribed on his tomb, but his name, the dates of his birth and death, and the single word,

'DÉSILLUSIONNÉ.'

---

1   Constantin Volney (1757–1820): *The Ruins, or A Survey of the Revolutions of Empires* (1791, 1792), along with *Paradise Lost* (1667), Plutarch's *Lives* (1st century AD) and Goethe's *The Sorrows of Young Werther* (1774) served as the texts to educate Frankenstein's creature. Volney's travels among the ruins of Egypt and Syria and his study of comparative religion provide him with lessons of reason, mortality, and equality, to lead him to a renovated France and a new, free humanist society. For Shelley, who independently pursued similar themes in *Queen Mab*, Volney was a kindred spirit.

Select Bibliography

Texts by Peacock

Brett-Smith, H.F.B and C.E. Jones, eds. *The Halliford Edition of the Works of Thomas Love Peacock.* 10 vols. London: Constable, 1924–34; rpt. New York: AMS, 1967.

Garnett, David, ed. *The Novels of Thomas Love Peacock.* London: Rupert Hart-Davis, 1948; rpt. in 2 vols. 1963.

Joukovsky, Nicholas A., ed. *The Letters of Thomas Love Peacock.* 2 vols. Oxford: Clarendon, 2001.

Mills, Howard, ed. *Memoirs of Shelley and Other Essays.* London: Hart-Davis, 1970.

Peacock, Thomas Love. *Headlong Hall, Nightmare Abbey, Maid Marian, and Crotchet Castle.* Standard Novels, No. 57. London: Bentley, 1837.

———. *Nightmare Abbey.* London: T. Hookham Jr. and Baldwin, Craddock & Joy, 1818.

Wordsworth, Jonathan, ed. *Nightmare Abbey* [facsimile of 1818 ed.]. Oxford: Woodstock Books, 1992.

Wright, Raymond, ed. *Nightmare Abbey and Crochet Castle.* Harmondsworth: Penguin, 1969.

Critical Commentaries and Works Cited

Altick, Richard D. *The English Common Reader: A Social History of the Mass Reading Public, 1800–1900.* Chicago: U of Chicago P, 1957.

Bate, Jonathan. "Apeing Romanticism." *English Comedy.* Eds. Michael Cordner, Peter Holland, and John Kerrigan. Cambridge: Cambridge UP, 1994. 221–40.

Baulch, David M. "The 'Perpetual Exercise of an Interminable Quest': The *Biographia Literaria* and the Kantian Revolution." *Studies in Romanticism* 43 (2004): 557–81.

———. "Several Hundred Pages of Promise: The Phantom of the Gothic in Peacock's *Nightmare Abbey* and Coleridge's *Biographia Literaria.*" *Coleridge Bulletin: The Journal of Friends of Coleridge* 25 (2005): 71–77.

Brooks, Harold. "A Song from Mr. Cypress." *Review of English Studies* 38 (1987): 368–74.

Brown, Nathaniel. "The 'Brightest Colours of Intellectual Beauty': Feminism in Peacock's Novels." *Keats–Shelley Review* 2 (1987): 91–104.

Burns, Bryan. *The Novels of Thomas Love Peacock.* London and Sydney: Croom Helm, 1985.

Butler, Marilyn. "Druids, Bards and Twice-Born Bacchus: Peacock's Engagement with Primitive Mythology." *Keats–Shelley Memorial Bulletin* 36 (1985): 57–76.

———. "Myth and Mythmaking in the Shelley Circle." *ELH* 49 (1982): 50–72. Rpt. *Shelley Revalued: Essays from the Gregynog Conference.* Ed. Kelvin Everest. Totowa, NJ: Barnes and Noble, 1983. 1–19.

———. *Peacock Displayed: A Satirist in His Context.* London: Routledge, 1979.

Campbell. Olwen Ward. *Thomas Love Peacock.* London: Arthur Barker, 1953.

Chandler, Alice. "The Quarrel of the Ancients and Moderns: Peacock and the Mediaeval Revival." *Bucknell Review: A Scholarly Journal of Letters, Arts and Sciences* 13.3 (1965): 39–50.

Chandler, James. *England in 1819: The Politics of Literary Culture and the Case of Romantic Historicism.* Chicago: U of Chicago P, 1998.

Clemit, Pamela. *The Godwinian Novel: The Rational Fictions of Godwin, Brockden Brown, Mary Shelley.* Oxford: Clarendon, 1993.

Coleridge, Samuel Taylor. *Biographia Literaria or Biographical Sketches of My Literary Life and Opinions.* 2 vols. Ed. James Engell and W. Jackson Bate. *The Collected Works of Samuel Taylor Coleridge.* Vol. 7. Princeton: Princeton UP and London: Routledge & Kegan Paul, 1983.

———. *Lay Sermons.* Ed. R.J. White. *The Collected Works of Samuel Taylor Coleridge.* Vol. 6. Princeton: Princeton UP and London: Routledge & Kegan Paul, 1972.

Colmer, John. "Godwin's *Mandeville* and Peacock's *Nightmare Abbey*." *Review of English Studies: A Quarterly Journal of English Literature and the English Language* 21 (1970): 331–36.

Crabbe, John K. "The Emerging Heroine in the Works of Thomas Love Peacock." *Zeitschrift für Anglistik und Amerikanistik: A Quarterly of Language, Literature and Culture* 27.2 (1979): 121–32 .

———. "The Harmony of Her Mind: Peacock's Emancipated Women." *Tennessee Studies in Literature* 23 (1978): 75–86.

Cunningham, Mark. "'Fatout! Who Am I?': A Model for the Honourable Mr. Listless in Thomas Love Peacock's *Nightmare Abbey*." *English Language Notes* 30.1 (1992): 43–45.

Dawson, Carl. *His Fine Wit: A Study of Thomas Love Peacock*. London: Routledge and Kegan Paul, 1970.

——. "Peacock's Comedy: A Retrospective Glance." *Keats–Shelley Memorial Bulletin* 36 (1985): 102–13.

——. *Thomas Love Peacock*. Profiles in Literature. London: Routledge and Kegan Paul, 1968.

Donovan, J.P. "Thomas Love Peacock." *Literature of the Romantic Period: A Bibliographical Guide*. Ed. Michael O'Neill. Oxford: Clarendon, 1998. 269–83.

Dyer, Gary. *British Satire and the Politics of Style, 1789–1832*. Cambridge: Cambridge UP, 1997.

——. "Peacock and the 'Philosophical Gas' of the Illuminati." *Secret Texts: The Literature of Secret Societies*. Eds. Marie Mulvey-Roberts, Hugh Ormsby-Lennon, and Michael Foot. New York: AMS, 1995. 188–209.

Erickson, Lee. *The Economy of Literary Form: English Literature and the Industrialization of Publishing 1800–1850*. Baltimore and London: Johns Hopkins UP, 1996.

Fain, John T. "Peacock's Essay on Steam Navigation." *South Atlantic Bulletin: A Quarterly Journal Devoted to Research and Teaching in the Modern Languages and Literatures*. 35.3 (1970): 11–15.

——. "Peacock on the Spirit of the Age (1809–1860)." *All These to Teach: Essays in Honor of C.A. Robertson*. Eds. Robert A. Bryan et al. Gainesville: U of Florida P, 1965. 180–89.

Felton, Felix. *Thomas Love Peacock*. London, Allen and Unwin, 1973.

Godwin, William. *An Enquiry Concerning Political Justice*. 2 vols. 1793; rpt. Oxford: Woodstock Books, 1992.

——. *Mandeville*. Ed. Pamela Clemit. *Collected Novels and Memoirs of William Godwin*. Vol. 6. London: William Pickering, 1992.

Goethe, Johann Wolfgang von. *The Sorrows of Young Werter*. 1789; rpt. Oxford: Woodstock Books, 1991.

——. *Stella: A Play for Lovers*. trans. London: Printed for Hookham and Carpenter, 1798; rpt. George Canning, George Ellis, and John Hookham Frere, *Parodies and Other Burlesque Pieces With the Whole Poetry of the Anti-Jacobin*. Ed. by Henry Morley. London: G. Routledge, 1890.

Haley, Bruce. "Shelley, Peacock, and the Reading of History." *Studies in Romanticism* 29 (1990): 439–61.

Hazlitt, William. *Liber Amoris and The Spirit of the Age*. Ed. Duncan Wu. *The Selected Writings of William Hazlitt*. Vol. 7. London: Pickering & Chatto, 1998.

Hoff, Peter Sloat. "The Paradox of the Fortunate Foible: Thomas Love Peacock's Literary Vision." *Texas Studies in Literature and Language* 17 (1975): 481–88.

Hogg, Thomas Jefferson. *Memoirs of Prince Alexy Haimatoff*. Intro. Sidney Scott. London: The Folio Society, 1962.

Holmes, Richard. *Shelley: The Pursuit*. London: Weidenfeld & Nicolson, 1974.

House, Humphrey. "The Works of Peacock." *Listener* 42 (8 December 1949): 997–98.

Howells, Coral Ann. "*Biographia Literaria* and *Nightmare Abbey*." *Notes and Queries* 16 (1969): 50–51.

Hunt, John Dixon. "Sense and Sensibility in the Landscape Designs of Humphry Repton." *Studies in Burke and His Time* 19 (1978): 3–28.

Jack, Ian. "Peacock." *English Literature 1815–1832*. Vol. 10. *The Oxford History of English Literature*. Oxford: Oxford UP, 1965.

Jackson, H.J. "What Was Mr. Bennet Doing in his Library, and What Does It Matter?" *Romantic Libraries*, ed. Ina Ferris. *Romantic Circles* <http://www.rc.umd.edu/praxis/libraries/jackson/jackson.html>.

Jones, Frederick L. ed. *Letters of Percy Bysshe Shelley*. 2 vols. Oxford: Clarendon, 1964.

Joukovsky, Nicholas. "Peacock before *Headlong Hall*: A New Look at His Early Years." *Keats–Shelley Memorial Bulletin* 36 (1985): 1–40.

———. "Peacock's Sir Oran Haut-ton: Byron's Bear or Shelley's Ape?" *Keats–Shelley Journal* 29 (1980): 173–90.

Keats–Shelley Memorial Bulletin 36 (1985). Special Issue on Peacock.

Kelly, Gary. *English Fiction of the Romantic Period 1789–1830*. London: Longman, 1989.

Kennedy, William F. "Peacock's Economists: Some Mistaken Identities." *Nineteenth-Century Fiction* 21 (1966): 185–91.

Kiely, Robert. *The Romantic Novel in England*. Cambridge, MA: Harvard UP, 1972.

Kiernan, Robert F. *Frivolity Unbound: Six Masters of the Camp Novel —Thomas Love Peacock, E.F. Benson, Max Beerbohm, P.G. Wodehouse, Ronald Firbank, Ivy Compton-Burnett*. New York: Continuum, 1990.

Kjellin, Håkan. *Talkative Banquets: A Study in the Peacockian Novels of Talk*. Stockholm: Almqvist, 1974.

Klancher, Jon. *The Making of English Reading Audiences, 1790–1832*. Madison: U of Wisconsin P, 1987.

Krieger, Murray. "The Arts and the Idea of Progress." *Progress and Its Discontents*. Eds. Gabriel Almond et al. Berkeley: U of California P, 1982. 449–69.

Leavis, Q.D. *Fiction and the Reading Public*. London: Chatto & Windus, 1965.

McKay, Margaret. *Peacock's Progress: Aspects of Artistic Development in the Novels of Thomas Love Peacock*. Stockholm: Almqvist & Wiskell, 1992.

Madden, Lionel. *Thomas Love Peacock*. London: Evan Bros, 1967.

Mee, Jon. *Romanticism, Enthusiasm, and Regulation: Poetics and the Policing of Culture in the Romantic Period*. Oxford: Oxford UP, 2003.

Mendelson, Anne. "The Peacock-Meredith Cookbook Project: Long-Sundered Manuscripts and Unanswered Questions." *Biblion: The Bulletin of The New York Public Library* 2.1 (1993): 77–99.

Mills, Howard. "The Dirty Boots of the Bourgeoisie: Peacock on Music." *Keats–Shelley Memorial Bulletin* 36 (1985): 77–88.

——. *Peacock: His Circle and His Age*. Cambridge: Cambridge UP, 1969.

Mulvihill, James. "A Prototype for Mr. Toobad in Peacock's *Nightmare Abbey*." *Notes and Queries* 49 (2002): 470–71.

——. "'A Species of Shop': Peacock and the World of Goods." *Keats–Shelley Journal* 49 (2000): 85–113.

——. "Peacock and Perfectibility in *Headlong Hall*." *CLIO: A Journal of Literature, History, and the Philosophy of History* 13 (1984): 227–46.

——. "Peacock, Monboddo, and the Dialogue." *Notes and Queries* 35 (1988): 310–11.

——. "Peacock's *Nightmare Abbey* and the 'Shapes' of Imposture." *Studies in Romanticism* 34 (1995): 553–68.

——. *Thomas Love Peacock*. Boston: G.K. Hall, 1987.

———. "Thomas Love Peacock's *Crotchet Castle*: Reconciling the Spirits of the Age." *Nineteenth-Century Fiction* 38 (1983): 253–70.

Pinkus, Philip. "The Satiric Novels of Thomas Love Peacock." *Kansas Quarterly* 1.3 (1969): 64–76.

Polhemus, Robert M. *Comic Faith: The Great Comic Tradition from Austen to Joyce.* Chicago: U of Chicago P, 1980.

Prance, Claude. *The Characters in the Novels of Thomas Love Peacock, 1785–1866, with Biographical Lists.* Lewiston, NY: Mellen, 1992.

Priestley, J.B. *Thomas Love Peacock.* New York: Macmillan, 1927.

Raleigh, Walter. "Thomas Love Peacock." *On Writing and Writers.* London: Edward Arnold, 1926. 151–54.

Robinson, H.M. "Aristophanes, Coleridge and Peacock." *Notes and Queries* 26 (1979): 232.

Rudinsky, Norma Leigh. "Contemporary Response to the Caricature Asterias in Peacock's *Nightmare Abbey*." *Notes and Queries* 24 (1977): 335–36.

———. "Satire on Sir John Sinclair before Peacock's Asterias in *Nightmare Abbey*." *Notes and Queries* 23 (1976): 108–10.

———. "A Second Original of Peacock's Menippean Caricature Asterias in *Nightmare Abbey*: Sir John Sinclair, Bart." *English Studies: A Journal of English Language and Literature* 56 (1975): 491–97.

———. "Source of Asteria's Paean to Science in Peacock's *Nightmare Abbey*. *Notes and Queries* 22 (1975): 66–68.

Sage, Lorna, ed. *Peacock: The Satirical Novels.* London: Longmans, Green, and Co., 1976.

Salz, Paulina June. "Peacock's Use of Music in his Novels." *Journal of English and Germanic Philology* 54 (1955): 370–79.

Schmid, Thomas H. *Humor and Transgression in Peacock, Shelley, and Byron: A Cold Carnival.* Lewiston, NY: Mellen, 1992.

Schwank, Klaus. "From Satire to Indeterminacy: Thomas Love Peacock's *Nightmare Abbey*." *Beyond the Suburbs of the Mind: Exploring English Romanticism.* Eds. Michael Gassenmeier and Norbert H. Platz. Essen: Blaue Eule, 1987. 151–62.

Smith, James. "Peacock's Mr. Asterias and 'Polypodes': A Possible Source." *Notes and Queries* 51 (2004): 157.

Spedding, James. "Tales by the Author of *Headlong Hall*." *Edinburgh Review* 68 (1839): 439–52.

St. Clair, William. *The Reading Nation in the Romantic Period.* Cambridge: Cambridge UP, 2004.

Stewart, J.I.M. *Thomas Love Peacock*. Writers and Their Work No. 156. London: Longmans, Green and Co., 1963.

Struever, Nancy S. "The Conversable World: Eighteenth-Century Transformations of the Relation of Rhetoric and Truth." *Rhetorical Traditions and British Romantic Literature*. Ed. Don H. Bialostosky and Lawrence D. Needham. Bloomington: Indiana UP, 1995. 233–49.

Tausky, Thomas E. "Peacock and the Peacock Papers." *Studies in Canadian Literature* 5 (1980): 5–22.

Tedford, Barbara W. "A Recipe for Satire and Civilization." *Costerus: Essays in English and American Language and Literature* 2 (1972): 197–212.

Tetreault, Ronald. "Shelley at the Opera." *ELH* 48 (1981): 144–71.

Van Doren, Carl. *The Life of Thomas Love Peacock*. New York: Russell & Russell, 1966.

Walling, William. "'On Fishing Up the Moon': In Search of Thomas Love Peacock." *The Evidence of the Imagination: Studies of Interactions between Life and Art in English Romantic Literature*. Eds. Donald Reiman, et al. New York: New York UP, 1978. 334–53.

Ward, William S. "Contemporary Reviews of Thomas Love Peacock: A Supplementary List for the Years 1805–1820." *Bulletin of Bibliography* 25 (1967): 35.

White, Newman Ivey. *Shelley*. 2 vols. London: Secker & Warburg, 1947.

Will, Peter, trans. *Horrid Mysteries. A Story Translated from the German of The Marquis of Grosse*. 4 vols. London: Folio, 1968.

Woolf, Virginia. "Phases of Fiction." *Granite and Rainbow*. London: Hogarth, 1958. 130–35.

Wright, Julia M. "Peacock's Early Parody of Thomas Moore in *Nightmare Abbey*." *English Language Notes* 30.4 (1993): 31–38.